THE WORLD UNDONE

THE PROTECTOR GUILD BOOK 8

GRAY HOLBORN

ISBN: 9781963893076

Edits by: CopybyKath

Cover by: DamoroDesign

AUTHOR NOTE

As an author, I love nothing more than when readers connect with the stories I tell. That said, nothing is more important than protecting your mental health and reading difficult content in a way that can best support it.

This book deals with material that may be difficult for some readers to engage with. Please visit my website for a list of content warnings.

1

MAX

"You look fucking exhausted." Izzy's nose scrunched in concern as the toe of her boot kicked up some loose dirt on the path.

I narrowed my eyes. "You know, that's not generally something a girl wants to hear first thing in the morning." I pointed to the dark circles under her eyes, fuller and more visible than I'd ever seen them. "Besides, you're not exactly looking spry and wide-eyed yourself."

It was great having Izzy around, even if I hadn't had much time to hang out with her since the whole burning-down-The-Guild-Headquarters-and-turning-all-of-our-lives-upside-down thing.

There was a hardness, a darkness around her edges that wasn't there before.

Izzy was the person I always associated with love and light and giddy happiness. That's how she always made me feel when I was around her, anyway.

But this world wasn't really suited to those things anymore —not when we were at the fucking heart of it, fighting our way through with tooth and claw.

And as bubbly and kind as Izzy was, she could also be a fucking force when she wanted to be. The best of both worlds, wrapped up in one package.

The girl who'd taken me shopping and snuggled into my side during countless vampire moviethons was hardened now.

Like I was, I supposed.

Heading a secret spy initiative against The Guild from inside the belly of the beast would do that to a girl.

Still, in a perfect world, she wouldn't need to wear such tarnished armor or be plagued by the nightmares I knew haunted her now. I could see her wariness in the lines of her posture, the dark, distant look that would occasionally eclipse the light in her eyes. Even when she tried to hide it, I knew it was there.

I shouldn't be surprised that she was concerned about the same shadows haunting me.

I took a deep breath, embracing the cloying chill that kissed the tip of my nose. It was strange, these moments of peace—how at odds they were with the world I knew now.

Part of me wanted to linger here, on this worn path with Izzy, forget about everything else for a little while. I wanted so desperately to protect all of my friends from the difficulties that inevitably lay ahead, but I was powerless against them.

She shoved my hand away with a dark laugh. "Yeah, I guess ushering in the apocalypse doesn't exactly come with a girl's proper dose of beauty rest. We're all exhausted, but that's not what I mean."

I yawned, as if proving her point. "I've been using what energy I can spare to help heal everyone. That's probably what you're picking up. It'll pass. Eventually."

A lot of the people we'd pulled from the labs were in rough shape. I couldn't help much with the mental and emotional trauma—of which there was undoubtedly a lot—but I did what I could for the physical.

Even that was limited though.

My ability to heal people outside of my bond group was minimal at best. Magic feasted on emotion, on connection. That kind of thing couldn't be forged falsely, no matter how badly I wanted to help everyone else with the ease I healed Six.

Still, that didn't stop me from draining my strengths day in and day out to try. It was the least I could do after bringing so many people here and draining the Lodge's resources.

She sighed, deep and heavy, and I felt her studying me from the corner of her eyes, a shrewdness piercing through the mask of levity she tried so hard to don. Izzy was the sort who could be down to her last morsel of food, and she'd still be concerned that those around her weren't getting enough to eat.

The girl was a titanium fucking needle in a burning pile of hay—one of a kind, and she came out forged stronger from the flames.

"Maybe. And I don't doubt that using your power is draining. Or that your team is draining you in other, more...pleasant ways." She shot me some knowing—and approving—side-eye. "But there's something more than that going on with you—" she scrunched her nose again, lost in thought, "something deeper, not just physical. An existential sort of exhaustion. So do me and favor and just level with me. Are you doing okay? Shit storm aside, I mean, obviously? You'd tell me if I had to worry about you, yes?" She snorted, "apart from how much I already worry about you, that is."

I took a deep breath and considered the question, weighing the possibility of answering as honestly as I could. But the truth was, I had no idea what 'okay' even looked like anymore. It wasn't a form I'd had the luxury to wear in a long time.

Every chance we had to take a breath, it was like we were pulled back under by another surprise wave—the new one often larger and angrier than the one before it.

We rarely caught a break. Drowning felt like an inevitability these days. It was just a matter of how long we could stave it off. But an umbrella couldn't hold long against an ocean.

Exhausted didn't even begin to cover it.

She gave me space and time to articulate my answer as we walked a long, winding path through Lake Cadaver's grounds.

Yes, that name was ridiculous and ominous as fuck—they clearly needed someone better on the marketing team. There was a reason everyone just called it 'The Lodge'.

I supposed it benefited us now though—kept the tourists away.

Well, the bad marketing *and* the protective magic surrounding the place helped keep the tourists away. Not that anyone was particularly forthcoming about how the latter worked. Charlie and her community enjoyed their secrets and privacy as much as we did.

Izzy'd finally been given clearance and permission to visit the medical building housed here.

Though, to be honest, medical building was a little generous. It was mostly a repurposed house with outdated supplies and not enough beds to corral all the new patients.

Bishop was a bit of a stickler for the rules. In that, when we flipped everything upside down, he took it upon himself to make a bunch of new ones.

Considering Izzy and I had doubled the number of occupants on this land, I couldn't exactly fault him for trying to maintain some semblance of control and organization, no matter how futile and frivolous it seemed to us at this point.

She bumped her shoulder with mine, reminding me I hadn't responded yet.

Right. How was I?

How the fuck was I supposed to know the answer to that question?

"I've been sleeping," I said, considering how much I wanted to share. But the hesitation dripped away as instantly as it had come. This was Izzy. She'd put herself on the line countless times for me—and she'd implicitly trusted me when I reached out to her the night we ambushed The Guild.

She was the real reason we were able to save so many of the demons locked deep in the labs. I may have burned it to the ground, but she was the one who'd done all of the heavy lifting before that. The moment after she'd woken up from our dream, she initiated things there instantly, corralling the protectors she trusted and manipulating those she didn't away from the grounds.

The girl deserved the truth—always. As long as I was able to give it to her, anyway.

"But most of my dreams end up as these horrible, almost tangible nightmares—not like with the dream walks, different somehow—and when I wake up, I'm at the lake. More exhausted than when I went to sleep in the first place."

Sometimes I even woke up with what must have been deep scratches and gouges in my arms and legs—the cuts from my nails long healed, leaving only crusted blood as evidence of the injuries.

"Like," she stopped walking, "literally at the lake?" She pointed her thumb over her shoulder, back the way we'd come. The air was filled with the soothing brine of it. "The giant one over there?"

I nodded.

Most nights, I was lucky and just woke up on the rocky beach, gasping for breath. But occasionally I'd come to, doused fully under water, with a rush that made it feel like I was only a few seconds away from drowning. "The guys and Dec started locking my door, but we learned pretty quickly that strategy doesn't work."

Neither did literally handcuffing my arm to one of them throughout the night—which they'd also tried. Twice.

Izzy tilted her head, gray eyes locking onto mine. "I suppose that teleporting makes most methods of jail or observation useless, huh? Sort of throws the typical rules of sleepwalking out the window."

I snorted. She'd figured out that flaw in our plan considerably faster than the rest of us had. We went through the entire experiment before reality smashed it to smithereens in our faces. "Was worth a try."

"I mean, I suppose it's better than waking up in the middle of a volcano pit—or in the clutches of The Guild Council, but still, it's weird. And weird these days always seems to mean something, doesn't it?" She read the confusion on my face and snorted. "Oh please. There are no coincidences where you're concerned. Everything is...something. So why now? Why the lake?"

I shrugged, remembering the first time it had happened.

I'd dream-walked to Lucifer.

A cold shiver ran down my spine at the memory of it.

Lucifer's ritual to save the world would *most likely* save the world. In theory, anyway, but it would also end in my death.

I still hadn't found a way to tell the others about that particular puzzle piece. Partially because I already knew I'd go through with it anyway, regardless of what they had to say.

What was the point in living, if the entire world collapsed as a result? If it risked every person I cared about?

At least I could go out saving as many people as possible—giving everyone I loved a chance to live their remaining days out in a peaceful, stable world. When I really thought about it, there was no better way to die.

It was how Cyrus had spent his last breaths, even if I wished down to my marrow that he hadn't.

Which was how I landed on the primary reason I hadn't told any of them the truth of that dream.

They'd fight me on it. I knew they would.

I would have stolen Cy's choice the instant it emerged from his lips, if I'd been given the chance.

But I also knew that they'd all lost so much already. I wasn't ready to completely shatter the small bit of bliss we'd been able to carve out for ourselves here since that night. It had taken us all too long to find each other—to break down the walls we'd all erected around ourselves for protection, to let each other in.

We were finally all in one place, finally together. It seemed cruel to shatter something so fragile now.

I needed more time.

I'd tell them, of course, but I wanted the chance to unwind a little, to enjoy being with them for a bit—before shit hit the fan. Again.

I mean, it had only been a week since we took down Headquarters, but it had flown by in a rush. As exhausted as I was, my body was still high on all of the adrenaline and chaos around us.

"You're not telling me everything." Izzy tracked my every movement, like she had a radar in tune with every muscle twitch, but she didn't fight me, didn't press for more.

Instead, we started walking towards the med center again, taking the long, winding way so that we could enjoy each other's company alone for a few more moments. We were never alone. Always busy. Always stumbling from one problem or issue to another. Always surrounded by other people, watching us with half curiosity, half trepidation.

I missed our movie nights something fierce.

"And I won't force you to say more until you're ready," she continued, "but I'm here to listen whenever you are. I just ask that you keep that in mind. You don't have to carry everything by yourself, you know?"

I wrapped my arms around myself to repress the chill. Her stare could strip me bare, layer by layer, and see all the dark and twisty things I tried to keep shoved into the back of my mind for perusal at a later date. Things I tried to hide even from myself.

It was infuriating.

But it was also comforting in a weird way too. As chaotic as the last year had been, I'd made some true connections that I wouldn't trade for all of the world.

In this case though, she wasn't completely right. I did have to carry this one thing on my own. This sacrifice was mine and mine alone to make.

I wasn't ready to tell her about my conversation with Lucifer, but I did compromise and update her on the things Six and I had been working on up until we freed Atlas.

She did the same, with her work infiltrating The Guild from the inside. It was a surprisingly brief story.

Her time at The Guild without me had been 'productive but single-focused'—with the new, heavy surveillance, they weren't able to do much but hack into some of the servers—thank you Arnell—and collect names and leads of those who might be willing to fight with us when shit hit the fan.

And hit the fan it did. There was flying, ricocheting shit everywhere. It was a goddamn masterpiece of shitty abstract art.

Of course, to me, what they'd been doing didn't sound single-focused at all—Izzy and Ten were fucking badasses and did more than we could ever thank them for while we were away from Headquarters. But they'd hit a lot of obstacles and dead ends. Izzy brushed most of their troubles off, eager to hear my adventures and weave them through with her own suspicions and conjectures.

We were both far more eager to hear the other's story, less so to tell our own.

She did promise to get me the tedious notes Arnell had been keeping on the council's movements as soon as she could. Something we'd no doubt need very soon.

"So, three things for his mysterious ritual?" She twisted a strand of dark hair near her collarbone—it had grown a few inches since I'd last seen her, another glaring reminder of how skewed time got whenever I visited hell—as she let the information settle over her. "The catalyst—which is you, your power at full charge," she put one finger up, counting along, "the nexus, and the abraxas."

I nodded, adding a soundless, *and my death* to that list.

I'd pull the magic encasing the shadow realm through me, the perfect catalyst, repairing and restoring it, or dissolving it altogether.

I wasn't sure which. No one was. Not even Lucifer.

That was part of the problem with an impending apocalypse—we were in pretty uncharted territory. The history books couldn't tell us much.

Not least of all because The Guild didn't exactly keep objective—or accurate—tellings of history.

"And we know where the abraxas is," she continued, grimacing, "or at least who has it."

The council, though I had no idea how we'd get access to it now.

I'd found it while spying on Atlas's bonding ceremony with Reza, but there was no way the council was just keeping it at Headquarters. Now that I had a scent for it—a spidey sense of sorts—I would have been drawn to it if they were.

Six, Darius, Ro, and I had finally agreed last night that the next step was to have a conversation with some of the elders here now that things with the new arrivals were leveling out a bit, to eke out as much information as we could about The Guild council. It was something none of us knew very much about.

That was by design, of course. Protectors were very secretive about their governing body and what it did—most went their entire lives knowing next to nothing about the group of people that ruled them beyond the location-specific teams that trickled down orders.

Until a few months ago, I thought Seamus, Cyrus, and Alleva were as high up as things went.

Fuck was I wrong.

"Your powers have grown considerably since I last saw you," she continued, her gaze dipping to my neck, where the dark, iridescent, abstract patterns were etched into my skin, creeping along the collar of my shirt.

My cheeks heated at the knowing look on her face. Having all of Six here, together, finally giving in to the intimacy and vulnerability of being bonded, had transformed things considerably.

We'd been so stubborn, resisting it. Deep in the night, when I was trying to fend off nightmares, guilt still clutched at my chest. We'd given up so much time together trying to fight off the inevitable. And now, after everything, I'd only get to have them for a short while.

It was profoundly cruel.

I wasn't sure which was worse—soaking up every stray second I had of them, deepening our connections, just to break their hearts at the end, or pulling away now to lessen the blow.

I scratched absently over the lines of shadow magic. When I focused on the mark, I could almost feel it pulse, the magic there both familiar and not. Strong. Powerful.

All five of the others had the mark now too—none of us knew the limits of our bond, or what this kind of power meant.

It honestly terrified the shit out of me.

True bond marks, woven naturally with shadow magic, hadn't existed in centuries as far as any of us knew. And they were typically only associated with incubi and succubi. Darius had never heard of vampires bearing the mark at all—let alone protectors.

But here we were. Ours had simply flared to life, growing

darker and more mysterious by the day—their presence impossible to ignore.

Izzy exhaled. "But how do we find this nexus point?"

That was the million-dollar question.

From what Lucifer had guessed, the nexus was at the juncture of the two realms—probably where the power of the shadow realm was first manifested or where it was anchored now.

By my ancestors apparently.

Which meant our best bet was learning more about my mother's family, tracing it back as far as we could. With any luck, that family tree might lead us to an answer. Or, at the very least, a path towards finding an answer.

"Saif Azar." The name felt strange on my lips, and a stabbing grief pierced my chest at the memory of when I first heard it. "My mother's twin. According to Cyrus. Though I don't have much more to go on beyond that. I'm hoping that he might have an idea of where the nexus is, or that he'll be able to at least point us to someone that does."

Izzy stretched her arms high, joints cracking loudly as she let out a humorless sigh. "Well, we never really have much to go on, do we? Lots of guess work, lots of twists and turns. But we'll get there. One step at a time, that's all we can do. The alternative is, well—" she shrugged, letting the depressing thought dissolve between us.

I didn't miss the way she repeatedly used the word *we*. The demand in her phrasing was just as clear as the one lingering in the dark threads of her eyes.

Whatever the next steps were, she would be at my side.

She was done being left in the dark, separated by circumstance and necessity.

And honestly, I was done leaving her in the dark.

I could feel some of the tension slipping from my shoulders. For the first time, I had everyone I needed here—Izzy, Ro,

Darius, Six. While worry never went away—how could it in a war like this—it seemed lighter to carry, easier to calm, when I had them all with me.

But things were hectic. This was the first time since our arrival that Izzy and I had time alone to talk.

Everyone had been exhausted, building new housing and protections for everyone we'd brought in from Headquarters. Not to mention that Charlie, Bishop, and the others in charge here had developed a pretty rigorous policy on keeping the new recruits separated until they could vet everyone and make sure that we hadn't accidentally brought anyone unsympathetic to the cause, Trojan Horse style, into this close-knit community they'd created.

How they did the vetting? I had no idea. I didn't have the clearance. But I knew it wasn't with the kind of callous torture The Guild swore by. From Izzy's experience, it mostly seemed like a deep, exhausting discussion, making sure everyone was safe for the community here.

It was frustrating at times—relying on their process and staying out of it when they asked. And while it was incredibly difficult to have the patience they requested, I understood why they were so protective of this place, of the people here. The Lodge was an oasis in a pool of confusion—it wasn't perfect or easy, but it was worth preserving, protecting. It was the kind of thoughtful community I'd always assumed The Guild would be.

"So, any ideas of where Uncle Saif is?" she asked, a small grin twisting the corner of her lips.

I snorted. "Of course not."

"Oof," Izzy stumbled, laughing quietly as a small redhead—no older than eight or nine—went zooming past us at high speed, face split into a giant grin as another child I didn't recognize chased him.

Children—several—were living here. That upped the security stakes considerably.

We were encroaching on this peaceful haven they'd carved out here, and we'd brought the fight they probably weren't expecting for years to them immediately—and to their front door.

It was a lot.

Izzy nodded to the large building in sight ahead of us. "This it?"

He did what? Why haven't you said anything?

"What?"

She snorted. "Girl, we need to get you a coffee. I said, 'Is this it?' The med center?"

She's exhausted. She has enough to worry about.

We still need to tell her.

The words were hardly even a whisper. I spun back towards her, eyes narrowed. "Tell me what?"

Lines carved through Izzy's forehead as she took a step closer to me. "You okay, Max? You've got that face on."

I shook my head, trying to clear it. Maybe I really was reaching a breaking point with my exhaustion. "Yeah, sorry. Coffee would be good after this."

My stomach clenched at the sight of the unremarkable building in front of us. It seemed quiet, normal even—brown walls and roof, small patio. I knew that once we crossed through the doorway, we'd be met with chaos and pain and confusion.

The med center was wildly understaffed.

Eli had been looped into working here most days, since he was the best at field medicine in our group by far. Each night, he'd come home drained and exhausted, a walking ghost with barely enough time to eat a bite of food before he crashed into a deep sleep and started the whole thing all over again. But he never complained, never took a day off—and as much as it hurt to see him so tired, I couldn't help but love him even more for how much of himself he was willing to give to help out here. He tried to pretend he didn't care about people, but his actions proved otherwise.

The demons we'd rescued were in pretty bad shape. And since we didn't exactly know the details of what they'd been through, it made it incredibly difficult to help them.

But they weren't the only ones.

Seamus was still in isolation, and I hadn't even been permitted to see him.

Until today.

And Sarah—

My chest pinched at the memory of her that night. Lost and confused, trapped inside of herself like Atlas had been.

I took a deep breath as my fingers wrapped around the cool metal doorknob. With a quick glance at Izzy, I exhaled. "Brace yourself. It's not exactly pretty on the other side of this door."

She laughed; the sound more haunting than humorous. "Nothing ever is anymore, is it?"

2

MAX

Like a veil had been lifted, the quiet calm of the grounds disappeared the moment we stepped inside. Chaos didn't even begin to describe the med center.

Sounds flooded me, cluttered and competing for my attention until they all just blurred into unintelligible noise.

"Fuck," Izzy muttered, her eyes wide as she took the place in. "You weren't kidding."

"Nope."

Compared to the high-tech labs and the med center at Headquarters, I wasn't sure this small log cabin could even be called such a thing. There were a handful of rooms, a cellar downstairs, and that was about it.

Beds were crowded and cluttered twenty to a room, packed tightly together like sardines. Most of the equipment was outdated, and the chorus of moans and screams from the patients locked in the terror of their trauma—both physical and mental—echoed on a constant loop. It was the soundtrack of nightmares.

Eli was already here, running from bed to bed, his arms

covered in splotches of red, despite the crisp, clean latex gloves he changed between each patient. My eyes found him instantly, like they'd been searching him out the moment we'd stepped through the door—my body aware of his presence long before my mind.

A grunt pulled my attention in the opposite direction. "Thought I told you to stay home today."

Somehow, even surrounded by the agony and horror of the room, I smiled.

A small face, mapped with wrinkles, appeared at my side. "Morning, Greta."

She grunted again, shaking her head with affectionate frustration. "Bentleys never have been much for listening, have they?" Her hand reached for Izzy's, giving it a small squeeze. "Good to see you again, Isadora. Though not at all surprised to find you here on your first day with amended clearance."

Izzy winked. "You too, you old bat. Put me to work today, okay? I've been bored senseless locked up in those rooms. It's nice to finally stretch my legs."

Finding out that Greta had been working at the Lodge for months was a downright gift from the gods. It wasn't entirely a surprise though. She'd always had a spark of rebellion about her and had bent the rules of The Guild from the very moment I met her. Maybe that was why I'd taken an instant liking to her.

She had a way with patients, her personality and bedside manner molding to whatever each person responded best to, what they needed. Without her help, we would have lost dozens of those we brought back here from The Guild. Something about her presence was like a balm for the soul.

She snorted but walked off without complaint. I was never able to get more than a sentence or two at a time from her. She was spread too thin. Even with all the volunteers in here, it wasn't enough. "Heard you got clearance to check on Seamus this morning. Charlie's down there now," she called back, her voice nearly swallowed by the chaos of the room. She nodded to the end of the hall where I knew a heavy, metal door was sitting. It wasn't enough to keep me out, but I'd done my best to honor their wishes here, to stay out of their way as long as I could. "Bring Eli with you. The kid's going to fall over if he doesn't take a break. And he listens to me about as well as you do."

"You're one to talk," I muttered, receiving nothing but a loud, cracked chortle in response.

Greta wasn't exactly a spry young thing—she'd retired twice over already—and I was fairly certain she didn't sleep. Like, at all. Still, she seemed to have more energy and stamina than the rest of us combined. If she kept up her current pace though, she was going to burn herself out.

I'd need to get her full story one of these days. I had a feeling it was a captivating one—but there hadn't been much time for friendly conversation since I'd found myself on The Lodge's front steps. Other than the look in her eyes when she'd first found me here, the warm hug that had me melting into a puddle of tears, her condolences pressed into me without a word, we'd hardly had time to truly reconnect.

Eli's dark gaze replaced hers as he wrapped me into his own tight, warm hug. His nose pressed into the curve of my neck as he took a slow, deep breath. My skin tingled where it met his. I felt him relax against me, the tension lining his body softening just a touch.

He pressed a soft kiss to my forehead before pulling away and sparing a brief glance to my left before his eyes found mine again. "Good to see you, Izzy. Welcome to the shit show. I hope you have a strong stomach."

She arched a brow, surveying the room. "I've seen worse."

A soft grin tugged at his mouth as he pulled me against him until our sides lined up, glued together.

I didn't fight it. My body craved his, just, I imagined, as his craved mine. And despite living in the same small cabin and working together here, we hadn't had much time to simply exist with each other.

We spent all of our days here in this small wooden box, tending to patients and helping Greta, and most of my nights were spent hovering over Atlas, trying to help him find his way back to himself—back to us.

Was it weird to miss someone I technically spent most of my time with? Because I did.

The small grin faded from his face as his eyes found mine. "Ready?"

I nodded, grabbing his hand and giving it a soft squeeze.

Eli saw his father every day, but I knew that each visit stabbed at him.

"Hi Max." A small mousy girl emerged behind Izzy, her expression hesitant as she studied my best friend. We weren't sure how old she was—no more than nine or ten, most likely—or what exactly she'd been through, but it took her a while to warm up to strangers.

For a vampire, she was incredibly timid.

I smiled at her. "Hi Ellie. This is my friend Izzy. Without her, we would have never gotten everyone out of The Guild labs. She could use your help and expertise today; think you can show her the ropes?"

Ellie's posture straightened, her expression growing both serious and eager with the promise of an important task. She'd been released from the med ward a few days ago, but she didn't seem to have any family or friends here. None that were conscious anyway. And she still didn't trust us enough to give up many details about her life.

Instead of claiming one of the free rooms in the resort, she asked to stay at the med ward, insisting on helping everyone here. Most of the vampires wanted out of this building as soon as possible, what with all the blood around, but Ellie seemed largely unbothered.

She was too young to be of much use with the medical side of things, but she'd grown fond of reading stories to the patients who got restless and fetching things for Greta and the others.

"Nice to meet you, Ellie." Izzy extended her hand to the girl. "Where should we get started, boss?"

Ellie's eyes widened, brimming with admiration and the first spark of excitement I'd seen from her since she arrived. She grabbed Izzy's hand and led her towards one of the supply trays.

"I'll catch you guys later," Izzy called back with a wink. "I think Ellie and I have things handled here for now."

Izzy didn't have a ton of healing experience, but she'd do whatever she could here, offer as much of her assistance to the people who did have training. It was her first day of freedom outside of her containment, and I wasn't even remotely surprised that she'd dedicate it to helping out until she fell over with exhaustion.

Eli pulled off his gloves and I followed him over to the sink to wash our hands in silence, the heaviness of our next stop settling around us both.

"Can we stop by Sarah's room first?" I bit my lip, trying my best to ignore the ball of fear already forming in my gut at the mere mention of her name.

"Of course we can." Eli's thumb pressed gently on my bottom lip, releasing it from my teeth. He lingered there a moment longer, stroking the soft, sensitive skin. "But don't get your hopes up. There haven't been any changes since yesterday."

I nodded, blinking back the film of frustrated tears clouding my vision.

Leading the way, I carved us a path through the various

hospital beds, winding down the hall until I got to the familiar wooden door. My stomach gripped at the sight of it, my body long familiar with the hours of failed attempts at healing I'd wasted in here.

I knocked softly, but I knew there was no point. Sarah wouldn't answer—or even respond to the sound.

Trying not to startle her, I opened the door slowly. This was the only relatively empty room in the med center. Other than Sarah, there were only two other people in this room.

Two days ago, there had been three.

I did my best not to wonder if there had been more locked in The Guild labs, prisoners trapped in the dark recesses of their own minds.

I was able to call to Atlas, to heal him enough to startle him awake and, together, we brought Sarah back with the rest. But in the darkest parts of the night, when I woke up trembling from my own nightmares, I couldn't stop my thoughts from lingering on the possibility that there had been more than the other three we'd found—shattered by the drude's power, fighting their way back to the surface.

An ache, deep and angry pulsed in my chest.

"There weren't any others," Eli said, his hand rubbing comforting circles on my back. I hadn't realized I'd spoken the fear aloud. "Darius cleared the cells. There was only Sarah, Atlas, and the other three. Any others who were down there had already met their death from the Nightmare, not your fire."

And now one of those three was gone.

I sniffed, wiped a stray tear from my cheek, and nodded before I walked over to Sarah's bed.

Not her.

I refused to let her meet that same fate. Atlas, Wade, Dec—they'd lost too many people already. I couldn't let them lose her.

Plus, a small part of me wondered if, when I was gone,

when the ritual was completed, they might be able to bond with her again—their original team reformed and whole. As much as the thought cut through my chest like a knife, the possibility that I wouldn't leave behind total desolation, that they'd have the chance for happiness again, soothed some of the weight on my shoulders.

So, unsurprisingly perhaps, this room was where I'd devoted most of my time and healing work. Still, I'd made very little progress.

These were the only injuries we weren't sure how to heal.

The paralysis poison from the tainted ones would disperse with time, and Greta and some of the others here had been trained in the med wards at The Guild.

While she wasn't familiar with every injury and torture the lab had applied in their recent months of desperation—she'd never spent much time with the prisoners of The Guild, her work had mostly been healing protectors who'd been attacked—she was able to ease most of the demons' pain and symptoms.

Most of it was a waiting game, however. Demons and protectors were strong—time healed most things that could actually be healed.

But not those afflicted with Sarah's torment.

Druden—Nightmares as they were also called—were uncharted territory for us all. So far Atlas was the only one who'd healed, and even then, I don't know that I could really call him healed.

He wasn't like the patients here, but he wasn't like himself either.

I shoved my worry for him to the back of my mind. I'd make sure to check up on him this afternoon. If I let myself linger too long on his pain—a hollow, deep presence I could feel echoing inside of my own chest—I'd be of no use to anyone.

Sarah wasn't on her bed. Instead, as she'd been each

morning when I'd arrived, she was huddled in on herself, pressed into the corner of the room. Her dark hair fell in limp waves over her arms and knees, several strands caught in her eyelashes. She didn't even have enough awareness to notice the nuisance.

Vacant blue eyes met mine.

With careful fingers, I cleared the stray hairs from her face. She didn't flinch from my touch.

She didn't react at all.

I set one palm against the side of her head, the other just under her collarbone.

I didn't know Sarah particularly well, and my power always worked better the deeper my connection to whoever I was trying to heal.

Outside of the bonds, Ro was the only person I'd been able to actually successfully heal—my connection to him being ironclad. But even then, I'd almost died from the exertion.

Still, I had to try.

Closing my eyes, I reached for Sarah in my mind, visualizing an invisible tether, not yet formed, trying to filter the few memories I had of her into it. My power flared, tingling in my skin, but it was listless and erratic, like it was unsure of where to go—or how to get there.

It was a feeling I was growing familiar with. One that sparked anger deep in my gut.

My teeth ground together as I tried—and failed—to swallow the frustration. I was useless against this darkness shrouding her. It was like trying to catch smoke in my hands.

I hated feeling useless. Hated knowing that Sarah was locked in this battle by herself and none of us could figure out how to reach her. How to save her.

Eli pressed in against my back, his fingers lightly touching my shoulder. I knew my healing powers wouldn't hurt him, but the brief possibility that they might pulsed through me all the same.

As if sensing my resistance, he doubled down and pressed his other hand to my other shoulder, his presence sturdy and strong as he worked out the tension in my muscles.

It took me a few minutes to notice, but slowly, I felt the invisible thread I'd conjured connecting me to Sarah—like, actually *felt* it. Not just imagined it like I had been for days. It was as tangible as any intangible thing could be.

A sharp breath pulled from my lips as I clung to it, trying desperately to shape and strengthen it, but it was like trying to shape a shadow without any light.

Still, it was something. More than I'd had any other time I'd tried to help her.

Eyes pressed shut, tight and eager, I called on what I'd learned about healing from Khalida—and, later, from Lucifer and Sam.

It was fractured and awkward, and something about my power couldn't quite locate the pulse of Sarah's, but I fought for collision all the same.

I opened my eyes and found hers locked on mine. They still looked vacant, not entirely recognizable as belonging to the girl I'd briefly known, but I had the distinct feeling that she was actually looking *at* me for the first time since we'd rescued her, rather than through me.

A breathy laugh of excitement pulled from my lips as I doubled down and pushed as much of my energy into her as I possibly could. I felt Eli's presence radiating over us both, infusing me with his quiet strength.

"Max," he whispered, but I barely heard it.

The brief flare of recognition I'd seen in Sarah's eyes was gone, and a wave of frustration with myself threatened to drown me.

I fought to cling to the thread of power, but it was fading.

"Max, that's too much."

My fingers tensed around Sarah, like they were searching for purchase, for other entry points.

"Max."

This time, there was a note of pain in Eli's voice, and I stumbled back. His hands weren't at my shoulders anymore—they were clutching his head, his face contorted in pain as he took deep, heaving breaths.

"Oh my god, I'm sorry," I crawled towards him, pulling his hands away and replacing them with my own. Had I somehow pulled energy from him? "Fuck, I'm so sorry. I don't know what I did. I wasn't thinking."

Finding the thread tying me to Eli took almost no time at all. It was strong and thick and as familiar to me as my hand.

"No, don't—I'm okay."

I ignored his protests, healing him quickly. I hadn't taken too much strength from him, and healing Eli from something so small came with an absurd ease when compared to my ragged attempts to heal Sarah.

The muscles in his face loosened. "Thanks, you didn't have to—"

"Eli, shut up. This is nothing. I'm sorry. I didn't realize what I was doing—sometimes healing puts me in a weird sort of trance." When I accessed that power, all I could think about was helping the other person, all self-preservation gone, every atom of my body ready to surrender for the cause if needed. Khalida had warned me of it—the power that came with healing others was addictive and all-consuming. Difficult to control. You lost yourself in it.

I stood up, pulling him with me, as I turned back to Sarah. I studied her for a long moment, searching for the small spark, but finding the same blankness I'd tried to fight all week.

Had I imagined it?

"There you are, Max." Charlie stood in the doorway. Her

lips pressed into a grim sort of grin—the smile unable to quite reach her eyes under the weight of everything she was dealing with. She turned to Eli and nodded. "Eli. I'm sorry I haven't been available to either of you for a few days. Things have been —" she scrunched her nose, "hectic, to say the least. As I'm sure you've both noticed."

Charlie was one of the leaders here. She'd welcomed us in —along with everyone else who'd been ostracized by The Guild or the outside world, whether demon, protector, or human. Charlie was mostly the latter, though she had some protector ancestry. Her partner, Bishop, was ex-Guild.

And apparently Atlas's cousin—long assumed dead. Small world.

I didn't know either of them particularly well, but they'd treated us with respect and kindness, even knowing that we were keeping secrets from them. That counted for a lot. Especially when The Guild operated on a platform of distrust.

"Good to see you, Charlie," I said and, surprisingly, I meant it.

We didn't know the people here well—Eli and I especially. We hadn't had the time here that Darius, Declan, Wade, and Ro had while we'd been briefly locked in hell.

Even so, I couldn't shake the innate trust that Charlie and those she surrounded herself with seemed to inspire and demand from me. There was something about her that called out to me, a kinship that I felt deep in my bones, even if it didn't make much sense from a logical standpoint. Trust was an expensive commodity these days.

But if I'd learned anything over the last few months, it was that I needed to trust my intuition.

"I heard you were going to see Seamus today. Thought I'd swing by and say hi, see how you were doing before I get on with the rest of my morning tasks, walk you down." She turned to Eli, compassion almost leaking from her pores. "Greta says you've both been helping tremendously in the med center this last week, we really appreciate it."

His fingers twitched in mine, and I knew he was uncomfortable under her praise. "Least we can do."

Charlie and Bishop had taken in everyone who'd followed us here. Bishop was protective of this place, understandably, and had instituted a rigorous vetting and acclimation process for the new recruits—they needed to make sure everyone who was here wanted to be here and understood the rules, the magic of this small community. The need to keep it, and the people here, safe.

But even through his surly facade, they'd also used all of the resources at their disposal to help everyone who needed medical attention, treating them all with the same attention and care they bestowed on their regulars here—without even questioning the utility or cost of it.

There'd been a few fights I'd heard about over the week, a vampire attacking another, a few protectors lashing out as well, caught between disgust and mourning over what they'd learned about The Guild.

Unlearning was a difficult thing. And they'd been indoctrinated in Guild practices and beliefs their entire life. It wasn't easy recognizing how many of those beliefs were built on lies. History was a fragile concept when you started to interrogate who penned it.

But it would all be worth it, all work out. I hoped, anyway.

The goal was, as Charlie had explained it, that this community could create a space for that unlearning—a space for people to come together and grow stronger through shared goals and values.

Even a trickle of hope could wield uncompromising power and strength, if given the chance to spark and grow.

Charlie nodded and turned out of Sarah's room, signaling for us to follow.

Without further preamble, Eli and I did just that. She unlocked the padlocked door at the end of the hall—the tech here wasn't nearly as advanced as what we were used to at The Guild. The lock wouldn't keep many people here out, it was a signal more than anything. But everyone honored the rules, trusting that, unlike The Guild, the people here were doing their best to keep everyone safe.

And from what I understood of Seamus's situation, these provisions were more for our safety than his.

The door opened into a dark stairwell that we descended in silence, until Charlie stopped at the base where another locked door stood. A single lightbulb lit the area, the glow of light warm and faint, highlighting the dust particles that floated in the air around us.

She turned around, her dark eyes latching onto mine. There was a spark of knowing there that I couldn't quite name, a sadness that burrowed deep into my bones. "I assume that Eli's been keeping you updated on him?" She grunted. "To be honest, I'm surprised you didn't break in here this week. Not like we could truly keep you out, even if we used every tool at our disposal to try. But I appreciate that you've been abiding by our protocol, as tedious as it may seem sometimes."

I nodded, leaning into Eli at my back. "I recognize that I've thrown a wrench into a lot of your plans here—created a lot of work and rushed things along at a pace that probably none of us were prepared for. But I'm trying to honor your rules and requests as best as I can, when I can."

She tilted her head, studying me, the smirk softening into something kinder, but still clouded over by a pervasive exhaustion.

"And as for Seamus," I tightened my grip on Eli's hand, "I'm up to date, yes."

Unfortunately, there wasn't much to be updated on.

Seamus was a werewolf now, but due to his age and the

severity and location of the bite, he was not handling the transition particularly well. More than that, there seemed to be something different about the wolf that bit him—and no one had any ideas or explanations as to what that difference was.

"I was just visiting with him. His memory," Charlie took a deep breath, her gaze cutting briefly to the thick door behind her before she turned back to Eli and shook her head. "I'm sorry, I can't even imagine—that must be very difficult for you."

"Better faulty memory than dead." Eli's voice was hard, but not unkind.

"Yes, well, Levi has been taking good care of him. He's in there now and has offered to guard during your visit today while Tex and Bishop tend elsewhere," she said. Eli stiffened next to me, his tension slicing into me. "I know you both can protect yourselves, but sometimes that's more difficult when it's your own family that you need protection from. Seamus has been a little—" her eyes narrowed as she searched for a word, finally settling on "volatile."

Eli's hand gripped mine. He'd been visiting Seamus every day, in the brief stretches that he was permitted, and each time he'd emerged from this stairwell, he'd looked a little more fractured, the pain echoing deep inside of me.

I'd found scratches carved into his side, noticed a few discarded shirts that had blood belonging to him. But he never spoke the words out loud—that Seamus had attacked him.

Of course, Darius knew for sure—his body often mirroring the strikes against Eli, thanks to the blood bond. Surprisingly, he never called attention to it, never complained or even said a word. He'd just look at Eli with unspoken compassion—their bond shaping into something surprisingly tender, given all of their bickering.

"I should be going though. I want to check in with Greta again before lunch, see what orders she needs sent out. I know we're low on a lot of supplies. I'm hoping we can send a team out for a run, now that things are settling down a bit."

I bit back a grin at the sarcasm that lifted her voice at the end of that sentence. I wasn't sure things would settle down here for a very long while. Maybe ever again.

With a soft smile and sympathetic glance at Eli, she left us there, waiting outside of the door.

I didn't rush Eli.

Instead, I turned around and looked up. He was always taller than me, but I had to really crane with him on a step above mine. I cupped his cheek and pressed a soft kiss to his mouth—one he met me halfway for. Amber eyes swallowed my focus as he studied me—open and vulnerable in a way that I'd only seen him a handful of times.

My heart skipped in my chest, and I tried desperately to resist the urge to kiss him again, this time with more heat. It had been a while since we'd last been together in that way, and I could feel my body hunger for him—could feel that hunger mirrored in him too.

Something had shifted irrevocably between us in hell—an openness, a trust. It's what allowed the bond to fully shape, and it was growing stronger every day—more solid, unwavering.

We'd wasted too much time hiding ourselves from each other, resisting the obvious connection between us. Now that those barriers were demolished, I wanted nothing more than to be consumed by him.

The heat in his eyes flared, the tension in the dim stairwell teetering on the edge. My stomach was tight, my breath quick.

I took a step back as he cleared his throat.

Later.

Seamus was waiting for us.

As was Levi.

I rapped my knuckles against the cool metal door, but the hinges creaked before I could repeat the gesture.

A soft glow of light washed over us as Levi stood before us.

Dark gray eyes locked on mine, the usual dark, mischievous gleam present in their depths, if clouded slightly by concern. "Max, good to see you again. Eli." His eyes didn't move from mine, like he was searching for something there. A chill ran up my spine at his perusal.

There was something strange about Levi, uncanny almost. In many ways, he reminded me of Eli—they both had a flair for arrogance, a desire to soften discomfort with teasing.

The same mouth.

But there was something else even more disconcerting about Levi, hard to place. A coldness that Eli didn't share, something almost feral—dangerous—buried deep.

I dropped the intense eye contact, trying to see into the room. Levi, unhelpful as ever, seemed unconcerned about stepping out of the way to let us through the doorway. "How's Seamus?"

"And why are you the one watching him?" Eli's tone was clipped with ill-disguised anger. He took a step down until he was pressed against my side. "I highly doubt he wants you here."

I stroked my thumb over the back of his hand.

Eli and Levi's relationship was a deeply fraught one. I had no idea if they'd ever find a path towards mending it, but now wasn't the time to lean into the inevitable explosion either.

Family trauma never really stayed truly buried, but hopefully they'd find a way to push it to the side with everything going on. They had no choice but to trust each other, to work together as well as they could.

Levi's eyes narrowed, but his focus was still on me. "Actually, wolfy Seamus seems to like me quite a bit. I'm one of the few who seems able to calm him. I'm here most days, whenever—"

The rest of the sentence was swallowed into silence, but we all knew the conclusion—whenever Eli wasn't around.

Eli definitely seemed to hate his brother, or what he represented to him at least, but Levi's commitment to keep his distance took a different shape.

The muscle in Eli's jaw twitched. If he clenched it any tighter, he'd crack a tooth.

I pressed my palm to Eli's chest while I sent a glare at his half-brother. "Enough of the baiting. None of us have the time or the energy for this shit. Let us in, Levi."

His lip twitched briefly into a grin, eyes narrowing on me for a long breath, but then he stepped to the side.

The room opened into a small cellar with dusty wine bottles lining one of the walls.

Seamus stood chained in the back corner, the thick metal rings around his ankles bolted deep into the concrete floor.

He was naked, likely from the constant warring with his wolf, shifting between bodies several times a day. The wound where he'd been bitten was still not healed all the way—it looked infected and deep. I kept my eyes on his face, noticing the dark lines of exhaustion creasing his eyes, the sweat coating his forehead. His breathing was ragged, his expression drawn in pain.

My chest squeezed at the sight of him, at the clear torment in his normally kind, gentle eyes.

"Hi, Dad." Eli took a few steps into the room. He stopped just out of reach of the chain's give.

Seamus's eyes narrowed and my stomach clenched at how much they reminded me of Cy's in that moment. "Eli?" His gaze cut to me. "Max? How are you? It's been months."

"I'm doing okay, all things considered." I didn't bother asking him how he was. The tension and pain were marked clearly in his posture, in every muscle twitch, in every line of his body.

"And Cyrus? Where is he? I thought he'd make his way down to see me by now?" He grunted, the sound caught between a strangled laugh and a moan of pain. "Stubborn prick."

My breath caught in my chest as Cy's name pierced through me like a spear. Eli and the others had warned me that Seamus's memory was unpredictable—sometimes he'd forget the last few days, sometimes he didn't seem to even remember who he was.

"He'll be here soon," Eli said, wincing slightly as he turned to me in apology.

I understood. There was no use putting Seamus through a grief that he wouldn't remember. If, when the war in his mind and body settled down a bit, he still didn't remember all that had happened, we'd tell him then. Right now, it was kinder to let him imagine his brother stomping around upstairs and raising hell.

As if a switch had been flipped, Seamus's face warped into something sharper, angrier. His brows furrowed as he glanced around the room, like he suddenly didn't recognize where he was.

"Unlock me." He turned to Eli, eyes fierce, hints of the soldier shining through. "Don't just stand there, boy. We haven't time for this. Get me out of here, they're coming." The chains rattled at his feet. I noticed a few scattered pieces of wood surrounding him—the relics of what was probably once a chair.

The violence of his pain was mapped across the cellar clear as day when I knew to look for it. Blood caked the ground in dark patches. Gouges had been dug out of the floor, lined with red vestiges from where his nails had peeled back, his blood soaked into the floor.

His body was battered and bruised—a surprising thing to see in a protector, but even more so in a wolf. I wasn't sure if these were new markings and injuries or if he just wasn't healing as quickly as we'd expected, beyond the bite.

"Now!" Seamus's teeth elongated, his dark eyes flashing bright with swirls of yellow and thick black ropes. Those eyes locked on me, the familiarity warped and angry. "You. You did this."

The metal of his chains clanged in vicious strikes, echoing around the room with his snarls.

"Fuck." Eli stepped in front of me, shoving me back a few feet. "Dad, you're okay. It's okay."

But by the tremor in his voice, I knew that even Eli didn't believe these words.

Strings of spit flew from Seamus's mouth as he screamed, the sound more animal than human.

Deep circles of red cut into his ankles as he strained against his restraints, his skin peeling back as it tore. Bones bent and broke at angry angles, skin and fur warring for real estate they couldn't both share.

My eyes watered as Seamus screamed in rage, in pain—the agony of the shift violent and loud.

"Dad," Eli held his hands up to his father, took a step closer. "It's okay, you're okay. Breathe with me, okay? One big breath in."

But he was too far gone, barreling on a path of pain that Eli couldn't reach.

Seamus's response was an ear-splitting scream-turned-roar as he lunged for his son. Any flash of recognition he'd had before now was eclipsed by a violent desire to tear his own flesh and blood to pieces.

The skin around his ankles ripped to shreds, peeling back even more as he used the force of his weight to free himself. It was enough to crack the bone, but I doubted he noticed it much anyway when his entire body was breaking and contorting, limbs elongating and shrinking, caught and confused in the shift.

I spun around to Levi, whose face was in shadow as he studied Seamus—half horror, half curiosity. "Is it always this bad?"

Levi shook his head, as Eli grunted out a soft, "No."

Levi's eyes widened as he took a step forward and reached for me. "Max, look out."

Eli fell back on his ass as Seamus ripped his chains free. "Holy fuck."

Seamus's feet were broken and bloody, but he didn't seem to mind. Instead, he lunged towards us, spit flying from his mouth like a rabid animal.

I shoved Levi off of me and jumped in front of Eli, conjuring a ring of hellfire around Seamus in one fluid movement. I had more control now and knew that I could keep the fire contained without burning anything too badly.

His eyes rippled, reflecting the crackling flames. For a moment, it looked like he might try to jump through them, but something about the shock pulled him out of it, woke him up.

The bright light from the fire highlighted the contusions and bruises along his body until it hurt to look at him. I narrowed my eyes and took a step closer to him, my face nearly touching the flames.

"What the fuck is she doing?" Levi's voice was hollow and low, dimmed by the low roar of the flames licking against my skin.

"Max, get away from him." I felt Eli at my back, his presence solid and unwavering as my flames shielded him.

My focus was drawn to the veins on Seamus's forearm— black, like ink, and rippling as if alive.

It was similar to what I'd seen in The Guild labs, identical to the magical energy moving underneath the council member's skin before he disappeared from sight.

"Is that—" I glanced up at Seamus's face, his eyes blown wide with horror at what he'd done. He took a few steps back, panting as he watched me, shame etched into every line of his face. I pulled the fire back, just as it would have swallowed his leg. The room grew dark and quiet without it.

"I'm sorry, I'm sorry, I'm sorry," Seamus repeated the phrase like a prayer, his body trembling as it shifted and locked back into his human form. "Please just kill me, just kill me, just kill me—"

His pleas echoed, ragged and anguished around the room.

I took a few steps closer to him, no longer afraid of what he might do to me, but I could no longer see the dark lines threading underneath the clammy smooth casing of his skin.

"Max, careful." Eli's arm pressed against mine, his blade hanging limp at his side. A small tremor ran through him before his body shifted into a fighting stance.

Seamus fell back on his butt, scurrying away from us like a crab. "Max? Who's Max?" His focus flung to Eli. "And you? Who are you?" Panicked breaths lifted in his chest in short, uneven gasps. "Where's Levi? Levi—do it, just do it. Plea—"

A low whistle flew past us, a dart landing deep into Seamus's arm. An almost smile pulled across his face, as his body relaxed, then fell into a slumber. I couldn't be sure, but I thought I heard him mumble a breathy "Thank you," before his eyes rolled back in his head and he stopped moving altogether.

Eli's fingers tightened over his blade as he spun around. In one swift motion, he had Levi pinned to the wall. A bottle of wine crashed at their feet, bathing the floor in another layer of crimson. "What the fuck did you do to him?"

Levi arched a brow but made no move to resist or engage with him. "What had to be done. When the confusion settles in, he panics, and then the shifts start pulsing through him. That back and forth—it exhausts him. It's literal torture—beyond what you can even imagine. The meds are the only way to help him rest." He shook his head, lips turned down in a soft frown, completely unconcerned that Eli had a blade pressed to his carotid. "I've never seen him that bad though. I don't know what triggered it, or if this is just the next stage. I've seen feral wolves before, but this is something else—something new."

The next stage?

My stomach tightened and it took everything I had to hold back the urge to vomit.

Fucking hell.

I knelt by Seamus, repositioning his arms and legs in a more comfortable posture. It was probably irrelevant, silly even, to fret over such a small comfort. The man had broken every bone in his body, over and over again—had willingly obliterated his ankles and feet trying to gain his freedom. A bit of stiffness from an awkward nap was the least of his worries. Still, it was the only thing I could help with.

I was sick of feeling useless, didn't know what to do with the jittering fear coursing through my blood.

I felt Levi's gaze on me, studying me and peeling back my layers in that way of his.

"You have very good control over those flames. That was impressive." He snorted, turning back to Eli. "Far better than your firework show, eh, brother?"

Eli stiffened, his blade drawing a small drop of blood from Levi.

Levi didn't seem to notice. Instead, eyes wide, he shook his head, oblivious to the fact that he was making the cut worse. "You haven't told her, have you?"

I closed the distance between us and put my hand on Eli's bicep, silently asking him to release Levi.

He dropped the blade but kept him pinned. He wouldn't meet my eyes. Instead, he glared at his brother with enough venom to make even me wither from the sight.

The two of them were locked in a silent conversation—

though conversation might have been a generous word for it—the muscle in Eli's jaw ticking with fury.

"Eli, what's going on?"

Levi arched his brow, looking partially intrigued, partially annoyed. "You really haven't told her? Why the fuck not?" His mouth curved like a scythe. "Don't want your girlfriend to know that you're stealing her powers? That you nearly burned the place down during one of your temper tantrums?"

Eli's arm drew back before I could stop him, his fist pounding into his brother's jaw with a vicious, resounding crack.

3

ELI

"Fuck," I shook my hand, appeased slightly by the fact that Levi's face was probably in more pain. But any appeasement dispersed the moment I turned towards Max, my stomach bottoming out at the look of hurt etched in plain text across her face. "Max, no—it's not like that."

She crossed her arms in front of her chest, her glare darting back and forth between me and Levi, like she couldn't quite decide who deserved her ire more.

I could. I fucking wanted to kill him.

"What's not like that? What's Levi talking about?" Her voice cracked, the sound like a shovel digging into my chest and ripping my heart out. "Why are you still keeping shit from me? I thought we were over this."

"Max, we are." I reached for her, but she took a step back.

"So, it's true then? You channeled my powers and didn't think to fucking tell me about it?" A glaze of tears coated her eyes, and I could practically feel the tightness in her throat from holding them back.

"No—" I pinched the bridge of my nose, trying to collect my

thoughts. "I mean yes. We are over this. We were going to tell you. We just wanted to wait until things calmed down. And this just took a natural backseat—after everything. You have so much on your plate right now and you're not sleeping—" my eyes darted to Levi. I didn't trust him—the less he knew about her powers, about her dream-walking, the better. He grinned, reading my hesitation with ease, then spit a dark spray of blood on the ground before wiping his mouth on the back of his hand. His teeth were lined with red, eyes glistening as they watched me until he looked more feral wolf than my dad. I took a deep breath, gesturing with my hands in a silent sign of "you know."

She took another step back, her eyes widening like I'd slapped her. "We?"

Fuck.

Fuck.

Fuck.

My heart hammered an angry beat against my ribs.

I was handling this with about as much grace as a goddamn intoxicated donkey. Where the fuck was Declan? She was so much better at this shit than I was.

I shot a scathing look at Levi. "Can you give us a minute please."

"By all means," he leaned against the wall, catching a bottle of wine he'd bumped into before another one met its demise on the ground "take all the minutes you need."

Clearly, he wasn't leaving.

Smug fuck.

I swallowed back the growing desire to punch him again, knowing full well it would just upset Max more.

I had enough working against me at the moment.

My jaw clenched so tight I could barely speak. But I managed a low, "without you," anyway.

Obviously without him. Fucking dick.

Levi grunted, a shadow of mirth flaring briefly across his expression. "I know what you meant, but I want to hear this too. Perfect little bonded team isn't as perfect as it seems, apparently. You can't pay for this kind of entertainment. And as amusing as Seamus is, this takes top billing."

That tic in my jaw was back with a vengeance, but instead of pushing the argument further, I turned back to Max.

I hated Levi, but that was personal, me-problem shit. Max didn't need to deal with it, and if we were going to stay here for a while, I needed to find a way to interact with him without exploding every time we shared air space.

Of course, it would be a lot easier if he wasn't constantly watching her, staring at her with a familiarity and interest that made my stomach crawl with boiling, unfamiliar rage.

I took a deep breath, focused my attention on Max.

I wasn't going to fuck this up.

Not again.

I was done fucking shit up with her.

"When you left in the middle of the night, when you went to Headquarters, I was fucking terrified that I was going to lose you. Like the forever kind of lose you. I needed to get to you, to save you, but—" I shot a look at Levi, remembering all over again that he'd made my life more difficult in that trying moment as well, "I didn't know how. And I got angry," I shook my head, trying to dispel the lingering memory of that acute fear, "like really angry."

"Eli angry? Shocking." Levi snorted, but he shut up when I cut him another warning look.

He raised his hands in mock surrender, but he didn't say anything else.

"And then I caught on fire." I grabbed her hand, the feel of her skin against mine calming the anxiety rushing through me, like my body needed to know at a cellular level that she was okay, that she was here, that I was hers. "Like your fire." I shook my head before clarifying, "not just *like* your fire—we're pretty sure that I actually conjured *your* fire. Somehow."

The soft wrinkle between her brows unfurled as her face settled into surprise. I took a step closer to her, cradling her face between my hands and blocking her from Levi's view.

If he insisted on staying for this, then the least I could do was obliterate his presence as much as possible. This wasn't about the smug asshole.

This was about me and Max. Protecting the bond that had grown more important to me than anything else in the entire world—more important, even, than my own life.

Her dark, beautiful brown eyes met mine, and I hated that there was a glassy film obscuring their usual warmth. Hated even more that I was, in part, the cause.

"I don't know how I did it and I don't know why it happened when it did. Maybe it was just a flare from when you were burning down The Guild, and I channeled it somehow through my own anger." My thumb grazed over the soft skin of her cheek, a steady rhythm to calm us both. "I haven't been able to conjure even a wisp of smoke since. Nothing happened. No one got hurt. I scorched some grass outside and that was it. After you brought Atlas and Sarah back, after you brought down Headquarters—Max, it honestly didn't seem that important. Not compared to everything else that we're dealing with right now, everything to come."

I stepped closer, inhaling the soft smell of her shampoo, using it to center me. "And the longer we went without saying anything, the more difficult it became to start—like in forgetting about the whole thing briefly, and then not saying anything, it had grown into a bigger deal than it was. Does that make sense?" I sighed, feeling the exhale low in my gut, fear over her reaction mingling with the easing tension now that this was out. There were no more secrets between us. She could reach into my thoughts and pull out anything that she wanted

—they were all about her—all for her, anyway. "I'm sorry. Truly, extremely sorry."

Her jaw was tight, and I rubbed my thumb against the sharp line of it, trying to soothe away the tension.

She didn't lean into my touch like she often did, but she didn't shy away from it either. I'd count that as a win for now, though I knew this wouldn't be the end of the conversation.

But hopefully it would be enough to hold her over until the others could join in.

I could see her mind working overtime, her eyes asking a thousand questions at once, like she couldn't decide where to start. She shook her head and pushed my hands away from her. "It's been a week, Eli. There were plenty of opportunities for one of you to slip in a quick, "Hey, Max, I channeled your powers, isn't that weird? We should probably figure that out."

"Fair point," Levi said with the kind of casual interest someone might employ while observing a mildly entertaining tennis match.

"That includes you too, Levi," she snapped. "You knew about this too and didn't tell me either."

He withered slightly under her glare, then stood up and took a step towards her. She raised her hand stopping him.

I bit back my smirk, then swallowed it completely when she turned that anger in my direction. "It could be dangerous; you could have been hurt. Eli, what if I've been unintentionally putting you in danger? Opened up a link or something that I don't know how to close, how to control." She took a step back, her gaze dropping to her hands, like they might spontaneously combust. "What if I hurt you?"

Fuck.

Of course she'd find a way to feel guilty about this—to feel responsible.

For something I'd done.

Something I'd kept secret.

"Max, no, you're not endangering anyone." I reached for her again, slowly this time, then closed the distance when she didn't move further away. I pressed my lips softly to hers, then whispered against her lips, ignoring Levi entirely. "I promise. No more secrets between us. It won't happen again."

Her expression shifted, flattening out, then she dropped her eyes from mine, offering only a nod in response. "Yeah," there was something lingering there—something I couldn't put my finger on. When she opened her mouth like she was going to say something else, my stomach clenched with fear. But she just shook her head, gave me a weak smile, and said, "Okay, no more secrets."

"Well," Levi brushed some invisible dirt from his pants. "Now that the lovers' spat is through—and far less climactic and entertaining than I'd hoped—and since Seamus is likely going to be under for another couple of hours, I should probably take you both to the meeting."

Max's brows furrowed as she stepped around me to get a better look at him. "What meeting?"

Levi gave her a lazy half-grin, his eyes once again locked on hers like she was all he saw.

I didn't blame him, but it still fucking infuriated me.

I'd never hated-hated Levi, beyond my own jealousies and baggage about my mom. I was emotionally aware enough to understand that my dislike wasn't personal—he'd had about as much say in our familial circumstances as I'd had.

But then he went and set his sights on Max, and that dislike shaped into something sharper, more solid.

Then again, that was just a different kind of jealousy. One that resonated deeper.

"It's about time you and your team are let in on what we know." He shrugged. "Part of it, anyway."

A familiar spark of excitement lit her face and my stomach flipped at the smile she gave him.

But then she turned that smile on me, and any petty jealousies slipped away. Even with his flirtations and attempts to garner her attention, Max had never once looked at Levi the way she looked at me.

When she looked at me like that, I couldn't move, could hardly breathe.

It was equal parts intoxicating and terrifying.

I used to be suave, have game.

Now, I was a puddle of goo in the palms of a girl.

What the fuck had become of me?

"Let's get the others before we go." Her smile dimmed slightly. "Do you think we'll be able to convince Atlas to leave his room?"

My stomach tightened for an entirely different reason, one much less pleasant. "We can try."

4

ELI

Thankfully, Levi ditched us as soon as he'd delivered us to the meeting. We found ourselves in a small room at the back of Charlie's restaurant—it was crowded and cramped but had been repurposed into a cluttered conference room of sorts.

He didn't say so, but I knew he was going back to sit with my father, and as much as I wanted to hate him for encroaching, for being the one my father seemed to turn to in those moments when he lost himself, I was also grateful that my dad wouldn't be alone.

Atlas was locked next to Max, a silent sentinel.

He still hadn't spoken much to the rest of us, but every day he seemed to be getting a little bit better, a little more like himself. The problem was that Atlas was a bit of a quiet, surly loner even when he was his usual, brooding self. That made gauging any improvement in his mental state difficult.

He didn't leave his room, other than to use the bathroom. Max crawled into bed with him each night in an effort to help comfort him, to combat some of the lingering dread tugging at his mind.

It was almost like he was relearning how to fit inside of his skin, his world—and she was the key to helping him do it.

I had a feeling that the dark shadows that seemed to encase him would linger for a long time though. None of us really knew what he went through, and Max didn't talk too much about the glimpses she'd seen in her dreamwalks to him. She didn't want to betray his trust, to tell his story.

I respected the hell out of her for it, but respect and understanding did nothing to quell my curiosity or my concern.

But I knew from the brief things she did tell us—the fear that flickered in her expression whenever we brought up his name, the way she spent most of the evenings in his room, trying to coax him out of his shell and soothe whatever invisible scars he harbored, her obsession with healing Sarah—that what he was going through would take time.

Maybe even a lifetime.

Honestly, it was something that he actually let her see him like this. Atlas wasn't one for being comforted, for allowing someone to see him in his most raw and vulnerable state.

I supposed I shouldn't have been surprised though. Max had that effect on us all. The ability to get in and truly *see* us— even the parts of us we wanted to hide. It's why we'd all been so fucking terrified of getting too close to her. The fear that she'd see the worst we had to offer and leave.

She hadn't though. And I was beginning to realize that we'd done her a disservice in assuming she was the kind of person who'd bail.

Atlas wasn't himself, but the fact that he was letting Max get a glimpse of the pain he was enduring had me confident he would be himself again.

One day.

Ideally it would happen before the impending apocalypse, but we couldn't afford to be picky.

He shifted awkwardly, limbs stiff, and I knew it took everything in him not to run back to our cabin, back to the dark shelter of the room he'd taken over. This was the first time since his return that he'd left, the first time he'd settled into a room all of us occupied. His discomfort shone through every muscle twitch, every nervous sidelong glance at us.

A door opened and Charlie and Bishop walked in. Behind them was a tall white man with dark red hair knotted in a bun on his head, and an East-Asian woman with a sharp, black bob. I hadn't seen either of them around the Lodge yet.

And I didn't give either of them much attention because it was the last person who walked in that made my stomach bottom out.

Evelyn.

I'd done a damn good job of avoiding her when she was at Headquarters, and an even better job since arriving here.

But apparently that avoidance spree was ending now.

Her eyes locked on mine, her lips lifting into a small, tentative smile, but it disappeared when I offered her blankness in response.

It took everything I had to swallow the anxiety lodged in my throat, my chest damn near like a vise at just the sight of her.

An unfamiliar emotion flashed across her expression—hurt, maybe—before she covered it up with the usual protector mask and greeted the others with a stiff nod.

"Thanks for joining us." Either oblivious to the tension or kindly ignoring it, Charlie smiled before gesturing to the mismatched swivel chairs surrounding the large, wooden table we were all hovering around. "Why don't we all take a seat and get comfortable?"

Without a word, we all shuffled to an available chair. It was an almost comical moment of musical chairs, each set of hinges squeaking loudly under the weight of bodies. The room was a far cry from the command centers where we'd received our mission at Headquarters.

It wasn't until all the other spots had been taken that I realized the only available seat left was directly across from my mother.

Fuck today.

I bit the insides of my cheeks and gripped the arms of the chair, trying like hell to keep my face blank, even as my traitorous fingers trembled with anxiety.

In that moment, I hated myself. Hated that I couldn't swallow back my own bullshit and wear the mask I'd spent a decade perfecting. Hated that my mother had this effect on me. I felt so small, powerless in her presence. Like I was suddenly the same little boy she'd abandoned all those years ago.

There were more important things going on, and I so badly wanted the strength to push all my personal shit aside.

Max lined the side of her foot against mine and I froze, briefly, before relaxing and leaning into the soft pressure of hers in thanks. The simple reminder of her presence, that she was with me and on my side, was like a fresh gulp of water after weeks in the desert.

"This isn't all of our community representatives," Charlie started, glancing around at everyone, her eyes wide and shining with warmth, "but it will do for our purposes today."

"And what purposes are those?" Darius asked, his voice uncharacteristically frigid. I hadn't spoken to him much over the last week—all of us were spread thin, busy helping out in various capacities around the campgrounds—but something about him seemed a little...off.

Tense.

Hungry.

He hadn't bothered taking a seat. He was the only one standing, leaning against the wall behind Max's chair. Typically, I'd find his obnoxious behavior, well, obnoxious, but right now I was honestly glad to have one of us at Max's six. The girl attracted danger and enemies like no one I'd ever met. And while I trusted Charlie and Bishop reasonably well, I hadn't met everyone who lived in this small community. We were outnumbered and in the middle of nowhere.

Bishop's dark gaze drilled into him. Whatever animosity he'd once harbored for the vampire was still very, *very* much alive, but Darius paid him no attention.

"Well—" it was strange, I hadn't really heard it in years, but Evelyn's voice—soft but sure—cut through me like a goddamn knife. I tensed at the sound of it. There had been so many nights I'd woken up wishing more than anything that that voice would come comfort me back to sleep and ease the nightmares away. But she was the one who'd caused so many of those nightmares in the first place. Max squeezed my knee under the table, and I did my best to relax into her touch. "This is war, isn't it?" Her hazel eyes cut to Max. "Or are we going to pretend that burning the primary research station of The Guild was just an unconventional greeting card?"

There wasn't judgment in her tone, if anything, she sounded almost impressed. Intrigued, at the very least.

She studied Max for a long moment.

Max met her stare, unwavering, and I could feel her anger on my behalf directed like a laser towards the woman. She had no reason to hate Evelyn—except that she'd hurt me.

Evelyn's mouth twitched into an amused grin, but it dissolved into her usual mask almost as quickly as it had appeared. "I don't think we've formally met yet, Max Bentley. But I'm Evelyn. I've heard a great deal about you."

Max's lips flattened. "I've heard a lot about you as well."

"Yes, of course." The angles of Evelyn's jaw tightened as she listlessly arranged some papers and files sitting in front of her. "I'm sure you have." She leaned back into her chair, the rickety groan echoing in the tense silence.

I could feel my team's eyes on me, waiting for me to react, to blow up. But I swallowed my anger, using Max's touch to anchor me. My past was nothing compared to what we were up against—it was time for me to swallow it as best as I could.

Evelyn cleared her throat, then her face softened as her focus turned to me. "I hear you're coming from visiting with Seamus. How is he? I haven't been down to see him yet today."

I snorted. "Are you suggesting that you suddenly care?" The words slipped out before I could reign them in. The petulant, childlike tone of my voice had shame licking at my spine. This wasn't who I was, not anymore. I hated that two seconds in a room with her sent me back to adolescence.

"Of course—" pain flashed across her face, her eyes framing in soft wrinkles as she narrowed them. "Eli, of course I care."

I swallowed the retort on the tip of my tongue and nodded. "He's not good, but he's strong." I met her eyes, adding, "and he's survived through worse. He'll get through this too—and be stronger on the other side of it."

There was no mystery as to who had caused the deepest ache in his life.

It certainly wasn't a wonky werewolf.

"Yes, well, we're doing everything we can. Levi tells me that there's been some signs of improvement. He's getting stronger, the—"

"Enough." I only whispered the word, but it seemed to echo through the room like a bell. My chest was tight, heavy, like it was being crushed by a fucking semi. "I won't discuss my father with you. Is he why you called us here? Or are there other things we can discuss?"

Boundaries. Boundaries were good.

Her eyes dropped down to the table, the apples of her cheeks flushed bright with pink. "Right. Yes. I understand." She cleared her throat. "I apologize for overstepping."

The man with red hair smiled awkwardly, catching on to the tension and clearly trying to dispel it as gracefully as possible. "Perhaps it would be best if we got introductions out of the way. My name is Jace. I've been a part of this community for two years." He turned to Max, his smile widening until it was almost absurdly bright. He was a disarmingly good-looking dude. "And I'm already a big fan of yours, Max. My little sister was locked up in those labs. I didn't think I'd ever see her again. I owe you a great debt."

That caught Max's attention, and pulled her quiet, withering glare away from Evelyn. "Is she okay?"

Jace tilted his head back and forth, his smile flattening a bit. "As okay as can be expected. She was stuck down there for nearly six months—very few succubi are lucky enough to survive protector—" he grunted, "what do they like to call them? Tests? Well, whatever the semantics, very few survive their particular brand of torture that long. But she's strong and somehow managed it. We are eternally grateful to you."

Max straightened up, her eyes brightening. "You're an incubus?"

I noticed Wade lean forward a bit as well, unable to hide his own intrigue. Incubi were rare. Other than Wade, I'd never encountered one. Not knowingly anyway.

But that definitely explained why the man was so pretty, the charisma nearly dripping from him.

He nodded. "Yes. We grew up in the hell realm but spent most of our lives on our own. Easier to survive that way—to blend in."

The woman on his right arched her brow. "And I'm Haley. Vampire."

So, Charlie and Bishop weren't kidding when they said that this place was a large mix of supernaturals from all corners of the world.

We rattled off our names, and while Jace gave each of us a jovial nod, Haley hadn't taken her eyes off of Max. Not even to blink.

"You bear the start of a bond mark." Her eyes narrowed on

the small iridescent curve that had grown up the smooth column of Max's neck, where few shirts could cover it completely. "So the rumors are more than rumors then? You are a true bond pack. Like the kind of the old days?"

Max shifted uncomfortably, eyeing me out of the corner of her eye.

I could almost feel the outline of my own mark pulse under my shirt from the heavy intrigue on the woman's face. We all had them now. They were growing more solid, more undeniable with every day that passed.

The collective weight of everyone's gaze was heavy, like they were all trying to find the marks that weren't on display, like they could see beneath our clothes if they stared hard enough.

"Yes," Max said, offering them nothing else. She was hesitant, careful, and I could feel her desire to protect us flare against my skin—bright and hot like the sun. For once, I understood Icarus's temptation. What a way to go.

"Yes," Jace nodded, "I can feel it, emanating from you all. Such a large group, too."

I cleared my throat, uncomfortable discussing our bonds— it was a sacred connection between us, the only thing anchoring us through the chaos of this new world. That we were casually chatting about them in front of my mother, who'd deliberately and knowingly broken her own, albeit fabricated bond, made my skin itch with disgust.

"And your powers." Haley's sentence hung in the air, not a question but more an invitation to elaborate.

"Not important." Darius's voice was clipped. I'd almost forgotten that he was hovering behind us.

Jace nudged Haley's arm as her stare focused on Darius, curiosity evident even in the blankness of her stare.

"And you," she said to him, "are more than you seem as well."

Darius offered her nothing but a scathing glare in response.

"Right," Jace started, the word layered with a tense chuckle, "let's establish some trust here first, we're all on the same team. It's paramount that we learn to trust each other if we're all going to be working together. At the risk of sounding like a narrator from a fairytale, dangerous shit is afoot. There's a lot of uncertainty, uncharted water in our future, and it's best we go in knowing who the true enemy is—The Guild Council." He arched a brow, his focus turning to each of us. "Sound fair?"

"We'll see," Dec responded. She was sitting on my other side, and I'd caught the several death glares she'd shot my mother. Dec liked to pretend that she didn't give a shit about anyone, but she was protective as fuck—and she'd seen first-hand the damage that Evelyn had done to both me and my father when she'd left us.

And Seamus had been like a second father to her too over the years.

I felt unexpectedly warm with the support system surrounding me. I always knew my team had my back, but things had shifted lately, grown stronger—unshakeable.

We'd literally been to hell and back for each other. That kind of shit changed things.

My mother abandoned me, and I'd been unknowingly terrified that the family I'd chosen, my team, might one day do the same.

But I wasn't anymore.

They'd be with me to the end. It was the only thing I was sure of these days and, honestly, it was a pretty fucking magical feeling.

"Obviously things are going to shit," Jace continued with a soft chuckle. "The world, I mean. It's very clear that something big is changing and The Guild has been in denial of it for years. Or deliberately hiding it from their own. The magic is changing, I can feel it. Taste it, almost. There was a reason my sister and I took our shot and escaped the hell realm when we did.

But things aren't necessarily better here, and they're about to get worse, aren't they?" He nodded to Max, then Wade. "You're tied to the same magic, so I'm sure you can feel it too. The magic that separates the realms is starving."

Max leaned forward slightly. "What do you mean, starving?"

He tilted his head, like he was searching for the words. When he finally landed on them, they came out clear, sharp, full of warning. "That kind of magic feeds on blood, on violence. It's why hell is such a chaotic, dangerous world. Why this one is mirroring it at a rapid, accelerating pace. The barrier is warped, that violence is echoing and reflecting in this world now too."

"This world has always been a violent one," Wade said.

Jace smiled. He seemed oddly relaxed for someone discussing the end of the world. Then again, that kind of disarming demeanor was the razor-sharp weapon of an incubus.

They were better at controlling their emotions, at reading others than most.

"You're not wrong. But it's gotten worse and will continue to get worse. We don't fully understand why it's happening, but we can no longer deny that we are on the edge of some sort of existential threat. All of us. And while it was caused by The Guild long before any of us were around, it's clear that The Guild has no intention of cleaning up their mess—as per usual —nor do they likely have the power to do it even if they wanted to. Their strength and their numbers have been diminishing for years—a sacrifice and consequence to the power they've long misused."

Max glanced at me, then the others, all of us silently checking in, unsure of how much to tell them. She took a deep breath then nodded. "The barrier between realms is collapsing. It's possible that when it reaches a tipping point, everything—

and everyone will be destroyed. Sucked into some kind of magical black hole." She exhaled, eyes darting from face to face in the heaviness. "We don't really know our odds of keeping that from happening but we're doing everything we can to try."

The room was silent, heavy, as they all took in the blunt statement. It was the kind of doom and gloom announcement that seemed almost humorously exaggerated. Only we knew now that it wasn't.

I wasn't sure we could truly, unequivocally trust these people. I'd never forgive my mother for what she did to my father, but that didn't mean she was evil beyond our personal dynamics.

If we were going to live and work with them, it was only fair that they knew what they were up against, I supposed.

Clearly Max did too.

Haley still watched Max, unblinking and ethereally still, but she didn't flinch at the direness of the message. If anything, she only sat up straighter, a fighting fire growing in her dark eyes.

"You seem confident in the validity of this information." Bishop unconsciously swiveled his chair a few inches closer to Charlie. "We've guessed at it, naturally. Jace and some of the others who've traveled between realms in recent years have mentioned the fluctuations. And of course, we've been tracking fractures and tears between the realms when we hear about strange activity—" his focus locked on Max, distrust clear in the tension lining his body, "but how did you come by this information?"

Max met my eyes, then the others. We all nodded.

The decision was clear—surprisingly easy to communicate with just a glance—conceal what we needed to but share as much as we could.

Everyone's life was in danger, we were past the point of keeping things secret from those we could trust. Miscommunication only ever created more problems.

And while our trust could only extend so far, Charlie, Bishop, and the others here had taken us in and created the kind of community The Guild had only pretended to foster.

When we'd brought them a bunch of injured and tortured demons, and voluntarily exiled protectors, they bent over backwards offering their resources and help.

They deserved the truth, the chance to decide whether they truly wanted a part of this war or not. Because honestly, that was the truth—this was a war. We just weren't entirely sure on how many enemies there were, or how to fight the ambivalence of unstable magic. But if we wanted to survive, to save as many people as we could, we'd have to try.

Because while The Guild was the most tangible threat at the moment, the real battle was going to be against the unstable magic—a disaster they'd created through greed, one that we'd be responsible for preventing further fallout from.

I saw Max fidgeting with the hem of her shirt out of the corner of my eye. "We've been to the hell realm; we've seen what's happening."

"What?" Charlie's eyes widened. "How?"

"Several times, actually, because—" Max took a deep breath, "because, the thing is," she cleared her throat, "the thing is, I'm Lucifer's daughter. Most of my power comes from him, some from my mother's line of protectors. Something about my birth might have triggered things, we aren't really sure on the details. Most people who have them are dea—" she paused for a beat, the five of them stunned. She took a deep breath and pressed on. "Um, right. But we also know how to fix it. To keep the barrier from taking out both realms." She scrunched her nose. "Maybe."

Jace opened his mouth and closed it a few times, the first to recover from Max's revelation. After a few seconds, he finally pushed out a word. "Maybe?"

"The devil is real?" Charlie's complexion dipped into an ashy gray, so at odds with the usual warmth. "Seriously?"

Out of the corner of my eye, I saw Evelyn was preternaturally still, her expression not revealing surprise or much of anything really. She was always so good at swallowing her emotions, spitting them back out as an empty canvas when she needed to.

Max smiled sheepishly.

"Yes, but not like you think," Wade clarified. "He's not evil or anything. At least we don't think so. His motivations are slightly unclear, but we think we can trust him. For now. And if his predictions about the hell realm are true, we don't really have a choice."

Charlie took a deep breath. I could see her wrestling with the information, her mind moving a mile a minute. She wasn't really born into this life, hadn't even learned about the supernatural world until a few years ago. I imagined this was especially jarring for her to hear.

She exhaled, long and deep. "Okay. Well, assuming he's not as evil as I'd imagined my entire life, does Lucifer have an actionable plan for how to fix things?"

Fear was etched into every line of her face, but there was also determination. It was damn impressive how well she was handling things. How well they all were.

Better than I had when I'd had to metabolize the same news.

I resisted the sudden urge to glance at Evelyn again, though I was strangely tempted to see her reaction unfold to all of this. Vestigial attachments to an old life, perhaps.

Charlie's hand unconsciously dropped to her stomach, then she shared a brief, intimate look with Bishop.

They hadn't mentioned it to any of us, but I had a feeling they had a very specific motivation for ensuring a more stable and peaceful future.

"First, we need something that The Guild stole many centuries ago." Max's voice was strong, decisive, and, with an almost indecipherable ripple, the atmosphere of the room instantly shifted from shock to action. "A stone—shadow magic made solid. They use it to forge their bonding ceremonies."

"They do what?" For the first time, Jace looked almost cross, the vestiges of rage, the clear threat of his power—circling like smoke in his dark green eyes.

Evelyn nodded, drawing my attention, blinking like she was coming out of a trance. She straightened her posture—any lingering feelings she had from earlier were buried under the commanding mask of someone devoted to a new, top-secret mission. "I think I know what stone you're referring to. They didn't use it for those purposes initially, but they've resorted to that in recent years, after losing their paired blade. I've seen it once, but it's kept under heavy protective detail. I don't know much about it—only that it never leaves a council member's sight. It won't be easy for us to get a hold of, especially if they believe you're after it." She shook her head in disgust. "It's taken a while to confirm, but on one of my last missions with them before," she waved a hand in Max's direction, "you know, the fire, I confirmed some of my deepest fears—that they've warped the magic they were sworn to protect. After looking at Greta's notes on some of the patients she's taking care of, it's becoming clearer. Not only have they found a way to pull magic from demons, they've found ways to mobilize it for their own uses. Beyond what they've been telling us—" she shook her head, "even those of us with unseasonably high clearance."

"They've what?" Darius gripped the back of Max's chair, echoing Jace's anger with far more volume. His fingers tore holes through the leather lining, white filling poking out at odd angles. He didn't seem to notice.

Every muscle in Max's body froze.

Evelyn's mouth flattened into a thin line. "They used to

drain the blood from the demons they kept in captivity and feed it into the realm, through the stone. The barrier, the ether, whatever the hell we want to call it—it requires power to maintain itself—from this side of the veil too. For years, the only power we've had access to is blood—protector and demon. Protector blood has become diluted over the centuries, warped —weak. And eventually, through decades of research, trial and error, Guild scientists realized that not all demons had the same magic." She glanced apologetically at Jace. "With lust demons, for instance, they noticed something different. They're rarer than vampires and werewolves, partly because they're harder to identify and capture, and partly because protectors often fall victim to their power without realizing it. But with the influx of attacks and activity over the last decades, their research began to accumulate and take shape. This—shadow magic, did you call it? They were able to identify and isolate it in a succubus about a year or so ago—and, more recently, a new demon they captured. One who feeds on fear and is somehow able to harness demonic energy of other forms and transform it into this shadow magic. My clearance was high, but I still only caught small threads of information from my infiltration. They're unfortunately very good at keeping bits of information separate and isolated, so that even the people working on it hardly know what the larger context or body of knowledge they're contributing to is. It didn't make much sense, collectively, until recently, when we've had better opportunities to fill in the gaps—and now, it seems obvious what they're doing."

"It's why The Guild has always preferred capture over kill —" Bishop directed his attention to Atlas, like he was searching for the cousin he used to know behind the darkness. He wouldn't find him. The Atlas he knew was practically just a kid —he'd been through a lifetime of pain since then, molded into something new. "Why they've doubled down on that more recently. They're trying to find a way to maintain the imbalance they created centuries ago—to fix their now undeniable mistakes. Only they want to do so while in a way that will keep protectors on top of the food chain so to speak. They want to maintain control of the power."

Haley's lips dipped with disgust, the first fracture in her indifferent expression. "As insufferably evil as always, in other words."

Evelyn nodded. "But this last year, they've become even more consumed by fear, and that's translated to only more greed. They've read the writing on the wall and decided to give themselves the best chance of survival they can."

"What are you saying exactly?" Declan asked.

"I can't confirm it, but I have my suspicions that," Evelyn took a deep breath, her shoulders sagging slightly, "they've actually found a way to inject themselves with this shadow magic, effectively imbibing them with the strength and power of demons. Attaching themselves to the magic of the barrier. Guild researchers have always been invested in understanding the supernatural world. That very thirst for power is the reason the hell realm exists at all. Demons have power and The Guild wants it. Recent events and fears have pushed that research to new extremes—turning that very power into a weapon they can use to protect themselves if the world turns hostile towards them."

"And how exactly is it that you know this?" I asked. "My father hasn't mentioned it before."

"He's lost council trust in recent years, more so in recent months. He wouldn't have access to that information. And with his connection to Cyrus, the council has always been hesitant about letting him in deeper." Her eyes met mine, sad and hazy with emotion and history I didn't want to untangle. "Even with my level clearance—I'm still unable to confirm. But I've heard rumors, seen glimpses of it firsthand."

"So have I," Max said. Her focus was on Evelyn. "When we were leaving the lab, we ran into a member of the council—at least I'm pretty sure he was a member of the council." Her eyes closed, like she was trying to visualize the memory, make it solid. "His veins were dark black, the same kind of sludge-like liquid we noticed them siphoning from some of the demons. Not exactly pure shadow magic, but an essence of it definitely lingered in there. When I focused on it, I could sense it was more than blood they were draining."

She'd mentioned this run-in a few days ago, but now with this new insight, the direness of it all sank in.

"He teleported away—something very few demons are able to do, especially outside of the magic encasing and pulsing through hell. There's a reason lust demons need access to hell's power to engage with their own."

"Like you can, you mean." Haley's voice was emotionless, but I tensed at the unfulfilled accusation.

Max only nodded though, taking her point. "Yes, like I can. I wasn't sure what I was seeing at the time, but this makes sense now. They're scared—they know shit's going to hit the fan so they're taking the magic and trying to save themselves."

My teeth hurt from clenching them so tightly.

"And—" Max paused for a beat before she inhaled sharply, "oh my god. Seamus." She squeezed my thigh under the table, her eyes wide as she turned to me. Panic pooled low in my gut, like my body knew what she was going to say before my brain did. "Today, there was a moment, when the light of my hellfire hit just right, that I could have sworn I saw his veins turn black. What if that's the reason his shift is so difficult?"

Evelyn's face clouded in horror. "You think he wasn't just bitten by a werewolf, but one infused with this distorted shadow magic somehow?"

"Is that possible?" Wade asked her. "Have you seen anything like that when working with them?"

Evelyn shook her head. "I know they've been doing a lot of experiments. They've been more or less throwing spaghetti at the wall, hoping something sticks before it's too late—before they lose everything they've spent generations—centuries—cultivating. People don't let go of power easily. That kind of fear inspires bold, unprecedented action. Now that I know more about what our world is facing, it's not impossible to imagine they'd do something like this. I just don't know what it could mean for us—or for Seamus."

"And now the greedy fucks are throwing their people under the bus to save themselves—the rest of the world they're supposedly sworn to protect be damned." Darius's voice was dangerous, the look in his eyes wild with anger.

If I didn't know him as well as I did, my hackles would be up—as it was, I only shifted slightly, uncomfortable with him standing behind me.

Never have your back to a predator. Blood-bonded to me or not, Darius was no prey.

Bishop's hand moved below the table, and I knew with a deep certainty that he'd wrapped it around the blade at his thigh—eyes locked onto Darius.

Charlie rubbed his shoulder, and he loosened up at her touch, just slightly.

"If this is true," Haley leaned back in her chair, brow arched, "getting this stone will be more difficult than anticipated. They'll be hard to kill."

Max smirked. "So am I."

5

———

MAX

"Do we have any idea how many council members there are?" Wade asked. "Even with Tarren as a father, I learned surprisingly little about how they work. I couldn't even name one of them to be honest."

Wade didn't even flinch when he mentioned his father's name—his eyes were cold, expressionless.

He hadn't said much after I told him that Atlas killed their father. I left the gruesome details out, waiting to see if he wanted specifics.

Other than a resounding "Good, if he didn't kill the fucker, I would have," he'd been oddly silent on the topic.

Still, I knew from experience that grief was a gnarly little dickhole that snuck up on you, often when you least expected.

Tarren was an asshole. And he was an absolute prick to Wade especially.

But he was still his father—and the only one he'd ever get.

Evelyn nodded. "That's by design. But as of now, from what I can tell, there are seven." Her lips twisted into a satisfied grin. "And I know where we can find three of them." She shrugged, her lips wavering slightly. "It's not much, but it's a start."

Eli glanced at her briefly before his focus landed firmly on the wall behind her.

He didn't seem able to look at her for very long, but he kept sneaking glances every few minutes, whether consciously or not, I wasn't sure.

I rubbed my chest, like I could feel his anxiety trapped there, dying for release.

Dealing with his mother and brother both in the same hour was no easy feat.

"Isn't your double agency shot now though?" he asked, his voice quiet. "I imagine they'll change all of their whereabouts if they think you've turned on them."

Her lips curved into a tentative smile as she glanced at him, probably pleased that he was addressing her with less venom in his voice this time.

I couldn't help but ache at the way she looked at him—so much longing, so much pain. I knew very little about her, outside of the few details Eli had shared what felt like a lifetime ago. She'd broken her bond to Seamus and left him and Eli behind—apparently to live with Levi and her second family.

She'd hurt him. Badly enough that he lived most of his life refusing to let anyone get close enough to carve another crater deep into his chest—a similar, festering wound of abandonment.

But something about the way her eyes softened with regret whenever they landed on him told me that there was more to their story than I realized. Maybe even more than Eli himself knew. It wasn't the sort of look I imagined a woman giving a son she didn't love.

She'd abandoned him, yes, but there was true affection—love—in her eyes. Even when his only broadcasted anger and hate back at her.

She cleared her throat and sat up straighter, pride sharpening her posture. "Not if they think I'm dead."

"You faked your death?" I asked. It was a smart move, and I couldn't help but be mildly impressed by the woman in front of me, as much as I hated her for hurting Eli.

Like most women in The Guild, she had an iron strength. It was impossible not to respect that.

"Borrowed the idea from a friend." She glanced at Bishop, and I noticed that her smirk mirrored Eli's almost identically.

Bishop grunted.

"Well, that's good news at least," Declan said. I noticed she'd scooted herself closer to Eli too, and kept glancing at him from the corner of her eye, like she was getting ready to throw herself between him and his mother if it came down to it, to protect him from the pain that was lining every tense muscle in his body. "If they think you're dead, they won't invoke any kind of protocol to revoke your access. So now it's just a matter of using whatever intel you have to find the stone. We can start by going after the three council members you have access to."

"It might be a little more difficult than that." Charlie's teeth snagged on her bottom lip as her eyes caught mine.

"What do you mean?" Eli asked, that muscle tic in his jaw was back again. He narrowed his eyes. "What aren't you guys telling us?"

"Have any of you watched the news since the fire?" Haley asked, her thin brow arched. "Read a paper?" Her eyes met mine, widening slightly. "Checked social media?"

"Apparently not," Darius said, his voice laced with gravelly impatience.

Charlie cleared her throat, turned to Bishop, then Evelyn, like they were deciding who was going to be the bearer of bad news. Because of course there was bad news. There was *always* bad news.

"The Guild controls most human governments." Jace ran his thumb over his lips, as he fought for a way to frame whatever he was struggling to say. "In almost every way that counts anyway."

I'd suspected as much, though no one had ever blatantly laid out the details as to how they managed that. Protectors and demons did a reasonably good job of hiding their tracks, but none of us were perfect. Having a hand in human governments would certainly help keep the supernatural communities flying under the radar. Especially in the age of the internet.

I nodded, urging him to continue as he locked eyes with Haley.

She exhaled, then turned to us. "Look, no use sugar coating it—you guys are all wanted."

"Wanted?" I asked. "By whom?"

She snorted. "Take your pick. Literally everyone. You're blacklisted everywhere—any camera so much as picks up a glimpse of you and they'll know where to find you."

I felt Darius tense behind me—it wasn't a movement so much as lack of movement. It was in those moments it became abundantly clear that he was a vampire. It was the kind of stillness that came right before a predator chose when to strike.

"So leaving here is going to be a problem," Haley said, her voice infused with a long drawl like spelling this out for us was going to prove more tedious than she'd anticipated. "If you leave, you risk bringing The Guild to our front door. That would jeopardize everything we've built here—everyone we're protecting. We won't have many chances to get this right, and once we go after one of them, we'll have shown our cards."

Eli shrugged. "Max can teleport. Unless the government is keeping some seriously advanced—and magical—tracking equipment secret, I don't think they can catch her even if they wanted to."

"You misunderstand. It's not just your group." Bishop scrubbed his hand over his face. I wondered how long it had been since he'd gotten a decent night of rest. I had a feeling he hadn't had one since we barged back into his life. "It's everyone who left that night—everyone who they think might have turned on them." He shrugged, then shot me a quick glance. "You're just at the top of what is a very long list."

Charlie's nose scrunched in sympathy. "One of the reasons the vetting process has been so extensive this week—we can't let anyone you've brought in leave this place and then come back until we figure out how to handle the intricacies of all of this. There's too much risk to the people we're protecting here."

"It's propaganda, a corralling strategy," Evelyn said. She shuffled some of the papers in front of her before stuffing them into a manilla file. She hadn't looked at them once since we sat down. I had a feeling she had every word memorized, that she'd pored over every ounce of information she could get her hands on—she had that vibe about her. Reminded me a bit of Seamus in that way. "They're hoping one person steps out of line and they'll draw a perfect link back to you. Also makes sure you can't recruit anyone else from any of the other campuses. You appear like bad guys to the world at large, and it will remain that way so long as The Guild maintains power of the media and humans in powerful positions." She looked up at me, smiling that Eli smirk of hers. "They're terrified of you, which is good, but it also makes them desperate. Desperation can be dangerous. We haven't seen them pull strings to this level—" she considered for a moment, then shrugged, "well, ever, as far as I can tell. They control the human governments, keep an eye on things and make sure that the secrets of our world remain hidden, but they rarely intervene in any real way. But now, they've instituted a full-on hunt—with every arrow aiming for the target they've drawn on your back."

"How...flattering?" My brain felt like it was working a mile a minute, trying to understand and outline all of the myriad ways this would make our next mission even more impossible than it already was. I suddenly felt very claustrophobic, knowing that

I'd lost anonymity, that I'd be watched—hunted—wherever I stepped.

"Don't worry, we've got your back and we're working on ways around this. Just might take us a while," Haley said, her tone strangely calm, like this was just another day, just another run-of-the-mill meeting and reveal. Oddly, it helped ease some of the anxiety unfurling in my gut. "We're mostly telling you so that you don't just leave on some secret heroic mission that will just get everyone killed—yourselves included—and because we'll need your help calming those recruits who followed you here. We can't have them balking now that their names and faces are plastered on every local news channel with the label 'dangerous' printed above their heads." She gave me a stiff nod and smile—but a smile on her looked more like a promise of violence than friendship. She tilted her head. "I have ways of keeping them docile if needed, but I prefer saving those particular skills for the enemy."

I found myself deeply invested in making sure none of us ever ended up in that "enemy" category of hers. She wore that same edge of violence that Darius often donned—only where it excited me on him, on her, it only reminded me how acutely dangerous vampires were.

Jace ran his hand roughly over his jaw. "We're sheltered from a lot of things here, but that doesn't mean things aren't getting worse. There've been unexplained earthquakes and other catastrophic events happening weekly at this point. Things are not going well for humans—the secrets of our world are growing more and more impossible to keep hidden. People are disappearing, ending up dead, attacked by creatures they've only encountered in movies and nightmares, caught in territory wars and fights for freedom."

My stomach clenched with a new wave of fear. I'd been so focused on my team, The Guild, hell, demons. I'd hardly given humans more than a passing thought, but of course they were affected by what was happening. How could they not be?

"Not to mention the increasing number of tears between realms that have been cropping up around the world," Jace continued, "unregulated portals that will have consequences we can't even begin to imagine. We probably only know about a very small fraction of them as it is. Humans are finding themselves confronted with supernatural powers and demons who are only trying to learn how to exist in this realm after escaping hell. Humans may not know about our world, or have the language yet to understand or explain what's happening, but they're not unintelligent.

"Even they can feel the magic changing in the air. It's static, electric. Time is not on our side. We don't have the resources to fight what's coming while protecting their gentle sensibilities and world views." He folded his arms in front of his chest, the jovial humor now gone from his expression, revealing some of that lethal power incubi kept tightly latched. He was just as dangerous as Haley—but that was the power of incubi. They pulled you in close with smiles and promises, so when the time came to strike, you were almost begging for it, laying your neck out to be sliced.

Instead of finding myself terrified by these two new acquaintances, I was excited. They were a formidable pair to fight alongside—and the stronger they were, the better their chance of survival.

"So," Haley continued, "to protect themselves, The Guild will do everything it can to mobilize humanity against you. Humans tend to react poorly to fear. In some ways, they become even more dangerous than supernaturals. They need a target—someone they can hate when they are afraid. Right now, that target is you. And The Guild is taking care to paint it with as much precision and detail as possible."

Eli snorted. "We're the ones who are trying to save them—to keep the realms from literally collapsing in on themselves."

"Yes," Charlie tilted her head to the side, "but they don't know that. And we don't have the power or ability to spell it out for them en masse. The Guild does. And history's shown time and time again that those who wield that kind of power shape reality."

"We start planning immediately then." I clasped my hands together, trying like hell to keep the panic coursing through my body from revealing itself in the soft trembling of my fingers. I needed to be strong—this fight would be too big to tackle if I let the odds of our success weigh too heavily on my mind. "The more time they have to get ahead of this shit, to mobilize the human world and the rest of the protectors against us, the more impossible this mission will become." I turned to Evelyn, steeling myself. I had no idea if my powers were at the level Lucifer needed them to be for his ritual. But we couldn't wait much longer. And in the meantime, we needed to locate the stone and the nexus. "The information you have on those three council members—gather it. The more we know about them all, the better our chances. Finding that stone needs to be our number one priority. And maybe we'll stand a better chance if we strike before they even realize we're looking for it."

She didn't blink as she studied me, her expression unreadable. After a long, drawn moment, she nodded, her fingers tightening around the edges of the folder in front of her. "Once we hit them, we lose all element of surprise, so we'll need to be strategic about where we start as well. The more time and room we give them to hide what we're after, the more infinitely difficult this will become."

I didn't like the woman, but she had a good point. Something about having her level-headedness in the room, when the rest of us were so quick to lash out, was calming—almost like Cy or Seamus were in the room with us.

"Alright." Jace stood, stretching, his good humor already shifting back in place, like a filter he could just switch on and off. Was that an incubus thing or was that a Jace thing? If the former, I needed to learn that shit. I had the unfortunate habit of broadcasting my emotions like a goddamn siren. "Let's adjourn for now and we can discuss details tomorrow afternoon, once Evie has the intel we need."

Evelyn grimaced at his jovial familiarity, which just made Jace's smile widen, both seductive and lethal. When he winked and she flushed, I wondered if the two of them had a past...or a present.

I stood with the others, my thoughts racing as I tried to process everything we'd just learned.

I felt Darius inch closer to my back, his energy wilder than it usually was, darker as it lapped against me. It had been building for days, but between the med center and Atlas, we hadn't had much time to chat—and any time I broached an even remotely serious conversation with him, he'd immediately loosened up and changed the subject.

When I moved towards the door, Evelyn's eyes latched on to mine again.

"Max, a word if that's okay?"

Charlie and the others filtered from the room, but my team stopped in their tracks, folding around me.

Evelyn cleared her throat. "Alone, if you don't mind."

Darius stiffened, and I watched the muscles work in Eli's jaw.

No. Like fucking hell I'm leaving her with you.

I could have sworn I heard Eli speak the words, harsh and rigid, but his lips were firm, unmoving as he glared at his mother.

Coffee.

Izzy was right—I desperately needed a good night's sleep.

But until then, I needed to get better about properly caffeinating.

I ran my hand over his back and nodded. "Yes, that's fine. I'll meet you guys out front in a few."

For a moment, I wasn't sure Darius and Eli would leave, but I focused on them, trying like hell to convey that I'd be okay—I promised—with my eyes, that I'd call them if I needed anything.

I could fucking light the building on fire or teleport outside of it if I needed to for crying out loud. My safety wasn't a logical concern right now.

Their eyes widened briefly, Eli's lips parting in a soft shock.

Darius gripped his shoulders, sent a dark look towards Evelyn, and pushed him towards the door, whispering a quiet, "not here."

Eli shook his head, like he was dazed, but then he respected the clear request and allowed Darius to move him gently away from me.

His hand lingered on the doorframe, like he was second-guessing it, but he fought the resistance and his fingers peeled away one-by-one, until he closed the door behind them both.

It was strange, being in this room alone with Eli's mother—she seemed smaller somehow, no longer surrounded by her friends, sadder almost.

She stared at the file clutched in her hand and nodded for me to sit back down.

I took the seat across from her, the chair still warm from Eli sitting in it.

"What can I do for you?" I broke the awkward silence, not entirely sure how to act around this woman. I hated her for what she'd done to Eli, but I also knew that, right now, she was our best chance at going after The Guild. We needed her. And, as much as I hated her on Eli's behalf, I also wanted her to like me. It was an irrational, annoying desire that I did my best to shove down and ignore—but she *was* the mother of the boy I loved. Part of me desperately wanted her to think I was good enough for him, even if she wasn't.

She didn't look up from the folders in front of her, but her lips pressed into that Eli-smirk again. My stomach clenched at the sight of it. It was just as disconcerting as seeing Wade's eyes set in Tarren's face. Features I adored in my team, set in the faces of parents who'd treated them cruelly. It was unsettling, to say the least.

For a moment, I studied her, hunting for more traces of her son on her face. On the surface, she didn't obviously share any of his features. Her hair was cropped in a severe reddish-brown bob, several shades lighter than Eli's. Her eyes were hazel, the greens weaving through threads of brown, where Eli's held more golden tones. Her build was more petite than most protectors, her skin a shade or two paler than his.

When she was stationary, it was only her mouth that immediately gave their relationship away—both had the same shape, the same smile. But when she moved, the similarities between them became more obvious. Their expressions in motion carved clear lines of connection—the arch of her brow, the teasing intelligence behind her eyes. Eli was etched into her plain as day in the moments between frames.

"I was hoping we might have a few minutes to talk," she started. For a moment I wondered if she was as nervous in my presence as I was in hers. If that yearning for approval that I felt echoed in her. She cleared her throat, pushing on, "Levi is quite fond of you, and Eli—" her voice cracked on his name, but it was only a brief break in the armor she wore with a fluid confidence, "I thought I should meet the girl bonded to my son. Especially when she's tangled up in more danger than perhaps anyone in the world right now—and therefore so is my son, right along with her."

My jaw clenched. "Oh?"

It was the only word I could bring myself to say. I swallowed back the anger raging through me on Eli's behalf. She'd hurt him, left him. Seamus too. What right did she have to fill the role of protective mother now?

But some of my own guilt lingered amongst it. She'd, perhaps unknowingly, tugged at a fear I'd been doing my best to keep tightly coiled. I couldn't control the fact that I was Lucifer's daughter, that I was the catalyst between realms.

That didn't mean I wasn't absolutely terrified about what that meant for my team. The stronger our bonds became, the more danger I put them in, whether intentionally or not. I was an anchor and with every touch, every moment we spent together, every wall we knocked down, the bonds became ropes tying them to me. I could already feel that rope turning to steel —unbreakable.

The only way I could survive the fear of what I'd eventually have to do was by convincing myself that when it was time for me to sink, those tethers would uncoil and gracefully release. Otherwise, I'd have to cut them myself.

Evelyn narrowed her eyes as she watched me, glassy amusement evident in their depths. "You don't like me very much, do you."

It wasn't a question, merely an observation—no hurt or accusation lacing her tone.

I tensed, but I didn't deny it. I couldn't. "Do you blame me?"

She deflated slightly, the chair squeaking pathetically as she leaned back into it, like it was expressing some of the sorrow she couldn't. The harshness of her presence softened, like a statue grown weary from years of weathering.

"No, I suppose I can't, can I?" Her fingers picked at the worn fabric on the arm of her chair as she wrestled with some emotion I couldn't quite parse. Like Eli, she was difficult to read. "You may not understand it, Max, or even believe it, but I do love my son. Both of them. Fiercely. More than anything in the entire world."

I bit my lip, trying to keep my doubts from spilling forward.

Her eyes shot to mine, clearly seeing them written on my face regardless. She sat up, the sleek, powerful mask back in place. "You shouldn't pass judgment on things you don't understand. Has our world taught you nothing in your brief exposure to it?"

I arched my brow, but swallowed my tongue, uncomfortable with speaking about this without Eli present.

"You love him too," she nodded, adding more to herself than to me, "that's good. You wouldn't be filled with that righteous anger if you didn't care for him. I'm glad he has you."

The silence stretched so long that it became uncomfortable, thick with the awkwardness of the situation—until I couldn't take it for another moment.

So, I told her the truth.

"I don't like you, no. How could I after what you've put him through?" I took a deep breath. "I can also concede that I don't know the details of your past. But that doesn't matter, not with everything happening. Family trauma is a whisper into the void compared to what we're up against. I do believe that you are here because you believe in this place—in the truth. I will work with you, to save as many people as we can. So will Eli, no matter how much doing so pains him."

"What I've put him through," she echoed, nodding, her lips quivering slightly as they formed the words. "I have put that boy through more pain than he's ever deserved, there is no question there." Her voice was soft, filled with a sadness that twisted inside of me. I hated myself because, in that moment, I didn't hate her. I couldn't. No matter how badly I wanted to on his behalf. I understood the grief that lingered inside of her, that sense of loss. "I don't owe you an explanation, Max, though I do owe him one. Seamus too. Despite what you may think you know, I care deeply for them both. Leaving them was the hardest thing I've ever done," the side of her mouth curved into a sad smile, "and I have lived no easy life."

"But you did—" I said, "leave them, I mean."

She nodded. "I did. I had to." Her head tilted as she watched me, and suddenly it seemed as though she could see every errant thought in my head, reading me with far more ease than I could her. "But is it so impossible for you to imagine? Loving more than one person at once? Loving someone that everyone in your life tells you that you shouldn't? Forsaking that life for one that keeps those you care for safe, alive, even if doing so breaks your heart in half?"

My breath caught in my chest. I didn't know who Levi's father was, why she couldn't be with him and Seamus, like I was with my team.

I wanted to ask her questions about her past, about why she left, why she chose Levi instead of Eli, but I realized as soon as I opened my mouth that she was right—she didn't owe me these answers. And pulling them from her when Eli wasn't here felt like a betrayal that I'd never forgive myself for.

I was already betraying him as it was—betraying them all— every moment that I didn't tell them the truth about Lucifer's ritual.

When it came down to it, I'd end up leaving him just as she had.

"You're right," I said, my throat suddenly raw, "I don't know the details of your situation." I considered her for a long moment, the version of her I'd conjured in my head reshaping into someone more complex than I'd imagined before. She was no longer this phantom figure—the original antagonist in Eli's story. Now, she was colored in shades of gray, like us all, I supposed. There were no perfect heroes or villains in this story. "But if you truly love Eli as you say you do, you owe him that story—your truth. If he wants to hear it, that is." I licked my lips. "And until he does, you should understand that my thoughts about you don't matter. As far as we're concerned, Eli is my priority, not you."

She nodded, considering me for a moment. "Fair enough. I'm glad to know that if he doesn't want me in his corner, he at least has you there."

We were silent for a few long moments, but before I could break the heavy stretch, she beat me to it.

"You remind me of her, you know. It wasn't immediately obvious at first, but the signs are there if you know to look for them. You have her fire. Her fierce loyalty." The shadow of Eli's smirk reappeared on her face again. "Her stubbornness."

The words hit me like an iron bar to the gut.

"Like who?" I asked, even though I knew the answer. There could be only one.

She looked up, the smirk turning into something softer. "Your mother."

"You know who my mother is?" I wracked my brain, trying to remember who all I'd told. But it was only my team, my friends.

Hurt flashed sharp and hot in my belly—had everyone known about Sayty? This whole time I'd been a part of The Guild, had people been seeing her written into my features, the way I saw Eli mapped into his mother's? Was I the only one Cy had kept this secret from—the one who cared most about uncovering it?

She nodded, her expression distant, like she was trapped in a memory. "I didn't know Sayty nearly as well as Cy did but, yes, she was around our team a lot and we were friends, more or less. When you joined The Guild, I had my suspicions about who you might be, why he'd taken you in—he'd always had such an uncharacteristic soft spot for her." The sharp corners of her eyes softened. "It was sweet. Seamus never confirmed, of course. He'd never go against his brother's wishes, even for me—but seeing you now, it's undeniable."

Her stare met mine, harsh and unrelenting. "If others don't see her in you, it's because they aren't looking. The Guild hated her, did everything they could to erase her from our collective memories. But she was a good person, Max. And so was Cy. I don't know what happened to her in the end, but I'm glad that you had him, and that he had you—and I'm sorry that, like her, he was taken from you too." I had to turn away from the compassion pooling in her eyes, unsure what to do with it. "I'll admit, the thought of Cyrus Bentley parenting an orphan girl is a surreal, amusing one. I'm truly, very sorry that he is gone. We didn't always get along or see things the same way, but the world certainly grew dimmer when he left it."

My throat was tight, words difficult to form. I swallowed, blinking back the film over my eyes. But a flash of hope sparked at what this meant.

Evelyn was perhaps the only person in this realm who knew my mother.

"My family—" I licked my lips, the phrase sticking strangely on my tongue when used to refer to anyone other than Cy and Ro, "Sayty's family, I mean. Do you know them? Cy said she had a brother—a twin. Saif. Have you met him?" My fingers drummed anxiously on the cool tabletop. I pulled them back to reign in my nerves, my desperation. "Or her line of protectors— could you point me to any of them?"

Her brows lifted slightly, the only evidence of her surprise. "I didn't know that Sayty had a brother, no." She paused, considering, "In truth, I knew very little about her in general— and almost nothing about her family, where she came from before The Guild." She shook her head, "Even the council has sparse details of where—who—she comes from."

That small spark of hope dimmed, until it died out altogether. "Right. It was a long shot."

"But I do know several people from other lines of protectors." She smiled, her brow arching slightly. "In fact, so do you."

I sat up straighter, folded my hands nervously in my lap. "I do?"

She nodded. "And you don't have to go looking far at all."

"I don't?"

"From my understanding, The Lodge and Lake Cadaver are owned by one of these lines. Protectors who split from The Guild many years ago, as far back as records go, who have long hated what that institution stands for—it makes sense that they would be the foundation of the group building a resistance against it, does it not?"

"Charlie—" I started to ask, but Evelyn shook her head.

"I don't really know the details. Protectors, and supernaturals in general, are private people. Trust is a complicated practice when lives are at stake. But from what I understand, Charlie doesn't own this place. She's just inherited the restaurant from an absent uncle who passed years ago. The traces of protector in her blood, however, I assume are from such a line, yes." She paused for a moment, her smile reaching all the way to her eyes now. "I hear you are particularly fond of our nurse."

"Greta?"

She nodded again. "She worked at The Guild for most of her life, but she did not grow up there. Her family is from a line of protectors who turned away from The Guild. And she was always quite fond of Sayty. She might be a good place for you to start on this search."

I chewed on the information for a moment, revisiting my memory of Greta and laying this new insight to her past on top—an overlay that provided new depth.

Did she know that I was Sayty's daughter? She'd taken an instant liking to me, seemed to trust me from the moment I stepped foot in The Guild's med ward. There was also something different about her—she always seemed to be just a little bit, I don't know...*more* than the other adults at Headquarters. Cy had said that protectors from that line—or those lines, perhaps they'd branched even further over the years—had a different kind of power, a different kind of magic. One that hadn't diluted over time like The Guild's, because it honored balance rather than destroying it.

Was that what I'd been sensing in her—a likeness, a familiarity, a connection to my mother's community?

Why hadn't Greta ever said anything to me?

Evelyn's head tilted to the side slightly, sympathy etched into the soft lines around her eyes. "I know how alluring uncovering the past might be for you, Max. How tempting it is to dig out a family history when you've just laid a part of your family to rest."

My stomach tightened at the warning, laced with pity.

"Find the answers you seek, but make sure they don't come at the expense of what truly matters right now." She took a deep, steadying breath, like she was folding the sadness encasing me back into herself. Then she pulled a thin file from inside the larger one in front of her, and slid it across the table until the words printed on the tab were face up for me to read.

Max Bentley.

I glanced up, not bothering to hide my surprise. "What is this?"

"Levi found the information they have on you, during one of his clandestine perusals of Headquarters."

I grunted, not bothering to ask how Levi always seemed to be in places he shouldn't be—how he always seemed to walk away undetected, unscathed. I knew she wouldn't answer.

"I didn't want to scare you, to drop this bomb in front of everyone." She scrunched her nose, leaning back in the chair. "I know how uncomfortable it can be to have that kind of spotlight on you when you're trying to process so many big things yourself. It seemed only fair that you decide when and with whom to share this information—to process it before everyone jumps into action."

"What does this say?" I asked, staring at the closed file like it might explode if I touched it.

She considered me for a long moment, ran her teeth gently over her bottom lip, like she was finding a way to coax the words out. "Since the night of Cy's death, it seems the council has devoted a significant amount of their resources trying to uncover exactly what—or who—you are. I don't know how, but they know the truth now, or something close enough to it. They may not know with scientific confirmation that you are Lucifer's child specifically, but they suspect it. And they know that you are at the heart of things, that your power is connected to the hell realm's."

My focus drifted up from the folder until I met her eyes—unwavering and sure. She hadn't reacted when I'd told Charlie and the others the truth about my father. At the time, I thought it because, like most protectors, she was uncharacteristically good at bottling up her emotions.

"You knew—Levi too."

She nodded. "Like I said, Levi was able to get this information and, after sitting on it for a few months," she grunted, rolling her eyes, "he gave it to me." The amusement and gentle affection for her son melted into something sharper. "But there's more in that file Max, than just a hypothesis about your father. The council wants you. More specifically, they want your powers. And they will do whatever it takes to get them. To harvest your power and use it for their own purposes. I suspect that they'll tell the rest of The Guild that they'll use them to repair the realm, to restore the balance—that you alone are responsible and to blame for the tearing of worlds, that they are the only thing standing between you and the death of us all."

My blood turned cold, every muscle in my body freezing

until I was half-convinced that even my heart had stopped beating its steady rhythm.

Her jaw stiffened. She held my stare, hard and demanding. "You can't let them capture you, under any circumstances. If they drain your power, if they find a way to harness it, they will mold it into something for their own needs. Judging from the words in that file, they hope that your power will find them a way to not only trap all demons in hell irrevocably, but to eradicate them entirely. Until theirs is the only power left." She tilted her head a few degrees, "do you understand what I'm saying, Max?"

I swallowed, my throat thick and scratchy. If the choice came between my death and letting them steal my power, allowing them to use it to further their own, there was only one choice.

I nodded.

It was an easy concession. This would inevitably end in my death anyway—that was the lot of holding this power, of being a catalyst.

"You don't seem entirely surprised by this possibility," she said, as if she had plucked the thought from my brain. She leaned closer, her voice hardly a whisper. "This plan of yours. This power you wield—" her eyes narrowed as she studied me, "it only leads to one conclusion, doesn't it?"

I cleared my throat, my lips parting.

Her posture slumped, her expression horrified as she read the truth that I couldn't voice on my face. "Do they know?" She paused, reigning in her emotions until her expression hardened again. "Max, does Eli know that you'll—"

Die.

She let the word drift in the air between us, heavy and unspoken, but loud as a roar all the same.

I shook my head, my eyes darting to the door, where I knew they waited only a few walls away.

Her expression fell, a sadness pulling down at the corner of her eyes, her lips—whether for me, or for the grief her son would inevitably be put through, I wasn't sure.

"I'm sorry," was all that she said.

I nodded, unable to latch onto any words.

"You're so young. You don't deserve the burden that you bear." Her hand reached forward until it found mine across the table. Her skin was cool to the touch, soft—unexpectedly comforting. "But they deserve the truth—the chance to say goodbye, when the time comes."

My vision blurred as I fought back tears, emotion clogging my throat.

When the time comes.

It hadn't escaped me that the harder I pushed to go after the council, the closer we got to uncovering the stone, the more I bonded to my team—that I was simultaneously pushing the needle closer to my own end.

I nodded, feeling a rebellious tear carve a path down my cheek.

I wiped it quickly with a sniff.

They did deserve the truth, I just didn't know how to give it to them.

Because once I did, everything would change.

Because once I did, I'd have to do the very thing that made me hate every last drop of power that I had.

I'd break their hearts.

I'd spent months convincing each of them that hurting them was the last thing I'd ever do.

And, as a twisted and cruel fate would have it, it would be.

6

———————

DECLAN

The cabin was dim as Max paced back and forth through the small living room. It seemed even more cramped than it usually did, with all of us huddled together.

I could feel her anger, her fear lap against my skin, rough like a cat's tongue.

She hadn't spoken a word since emerging from the pseudo conference room with Evelyn.

It had been a quiet, uncomfortable trek back, all of us lost in our thoughts as we processed what we'd learned.

Eli had the foresight at least to let us know about his talk with her—that she knew about him channeling her fire and that she was pissed that we'd kept it from her. He leaned against the wall now, his gaze hard and focused on a worn patch of carpet with a small stain on it, like that small stain might somehow have the answers to the universe baked into it, waiting to take shape.

Atlas, as he'd been since his return from captivity, was quiet. He sat on the ground, long limbs folded in sharp angles, his eyes tracking her every movement, back leaning against the wall, face otherwise unreadable.

Wade and Darius kept glancing in my direction, the three of us silently trying to figure out what to say. What to do.

I took a deep breath and decided to take one for the team. I rose from the couch and took a step towards her. "Max. Can we talk about this?"

"Have the rest of you channeled my powers too?" There was no anger in her voice, but somehow that made it worse.

Just hurt.

Just fear.

She wasn't mad at us, she was mad at herself. I just didn't understand why. Something had been off the last week, and I'd chalked it up to left over adrenaline from the jailbreak at Headquarters, but now I wondered if there wasn't something else underlying it all.

I shook my head fast, catching the others doing the same from the corner of my eye. "No. None of us. Just Eli, and just the one time." I turned to him, second guessing myself. "Right?"

He nodded.

It was such a strange, new thing for me, for us all—trying to maintain and manage the feelings and experiences of everyone. All five of us were tied to Max now, and it would take work and practice, and probably a few fucking missteps to boot, to keep things as smooth and peaceful as possible.

She paused mid pace, folding her bottom lip against her teeth as she sniffed, then nodded, and resumed her pacing again. "Good, that's good. We need to find a way to control that."

"That would require that we understand why—" Darius turned his angry stare on Eli, "and how—it happened in the first place."

He hadn't been there, hadn't seen what Eli had done. And when Wade and I filled him and Atlas in this morning, he'd been livid. His anger spilling out of him like a leaky faucet, until I was certain the only thing keeping him from tearing Eli's head from his spine was Max—and the small problem that killing Eli would effectively end his life too.

Atlas hadn't really reacted, though I could see something shift behind his eyes, processing, thinking. Usually, I could read him like a book, understand every twitch, every unspoken thought—but since his return, it was like that familiar book had been translated into another language. He was here, the Atlas I'd always known, I just didn't have the same access to him that I used to. His thoughts were closed to me now.

I wished like hell it didn't bother me as much as it did. But he'd been my lifeline when I moved in with my aunt, my family. When my entire life had imploded and I'd moved to a new country, his solid presence, unwavering support, had kept me steady.

My stomach had been tied in knots over the fact that I didn't seem to have the ability to do the same for him now.

We were all finally in the same place—for the first time in what felt like forever—but we'd been through so much, we'd been so transformed by the trauma of it all, that I wasn't sure how to hold us together. It was like, if I breathed too hard in the wrong direction, we'd all fall apart, the history holding us together dissolving until there were no threads left to tie.

Max.

She had become the thing that held us together. I just had to hope her grip was stronger than mine.

"I'm not holding you together," she said, her brows furrowed. "Don't be ridiculous, Dec."

"Oh, I—" I hadn't realized I'd spoken that last part out loud.

"What?" Wade asked.

Darius stiffened, his focus darting from me to Max, eyes narrowed.

Max shook her head. "It's just so much—too much. So

many things to do. So many obstacles. We'll be fine, I just need to process, just need to figure out—"

I wasn't entirely sure what she was talking about. "Is this about your conversation with Evelyn? Or about what we learned before that—that the human governments have drawn a target on our back?"

She grunted. "That, and the fact that the council is making plans to drain my powers and use them for gods know what nefarious purpose."

I blinked a few times, willing myself to focus. Her lips hadn't parted when she'd spoken those words. The sound was clear, her tone laced with the wobble of anxiety, but her lips were pressed tightly together, the line firm, unmoving.

I glanced at Atlas and saw him straighten slightly, his head tilting in question, as he focused on her.

"The council is trying to do what now?" Wade took a step towards her, his gaze drifting between her mouth and eyes, like he was trying to decide whether he'd missed the same thing I had.

"I didn't—" Max stopped pacing, every muscle in her body still, "I didn't say anything about the council."

"Except you did," Wade took a slow, deep breath, confusion and concern mapped out clear on his face, "just now."

"She didn't say that," Darius said, his brow arched as his eyes darted briefly to Eli and then back to her, his body unconsciously leaning towards her, "she thought it."

"I," she frowned, "what?"

"It's the bonds," he clarified, shaking his head like he couldn't quite believe it, "I thought I was imagining it earlier, when we left the meeting, I could've sworn—but now, it's undeniable."

"What?" Max repeated, a small tremor in her voice this time, her skin a shade paler as her gaze darted between each of us. "Are you saying you can hear my thoughts?" She took a step back from us all, panic pulling her breaths in harsh, uneven rasps. "They're just being broadcasted to you? All of them? Can you hear what I'm thinking about right now?"

It was clear from her reaction that she wasn't exactly elated by this development, and I could tell there was something she was trying to keep locked down—but I knew how that went, the moment you tried not to think about something, it was all you could think of.

She deserved that privacy. We all did.

"No," I said, desperate to ease her reaction. "I think Darius is right—but it's only in clips. When you're feeling particularly strongly about something, maybe? Or maybe it comes in the form of what you're feeling. I'll occasionally feel anxious or excited and not entirely understand where it's coming from—maybe it's the same thing that caused Eli to channel your flames. Like during heightened moments, we become more connected, almost like a distress signal or something."

Darius nodded, his jaw tight. "The bonds are solidifying, but at a speed that outpaces our control of them. I've heard stories of this happening, in the old days—but I never believed they were true."

"So how do we control it?" There was a nervous tremor in her voice.

Darius didn't respond, and neither did any of the others. Which meant we didn't have a fucking clue.

Maybe we controlled it the same way all supernatural powers were controlled.

Practice.

Intention.

I closed my eyes, tried to calm the excited thrum of anxiety drumming through my body. I focused on that feeling I had, deep in my chest, that never-ceasing awareness of her, the desire to be close to her, to twine ourselves together. I breathed in, focusing on her scent, on the visual of her I conjured in my mind.

When she healed us, she often spoke of the bonds between us as if they were physical—tethers to tug on in her mind.

I conjured that feeling of her, braided it with the image of a long rope that extended out from me and reached for her.

I breathed into it, feeling it expand and contract and vibrate with my breath.

We'll figure it out.

I thought the sentence as hard as I could, enunciating every syllable in my head as best as I could, so that it was more than just my vague emotions that traveled along the wobbly thought-rope.

She gasped and I opened my eyes. Her lips were parted in awe, her focus on me.

"Did it work?"

She licked her bottom lip and nodded, too stunned for words.

My eyes latched onto the smooth column of her throat as she swallowed. I couldn't help but feel like there was something heavy there, something she was trying desperately to bury deep inside of herself. Shoved so far down that none of us could reach it—that even the mate bonds were unable to pluck it from her thoughts.

"Did what work?" Eli asked, stepping between us like he was missing something.

"I think the connection becomes stronger when we focus on it, when we try to filter our thoughts with intention," I started, shoving him back so that I could see Max again. "And maybe sometimes, when we run away with our thoughts or lose that control over them, they shake loose and slip through the connection on their own."

Max took a deep breath, relaxing, and that ease slowly settled over me too, over us all.

I wasn't sure she was even aware of that—how in tune we all were with her heightened emotions. It was like I'd developed a seventh sense. One that was reserved entirely for her.

"Okay," she whispered, nodding, "I can work with that."

"If we work on controlling it—" Wade started, that studious expression of his—that I'd seen only rare glimpses of since his descent into hell—making an appearance, softening his features until he looked more like the gangly younger kid who followed me and Atlas around like a lost puppy. The memory squeezed at my chest, knowing how much trauma he'd endured to sharpen those edges. "Maybe we can eventually use that to our advantage."

"You mean not just block the connection or learn to tune it out, but use it?" I asked.

Darius shrugged. "Could be useful. We get separated from each other often enough that having a built-in cellphone line would certainly make things easier."

"Can you hear each other's thoughts or just mine?" Max swallowed, her eyes darting around the room, but hesitating to linger on any of ours for too long.

I turned to Darius, closed my eyes, and tried to focus my thoughts in his direction. I had no fucking clue what I was doing, but I shot the words out anyway.

You're a fucking twat.

Max snorted, but Darius just studied me, eyes wide and confused.

"What?" he asked, nostrils flaring slightly at my smirk. He turned to Max, some of the darker shadows that had clouded his temper these last few days clearing just slightly. "What did she say?"

"That she's very fond of your friendship," she responded, face split into a shit-eating grin that instantly seemed to lighten the tension in the room, briefly, as those moments often were these days, before it melted back into concern. "Clearly just me then." She took a deep breath, studying the vampire. "Unless reaching each other will just take more practice, more effort. Like if you speak to each other through me somehow?"

"Possibly. And if we can share each other's powers and strengths," a small grin tugged at Wade's lips, and I could tell that he was excited by this untapped knowledge, the need to puzzle out the rules and understand it, "that wouldn't be the worst thing either. Would take some of the pressure off of you, Max. Give us a better chance of helping you, keep us from getting in the way."

"What if I hurt one of you though? I hardly have control over my powers as it is—we don't know what will happen if I just start blasting them through to you."

"Lucifer has said that you're a catalyst," Darius studied her, his chin balanced on his fist as he paused for a long beat, not unlike Wade in his curiosity, "which means you're literally made for siphoning magic, for the push and pull of it. And we're—"

"Made for you," Wade finished, indigo eyes sparkling with affection. "Your powers have never hurt us, Max—only healed."

Max considered him for a long moment.

"Okay," she said finally, a soft smile relaxing some of the tension wrinkling her forehead. "We can try."

Especially if channeling my powers can help keep you all safe.

The last sentence came not from her lips, but her mind.

I met the others' eyes, all of us trying to stifle a grin.

"I said that in your heads, didn't I?" she asked with a sheepish slump. "Shutting the connection down is going to take as much work as opening it, I think."

"Probably," Wade said, "but I'm okay with you sifting through my thoughts in the meantime." The salacious wink he punctuated that sentence with made it abundantly clear what kind of content those thoughts would be broadcasting. And the blush coloring Max's cheeks meant that he'd either successfully spoken to her through their link or she'd conjured some of those thoughts on her own.

I stifled a groan, hoping like hell none of his dirty thoughts filtered down to me. The last thing I needed was these dickheads broadcasting their horny 24/7 directly into my brain. When I turned to Eli, I shivered at the thought, having unintentionally walked in on more than enough of his encounters to know I wanted nothing to do with them.

"Now that I know it's there, that we can use the connection, it doesn't feel that dissimilar to the kind of control we can wield in dream-walks," Wade continued, thankfully oblivious to the cringey turn my thoughts had taken. "I think you'll be able to use it at will in no time."

She took a deep breath, and sat down next to Eli where he'd settled on the couch.

My own tension eased with hers, and when I glanced at the others, I knew they felt it too.

Everyone except for Atlas. If anything, he seemed only more uncomfortable.

When his dark eyes met mine, the threads of gold nearly invisible from this angle, I understood. His thoughts were darker than most these days, he seemed half with us, half trapped in the nightmares the drude had locked him in.

Max had freed him from the worst of it, but the wounds left from those memories were as strong as they were invisible.

He wouldn't want Max anywhere near there. Wouldn't want her to know or feel the true depths of the pain he was in.

It was, perhaps, the most sure I'd been about any of his thoughts since his return. The first time the connection between us felt clear—not quite as pristine as it had always been, but an echo of it. My best friend was still there. Buried and burdened, perhaps, but he wouldn't be forever.

I walked over to him, slid down the wall until I was sitting just a few inches away, careful not to accidentally touch him.

He flinched anytime one of us got too near.

I was honestly just excited that he'd spent this much time in the same room as the rest of us.

He tensed at first, uncomfortable with my proximity, but that tension relaxed slightly—not entirely gone, but melting.

It was a start.

I didn't know how to voice the words, didn't want to call attention to his fear, but I knew Atlas would find it easier than the rest of us to shut the connection down, to block his thoughts from Max. He had a lifetime of repressing his emotions, his wolf, his desires down as far as they would go. Something told me this would be no different.

Of the six of us, Max was the one who wore her emotions most vividly on her sleeve—it was one of the things that had drawn me to her instantly. The vulnerability, the complete ease with which she could be herself—free of judgment, of concern for what others might think of her.

I settled on a vague, "we're all pretty good at suppressing ourselves, it's one of the first things The Guild trains us to do, so I don't think that temporarily closing the connection will be the difficult part. Opening it will probably require more muscle flexing."

As if he knew that was just for him, Atlas's fingers twitched, his head nodding slightly. He turned to Max, the temporary reprieve making way for something sharper.

"What did you mean before," he rasped, his voice quiet from disuse, "that the council wanted your powers."

Max took a deep breath, leaned up against Eli, her head resting on his shoulder as his fingers drew circles on her thigh.

It was strange, all of us being in love with the same girl, but I didn't feel even a spark of jealousy as I watched them together. It made me oddly happy to see Eli—a man who'd spent his life using and being used by women to suit sexual whims and quell boredom—out of his mind in love with this girl.

"Evelyn and Levi," she started, locking her fingers through Eli's as he froze. Any negativity coursing through him visibly and instantly withered away at her touch, her effect on him tangible and evident in every line of his body. "They found a file on me. Apparently after I disappeared—" she cleared her throat and stood up, walked over to the kitchen table to grab the file she'd anxiously creased in several places on our walk home, and dropped it soundlessly in Eli's lap. "The night of the ambush, they started to puzzle out who I was. And now that they've found ways to infuse themselves with shadow magic, Evelyn is concerned that they might have a way to either use— or steal—mine."

"Well, great," Eli muttered, as he flipped through the documents, his brows furrowing and his expression growing darker with every line that he read. When he was through, he passed it to Wade, each of us scanning in turn. "I was hoping things wouldn't start getting simple and easy for us."

"How did they get this?" Darius asked, when it was his turn to peruse the pages. "Was her clearance really this high?"

The breath caught in my chest as I stiffened.

Fuck. We hadn't told him.

How the hell had we forgotten? Had things really become so chaotic that this had slipped my mind for days?

"Erm," I started, suddenly upset that Rowan wasn't here to help with the delivery of this less-than-super news. "I think Levi is more than just a protector."

The ruffling of papers silenced and I felt everyone's eyes fall to me.

I didn't look at them though, focusing only on Eli.

He was still, expression giving nothing away, the hand not holding Max's now in a white-knuckled grip. Honestly, it was sort of surprising. He wasn't known for exercising restraint, not when it came to his family. And he'd already been pushed to the edge as it was today.

"What do you mean?" Max asked, her entire side pressing into Eli, soothing the turmoil that I knew she probably experienced as strongly as if it was her own. Another element of the bonds we'd need to understand.

I picked at the carpet lining the floor between me and Atlas, searching for words. I should have told Eli immediately, but in all of the chaos, I honestly hadn't thought about it. And he had a short fuse when it came to his family—a fuse that was always threatening to spark between Seamus struggling and Levi and Evelyn always being around. The last thing we needed was him spiraling because of this and accidentally lighting the cabin on fire.

Atlas's foot slid slightly until the side of his boot pressed gently against mine. It was a small gesture, but my chest squeezed at his small encouragement, his solidarity.

"We've been on a few missions with Levi," I started, trying to fully remember the details. He never confirmed anything, of course," I shot Eli a weak smile, "I mean, you know how he is. Loves being all mysterious and probing and shit. But it was clear that he was something...*more*. All I know for sure is that he seems to have the ability to blur or compel human thoughts, but he also suggested that he could do the same with protectors, with supernaturals as well. I think—" I cleared my throat, the sound uncharacteristically loud in a room where I could suddenly hear a pin drop, "I think that's why they've allowed us near this place in the first place, why Levi was always able to slip in and out of Guild life whenever he wanted, without anyone ever calling him on it—because he could erase whatever interactions he didn't want sticking. He's always existed as a sort of phantom in The Guild—no team, no friends, no clear role, slipping through the seams like a shadow. I think this is why—" I shrugged, "or, at least, how."

"He can do what?" Eli's voice was hollow, his dark eyes vacant.

"Seriously?" Wade leaned his head back, letting out a long exhale. "Is everyone a demon now? I can't fucking keep up."

Max's face scrunched up in confusion as she turned to Darius. "Vampires can do that, right? Light compulsion, I mean. With humans at least?"

"I'm pretty sure Lucifer, and other higher demons can as well," Wade added.

"Vampire compulsion is rare, and difficult to master," Darius started. "It also can't be employed at the level Declan is suggesting. At least not on protectors to the extent it would allow us to get past Guild security protocols, and definitely not on demons. Memories are very complicated, they are tied to our identities and once you pluck or change one, there is a ripple effect. No single memory exists in a vacuum. It's why vampires rarely bother with it outside of blurring the thoughts of humans they feed from. More trouble than it's worth and it can lead to Guild capture when done poorly." Darius arched his brow as he turned to Eli. "You know who his father is?"

Eli swallowed then shook his head. "They never told me." His voice was hoarse, shaken. "And, honestly, I never swallowed my pride long enough to ask."

Darius turned to me, his hair disheveled, eyes feral. "And I'm guessing he didn't give you any clear answers, or outline his family tree during this big reveal?"

I snorted. "Have you met Levi? Getting a straight answer out of him is about as common as spotting a unicorn on the side of the road."

"Hellhounds exist," Wade said with a shrug, "who's to say unicorns don't as well?"

"I've never seen one." Darius paused for a moment, not bothering to hide his curiosity as he considered the possibility, "but I suppose after everything, we can't exactly rule them out, can we?"

"Not the point." Max shook her head, a reluctant grin

tugging at her lips. "Levi's part mystery demon. That explains how they've been able to get as much intel as they have here, why they've been willing to give us a chance—to trust us as much as they have." She frowned, "but that also means—"

"That we don't know the limits of Levi's strengths—or how much we can trust him not to use them against us if we become a threat," Eli added, his face growing paler with each passing minute.

I shuddered at the thought of Levi erasing or muddling my memories.

But I didn't miss the way that Atlas's face softened, just a touch, like the idea of forgetting was laced with equal parts fear and hope.

7

———

MAX

My head hurt. I could feel and hear the blood rushing through my veins. It didn't even feel like I was living inside of my body. My skin was tight, itchy, like I didn't quite fit into it the way I usually did.

I knew why, knew that my secret was eating me alive. I needed to tell them the truth, but I had no idea where to start.

'Hey guys, just so you know, I'm going to die,' just seemed like a ridiculous thing to blurt out in the middle of the cabin's living room.

But now that I knew my brain was randomly broadcasting announcements to them, the pressure was worse. The last thing I wanted was for them to find out that way.

"Fuck," I muttered, pacing back and forth in the small bedroom Declan had been occupying.

I spent most of my nights with Atlas, not really talking much—or doing anything more physical than that—just lying together, soaking up the silence and the warmth of each other. He never directly said so, but I knew that my presence helped soften some of the fear and sadness still tormenting him.

I knew from my own experience that sometimes, when you were sinking, the quiet presence of someone close by helped open your chest, your throat, enough to pull in a desperately needed gulp of air. I'd be that for him for as long as it took.

He didn't say much, but I didn't push for much more than that either.

Being near him had been helpful for me too though, after all of the time we'd spent apart, the time we'd spent denying the connection between us. We both had fresh wounds that needed to heal.

But between nights with Atlas and my attempts at healing in the medical building, I didn't have much alone time. I didn't even have my own room, now that I thought about it. After Atlas returned, Rowan moved out of our cabin and in with Arnell and the rest of Ten. He spent most of his time running training camps and exercises. Even with him gone, the cabin was still cramped and short a room.

Which meant that when I wanted to escape for a few minutes, there was no space to decompress and get my shit together. No place that really felt like mine, anyway.

Maybe that was why I kept finding myself out by the lake in the middle of the night.

"Max?" Declan's voice was soft, quiet as she pulled the door closed behind her, the gentle snap enough to make me jump.

The deep black of her hair and shirt made the gentle concern in her glistening green eyes impossible to avoid. It was a look I was growing more and more familiar with.

Dec liked to project a chilly demeanor to the world, but she was the core of the group—the most in tune with each of our needs, the first one to notice when one of us wasn't quite right.

At least she was that way with me. I swore she could read me like a goddamned book she'd memorized years ago and recited daily.

I took a deep breath, tried to pull my fear and anxiety back inside of myself, swallowed the lingering thoughts about my conversation with Evelyn, pulled the cyclical repetitions of Lucifer's ritual back before they burned her.

Her eyes narrowed as she moved towards me, hesitant and slow like she was afraid of scaring off a timid animal.

"Are you okay?" She exhaled sharpy, shaking her head. "I mean, *okay* probably isn't the word I'm looking for. Of course you're not okay. Shit's been abso-fucking-lutely wild lately. I'd be almost more concerned if you were okay. But—" she paused, searching for the right word, "You've just seemed a bit more off than usual the last few days. Distant, maybe? I know that what happened at Headquarters was a lot. I just want you to know that I'm here, okay? I love you. If you want to talk about any of it—"

I opened my mouth to respond, but I had no words to give her.

Tell her. Just fucking tell her goddamn it.

It was so fucking easy.

Dec, you're right. I've been distant because I love you too—I love all of you—and I'm terrified of letting myself get even a little bit closer because I'm going to die and the damage and pain my death will cause will only increase the closer I let you all in.

I wanted to let the words fall from my lips, but I couldn't.

Worse, even, I wasn't sure I could do it—that I could willingly leave them when the time came, knowing how much it would hurt them. Now that I intimately knew that kind of loss —felt the absence of Cy like a near-constant stab wound to the chest—being the cause of that kind of pain was my biggest fear. Even bigger than feeling it again myself.

What if I couldn't do it? What if I damned the world because I wasn't strong enough? What if, after everything, I'd let love become my greatest weakness instead of my greatest strength?

But I closed my mouth tight, swallowed the fear, my eyes welling with the unsaid words. My thoughts were clamped down. I used every ounce of focus I had—pulling on the dream-walking training I'd done with Wade and Serae, to keep those rampant anxieties from spilling into Declan's mind.

With the mate bonds taking on a life of their own, it was more difficult to hide from my feelings for her. Now that we'd acknowledged that connection, dove into the closeness—both physically and emotionally—I didn't want to go back to where things were before that.

I didn't want to pretend that her bright green eyes weren't the first thing mine fought to find every time I entered a room she might be in, that her every touch didn't make me drip with need, that the sound of her voice didn't make air lodge in my chest.

I wanted more of her, of them all, not less.

And I knew, truly knew, that the only way to achieve that was through honesty.

But not yet. I just wanted a little more time. Just a little more happiness before I changed everything again.

Didn't we deserve that? A moment of peace? Or some semblance of it at least? Even if it couldn't last?

She tilted her head, studying me, her eyes darting between mine as she took a few steps towards me. When her hand lifted and cupped the side of my face, a sob nearly broke free from my chest.

Her thumb traced my cheek bone, the pressure soothing and soft as she leaned her head in towards mine. The feather-light touch sparked through my entire body, traveling down my spine like a humming livewire.

"It's just been a tense few days," I finally managed, my eyes closed tight so that I didn't have to stare into hers while I circled the full truth I wasn't ready to tell. Instead, I offered her part of it. "And with the mate bonds solidifying—" I opened my eyes, until I found hers, my stomach clenching at the closeness of her, the smell, the realization that I could take a step closer and feel the intoxicating curves and lines of her body as they fit against mine.

Instead, I took a step back.

"Not that the bonds are a bad thing. That's not what I mean." I shook my head, tried to keep my thoughts from spilling out in a bumbling mess—something I would probably never master. "The power between us is amazing, sometimes it's all I can do not to focus on it, not to sink into you all and just sort of drown in the dizziness of it for a few days—weeks. But then I feel guilty—giving into that with so much shit going on, with the literal fate of the world at stake—it just feels wrong. And now, with you all in my head, with Eli channeling the powers—it's just a lot to process. I'm afraid of hurting someone, of hurting one of you. I just don't know how to do this—" I took another step back until the back of my legs hit the bed. I let the momentum pull me onto it, my body sagging into the mattress, the brief relief of weightlessness. I laid back, focused on the ceiling—a cobweb that hung draped over the light fixture. "I don't know how to be everything you want. Everything you all need. I don't want to fuck things up."

Dec's eyes narrowed as she studied me, processing. She tilted her head and took a step closer, until suddenly I felt naked in front of her, impossibly vulnerable under her perusal above me. "Why do we all do this?"

"Do what?"

She snorted. "Allow ourselves to be so consumed by the possibility of failure that we stop taking chances, stop letting ourselves sink into the few things that make us feel good, that make us happy?" Her eyes met mine as she hovered over me, the soft light framing her head like a halo. "Aren't you sick of it?" she shook her head, pinching the bridge of her nose. "I sure as hell am."

I was. But saying that you wanted to not feel fear wasn't the same as not feeling it.

"The world is quite possibly ending," she pressed on, "and I don't know what's going to happen. To any of us. You're under a literal world's worth of pressure, Max. But not from us. And I won't speak for the guys, but I will say that all I want is you—however much you want to give. And I don't just mean some caricature version of you that's all sunshine and rainbows. I want your darkness as much as I want your light, your bad days as much as your good. I just want you as you are. You can't mess that up." She tilted her chin up, "You understand?"

I nodded, unable to form any sort of intelligible response.

"Sometimes it can feel wrong to be happy in light of everything. It's hard to experience joy, desire, laughter, when there's so much wrong in the world. But that's when it's most important." She ran a hand through her long hair, and my eyes hungrily traced the way a few strands fell around the curve of her neck, her chest. I wanted to do the same with my fingers, with my tongue.

Her eyes sparked, like she felt that stray thought, even if she didn't hear it out right. "Sometimes happiness can be its own form of resistance." She grinned, brow arching. "At the very least, it gives us the stamina for the long run. A reason to keep going. This task we face is a marathon, not a sprint, Max. Don't be afraid to lighten your load every once in a while—the rest of us will take turns carrying it."

Her words ricocheted in my chest, carving their way in, making a home—completely impervious to my resistance.

"I have an idea." A small grin curved the corner of her mouth. "Stay here, okay?"

I nodded, but otherwise didn't move. As I watched the dust particles float above me, I heard the door open, the brief juggling of clanks in the small kitchenette, heard someone—

maybe Eli—mumble something to her, before she responded with a soft "night mate," closing the bedroom door behind her.

The light above me switched off, bathing the room in a dark gray haze, my vision blurring and adjusting to the sudden shift.

I heard Dec rustling through a drawer in the bedside table and sat up.

"What are you—" she pressed a finger to my lips, stopping the question before I could ask it.

Her eyes found mine and I could see a flash of excitement there.

She didn't pull her finger from my mouth, and something about the silent darkness, her closeness, the image of her leaning over me, sent a wave of desire flaring through my body.

My tongue instinctively parted to lick my lips, and I tasted her finger.

She exhaled, her breath minty and cool as it swept over me. As if emerging from a trance, she cleared her throat and pulled her finger away.

"No questions," she said, her voice filled with authority even in the soft whisper. The scratchy sound of a match striking turned into a sizzle as the soft glow of fire flared at her fingertips. "We're going to get you out of that head of yours for a few minutes, push you back into your body."

She set a small candle on the table, lighting it until the air around us was bathed in a soft glow. With a flick of her hand, the match went out, the soft smokey char curling in my nose. "Borrowed this from Mer. From a secret resource cabinet she showed me a few days ago—told me she keeps these stocked during the cold winter months." A seductive grin curled her lips. "It's body safe."

"Wha—"

She lifted a black bandana between us, folded it over a few times, then pressed it to my eyes. My heart started to race as she tied it carefully at the back of my head, gentle but firm.

The coconut scent of the candle was so much stronger as my vision blurred to black.

I shivered as her hands swept my hair back behind my shoulders.

I bit my lip, but her thumb gently released it, the touch pulling a breathy shudder from me.

"Your only job right now is to relax," she said, the soft sultry sound of her voice enough to make me clench my legs together. "We're going to work on embracing some of that happiness I was talking about. See if we can't pull you out of that doom spiral, okay? All of the bullshit, all of the challenges we face—those are tomorrow's problems. Tonight it's just us, just this. Do you trust me?"

I licked my lips and nodded, unable to find my voice.

"That's my girl," she whispered against my lips before hers ghosted briefly over mine in a soft kiss that sent a wave of flutters low in my belly. "If you want to stop at any time, just tell me. But until then, I only want you to focus on your body, on every sensation—on nothing else but that, okay?" She paused, waiting for me to respond, so I nodded again. "Just try to relax and just—*be*—okay?"

I nodded again. My nipples were already hard, my senses hyper alert, aware of her closeness and wanting it closer.

My heart beat like a rabid hummingbird in my chest—whether from nerves, excitement, or desire I couldn't quite tell. Could she hear it in the heavy silence of the room? Even my breathing seemed desperately loud.

Slowly, her fingers found the hem of my shirt, and she lifted it up. I raised my arms above my head, allowing her to peel it off of me, the fabric grazing my skin in featherlight kisses. The soft strawberry scent of her favorite shampoo clouded my senses as she leaned over me. Gods, I didn't think I'd ever tire of the smell of her—the way the soft scent blended with her natural sweetness.

The memory of the way she tasted had me salivating. It was like she'd been crafted from my deepest desires—desires I didn't even know myself well enough to ask for—and then offered up to me.

When my shirt brushed against my sensitive lips, I gasped, as if she'd kissed me. My sports bra followed suit, my skin pebbling with every touch of the cool air.

As if aware of my sensitivity, she playfully licked the peak of my left nipple and then blew a soft breath, cooling it.

My back arched against the bed, my body loudly begging for more, but she denied the request.

And of course, that only made the ache deeper.

I sensed her smug grin, even if I couldn't see it. Right now, I desperately wanted to taste it.

She peeled my pants off next, the maneuvering a little more clunky than my top as I leaned back into the bed to allow her a better angle.

Gently, she shifted me so that I was lying on my stomach, my head resting to the side on the pillow.

It was such a vulnerable position, not being able to see anything as I was splayed out before her, like a willing—and, let's be honest, fucking *eager*—sacrifice.

My stomach muscles tightened as the bed sank softly to my right, waiting with anticipation for whatever touch she was willing to bestow.

But the next sensation didn't come from her touch.

Liquid heat pooled on my lower back.

I inhaled a sharp hiss of surprise as the strength of the heat dimmed. The hot wax carved a small stream down my spine, dripping in branches along my side.

Her hands kneaded the oil into my muscles, and I couldn't even be bothered to suppress the low moan.

I felt some of the knots and tension fight against her fingertips, her knuckles, sighing in relief as each one gratefully lost that battle. She poured more of the candle along my upper back —the first hit of the heat, both unexpected and exciting. Then, with careful strength, she rubbed it into my shoulders, my neck.

I relaxed beneath her touch, savoring every massage, every featherlight touch of her hair as it tickled my arms, my back, the smell of strawberries mixing delectably with the coconut candle.

It shouldn't have been surprising—that Dec somehow seemed to know, to understand my body better than I did. Like she could anticipate and identify points of pleasure, of tension that I hadn't noticed. My skin sparked with waves of tingles, my toes curling each time she relieved a new ache.

When she dripped wax along my ass, my thighs, I jerked up slightly in surprise as the oil slipped between my legs, joining another liquid heat already soaking me from her touch. Her fingers dug into the back of my right thigh, starting closer to the back of my knee and growing closer and closer to an entirely different sort of ache—one I knew she wouldn't relieve. Not yet, anyway. And somehow waiting for that relief just made me all the more desperate for it.

I fisted my fingers into the bed sheets as her hand slipped between my legs—so very close to where my body was begging her touch—just to keep from grinding into her.

Every inch of me was alive and sparking with a pleasure that I couldn't contain.

"Fucking hell," I moaned as her thumbs traced either of side of my spine—starting at my neck and then ending at the apex of my thighs.

Need pulsed through me and I wondered, briefly, if it was possible to come from a massage—without her even once touching me between my legs.

"Flip over," she whispered into my ear, punctuating the

request with a soft nip of my earlobe that drew a pathetic-sounding mewl from my lips.

I did as she asked, lying on my back as I felt her eyes rove over me as if they were her fingers.

My nipples were hard peaks, and there was no denying that the wetness between my legs was more than hot oil. I could hear my breaths coming out in fast, heavy pants, with every moment of anticipation.

Not knowing what she was going to do next made every sound louder, every breath of air against my skin sharper.

The muscles in my abdomen tensed as she poured another small stream of oil along it. She rubbed it into my skin, her hands and fingers molding to the curves of my sides, my stomach—going lower, lower, lower with each stroke, but never quite reaching where my body was silently screaming for her to go.

The tops of my thighs felt hot and tight as she massaged into them, and I groaned in frustration when her thumb grazed over my pubic bone, denying again the release I was desperate for.

"Please," I muttered finally, the word a breathless prayer on my lips as my hand sought hers.

She pulled back, pressed my hand back to my side. She leaned over me, hair grazing my chest, as she whispered, a sultry, "Don't make me tie you up," as her teeth bit into my bottom lip, tugging lightly. I groaned as raging need shot straight to my core. "Because I will. Happily."

I grabbed the bedding, my grip so tight that I wouldn't be surprised if it tore.

"Good fucking girl," she said, clearly pleased with my hard-fought restraint. Her oily hands caressed my clavicle, my breasts, pinching my nipples lightly in reward. I could hear the coy grin in her voice, husky and low, and I desperately wanted to press my lips to the smug curve of her lips that I knew was there, even if I couldn't see it. I wanted to taste her smile, to devour it. Mine. All of her. Mine. "And good girls get rewarded."

The mattress shifted as her weight left, and I suddenly felt even more bare, more vulnerable without the softness of her thigh against me.

There was a soft clink as she reached for something on the side of the bed, like the sound of rocks against ceramic.

And then a sharp hiss tore from me when a wet chill circled my right nipple—the sensation made more extreme in contrast to the hot oil.

Ice.

My tongue wet my bottom lip as I bit down, a poor attempt to stifle my moan as she carved an icy path from my right nipple to the left, the cool stream left behind by the cube pooling along my sternum.

But when the weight shifted on the bed and she leaned over me, blowing a cool breath on my already-stiff peaks, I gasped.

The gasp turned into a low groan that I couldn't contain no matter how badly I tried as her lips closed around my nipple, warming the icy breeze with the heat of her tongue.

"Fucking hell," I whimpered, my fingers digging into the side of my thighs now, the bedsheets not solid enough to keep me from clawing at her.

The pain of my nails digging into my thighs helped center me, but the sharp pain only amplified the pleasure as her tongue traced the icy path to my other nipple.

My breathy gasps sounded pathetic and needy to my ears, but I hardly cared. I was putty in her hands, eagerly and greedily chasing every touch, every kiss that she let me.

She nipped and licked at my neck, my jaw, my earlobe as her hand slid the cube of ice down my stomach—and then lower, lower, lower, until it edged just above, and then over my clit, before it slid between my legs and dissolved completely, devoured by my heat—until it was just the light pressure of her finger against me.

I bucked, chasing more friction, my chest heaving with needy breaths as I bit down hard on my lip.

"Relax," she whispered, pulling her hand away. My skin pebbled as her breath caressed it. "Just focus on the competing sensations," she circled a new ice cube over my nipple, leaving it pressed against me and then moving it away in intervals I couldn't predict, "the way your body reacts," she moved the cube, keeping it flush against me, drawing down my stomach again, "the way it tries to chase the feeling." My thighs clenched as she kissed my ear, my neck, "Let yourself sink into it."

She dipped the ice between my legs again, and I nearly cried out with the pleasure of it—the heat of her fingers mingling with mine, both competing against the ice.

Her body lined against mine as she circled over my clit and when she moaned, the heat of her breath caressed my neck, echoing my own desire.

"Fucking hell, I want you," I gasped, my head turning towards her but all of my willpower focused on not chasing her mouth with mine.

Her breaths were hot, frequent against my cheek and I knew that this was no easy game for her either. I could feel her own desire lapping against my skin, as strong and demanding as my own.

She shifted away from me again, and I resisted the small whimper as I heard her shuffling around.

When her weight sank down on the mattress again, I felt her smooth skin against mine as she straddled me.

Her clothes were gone.

Fucking finally.

More of that. More of her skin, more of her.

I wanted to be completely engulfed by her—her touch, her taste, her scent.

"You have me," she whispered. "You have no idea how much you have me." And then she grabbed my hand and lifted it, pressing my fingers between her legs. Her thong was soaked, drenched with her own desire. "I don't think I've had a dry set of knickers since the day that I met you, Max." Our fingers twined and, together, we pulled her thong off. She pressed a kiss to my lips as she leaned over me. "You have no idea how badly I want you. What every kiss, every touch, every look does to me."

Gods, now that I could feel that she was naked, could feel the desire dripping from her, it seemed suddenly cruel that I couldn't see her. That I couldn't see the lust shine from her mesmerizing eyes, couldn't trace every quivering muscle with my stare.

"More," I whispered, because my brain couldn't fully form thoughts anymore. I just wanted more. More of her. All of her. It would never be enough.

She grinned against my lips. "Open."

I did as she asked, and she shoved the fabric in my mouth, the cotton wet and flavored with the salt of her. I groaned, taking in her taste, letting it float over me as she pulled back.

My breath caught as more hot oil spilled over me, coating my chest, my nipples. My gasps were muffled by the cloth as the path of oil spilled lower and lower, until it glazed over my clit, the brief flash of heady pain quickly morphing into a sharp bolt of pleasure that made me dizzy.

Her fingers massaged over me, the pad of her thumb circling around my clit, teasing—until, slowly, slowly, she pressed it against me.

I felt every throb pulse through my entire body, like a banging drum in my ear as my tongue soaked in the taste of her.

She slid two fingers inside of me, teasing and slow until she found a spot that had me arching off the bed, head leaning back into the pillow, moaning for more.

"Fuck," I whimpered, the word lost around the shape of her thong as I tilted my hip, seeking more friction.

Declan's breathy chuckle held less control than she'd had up until this point, but she still had enough left to pull herself back, to pin my hips back down to the bed with her hands.

I felt her indecision in the pressure of her fingers as they dug into me, until, as if she didn't have the composure to continue holding herself back, she pulled the thong from my tongue and replaced it with her own.

This.

Yes.

So much this.

My tongue greedily slid against hers. The edible candle wax made her taste even sweeter than usual. Her thigh slipped between mine as she ground her hips into me, both of us a tangle of oil, limbs.

"Fucking hell you feel good," she whispered, like a prayer, her breathing as uneven as my own, my leg already slick with her desire.

Her lips found the side of my jaw, my neck, as she licked and teased me with her teeth.

My fingers dug into her hips, her back. When I slid my hand between us, my finger gliding through her slickness and slipping inside of her, I couldn't wait any longer. I wanted to look into her eyes when she came.

I shoved the blindfold off and over my head.

For a moment, I thought she was going to argue, but the fight died on her lips when she registered the pure hunger in mine. Her eyes were wild and blown wide with lust, holding mine as I slid down her body and dipped between her knees.

"I need to taste you." I hardly recognized the sultry tenor of my own voice—it was pure need, pure lust. "Properly."

She opened her mouth, ready to argue, trying to maintain her careful control of the scenario, but the second my lips closed around her, all potential fight dissolved on her tongue as mine slid over her, lapping at her soaked core, my tongue circling, then running over her clit.

"Oh," was the only sound she managed to make as I licked and sucked her like she was the only good taste left in the world—because right now, she was.

All I could see was her, all I could feel, all I could think. Fucking hell.

Her back arched as I slid two fingers into her—and then, I froze.

I could feel her pleasure rolling through me, as if it were my own. Every tingling sensation reverberating through me. She was on the edge—and I knew that with a vivid certainty because I was too.

Our orgasms were building and amplifying each other's.

More so than I'd ever experienced with my succubus powers before. Every lick, every touch, every sensation echoed and pulsed through us both.

Taking advantage of my surprise, she gripped me by the hair at the nape of my neck and pulled me roughly to her. Her lips found mine as our hands warred for real estate over each other's bodies. I traced her neck, her side, her chest, her ass, her thighs. Neither of us could get enough.

"Why does this feel so good?" She moaned into my mouth as her fingers slid over my clit, "gods I can feel your every pulse of pleasure."

I moaned, unable to form any words. Like me, I could tell she wanted all of me at once, every sensation elevated and demanding, our skin on fire as we melted together. It was like a fever dream, everything heightened. We were drugged with it.

I slid myself against her, grinding slow and teasing as we met. Our lips parted on a gasp and we swallowed each other's moans. But the teasing only lasted a moment—my vision blurred when she let out a whimper, both of us overcome by an urgency that had been steadily growing until it outpaced our patience, our tenuous game of control.

Her hips moved in time with mine, both of us slick and hot and filled with a need that was unlike any pleasure or lust I'd ever experienced before. Just from fucking rubbing ourselves on each other's thighs. As one, we went over the edge, our limbs and hair coiled together as the orgasm rippled through us, a livewire of feedback braiding us as one. She shuddered against me, in time with the blood pulsing through me, until we both collapsed, unmoving.

After a moment, when we'd both finally almost caught our breath, she dipped her hand gently between us, fingers circling slowly around the sensitive skin. She hardly even touched my clit before another orgasm followed the first, striking us both, leaving us both panting and dizzy.

Holy hell.

Holy hell is right. Only she didn't speak the words, they filtered through her thoughts into mine, loud and clear as day. The bond connection between us was blown wide, every thought, every feeling echoing and amplifying between us.

She arched a brow, a mischievous smirk on her face as her hand grazed along my side until she found my nipple. Her thumb teased the peak before she pinched.

Both of us clenched our thighs around each other as a bolt of need rolled through us.

Doesn't do much for longevity, and I don't know how many times I can come before passing out, but I am very willing to test those limits, she thought, before she ground herself against me, entangled and seeking more friction as another climax pulled from us both.

This one was different, even stronger than before, and it

echoed between us, amplified by whatever final shields in the bond were temporarily abandoned.

My vision blurred, my lips finding hers as we rode the waves in whimpers and screams. And like a magnet, my palm pressed against her. I slid two fingers inside of her, stroking the spot I knew would make her melt—like her body was a map only I could read.

Because it made me melt too.

"Oh," she said, both of us groaning as we slipped into another orgasm. Only this time, warm liquid rushed from us both as my vision blurred from the intensity of it.

Too much, it was almost too much. But fucking hell, I never wanted to stop this feeling.

Fuck.

Yes.

Fucking hell.

Oh my god.

Thoughts and sensations that couldn't be made into words flooded my mind but I could no longer tell which belonged to whom.

My bones were jelly and we remained in a puddle of each other's limbs until the intensity of the feeling faded into a soft echo—still not entirely gone, but quiet enough that I had control of my limbs and was able to form words again.

"That was—" I huffed, searching for some way to describe it other than the most mind-blowing sex—hell, experience—I'd ever had. Maybe I wasn't actually able to form words yet.

"Yeah," she exhaled, her lips tilted into an intoxicated grin. "That...was."

I cuddled into her, mesmerized by the feel of her body against mine, the way that we seemed to fit together, effortlessly. My skin cooled from the liquid coating us—a mix of oil, sweat, and the product of our lust. It felt like a badge, a monument to all we'd just experienced.

"I've never done that before."

I knew that she meant the squirting even though there was a lot about the last few minutes I'd never done before.

I grinned into her neck. "Same."

My lips pressed into the spot where her neck met her shoulder and my tongue peeked out, already missing the taste of her.

"Mmm," she hummed, leaning into the feel. "Next time you squirt, I want my head between your thighs."

Fucking hell, just the visual of her beneath me, lapping me up, the simple promise of it, sent another pulse of need through me as I dug my fingers into her hips.

My mind was as jelly-like as my body, and I realized suddenly that she'd accomplished her goal. All I could focus on was this moment, on her, on the sensations flooding my system —every touch, every taste.

Hell, I was even greedily collecting every tiny whimper, moan, word, breath that she made like it was gospel.

And I was relaxed.

Happy.

Her own joy met mine in a crash and washed over us both.

She was right. Tomorrow. We'd deal with everything in the morning, but we needed moments like this, to feel connected— to remember what we were fighting for in the first place.

My thoughts started to feel more like mine again, and when I focused on the connection, I worked to close it—not completely shut it off, but shove a curtain over it. We couldn't lay in a cycle of orgasms forever. No matter how pleasant that sounded.

A heavy knock sounded against the door and I stifled my groan of frustration. I wanted to sit in this bubble of bliss for as long as I possibly could.

"Ignore it," Declan mumbled, her eyelids closing as she nuzzled into the pillow, her arm clinging around mine.

For a moment, I considered it.

But the knock came again, harder this time.

I took a deep breath before hauling myself up. "Hang on."

A gray towel hung on the back of the door, so I grabbed it and wiped myself off before handing it to her to do the same.

I pulled a shirt over my head and started fishing for my pants.

With the battle lost, Declan groaned and followed suit, heading to a pile of clean clothes for a pair of dry underwear—her soaked thong a lost cause she clearly had no intention of reviving.

I waited for a moment, my hand on the doorknob, making sure she was dressed and decent before I swung it open. "Wha—"

I swallowed my question at the dazed look on Eli's face.

His arms were spread on either side of the door frame, like he was physically restraining himself from barging in.

Declan shifted behind me, gasping as her eyes locked onto him.

I followed her stare to Eli's dick.

There was a stark, very obvious wet spot on his light gray sweatpants.

Eli made no move to cover it up, and if he was at all embarrassed, there was no trace of the emotion etched into his face. His eyes were all heat as he watched my realization unfold.

"Fanghole took the shower before I could," he shook his head, then turned to Dec briefly with a bemused, teasing glance before he looked down at his crotch. "First orgasm took me by surprise, clearly. But yeah, I take it back. Our immediate priority should be us getting a better grasp on this whole connection thing. ASAP."

Oh.

Apparently mine and Dec's connection wasn't the only one that had been blown wide open.

He took a step towards me, eyes tracing me from head to toe and back again—a scan that I could feel like a caress. I tried to ignore the flutter low in my belly as I clenched my thighs together. Sandwiched between them both, a flare of desire started to reignite.

I wasn't sure if it was the succubus, the bonds, or some combination of both—but my libido was fucking insatiable tonight.

"That," he said, his eyes darkening as he took another step closer, hovering over me until my chest brushed against his, "or the rest of us need to clear the cabin when you get laid from now on." His focus held on my lips that I'd unconsciously just licked. He shook his head with a grunt before biting his own. "Unless we're all cool with dissolving into a group-wide fuck-fest each time."

The sight of him there, that look in his eyes nearly had me undone all over again.

"Because fucking hell, it took every last inch of self-control I had not to come in here and join in." He nodded towards the other room without taking his eyes away from mine. "If you'd have been in anyone's room but Dec's, I would have. The guys seem okay with simultaneously sharing sexy fun time with you, but I know Dec maintains a strict no-dick policy in the vicinity of her sexcapades."

"Sexcapades? Sexy fun time?" she snorted, face contorted in mock-disgust, "you sound like an adult film star from the eighties." She tilted her head, lips twisting in surprise as she studied Eli, while I did everything I could to swallow my laughter, "and a slimy one, who isn't exactly inspiring at his craft." She sniffed, "But other than forever lodging that undesirable series of images in my head, thank you for respecting a very specific boundary of mine, I guess."

"Wade nearly ripped the front door off the hinges in his haste to create some distance. I think his powers are even more sensitive to this particular element of the—connection." He shrugged, focus still centered on me, his arms straining like he still wasn't in complete control. "And I heard a loud crack from Atlas's room. Pretty sure he punched a hole in his wall trying to keep himself from coming in here. So, not that we paid a deposit on this cabin in the first place, as far as I'm aware, but —" that playful smirk of his made an appearance and I clenched my fingers into a fist at my side to keep from tracing it with my thumb, "if we did, something tells me that by the end of our stay, we won't be getting it back."

8

ATLAS

She was on the floor, dried blood flaking away in chips between her breasts, the dark gash in her neck nearly black with the depth of the gouge. Wade, next to her—a far less gory sight, but no less dead.

"It's not her," I whispered, "It's not him. This isn't real."

I blinked back the image, opening my eyes, trying like hell to fill my vision with any other scene, anything but the horror that filtered like a film, non-stop.

Night after night, never ending. I hadn't slept for intervals greater than twenty minutes in weeks.

The only thing that even allowed me those brief respites was the feel of her body pressed against mine every night.

She was alive. She was here. She was safe.

By some miracle I still couldn't grasp, we all were.

And when I could hold her, could feel the gentle dips and curves of her body, the warmth of the blood rushing beneath her skin, it became easier to push back against the narratives clouding my mind—her dead, all of them dead. I'd run my thumb down her neck, feel for myself that she was still alive.

It's a lie. It's a lie. It's a lie.

But she wasn't here right now, so arguing with myself was more difficult.

I jammed my head back into my pillow. "Stop it. Just stop. You're being fucking ridiculous."

My body was stiff with unfiltered anger. It was an infuriating thing—having my brain work against me, spinning lies and twisting truths. Even when I knew it was happening, I couldn't stop the nightmares from filtering through.

I was here. In this dark, cramped room—a room I'd spent days in. But I was also there, trapped in the cyclic scenes the drude had crafted in my mind. He'd carved new pathways, new memories that felt more true, more visceral than the ones I knew were my lived reality.

My vision adjusted and I could see the dark hazy bedroom, the outline of the dark bed frame, the base propped up and bolstered with a few pieces of mismatched wood—the only lingering evidence of that blissful night with Max.

But layered on top of the bed, this setting, I watched clipped segments of scenes that I knew, logically, weren't here.

I'd blink, and there was Declan, head sitting face-up several feet from the rest of her body—blink again, and there was Eli, fastened to the far wall with a sword through his ribs, head lolling lifeless on his chest, the blood flow so heavy that his white shirt looked solid red.

When I reached out, I could feel these phantoms, as solid as the blankets that covered my legs, could see his blood stain the tips of my fingers.

"It's not real," I repeated again. I closed my eyes, focused on the sounds surrounding me, separate from those gruesome scenes.

Max, was finishing up in the shower, the quiet hum of a song I didn't recognize in harmony with the gentle drum of water.

Eli—in the kitchen, popping a tab off a fresh beer.

Declan's gentle snoring in the other room.

I didn't hear Wade or the fanghole, but I'd heard the front door open and close a few times over the last hour or so.

They were probably out getting fresh air, trying to dispel some of the tension from Max's bond—something I'd been doing my best to ignore for the last fifty-two minutes and fourteen seconds.

Selfishly, I didn't want to ignore it. For a few blissful moments tonight, the visuals drifted away. And as relieved as I was for the reprieve, I was disgusted with myself. They came at the expense of witnessing the connection between Max and Declan.

Those pulses of pleasure that sifted through from her to me were strong enough to sever my nightmare reality from this one. But they did nothing to hollow out the guilt that sat low in my gut from the uninvited voyeurism.

They're alive. They're here.

I sat up, watching my door, my body craving the soft light that would appear through the crack when she opened it, shadowing her figure as she came in, closed it behind her, and then tiptoed gracefully to my bed.

I needed to feel her, here and solid and more real than those phantoms could ever be.

I spent most of my nights watching her sleep, the curves of her body lifting and contracting with each soft breath, the quiet pressure of her warmth against me.

We never started the nights so close together.

I didn't allow it.

I hadn't touched her like that, let myself feel her like that since that moment. I'd allowed myself one night with her in that way—but only one.

Feeling that sort of belonging, that sort of pure ecstasy of being inside of her seemed undeserved after everything I'd done. All of the pain I'd caused. I didn't want to taint her with the horror that lingered with me, the two worlds I occupied—I wanted her as far from those sights as I could get her.

But I was weak, my resolve only so strong.

And when she crawled into my bed each night, I instantly sought her scent, my muscles relaxing just from the smell of her. She'd whisper a few quiet words, I'd give one-word answers when I could manage them, and then she'd fall asleep, exhausted from all of her work in the medical wards.

My self-control weakened as the night grew darker, the horrors of my thoughts louder. I'd press myself close to her, my body humming from the small whimpers she'd make in her sleep, and press my face into the curve of her neck.

I wanted to suffocate in that space against her soft skin, the silence of the cabin surrounding us.

The nights when I woke up and she was gone—a midnight visit to the lake—I'd wake up gasping, drowning with fear that I was back there. That this place too, with my brother and my team, was just another trick of the drude, longer and more cruel than the others because of the sliver of hope it had given me.

When she was gone, I'd give up completely on sleep, leave the confines of the cabin to find her, the tightness in my chest settling only when I saw her climb back up the rocky beach, her eyes black as night, lost in a trance.

In those moments, when I could take a full breath at the sight of her, at the pure relief of it, I felt more in control of myself, closer to the man I used to be, the man I wanted to be again. For her. For them all.

It wasn't enough—as much as I desperately tried to lift myself out of the darkness, to talk to her and hold her the way that she deserved, the words wouldn't form. It was like I was trapped, only offered brief moments here and there of clarity.

I didn't recognize myself anymore.

It was a bit ironic—that I'd spent so much time thinking

that my wolf was the thing that would fracture me, cloud over and consume me.

Now, I missed that part of me—felt unwhole from whatever The Guild had done to quiet him down, to keep him from unfurling in my limbs, my thoughts.

My wolf lingered deep inside my bones. I could feel him, growing erratic and anxious with each passing moment that I didn't shift—but neither of us seemed able to do it. Reaching him was like trying to reach across an ocean, with nothing but my arm.

My limbs didn't work like they used to—as if they belonged to someone else. I didn't even recognize my own thoughts half the time, could hardly keep track of time passing or recognize reality from the dream world I'd spent months occupying.

The soft creak of the door hinge startled me—something that was usually difficult to accomplish with wolf senses.

"Is it possible you linger in the darkness because you think you deserve to?" she whispered to me, her voice rough and cracked in the dark room, as she slid between the sheets.

My skin came alive at her nearness, the desire to reach out and pull her to me almost impossible to resist.

Her gaze focused on the far wall, where Eli's pinned body had been replaced with hers. Her expression was unreadable, but her focus was precise. Could she see it?

Was I broadcasting these ghosts through the connection she'd blown open tonight?

My heart beat angry and ashamed against my ribcage as I fought to erase the visuals, to ground myself here.

No. This was my punishment, not hers. I wouldn't let her suffer it.

"Linger where?" I closed my eyes tight, trying like hell to push away the visual of her, now dead beside me, body angled and wrong, the piercing shriek of her scream as her body contorted and cracked still ricocheting in my mind—her joints only coming back together long enough to relive the torment and pain all over again.

That wasn't her. She was on top of that phantom, existing in this plane, alive and warm and good.

"No," I pressed my palms to my eyes, "no, no, no."

She gasped, her fingers gently closing around my wrist, pulling my hand back from where it clawed at my head. Her focus drifted to her lap, where the nightmare-Max's neck sat at a wrong angle, her other hand passing through the image like a ghost. She couldn't feel them like I could, they didn't take corporeal shape for her. Good.

"Is it always this bad, this loud?" she paused, her fingers trembling against me, "this real?"

Air pulled through my lungs in heavy pants as I fought the images and forced myself to look at her—to see the version that was next to me now.

Her hair fell in dark, clumped strands, still wet from her shower, the scent of her freshly-washed skin enough to make my dick strain in my boxers.

Not that the erection had ever completely gone down since she'd entered that bedroom with Declan.

I pulled my arm from her grip and swallowed back my desire as I carved more space between us. "What do you mean?"

The words came out nearly unintelligible, my jaw was clenched so tight.

Atlas?

The reverent sound of my name in her voice rattled through my head, competing with the terrified screams that usually took up that space.

Atlas, look at me.

My eyes widened when I realized what she was doing. I pushed back further in the bed, trying like hell to think of anything else—anything but those visions, anything but that relentless ache of grief. I didn't want her to see that, to feel that. She carried enough pain on her own. She didn't need to be burdened with mine.

"No," I said, teeth clenched as I curled in on my side, trying like hell to close my mind off. For a blissful hour tonight, fear and pain had been replaced by an intoxicating desire that I had no more control over than I did the darkness. I'd come twice, my body on fire with a pleasure that felt like a sin. Feeling Max's joy, her body alive and electric like that was a drug I'd never grow immune to—but I didn't want it if that connection came at the cost of my suffering filtering into her, of it becoming hers.

Atlas, she said again, the word like a prayer as her lips pressed gently against mine. I was too weak to resist the taste of her, minty from her toothpaste, but also uniquely her. *I'm not afraid of your darkness. Please don't shut me out. Not again, not anymore. I only want to see you—and for you to see me too. Please. You're not there anymore, and I'm here. We're here. We're both terrible at getting out of our heads, at staying out of these thought loops. But Dec was right. We can help each other—together.*

Her words were rushed, panicked, as they snaked beneath and then through my thoughts, replacing their clutch with hers.

So fight.

I know it's selfish to ask this of you, believe me, I know it. This isn't toxic positivity talking right now. The world is literally crumbling down around us, and I can't lose you again—not to fear and pain that's been wrung from you by people who couldn't see you, colonizing your every thought. They don't get to win.

You have to fight because we—I—I need you. So fight, Atlas. Please.

The plea filtered through my head, cracking and reverberating again and again, growing louder and louder until the memories of my nightmares seemed pale in comparison, effervescent—like fire turned to smoke, until it was nothing more than air.

Her own fear mingled with mine, taking shape until I could see the root of it.

The others the drude fed on weren't getting better. They were dying.

Max had been wringing herself out trying to help Sarah, but she couldn't.

She could only help me—but I had to meet her half way.

"Please," she said again, her voice whisper-soft with a tremble, "and not just for me—fight because *you* want that too—to find your way back to yourself."

"I don't know how," I said, hating the soft tremble in my voice, the hollowness of it. "I don't know how to exist like this."

She pulled back a few inches, her face still close to mine, but I found myself already missing the feel of her mouth against mine. "By letting me carry some of it."

"I don't—"

Her finger pressed against my lips, and even in the darkness, I could see the hardness lining her eyes. "Seeing you like this, holding it all on your own—" she shook her head, dropped her fingers back down to the mattress between us, "that hurts more than these visions ever could. They aren't real to me in the way that they are to you. They're yours, not mine. I just want you to talk to me, please. I think—" She blinked. The waterline of her eyes was damp with unshed tears, as her chin dimpled. "I think I'm losing Sarah. I can't bring her back because I don't have a connection with her. But I brought you back, because we are built to support each other, to carry each other. I can't lose you—not again."

Her sadness, her fear struck deep into my chest. There was no hiding from it, not when the bond was flaring between us, not when she was this close to me.

For a moment, her eyes held mine, encouraging me to dig

through, to feel the depth of her truth. She meant what she said.

"I don't know how to fix this," I whispered, afraid putting too much voice to the words would reveal the truth—that I couldn't. That I didn't deserve to be fixed. "I don't know how to fix me."

"You don't need to be fixed, Atlas. You just need to *be*. Talk to me. We haven't spoken about that night—about what happened, what you went through—none of it." The pain in her voice pulled at me like a bony claw. It only took me a moment to realize that it was pain she was feeling on my behalf.

She wasn't angry with me, not anymore—even after everything I'd put her through, put them all through, she'd forgiven me.

You are the only one still trying to earn your forgiveness, Atlas.

The words echoed in my skull, peeling back a thin but not unnoticeable layer of the gruesome reality competing with this one.

"I don't know where to start," I said, my voice unrecognizable to me. There was pain there, a deep sadness that I couldn't linger in or dissect for too long.

"What the drude put you through was horrendous." Her hand closed over mine, twining our fingers together, lending me her strength. "And your father—"

"Deserved to die," I finished for her.

I held no sadness for his death. There was no regret buried in my bones for handing her the heart of the man who'd broken hers.

"He hurt you," I said, "took something from you that can never be replaced."

The depth of her grief at the reminder of Cyrus, of what she'd lost, rippled through me. It was cloying and heavy, and braided with mine like a companion seeking refuge.

"Yes, he did." She nodded, her tongue peeking out over her lips as her eyes searched mine. I wondered, briefly, what she saw there. "But he hurt you too."

I clenched my jaw, the memory of him sacrificing me to the drude crashing forward, relentless. "I didn't have the kind of relationship with Tarren that you did with Cyrus. I don't mourn for my father the way that you do for yours." Holding sadness for that man would be a dishonor for all that he'd put me through—for all that he'd put Wade through. For what he'd taken from Max. "He doesn't deserve my grief."

"No, he doesn't." She rolled her lips together, considering, "but you do. You're allowed to let yourself feel that loss, even if it doesn't quite fit the way it might otherwise have."

My jaw clenched tight as her words rolled over me— through me. Sadness I hadn't even realized I'd been holding clutched at my chest.

Was it hers or mine?

I wasn't sure it mattered.

"If I'm sad about anything where he's concerned," my voice was rough, unaccustomed to having conversations like this. I never really let myself linger in my emotions, let alone share them with someone else. I was bad at it. But I could try to get better. For her. "It's at the idea of what he could have been. The knowledge that he will never become the father that Wade deserved. There is no redemption for him, even if he never deserved it."

"You deserved a father too, Atlas." She cleared her throat, eyes darting to mine, then away again, hesitant. "I want you to fight for yourself the same way you've fought for Wade. For me. For us all." Her focus dipped down to our hands, and I realized I was squeezing hers in a python-like grip. I relented, slightly, still unwilling to part with her touch altogether. "I think that's the only path back to healing. It won't be easy and it probably won't be linear, and I honestly know so little about druden, if the pain of your time in those labs will ever truly go away. But I have to believe that it will, because you deserve to be free from it. You deserve to be happy. I refuse to believe in a future where you can't feel joy. And in the meantime, we're all here for you, happy to carry the weight of that pain, to spread it out amongst us. Dec has given me a very important lesson tonight." From the feel of it, many lessons, but I didn't interrupt her with the quip. Couldn't speak through the emotion lodged in my throat right now even if I wanted to. "That's what a team does—" her eyes found mine again, "that's what a family does. And that's what we are. We're all we have."

I swallowed, my throat tight as the force of her love poured into me. It was overwhelming. And while I didn't agree with her—that I deserved happiness, that I deserved family, that I deserved her, after everything I'd done—her stubborn resolve burrowed into me, wrestling with my own resistance, loosening it, at least in part.

"I don't regret killing him," I whispered, the words ripping free from my lips before I could hold them back, "I only regret not doing it sooner. I wasted so much time. I've only ever wanted to protect them—Wade, my team, and now, you—and no matter how hard I try, I fail. I fail you all, every time."

She shook her head, her hand pressing into my cheek, soft and warm. "You haven't failed any of us, Atlas. Only yourself. We're here. We love you. You can't always be the one protecting us, you have to let us return the favor." She grunted, her lips quivering into a small smile, the shadow of it still enough to make my pulse kick, even in the darkness of the room. "Hell, your brother's been spending most of his nights secretly sleeping outside of your door, as if none of us can sense him there. And I don't think there's been a single second that Dec's been in the same building as you without half of her focus spent assessing you—checking constantly for ways to help ease your pain. Same with Eli." The smile grew sharper, her eyes sparkling with life. "Hell, even Darius wants to help, in his own twisted way. He threatened to disembowel someone two days ago when they suggested having you sequestered away in another cabin, isolated from us all until we were sure you weren't a danger."

Her thumb stroked against my cheek, and I pressed my face into her hand, letting myself sink into her touch, allowing myself for, just a moment, to set down the guilt and fear that had occupied every molecule of my body for months.

When I closed my eyes, I could almost see the bond linking us, could feel it coil between us, flaring to life as I let her in.

Her lips parted in surprise, but I could feel her too—and knew that I wasn't hurting her, that she wasn't rejecting these parts of me. Instead, we lingered there, together, my pain and months of grief braiding together with hers, familiar and different—a peaceful, warm companionship.

And as my burden lessened, I felt hers do the same—as if carrying each other's hurt brought us each comfort in some strange, unfamiliar way. The connection helped ground me, when I'd been afraid it would only destabilize me more than I already had been.

For the first time since the drude fell into my cell, the nightmares he wielded seemed exactly that—like nightmares. Removed from me, temporal, not of this reality. Mere shadows compared to the feel of her skin against mine, compared to the terrifying power of letting her carve herself into my most vulnerable places, making a home there as I did the same with her.

Slowly, my wolf awakened, stretching through my limbs and twining us together—suddenly made tangible and real again, where he'd been cast as an echo, an empty reflection for so long.

Affection flared, hot and sweet in my chest. At first, I

thought the feeling was coming from Max, from the bond. But it was me.

I let out a soft gasp of surprise, the feeling of relief almost overwhelming. I'd missed the wolf, this part of myself, more than I'd let myself see.

Connected to him and to Max, letting myself actually focus on the feeling of us lingering in the connection together, felt like finally seeing the sun, after years locked away in a dark cave. I felt more like myself than I had since Tarren cast me to the whims and cruelty of The Guild.

The shadows were still there, the phantoms of the night-mares still clouded my peripheral, but they no longer eclipsed my vision, my focus like they had.

And when I let myself meet her gaze again, it was like someone punched me in the gut—but it was a feeling I'd willingly seek out again and again. The pure, unbridled affection shining from her face, from every single pore of her skin, lapped against me—simultaneously saved me and made me feel undeserving of such light.

But I'd spend every last breath I had trying to be worthy of it, to earn even an ounce.

I slid my hand through her still-wet hair, letting the silky strands coil through my fingers and tangle me against her as I cradled the back of her head, tilting her face towards mine.

I wanted more of her light, I wanted it all—whether I deserved it or not.

This girl had been thrown into my life when I least wanted or expected her—but her presence was undeniable, every ounce of me lasered in on her every breath, even when I did everything I could to fight it, to resist it.

But I was a fool. There was no resisting her.

I was so fucking done trying.

And if she wanted me, as fractured and defeated as I was,

then—even though I'd clearly won some ridiculous lottery rigged impossibly in my favor—I wouldn't deny her.

This was love, this impossible-can't-breathe-can't-think feeling that held a grip on my chest from the first moment I saw her and refused to let go no matter how hard I fought it. It was stronger than me, stronger than the wolf—and I was so fucking grateful for that.

I was hers, from the first moment I laid eyes on her, a naive girl, sequestered in a small town that had no idea what kind of a gem it had, her lips pressed against those of some human boy who never stood a chance. My recollection of that day had always been hazy, the wolf's memories often separate from mine, like dreams that sifted slowly away, with each moment I was awake, until there were only a few stray grains for me to make sense of.

But this one was clear, came back in a rush, hitting me strong and unbridled. The possessiveness that took over me when I saw her with someone else.

I'd thought it was the human who never stood a chance—but it was me. I was gone the moment she turned her righteous fury on me and tried to kill me.

Love in this world was strange—volatile and violent, but it was tender too. And we'd been dressed up and dancing in all those parts this whole time, resistance futile.

I didn't need to voice the words, I'd given her full access to my thoughts, my feelings. I was laid bare before her, torn in pieces and leaving her to judge which parts were best to sift through and put back together in whatever version of the puzzle we could manage to salvage.

It didn't even bother me that the others might be able to see these pieces too.

Her lips pressed against mine, soft and tentative—the kiss gone as quickly as it came. Her deep brown eyes were glassy with unshed tears as they held mine, but I didn't need to stare into them to feel her, to understand her.

I was consumed by her, and still it wasn't enough—this insufferable hunger flaring to life with a vengeance for all the time I'd wasted not holding her, not touching her, not showing her that she was mine, ours.

The insatiable need and desire I'd felt since that day, that I pushed and resisted, only letting slip through in slivers and moments of vulnerability when the wolf and everything I suppressed with it pushed to the surface—I let it unfurl and curl around me, basking in it.

"Atlas," she whispered, her lips parting from the force of the heat building between us, all-consuming and demanding, without even a touch.

"I don't want to talk," I said, gripping her hair at the nape of her neck, pulling her closer to me until she could feel me hard and wanting against her, "you asked what you could do? How you could help? You have." I wasn't who I was before the lab, and I probably never would be. But I could craft a version of myself from the wreckage, and maybe that version would suit me even better than the original. The ghosts weren't gone, but I wanted to bask in their temporary absence, sink into my body, feel it for the first time in months, linger in the corporeal world. "Right now, all I want is to sink into you. I don't want to think, don't want to talk—I'm an open book to you now. I've carved my chest open and pinned back my flesh. You can have your way with me—poke and pull out all that you wish. I won't hide from you anymore, won't insult you enough to think I can protect you from anything—not when it's been you saving me all along."

It would take time, I knew that.

Tomorrow, I'd go with her to the med center, try finding a way to integrate back into the team, to help. It would be easier —pulling myself out of the darkness, next time I slipped back into its grip—knowing that their hands were waiting for me to grasp.

"With you, and for you, I will fight. Right now, you're the only thing I want to feel, this feeling the only thing I want to fight for—but I want more of it. So tell me," I pressed my mouth against hers, hot and wanting, pulling back only long enough to whisper across them, "can you help me with that, Bentley?"

9

MAX

A lightning bolt of desire shot down my spine, sparking along every nerve ending as he deepened the kiss, his tongue parting my lips until it was wrestling with mine—languid and hungry all at once.

Fucking hell, you taste good.

His words pressed into me with a growl, laced with a need and desire that matched my own—out of control, hungry, unyielding.

With the connection blown open, I could feel his lust radiate through me, could feel how difficult it had been for him to sleep next to me each night, without giving into this desire that lived in his bones at all times—as it did in mine. It hadn't been easy, both of us shrouded in a heavy blanket of need, trying to protect the other by ignoring it and setting it aside.

No more. Declan was right. Joy, pleasure—we needed to take these things while we had the chance. Who knew how much longer we would be able to.

I didn't understand how I could possibly want more after coming several times already tonight, how my body could still crave and go feral for every ounce of pleasure that was offered to it, but it did, and I did.

A deep growl pulled from his chest as he pressed me up against him, sealing our bodies as close as they could go, his dick thick and hard, straining against my lower belly as a relentless need echoed between us.

I tried to reign it in a bit, to exercise a little control over the bonds, closing them enough to keep us from coming instantly. Now that I knew what it felt like, could trace the edges of where I ended and he began, could feel my connection to the others, I focused, used the tools Wade and Serae had taught me—the succubus power that I was growing more in tune with each day, the mental compartmentalizing I'd become adept at crafting— to manipulate an ebb and flow, to quiet and close the mental connections without shoving them closed entirely.

He stilled for a moment, tongue against my teeth, as he sensed the shift. His heart beat rabid against his chest, a match to my own. "Wh—"

"It's okay," I whispered against him, reaching for the bond between us, tugging him closer, "just experimenting with a little more privacy this time."

When he felt our link flare back to life, he grunted in relief. "Stay with me."

I nodded, letting my reactions to his every touch, his every kiss flow back to him—he wanted the connection right now, wanted to escape being alone with his own thoughts.

Declan helped me understand how valuable that could be —sinking into intimacy, into your own body, when the mind grew too cloudy.

I'd do the same for Atlas, on his own terms.

My hands traced over his shoulders, his chest, his arms, his abs. I wanted all of him—to map and memorize every dip, curve, and hard line of his body.

His fingers gripped into my waist, and I could feel his struggle, that he was trying like hell to hold himself back, to be gentle, to go slow. I could feel what he wanted, and how he wanted it.

It was what I wanted too.

"Don't," I whispered, my voice deep and pleading as I slid my hand down the front of his sweatpants and squeezed the rigid outline of his dick. "Don't hold back with me." His breath shuddered against my lips. "I can take it."

He groaned into my mouth, but I could still feel his resistance.

I climbed on top of him, pulling him into a seated position against me, and tore his shirt down the center, the rip echoing around the silent room, my nails digging divots into his back as I bit his neck.

His breath came out in hot, raspy gasps, the feel of it against my skin sending a wave of shivers across my body.

When I pulled back, caught his eyes with mine, I saw the feral desire unfolded there. Pain. He wanted it. Wanted to relish in it. For once in his life, Atlas wanted to give up control.

To me.

The recognition, the feel and flavor of his lust washed over me, and I felt my succubus powers flare to life, saw the way his body trembled with excitement as the power swept over him.

He groaned, head falling back on the pillow as he sank into it.

When he reached for me, I pressed down his chest, keeping him locked there. I slid over him, my confidence blazing with every pulse of his desire I felt lapping against mine.

I started slow, teasing, light—my lips pressing gently to his, before I moved down his jaw, his neck, his chest. When I reached his nipple, I bit—hard enough to sting, but not break skin.

His dick throbbed against the wet heat between my thighs,

my underwear and shorts already drenched with my own desire.

My tongue traced a delicious path down his abs, stopping only at the low waistband of his sweatpants where the lines of his lower stomach dipped.

Shifting between his legs, I grinned up at him, his eyes glowing pools of brown and yellow, dick tenting his pants almost comically.

But when I pulled them down, any humor fell away, my mouth watering at the sight of him.

He wasn't wearing boxers and the light brown tip of his cock was already slick with pre-cum. His shaft was smooth, solid—the veins lining it angry with desire. I traced them with my tongue, groaning as I took him into my mouth.

It was almost too much to take, but I relaxed my throat, took him in until he slid down as far as I could pull him in, then pulled back, my lips suctioned tight around him until he was free again.

"Tell me what you want, Atlas." I hardly recognized my voice, the intoxication of his desire suddenly the only thing I could focus on—like my succubus powers had just been offered an all-you-can-eat-buffet. And she was fucking starving. "I promise that I'll give it to you."

In a flash he sat up, grabbed both of my arms, and flipped me. A surprised grasp ripped from my mouth, when I found myself on my back beneath him.

His eyes were wild and hungry, like a predator caught mid-hunt as they found mine—his prey.

I shot him a teasing smile as he ripped my shirt, just as I'd done to his.

I was wrong. We both were. He didn't want to be powerless. He wanted to play. To fight. The permanent push and pull between us, the unbridled rage and control restructured into desire. As it had always been, even when we couldn't define or recognize it ourselves.

My coy smile transformed into a sharp gasp as he slid a hand between my legs and cupped me, the pressure and heat of his palm against me enough to shred any control I had left in this scenario.

He smirked, an arrogant expression shaping his face, as he slid a finger under my shorts and ran it over me, the sound of my slickness loud and undeniable in a room punctuated only by our breaths.

"I want to see if we can get you even wetter than this," he brought his finger to his lips and sucked my desire off of it, lips parting like I was a flavor he'd been dying to taste for years, "think that's possible, Bentley?"

With his help, I kicked off my shorts and underwear, too locked in his stare to form words.

When he slid two fingers into me, his breath hot on my neck, I arched off the bed, digging my nails into his back as I chased the orgasm just out of my grasp.

A dark, rough chuckle laced the shell of my ear, sending a flare of tingles all the way down my shoulders. He pulled his hand away, fully fucking aware of what he was doing to me.

I panted, shamelessly trying to grind against him, desperate for more friction, more him.

But he pinned my arms to the bed, one on each side of my head, and stared down at me—his eyes were like fire, wild and dangerous, but I wanted to burn alive in their depths.

He set himself against me, an attempt to unravel me more, but he lost his composure as his dick slid through my wet heat.

I smirked before taking his mouth with my own.

He swallowed a groan and stopped, throbbing against me as I gasped into his mouth.

I wasn't sure how much more power either of us would have in this game, but I wasn't going down without a fight.

Gripping his shoulders, hard enough that my fingernails cut crescent moons into his back, I pulled myself up a few inches from the bed, grinding against him from below, and bit his ear lobe.

He collapsed onto his elbows, caging in me closer as he tried like hell to resist the intoxicating need to slip inside of me. It was a game of wills that I wanted him to win as much as lose.

He rolled his hips, pressing the tip of his dick to my entrance, and we both moaned, my body shivering with need as I resisted the urge to end this game.

I changed my mind. Instantly.

Losing would be better, I would happily relinquish my power for one more inch of him. I wanted to pull him inside of me, shatter around him.

His breath hitched and he pulled back, a strained but cocky smirk twisting his lips as he pulled away from me, his hand splayed on my chest to keep me pinned. "Giving up that easily, Bentley?"

Fuck. The hold I had over the bonds and my thoughts had slipped, but I was too far gone to shut down the connection completely.

I squirmed under his gaze as he studied me, his free hand tracing the curves of my body, down my right thigh, then back up the line where my right met my left. His thumb circled around my clit—enough to tease and hint at the pleasure he could bring, but only *just a taste*.

"A taste," he said, brow arching as he shoved my knees apart. "I think I will."

That look was back again, his expression wild and hungry —almost predatory as he crouched between my legs.

Without looking away, his tongue grazed over my core, until I wasn't sure what had me holding back a scream of pleasure more—that devout, hungry look on his face, or the way his tongue felt against me.

"More," I rasped, relinquishing control altogether. He'd won. This was a game I'd happily lose again and again, if it meant I got more of this. More of him.

More, more, more.

I rolled my hips, desperate for more friction, then let out a frustrated growl when he pulled his lips away from me, instead of adding more pressure where I wanted it most.

For a long beat that passed like a lifetime, he watched me, waiting for me to go still again as I strained towards him, a needy, pathetic whimper on my lips.

His fingers traced around me, sure to stay exactly half an inch away from every spot I wanted him most—but with the bond open, he knew exactly what he was doing, could feel every flare of pleasure that rolled through me, could control me like a pawn, read me like a book.

"Fuck you," I muttered, but there was no real power behind the chastise, because he cupped his palm against me, the pressure against my clit sending a searing shock up my spine. "Fuck."

But when I rolled against his hand, chasing more, he pulled back again, his focus so intense that his stare alone made my pussy clench—empty where I wanted it filled with him.

My skin was on fire, goose flesh pebbling every inch of me, my nipples so hard they could cut diamonds—but I knew he wasn't immune. I could feel his lust radiate against me, amplifying my own until each second of waiting for release just made me want it more.

Frustrated, I met his arrogant stare and slid my own hand between my legs, soaking my fingers with my own need. It felt good, but it wasn't what I wanted.

His eyes narrowed, lips curving in an arrogant smirk over me, and I knew that he knew—that an orgasm from my own hand would be a fraction of what he would give me.

Fucking prick.

I grinned, before sitting up a bit and wrapping my hand, slick and wet, around his dick, coating him with my desire as I stroked.

He gasped, body sinking a few inches closer to me as he fought to stay in control. Instead, he dipped lower and lower, until the tip of him was just a hair's breadth away from where my body wanted him most.

Arching my hips, I slid against him, gasping into his mouth as I slid the tip of his cock over my clit, and then took him inside of me—only an inch, just enough to tease, before I clenched around him and fell back on the bed.

It was a cruel trick though—because in teasing him, I only further frustrated myself.

His chest moved in heavy gasps as his dark eyes found mine again, I could see him fighting a battle for control—a battle both we'd both lose, eventually.

He slid lower, taking one of my nipples into his mouth. He bit down and sucked, the pain braiding with pleasure as I arched into him.

He bit down again as he cupped me, my ears ringing as I fought back the orgasm threatening to tear through me. Not yet. Not yet.

Pleased at my restraint, my sudden willingness to follow orders, he pressed a soft kiss to my lips before sticking three fingers inside of me, the sound of my slickness obscene in the quiet of the room.

Again? Fucking hell you're going to destroy me tonight, Max. I'm starting to think it's actually medically concerning how long I've been erect.

I gasped in shock, at the sudden sound and feel of Eli in my thoughts.

Atlas paused, expression confused.

"Eli," I said, my brain too foggy and body too much like jello to form any real words.

Atlas's gaze went dark and teasing as he wrapped a hand firmly against my throat—enough pressure to get my attention, to pull my focus back to him, but not enough to hurt. Too much. "I must not be doing nearly a good enough job if another man's name is on your lips right now."

"Not my lips," I gasped as his thumb pressed against my clit, "my thoughts. I'm losing control over the bonds."

"If he's going to be a voyeur," a wicked grin crossed Atlas's face as he watched me, "then tell him to come here and do it properly."

"Seriously?" I froze, both shocked by Atlas's invitation and turned on by the thought of Eli here too.

He arched an eyebrow. "Seriously." Then, he leaned back, sliding my legs over his shoulder as he studied me, unblinking. "I want him to hear my name on your tongue while you come on mine."

A ripple of pleasure pulsed through me as Atlas pressed a soft, chaste kiss to my clit, the message clear. No orgasm until he had an audience to fully appreciate the performance. And judging by that wicked spark in his stare, it was sure to be an earth-shattering one.

Award-winning, even.

My plea for Eli to get in here was sharp and fast, but he took little convincing.

The door opened and then closed again, two soft clicks as Eli made his way into the room. I could feel his shock at the offer lap against me, but it melted instantly into pure lust when he saw me spread and writhing before Atlas.

"Hold her down," Atlas demanded, not bothering with pleasantries.

Eli prowled towards us, silent as a shadow, then did as he was told, his firm hands pressing mine on either side of my head.

Atlas grinned, satisfied, then pressed his mouth to my core, running his tongue along my slit as his lips sucked and kissed around me.

"Oh gods," I whimpered, straining against the two of them as the feel of his hot mouth brought me to the edge. My nipples were sharp peaks, my flesh pebbled and sensitive. "Fuck, yes—Atlas."

Two seconds—that was all it took for the orgasm to tear through me like a lightning bolt.

Both of them groaned, Eli's grip faltering as he experienced the force of it, the waves of my pleasure pounding against them both with a hunger that wasn't even close to sated.

A hunger that only matched and amplified theirs.

They both shared a look with each other, something passing between them, decided.

Before I could ask, Atlas flipped me around until my knees and hands dug into the mattress.

Eli flung his sweatpants down, his cock springing free, eager and ready—the tip already wet and sticky with cum.

"Can you take us both, Max?" Atlas asked, the sentence a low growl against the shell of my ear as he leaned over me, his dick thick and already coated with me as it slid between my thighs from behind.

I nodded, mouth watering as Eli kneeled in front of me, eyes wild with need.

When I took him into my mouth, groaning around the taste of him, Atlas filled me.

Fucking hell they felt good.

My mouth pumped around Eli with the same punishing pace of Atlas's thrusts—our bodies coiled together, a mess of limbs and sweat, and a boiling desire that I couldn't wrap my mind around.

The bonds were blown open again, and every touch was magnified, electric, every breath or grunt that feathered across my neck as arousing as Atlas's fingers on my clit.

Eli's hands wrapped in my hair, holding the wet strands out of my face as he watched me take him in my mouth, reverence and lust mapped out in equal strokes across his expression as he pumped into me.

"Fuck, you're perfect." His body tensed, straining as he tried to hold back, to hold onto control for as long as possible. But when Atlas thrust deeper, and I moaned around his dick, his composure snapped. "Fuck, I'm going to come. This is too much."

I took him deeper, moaning, chasing my own orgasm, wanting it seasoned with the taste of his.

Atlas's fingers circled my clit, the pressure mounting—too much, too much, too much.

My fingers could only hold onto the edge of the cliff for so long.

When he grunted against my ear, the only sign of him struggling to hold on too, I lost it.

I saw stars, my ears ringing as the orgasm tore through me like a tidal wave, both of them filling me as they followed me over.

Atlas collapsed against my back, his knees weak, unable to hold him. I did the same against Eli.

We adjusted until I was sandwiched between them, Atlas spooning me from behind as I rested my head on Eli's chest.

I felt our heartbeat pulse through us as one, our skin heated and caked in sweat, both of them stroking my arm, my thigh, their touch and nearness like a balm, until I was lulled under the temporary promise that everything was okay—at least for now.

10

WADE

"How are you here?"

I turned to the voice and did a double take. "Serae?"

My aunt.

As usual, she exuded power, her hair in box braids, with gold beadwork that brought out the natural glow of her skin.

But while she always seemed powerful, in control, today there was something off—almost unraveled about her. Her posture was slightly rigid, poised for attack as her eyes darted to me, then around the dark room, searching for answers to questions I wasn't privy to.

The room we were in wasn't familiar to me, nor was it particularly opulent as our dream-walking meetings often were. She was fond of style, but this room was plain, decidedly lacking.

"I don't," I took a step closer to her, tension rubbing off on me as I searched for a door, a window, a place of weakness open for attack. "I don't know."

I didn't even remember sleeping, to be honest. I'd left the cabin, practically drunk on the power flaring through the group. It was too much for me to handle, the lust of them all magnified and vibrating against me as if it was my own—I needed to leave, to breathe.

While I'd grown stronger, better at recognizing and controlling the energy I fed on, something about the strength of it had been too much to resist, to lap up in small doses. So I left out of fear I'd drain them all of it.

Even still, I'd had to go a few miles out. The night was cold, but the heart of their...encounters made it hardly noticeable. I found a dark path through the woods and followed it, trying like hell to keep from running back to them—to her—to feed on them all.

"I was at the lake," I started, not sure that it really mattered. She had no idea where we were. "Walked to the other side to get some distance. Climbed up a goddamn mountain, but I could still feel her—the bonds, they're—" I shook my head, unable to find a single word or phrase that could adequately describe how strong the connection had been. Incredible? Terrifying? Neither seemed enough to truly capture how it'd felt. Even now, I could feel myself start to stiffen, just from the memory of it.

Hell, I'd had to jack off three times in the woods, just from the sheer force of that power. And coming in the dark, my jizz disappearing into the snow, while I was alone, wasn't exactly my idea of a good solo encounter. But I'd still come so hard that my vision blurred, my ears ringing from the intensity of it.

Not that I'd admit that part to my aunt. Succubus or not, I still needed some privacy where my sex life was concerned.

"I must have fallen asleep. I didn't realize you could reach me across the realm divide." I scanned the place again—the room was empty, save for two stiff, rather unremarkable chairs. "Not exactly to your usual taste, is it?"

"I can't," she narrowed her eyes, "reach you through realms.

This isn't my dreamscape, it's yours. You brought me here, boy, not the other way around."

"Not intentionally."

"Hm." She pursed her lips, then sat down in one of the chairs. "What's happened? Are you sure you're not in the hell realm? This shouldn't be possible."

"Positive. And, honestly, a lot."

Where did I start? With Atlas killing our father? With Max burning down Headquarters? With the Defiance? Our new half-baked plan to take out The Guild council?

Her head tilted to the side slightly as she watched me. "There's something different about you—your power, it's strong. More so than usual. Stronger, even, than the girl's was last time I saw her." Her tongue wet her bottom lip, as if she could taste it. "How?" She nodded to the other chair. "Sit. Tell me, what's going on in your world?"

I did as she asked, feeling awkward as fuck as I collapsed in the chair, my arms folded across my chest, as if that could dispel whatever power surge she was feeling. "The bonds have grown stronger."

Her dark brow arched. "Yes, obviously. Still, I don't know how you're able to reach me. Bonds grow strength, sure, but this—" she shook her head, eyes narrowed, "this is unlike anything I've ever felt." As if testing her point, she raised her hand, face contorted in focus for what felt like minutes. "I have no control here, my power unable to even suggest or move the room you've crafted." She leaned back in the chair. "Curious."

"It's not just my bond with Max," I started, not sure how much to share with her, but she was probably the only person who could offer us any clarity. "It's the entire group. We can hear her thoughts, and she ours, can feel her power, and one of us—" I watched for a moment, considering, "and one of us has even channeled her powers."

Her face flattened, no longer legible to me. With careful,

eerily graceful moves, she stood and walked over to me, crouching when she was a foot away. Her eyes, dark as night, bore into mine, searching for something.

"Um," I cleared my throat, unsure what to do under her perusal—something about her stare unsettled me, like she could see way more than I wanted her to. Like she could see parts of me that were off limits even to me.

With a hiss, she took several steps back, her movements jilted and awkward as her eyes widened—half shock, half horror.

"There's a new, deep strength in you. A strength that wasn't there before—distilled, powerful. I don't know the details of what Lucifer has planned for her, but I'd dare say she's nearly ready."

My stomach clenched at that. I knew that Max's power was the key to potentially saving the world—from keeping hell from downright combusting, but the lack of details we'd been given made me uneasy.

I trusted Serae, for the most part. But I didn't trust Lucifer.

"But there's a darkness growing there too, unsettled and hungry—unlike anything I've seen in a very long time. And power. Too much power. Something is off, something is festering, unbalanced."

"What do you mean?" I hated the fact that I could hear the anxiety lacing my voice.

She took a deep breath, closed her eyes, clearly focused, though she didn't come closer again. "It doesn't stem from you, but you might be the best tool to control it."

"How so? What is it?"

She shook her head, eyes still pressed closed, like she could somehow sense more clearly without her vision. "I don't know. But your power is strong, the girl is a siphon and a catalyst between you all. And you feed on energy.

"I feed on lust."

"Darkness, lust, they aren't so different. You feed on emotions, on passions. They come from many places. Whatever I'm sensing in you, it calls to me, which means you will feel it too, when you focus. When you search for it. You can draw it out, balance it before it corrupts you, before it corrupts your bond group."

"How?"

Her lips twisted into a smirk as she found her way back to the chair. "Same as you pull all energy, nephew. What destroys and corrupts others, can feed us. Our connection to shadow magic is unlike that which most other demons have. And the girl's connection is obviously even stronger. You and her will be the cure. Your bonded group is large, complicated...," she licked her lips, as if she could taste it, "powerful. It will fall on you two to keep the balance, the stability. It's a big job, but an important one—if you're to survive."

"That's all you can tell me?"

Serae wasn't exactly known for her specificity, but this was taking things to another level.

She shrugged. "This is unprecedented. I've had a long life, seen many things, but even I don't have the answers you seek, don't know the powers and limitations of this girl you've been tied to. Let the power guide you—linger in it, feel it, taste it, understand it. And once you have, you'll know what to do with it," she paused for a moment, before adding, "at least I hope so. For all of our sakes."

Fucking great.

We didn't just have the weight of the world on our soldiers, but some mysterious magic infecting our bond group. Could we not catch one single fucking break?

We sat in silence for a few moments, and I used the time to try and sense whatever darkness she'd picked up on, focusing as she'd taught me, but reading my own energy was more difficult than sensing that of others.

"Could it be from my brother?" I met her eyes. "Atlas was attacked by a drude, he's been off since Max rescued him." I winced. Off didn't really begin to cover it. I'd hardly spent any time with him since his return, but when I did, I found myself making excuses to leave. We'd both changed so much in the last few months, the gulf between us felt monumental. And closing it seemed like such a trivial thing to focus on in light of everything. "He's in pain—" I searched for a way to describe it, but came up wanting, "like...metaphysically, if that makes sense?"

"It does." Her jaw line was sharp as she nodded. "I don't think that's what I'm sensing in you, but I suppose that could be it. I have very little personal experience with Nightmares, and have never met someone who's survived an encounter with one untouched."

I shifted in my seat and pulled at a loose thread hanging from the bottom of my shirt.

The possibility that Atlas might be forever marred by the drude made me sick to my stomach, even in this dream world where such feelings should be left with my physical body.

"It was our father." I hated the taste of that word on my tongue. "He's the reason Atlas is suffering. The son of a bitch fucking fed him to the drude."

Serae took a deep breath, her lips stiff as she watched me. "I've always known that Tarren was a bad man. But it's hard to imagine that anyone would willingly put their children through what yours has put you boys through." Her chin lifted slightly, posture lengthening. "For what it's worth, and believe me I realize it can't be worth much to you, not now, not when you have so much else to worry about—but your mother would have never left you with him, if she'd had any say in the matter. We didn't agree on many things, but I know it would have killed her to see the pain he's caused you boys."

"He's dead now." The words held little meaning to me as I

spoke them. I searched through myself, expecting to find sadness, or at least regret that things ended the way they did between us. But all I felt was anger—and gratitude to Atlas for doing the thing I'd spent nights plotting in my head.

She said nothing to that, just continued studying me with that laser-like focus of hers. I knew she could see, and feel, the parts of the conversation I didn't feel like sharing or feeling. Serae specialized in reading people—had honed her powers to identify and isolate information and emotions in her subjects.

I shifted again, uncomfortable under her gaze.

"I didn't etch that for you," she finally said. Her eyes caught on my arm, where my bond mark curled beneath my shirt, and her face softened in awe. "No, that's a true mark."

She folded her hands in her lap, stiff like she was keeping herself from closing the distance between us to trace the lines.

I ran my hand over it, uncomfortable under her stare. "Yes."

Her body sank back into the chair, some of the earlier tension dissolving. "You are happy. I can feel how happy she makes you."

"She does. I am." I didn't bother trying to hide the love-sick grin on my face. "I feel a little guilty being as happy as I am, if I'm honest."

I hadn't intended that confession, but Serae had a way of pulling things out of me that even I didn't understand or realize until they were there, spilled out in front of me.

She tilted her head, the question silent but poignant all the same.

"With Atlas the way he is, with the barrier between worlds unraveling—it seems a bit selfish to have found happiness now."

She nodded, something unreadable in her eyes, "I understand where you're coming from, but I'm going to urge you to resist it. It is not selfish to be alive, to allow yourself the space to enjoy the few precious things life has to offer. I hope that you can hold on to that. Happiness is a rare gift these days. One few are afforded. It would be almost callous to turn your back on it, to reject a thing so many would give their lives for." Her eyes narrowed on me, seeing into the depths in that way only she seemed capable of. It was unsettling. "And you've been through a lot, Wade. It's not only happiness you feel—I can see the lingering pain in you, the anxiety that wraps around you and tightens like a snake. Love, happiness—understanding that you're worthy of both—just might be the keys to helping you become even stronger. We can't help others if we're drowning ourselves. Do you understand?"

I nodded, unable to find the words. Some unnamed emotion stuck in my throat, like a large iron golf ball. My eyes clouded over as I cleared my throat, fighting back whatever reaction was struggling to get out.

She came over to me and grabbed my hand in hers. Her skin was soft, warm, and sent a wave of comfort from the tips of my fingers to my spine. She pressed her free hand to my cheek, gentle but firm, until my eyes met hers.

"You have too much weight on your shoulders, my boy," she said, her voice a soft whisper that still held more than enough strength for the two of us, "and you always have. I know you haven't lived a happy life, that there have been many trials in your way. I wish more than anything that you had easier options, a different path behind and before you." Her thumb grazed my jaw as her hand fell back to her side. "But for what it's worth, I'm very proud to call you my nephew, my family. I only wish that I could have been there for you sooner."

She cleared her throat and stepped back, blinking rapidly, like she'd caught herself off guard with the statement.

Warmth enveloped me, the vise that usually gripped at my chest suddenly more like a hug than a hindrance.

I'd never met my mother, and my father was an absolute ass hat. I wasn't used to these conversations from family, this support, this advice—it was unfamiliar, uncomfortable, but it was also...nice.

As I watched her, she seemed more weary than usual. She was still regal and striking, but there was a guardedness that hadn't been there before, her posture less confident, less sure. Barely-perceptible lines framed the corners of her eyes—fragile concern where there'd once been only a teasing delight, a softening.

"What's happening in hell? With Lucifer?" I asked, feeling a desperate need to break the heavy silence between us, to make this encounter as productive as it could be. It wasn't often we had a glimpse into the other realm without being pulled to it— and it would be a shame if I wasted the opportunity to learn more about what we were up against. Our sad family legacy could wait for another time. "Is there anything you can tell me about him, about his plans for Max? Anything I can be doing to protect her?"

She took a deep breath, expression unreadable.

"You see things others don't," I pressed, hoping to leverage her sudden vulnerability and openness to more useful purposes, "please. You said you wanted to help me, and this is what I need help with right now. We have so little information about what's to come."

"I'm sorry." She shook her head, her nostrils flaring slightly as she tried to reign in some emotion I couldn't access. "I have nothing that can help you—I wouldn't deny you information if I had it, if I thought it could do you good. No one has heard from Lucifer in weeks, nearly a month now."

"A month?" That didn't make any sense. "Max hasn't been back that long. Not even two weeks."

She shrugged. "Time does not work here as it does there, you know this."

"Yeah, but usually days there are weeks or months here."

"Time is unstable, the magic out of balance. Do not be so arrogant as to think you can predict the way that it will move."

I swallowed my retort. "Fine, but what do you mean he's been missing for weeks?"

"I mean just that. It's not uncommon for him to disappear for long stretches of time." She exhaled, long and slow, and I could see the weight hanging over her shoulders—she was worried about him. They weren't exactly friends, from what I understood—I didn't think Lucifer really had anyone that could be called a friend in the traditional sense—but they weren't enemies either. "But something feels different this time. He was unwell for a while, weaker than usual—though I know that shouldn't be possible. Demons with his power don't become unwell in the traditional sense. But last time I saw him, he was coming undone. Consumed with research, with tracking people down that no one has heard word of in years." Her eyes locked on mine. "His magic is deeply connected to that which holds the realms together. At first, it seemed like his power, his strength, was growing since Max's birth, since she came of age—but now, it's as if he's being drained. I don't understand it," she grunted, brow arched, "and Lucifer has never been the type to be exactly forthcoming. Especially not when he's feeling vulnerable."

"What about Sam?"

She snorted. "Samael's about as easy to decipher as Lucifer —and perhaps even less forthcoming with information." She shook her head, the gentle clang of the beads she wore the only sound in the room. "I've known these men for a lifetime, yes— but more often it feels like I don't know them at all. It's one of the many curses of living in this world—we do not have the luxury of intimacy, of trusting others with our truest selves."

The last part was said more to herself than to me.

Her gaze locked onto mine, and as powerful as her stare was, I couldn't look away. "Be stronger than us in that way, nephew. Do not allow fear or insecurity to claw at you and gain purchase, do not be ashamed of the darkness that digs into you, of the anxiety you feel. Don't bury it down, don't ignore it. Emotions are powerful forces, especially for our kind. The faster you learn to embrace and use them, the better off you will be. Otherwise, they will suffocate you."

As if her words shaped reality, my breath caught, my lungs frozen in time no matter how hard I tried to pull in a gulp of air. Thick, dark water suddenly engulfed us both, until we were suspended in it, limbs frantic as we fought against the waves ripping us apart.

Serae's eyes were wide, laced with panic as she tried to scream for me—but where her deep, soothing voice had been before, there was now just a trail of bubbles and the harsh pounding of water.

I reached for her, fighting to pull her back to me, but the current had other plans. It ripped us apart, until she disappeared into the dark abyss, along with the room we'd been occupying.

My muscles tensed as I clawed into the water, trying to swim to her with a desperation that only made the lack of oxygen more apparent.

A powerful wave pulsed into me, spinning me in its grip until I couldn't tell which direction my aunt had been pulled in.

Instead, I swam and swam, searching for a light, the subtle hint of where the surface might be.

My head grew dizzy as I fought the urge to breathe in, to pull the water into my lungs, a deadly gulp of air.

My vision blurred until I started to see unfamiliar shapes in the water—dark shadows that I couldn't quite make out.

A frustrated sob lodged in my throat as I swam. This was a dream. I wouldn't drown here, I couldn't. Could I?

It felt so real, the life force draining from me. What if incubi

could actually be killed in our dreams—it would make sense
that the thing that gave us our power could also take it.

Max.

The soft curves of her figure filtered behind my eyelids as I
stopped fighting against the water, letting it lap at me, and carry
me gently where it willed—surrendering to a power I couldn't
beat.

She looked like she was dancing, her limbs lean and limber
as she moved.

A gentle smile tugged at my lips. At least she would be the
last thing I saw.

But my smile melted the moment I realized she was struggling against the current too, that it had her in its deathly grip,
just as it had me.

"No," I yelled, the word darting forward in a small wave of
soundless bubbles. No.

I fought against the water, dug my arms into the waves with
a relentless fury as I swam to her. At first, it seemed like every
inch I crept forward, she was pulled ten feet back.

I didn't give up. My limbs worked through the water with a
feverish strength, every muscle I had tearing and straining as I
fought to get to her. The distance was closing, slowly but surely
—a realization that only renewed the ferocity with which I
tried to reach her.

Until she was nearly in my grasp, one more stroke away.

When my fingers should have closed around her, everything went black.

I pulled in a deep breath, coughing up a lung as my body
regulated itself.

My fingers dug into the rocky ground beneath me as I sat
up. It was dark and cold, but I was dry as I surveyed my
surroundings. Trees cradled the rocky cliff as I tried to orient
myself.

It was a dream. I knew these woods.

This was where I'd come when I left the cabin earlier. It was quiet, the only sounds those of the animals who called this forest home.

I dug my palm into my chest, breathing in and out, slowly now as I fought the cloying pain there.

Dream-walks always felt real, but I'd never had one take shape like that before, and I hadn't had a dream I couldn't shape or control at all in months. Even Serae had seemed powerless against the current.

Fuck, I hoped she was okay, that she woke up.

And Max—

My breath caught again at the memory of her drowning. I closed my eyes, searching for that familiar link to her, expecting it to pull me towards the cabin. But something told me she was in the other direction.

Panicking, I ran, abandoning all reason and logic and following only the strange, unexplainable awareness I had of her. I stopped just at the edge of a small cliff, the rocks and twigs cascading into the lake below as I kept myself from following them over.

Fuck.

It was almost impossible to see—we were far from any lights, but when I focused on it, and let my eyes adjust, the lake below almost glistened with an ethereal light—I couldn't make out much but for some reason, couldn't look away. Until—

"Max?"

There was a figure, just below the surface, hair fanned out like a painting, suspended in the greenish-blue water that was always so impossibly clear that seeing twenty feet down wasn't unheard of.

She'd been sleepwalking out here, but never this far out in the lake, and never far from the main dock, where the water was shallower.

Without hesitation, I dove over the cliff. It was over thirty feet down, but the jump wouldn't kill me.

I crashed into the icy-cold water, black as night as I fought to find her. For a moment, I was convinced I was back in my dream, like one of those nightmares where you wake up from a dream, only to realize you've woken up into another one.

There was no current this time, the lake as still as it always was. I couldn't see, but I closed my eyes and let the bond guide my strokes. After a few minutes, my fingers brushed against something soft, solid.

I opened my eyes and saw her—eyes closed, suspended in the water like a girl in a snowglobe.

My hands closed around her arms and I swam, using the glow of the moon to guide us back to the surface. When we broke it, I cradled her head, trying with frantic movements to see if she was breathing, if she was awake.

Her body was cold as ice, and I prayed like hell it was because we were in a glacier lake and not because—

I shook the thought away. "Max?"

Her head lolled to the side and I caught it before it sank back below the surface.

Fuck. I needed to get her to the shore.

With hurried, awkward movements, I brought her there, reminding myself over and over again that the daughter of Lucifer certainly couldn't die from something as mundane as drowning.

As soon as it was shallow enough for my feet to touch the lake bed, I stood, cradling her in my arms, and ran the final twenty feet or so to the small beach. The water cascaded around us in loud sloshes as I fought to get us there quickly.

I set her down, gently as I could, and started to assess.

"Please fucking breathe. Please," my voice seemed disturbingly loud in the quiet of the woods, the clear panic lacing it enough to know that I didn't fully believe my theory that she was most certainly alive.

My vision clouded as I started CPR, pumping her chest and pressing air against her cold, soft lips, as I fought like hell to keep the fear back, to stay focused.

With a gasp, she coughed, a small fountain of water dripping down her cheeks. She turned over, eyes wide and panicked as she fought for more oxygen.

I fell back on my ass, relief coursing through my veins as her gaze fell on me.

"Wade?"

An anxious laugh tore from my lips, like my body didn't know what to make of the simultaneous fear and joy fighting for control of it. "You're okay?"

She nodded, brows bent in confusion as she took in our sorry state. Her hands curled around her arms as she shivered. "I'm okay. Guess that dreamwalk was a bit more intense than usual, huh?"

I pulled her close to me, not that I had much heat or warmth to offer her right now, and nodded as I breathed into her neck, letting the feel of her skin, her scent—now coated with the briny water—wash over me. She was okay.

She pulled her face back slightly until her nose was just an inch from mine. Rivulets of water dripped from her eyelashes, her hair, carving delicate streams down her face and neck. Her lips were a few shades deeper than usual from the cold, and the soft moonlight highlighted the sharp angles of her face.

After a night of resisting her nearness, it was no longer possible. I pressed my lips to hers, swallowing her soft hum of surprise, and drank her in.

My body heated from her touch, my dick stiffening as her lips met mine with a need and force that matched my own.

I gripped her close to me, my hands finding the gap between the soaked shirt and boxers she wore—my brother's, probably, he seemed to like her wearing his clothes—and pressed against her skin, both of us desperate for warmth and nearness as we fought for closeness.

She straddled me, deepening the kiss, her tongue hot and demanding, as she started to grind against me.

Would it always be like this? Would I always want her so badly—every molecule on fire at the touch of her, every thought consumed entirely by her? Because if so, we'd never get anything done.

But I was okay with that—more than okay.

A twig snapped somewhere in the distance, and we ignored it.

But then another ruffle followed, another twig snapped, closer this time, and we froze.

A dark figure emerged from between the trees, just a few feet away, its face cast in shadow, like the moon didn't dare shine on it.

Max tensed against me, then held her hand towards the figure, sparks of her fire dancing around her fingers in a heated glove as her eyes narrowed, focused. "Darius?"

11

MAX

He didn't move, and I couldn't quite see his eyes, but I knew with a fierce certainty that they were locked on me.

For a long, tense moment none of us so much as breathed.

The chill air whirred around me and I shivered, suddenly aware of how cold it was—and how drenched I was—now that the adrenaline and heat between me and Wade had dimmed from the interruption.

I climbed off him, my movements stilted and awkward as I held my hand between us, the fire casting deceptively pretty lights around the small clearing.

"Max," Wade stood beside me, in one fluid motion, his hand reaching for my shoulder, to pull me back, "don't. Something's—not right. He seems—" his eyes narrowed, "off."

He was right, I knew he was. But I also knew, with an unwavering clarity, that Darius wouldn't hurt us.

At least not intentionally. And if he tried, I could teleport us out.

Still, he seemed to be almost in a trance, standing there, an icy chill emanating from him that had nothing to do with the patches of unmelted snow on the ground.

If not for the bonds, I'd think it was his twin brother, Claude.

My mouth tasted metallic, seeing Darius stare at me with the same indifferent disdain that I was used to from Claude.

"Darius," I shrugged out of Wade's grasp and inched towards him, every step I took echoing loudly in the strange stillness. "Are you alright?"

When he was close enough for me to reach out and touch, I paused, afraid to scare him, like I was approaching a predator backed into the corner, the light from my hellfire dancing softly across his pale skin like we were sitting calmly around a campfire.

He didn't seem to see me though. His eyes were dark, like no matter how thick the flare of flames, the shadows refused to abandon their caress.

He was still and statuesque, not even the breath in his lungs moving his chest so much as a centimeter.

And if he'd been staring at me before, he wasn't now. It was like he was seeing *through* me instead, beyond.

I turned around, following his gaze, but saw only the serene calm of the lake behind us.

"What the hell's wrong with him?" Wade asked.

I felt his warmth at my side, as I turned back to Darius. Panic lodged in my chest, clawing up my throat as I tried to figure out what the fuck was going on.

The hairs on the back of my neck stood tall, and for a moment, I second-guessed my unwavering certainty that Darius wouldn't hurt us.

This didn't look like the Darius I knew. It was the shell of him, sure, but there was something strange, something uncanny I couldn't quite put my finger on. He didn't *feel* the same.

I knew he had been a little...unlike himself for days. But I'd brushed it off, assuming it was the general chaos we'd been trying to get control over. Now, it was clear there was something more, something I hadn't seen before, brewing below the surface, and I was cursing myself for not checking in sooner. I'd been so focused on Atlas, on the patients, and working with Greta, that I'd missed something. Something big, something important.

It was tangible. I could almost taste the offness solidifying on my tongue, the mystery just out of reach of my fingers.

A thick pressure built behind my chest as I fought to get through to him—the connection wasn't severed, exactly, more blocked or clogged than anything.

Did they make mate-bond plumbers?

I closed my eyes, focusing on the feel of him, trying like hell to carve a gap, a path back to him.

What the fuck was going on?

Darius.

The word echoed sharp, loud in my head, as I reached for him, for the bond.

For a moment, I wasn't sure it had worked, but then he blinked.

He took a step back, shook his head, shoulders relaxing then tensing again as he noticed his surroundings, as if awakening from a trance.

"What the hell?" Wade's voice was quiet, filled with tension.

"Max?" Darius took a step back, voice raspy and deep. He turned to Wade, sparing him a quick passing glance, before his eyes locked on mine again, the dark emptiness in their depths replaced by the familiar heat and intelligence I'd come to expect. But there was confusion there too, a childlike innocence I wasn't used to seeing there. "Where the hell are we? What happened?"

Wade's head tilted to the side as he studied him. "You don't remember walking out here?"

Darius's tongue peaked between his lips, wetting them, like he was nervous, confused. "No, I don't."

Wade's eyes narrowed. "What's the last thing you remember?"

Darius shook his head, swallowed, and my eyes traced the bob of his Adam's apple as he searched for an answer. It was rare to see him so confused, the usual confidence that bordered on arrogance nowhere in sight. "I vaguely remember leaving the cabin, needing some fresh air when," he glanced at me, cheeks heating slightly, an uncharacteristic shyness, "Max went into Declan's room."

"And then?" Wade pushed.

"And then this."

"That was hours ago." Wade's tone was stern, not exactly accusatory, but not far from it.

"Maybe I'm not the only one who's been sleepwalking." I turned to Wade, my arms curling around my body as I fought to find heat. The sky was slowly turning to a gray haze around us, and I knew we didn't have long before the day broke. "Do you think that habit is slipping through the connections too?"

The two of them stared each other down, Darius's timidness solidifying back into his usual lazy confidence as he recalibrated to the situation.

"Maybe," he said, though he didn't sound entirely convinced.

I tried to read him, but all I could feel was Wade's unsettled confusion, edging towards distrust. Darius was like a silent wall.

My connection to him didn't feel quite as destabilized as it had, he was reachable now and I *felt* him—he was just silent, standoffish.

"What were you both doing out here?" Darius pulled his hoodie off and cocooned me in it. "Wake up in the water again? You look like you're freezing."

I was.

"Sleepwalking," I muttered through the fabric. The material fell midway down my thigh, and I burrowed into the warmth. My stomach flipped as I took in the scent of him now surrounding me. "Nasty habit, sorry if it's rubbing off on you too now."

"She was further out this time," Wade said, casting me a glance out of the side of his eyes, "deeper under the surface. I found her, but I don't know how long she would have—"

He let the sentence die off there, and both of them took an unconscious step closer to me.

"Let's get home," Wade's hands ran up and down my arms in an attempt to warm me, completely ignoring the fact that he was also soaking wet and likely freezing just as much as I was, "get warmed up and then maybe steal another hour or two of sleep before the day starts and we begin tackling and testing the limits of these bond connections."

I shook my head. I wasn't tired. I had too much adrenaline from the day's events coursing through my veins. Lately, I was pleased with just a few hours of sleep each night. Nobody talked about how difficult it was to find peace enough to sleep with an impending apocalypse hanging over your shoulders. "Actually, can we swing by the med center first? We can grab some dry clothes there. I want to check on Sarah and make sure that Greta's okay. A few people went on a run and were supposed to bring in fresh supplies today, which means she probably hasn't had much of a break distributing it all—she always immediately puts everything to use."

If we were going to devote the morning to practicing power exchanges and siphoning, who knew when I'd get the chance to swing by otherwise. And while I'd joked about it earlier, I was starting to really worry about my favorite nurse. She was getting even less sleep than I was, and didn't even bother leaving the medical building anymore. Instead, she'd sleep in whichever thin bed was momentarily vacant. I was pretty sure she wouldn't even remember to eat if Charlie didn't have meals brought in three times a day for her and the patients doing well enough to consume solid foods.

"You sure?" Wade asked.

Darius shrugged. "I'm not tired, I can go with her if you want to go back to the cabin and rest."

Wade snorted, a gruff *no way in hell I'm leaving her alone with you right now* echoing in my mind.

A challenging smirk started to tug at Darius's lips, and I looped one arm through each of theirs and began dragging them back towards the well-trodden path before one of their typical pissing contests had a chance to commence.

I ignored the slick lick of heat down my spine as the two of them pressed in close to me, silent and strong sentinels that had my body humming and my mouth practically watering just with their nearness. The savage hunger pulsing through the bonds was going to strangle me if we didn't get a grip on them soon.

Eli was right, figuring out the limits of our connection needed to become top priority. Last thing we needed was me getting distracted by my own horniness during a mission.

A soft light lit the path, and we followed it in a heavy silence.

Even though Darius had awoken from whatever strange reverie he'd been in, I could still tell that he was shaken from it—could sense him sinking quietly into himself in that way of his.

It probably didn't help that Wade kept casting suspicious

glances at him out of the corner of his eye, almost like he thought Darius would snap back into robot-vampire mode if he kept him out of his sights for too long.

When we came to the familiar sight of the medical cabin, my blood froze. Something felt inherently wrong.

Darius tensed next to me, no doubt catching onto the shift in the air even before I did.

"What's wrong?" Wade asked, falling back into my side when my body acted like an anchor and paused mid-stride.

I started towards the med center again, resisting Darius's attempt to keep me back. "The door's wide open."

Greta would never leave the door open. It was freezing in these mountains, and there were beds of patients in the direct path of the draft.

Fuck.

Greta.

She slept most nights here, and I knew from experience that she was a light sleeper. She would have noticed if something was wrong, alerted us if she needed help.

Unless she wasn't able to.

My heart beat an angry drum, and I tried to swallow the premature panic threatening to escape. She was okay. Maybe she went out for a bit, forgot to lock the door, and a gust of wind or dazed patient had made their way outside, forgetting about the door entirely.

It was an improbable course of events, but not impossible.

I followed Darius's gaze to the ground.

Small red divots carved into the snow, the heat from the blood melting through the ice as it stained the ground.

"What the hell is that from?" Wade's posture straightened, and he took a subconscious step in front of me as he scanned the area, looking for any sign of life.

"Not what," Darius's voice was soft, but clipped, "who."

Finding blood inside of the medical center was nothing new, nothing unexpected. But Greta and the rest of us volunteers were pretty good about keeping it cleaned up, contained so as not to tempt any of the vampires around or startle anyone over the direness of some of the injuries we were treating.

"Where were you before you found us?" Wade asked, his eyes leveling on Darius.

"I don't know." Darius's jaw was tight, his hand clamping down around mine. "In the woods, I think. I wasn't exactly aware of myself, if you recall."

"This wasn't him," I said.

Wade's eyes softened, but I could see he wanted to push the matter.

"It wasn't. I'm sure of it."

I wasn't. Not empirically anyway, there was no evidence to suggest otherwise, but I knew Darius like I knew the others, like I knew myself. He may have walked a dubious path in the past, and maybe he made some questionable choices along the way, but I knew with a deep certainty he wouldn't do anything to compromise our safety here, to jeopardize our chance at saving everyone. The stakes were too high and he'd more than proven himself to us all.

"It could have been," Darius whispered, his voice cracking slightly—a sound that cut through me like an icicle.

"Looks like the path heads over there," Wade nodded, "opposite direction from where you found us. And there's a lot of blood here," he turned back to Darius, scanning him from head to foot, "none on you. Chances are this wasn't you. I doubt you would have cleaned yourself up mid-sleepwalk. Hopefully just a patient who decided to wander."

Darius's jaw was tight, and I could tell that he wasn't completely convinced, but he nodded once. "We need to go in there, see if anyone is hurt, find out what the fuck happened."

I took a step forward, ready to do just that—and was met

with resistance as they both reached for a shoulder and pulled me back.

"I can teleport." I shook out of their hold, ignoring their icy glares and tense postures. "And literally conjure hellfire. If anyone needs protection, it's them, not me."

Wade took a deep breath, his eyes meeting Darius's above my head, as the two had a silent conversation I wasn't privy to. As much as they liked to poke and prod each other, they'd developed the same silent repertoire and strategy that the rest of Six had.

"Fine," Wade bit out. "We go in together. But if anyone attacks, or anything seems even slightly out of place, no holding back. You get out of there and don't be wishy-washy about defending yourself, yeah?"

I turned to Darius, expecting him to be on my side, my shoulders shrunk when I found him watching me with the same steely resolve as Wade.

"Darius, you literally watched me burn down Guild Head-quarters single-handedly." I shot him a glare, but when I saw that neither of them was relenting, I let out a frustrated exhale. We were wasting time. I groaned. "Fine."

Without another word, we moved into the dark entryway of the building. The floorboards were coated in thick stripes of blood, and something in the air felt off—dark, almost.

Wade's hand moved towards the dagger that I knew would be fastened at his waist.

Several of the beds in this first entryway were uncharacter-istically empty, but most of them were filled with patients too deep in recovery and sleep stasis to be bothered by the frigid chill brought in from outside.

It's too quiet in here. I sent my thought through our bond link. *The hospital is usually a tornado of chaos.*

Darius nodded, and a ripple of pleasure went through me that I was getting the hang of this communication thing.

There was a small creaking sound and we all froze.

I turned back towards the cabinet at the far end of the room to find a pair of wide, familiar eyes set in the face of a young girl meeting mine.

"Max?" She opened the door wider, her lips trembling slightly as she ran across the room to me.

"Ellie?" Her name came out like more of a grunt as she collapsed into me, her body shaking in fear.

Wade and Darius inched closer to me, both of them looking at her like a potential threat.

I shot them a look and pulled Ellie back so that I could have a better look at her. "Ellie, what's going on? Where is everyone? Where's Greta?"

"I," she sniffed, her eyes welling with tears that I could see her struggling to hold in, "I don't know. Someone screamed about an hour ago, and I got scared and ran into the closet. I heard crashes, more fighting, and then after a few minutes, silence. I smelled blood. A lot of it. And something—unfamiliar. I—" her hand gripped mine, and because she was a vampire with a tremendous amount of strength, I felt my bones strain under the pressure, despite her age and size, "I was too afraid to come out and check."

My stomach sank with each word she uttered. What the fuck was going on?

"She's right. There's blood," Darius's nostrils flared, his jaw tight as he scanned over the remaining patients, "a lot of it. But it always smells like blood in here."

Everyone else was still and silent, their bodies lifting in the predictable, smooth cadence that came with their medically-induced sleep.

I shook my head and moved to the wall, flipping the light switch on. It wouldn't be enough to alarm them or wake anyone who wasn't already awake.

Blinking back the initial shock of the bright, hospital-style lighting, I noticed several sets of rumpled sheets on the bed, blood coating them all. A few of the light bed frames were flipped on their sides, medical trays and tools scattered around the floor in chaotic arrangements.

"Do you think someone had a nightmare or something, woke up not entirely sure where they were, and attacked?" Wade asked, though judging by the skepticism in his eyes, I knew he didn't think it was really an option.

I shook my head. There were at least five patients not present in this room that had been here this morning when Izzy and I had been by. And, judging by the state of the place, they weren't simply released. "There's more than just one person missing right now."

"And no one appears recently injured, like they were attacked and left to deal with the fallout," Darius said, breathing in deeply, like a perfumer trying to isolate scents. "No one left smells like they have a particularly new or recent injury."

I patted my still-drenched clothes, searching for a phone I knew wouldn't be there. Sleepwalking wasn't exactly conducive for leaving the house well-prepared.

The guys shook their heads and I knew they'd left without theirs too.

"Ellie," I turned back to her, noticing a few tear streaks carving down her cheeks—she'd lost the battle with holding them in, despite the tough set of her mouth as she focused back on me. I nodded to a set of drawers on the wall. "Second drawer down, there's an extra burner phone with several numbers programmed in. I want you to go find it and call every single number on that list until someone picks up, okay? Tell them to get here immediately and to be careful—someone's in the woods, and whether they mean to be or not, they're dangerous. Do you understand?"

She sniffed again, then wiped her cheeks with the back of

her hands. "Where are you going? You're not leaving me here, are you?" Her chin dimpled as she tried to contain her fear. "I don't want to be alone."

I shook my head and gave her shoulders a squeeze. "We're going to check the other rooms, see if we can find Greta or one of the other volunteers, make sure whoever caused this mess isn't in trouble or hiding in one of the rooms. After you make those calls, go back inside that closet, okay? We'll come get you when it's safe."

She nodded, posture stiffening and eyes hardening slightly. In a small way, she reminded me of me when I first arrived at The Guild, trying like hell to put on the facade of bravery when every molecule in my body was screaming at me to run and hide. Some days, I still wish I'd listened. "Okay."

The three of us left her to her task, our footsteps silent as we made our way to the back hall. I grabbed the ring of keys hidden in the lockbox and opened the door into Sarah's room, cringing as the hinges creaked.

A quick scan confirmed that she was still there, huddled in her usual corner. Okay.

Well, not okay by any stretch of the term, but at least she didn't seem to have any new injuries. She wasn't missing and whatever had attacked the others, seemed to have left this room alone. Probably because it was locked.

I turned, looking for her two roommates who were kept in here. Like her, they were silent and didn't react to the three of us hovering over them, their breathing erratic and heavy as they sank into themselves, prisoners to their own minds.

Satisfied that Sarah was still here at least, we left the room and made our way to the office and room that Greta and the volunteers usually tried to crash in for a few hours of sleep each night.

As I reached for the knob, it moved of its own accord.

Every muscle in my body tensed as the door opened.

I conjured hellfire in my left hand, preparing myself to use it if necessary.

I exhaled audibly when my focus fell on a familiar and chaotic mess of spiky hair.

"Greta. Thank gods."

12

MAX

Her eyes were wide and confused when they landed on me, but I pulled her into a hug.

She stiffened in my arms, but didn't push me away.

"I was afraid you'd been hurt. What's going on? What happened?"

She patted me awkwardly on the back, like she wasn't exactly sure what to do with my affection, and pulled away. Her eyes were dark and unfocused as she blinked, like she was in a bit of a daze.

"I'm not sure," her voice was raspier than usual, flatter almost, but I wasn't sure if it was because we'd woken her up from a much-needed rest, or because she'd been drugged. "What do you mean," an unfamiliar, worried quiver lilted her voice, the usual confidence and bossiness dissolved into something almost child-like, "has something happened? Are you alright?"

Darius took a step closer to me, crowding the poor woman. "You slept through it all?"

Her eyes narrowed, some of the concern dripping into

annoyance. "Obviously. I'm old, I need rest, you know? My hearing isn't what it used to be."

Greta typically had the habit of picking up on the barest of whispers, and was usually a light sleeper, but I didn't challenge her on it or call her out in front of the guys. She'd been working a lot lately—too much. Clearly it was beginning to take a toll on her.

I swore under my breath, cursing myself for not forcing her to relax a bit earlier. She was stubborn, and I knew it would take us locking her in a room for a day or two to actually force her to rest, but still—maybe I should've done it.

"There was an attack," I said, nudging Darius with my shoulder. He kept watching her, distrust etched into every smooth line of his face. I wanted to ask Greta about him too, about the strange fugue state he'd been in tonight, but it would have to wait. "We don't know what happened," I continued, "but several patients are missing. Did you send anyone home today?"

Her face relaxed, and she opened her mouth in an exaggerated but silent, "oh."

She tilted her head, as if considering for a moment, then nodded. "Yes, I did." She blinked at me, a few times, ignoring the glares coming from the vampire. "Five, if I recall."

Five. It was the number of empty beds I'd counted. I relaxed slightly. Maybe no one was missing?

"And the blood?" Darius's voice was steel.

Greta pursed her lips. "Blood?"

Wade's chest pressed against my back, his body a shield of solid warmth. "It's a mess out there."

"Ah," she let out an odd chuckle, "a few rough procedures tonight. Was going to clean up, but needed a nap first. I'll get to it now. Apologies, if I frightened you."

"Oh, that's all?" I let the words roll over my tongue, tasting them. A shiver ran down my spine as Greta's eyes met mine again.

Greta wasn't the sort to lie, but she also wasn't the sort to ever leave a room full of patients with the evidence of their suffering strewn about the floor.

I swallowed and stepped back, nodding. "Okay."

Something's off, I shot silently to the guys.

Obviously, Darius's voice rang through my head, and when I looked up at him, his jawline was sharp enough to cut glass, his eyes like daggers as he stared, unblinking, at Greta.

I knew he didn't trust her, but I did. If she was lying to us, it was because she was trying to protect us—or she was so over-worked that she had no idea what was going on.

"I just want to check on Seamus before we leave." I turned back to the nurse. "Is that alright?"

"I don't see why you need to do that," she said, her voice clipped, flat—missing the usual teasing warmth I was used to, "it's late. He's fine. Best not to disrupt him. You know how he can get."

I licked my lips, my mouth suddenly dry with an awareness just out of my reach. There was an inherent wrongness about this situation that I couldn't quite put my finger on.

"We'll be quick," I said, backing away from her and moving towards the hallway, "promise."

"Come back tomorrow—" her words were hurried, but still flat as she moved towards me. "Let the poor man sleep."

"I just want to see him once—I won't be on duty here today, and I just want to see him." I didn't add on that after she'd slept through everything Ellie had reported, I needed to make sure that Seamus was okay. That he wasn't harmed by whatever—or whoever—had caused a kid like Ellie to barricade herself in a closet.

"Max," Darius said my name on a low, warning growl, and I

knew that, like me, he was trying and failing to understand what was off about tonight, about Greta.

But at his warning, a soft grin curved on Greta's face, her eyes widening as they focused back on me. It wasn't like her usual smile —all coy and half-chastisement, like a mother both fed up with and charmed by her children. This one was strange, hook-like, as if her muscles were moving in a way she didn't quite have control of.

"Are you okay, Greta?" I took a step closer to her, "should you maybe go lie down again? Did you take something? To help you sleep, maybe?"

If she had, that would certainly help explain some of her behavior tonight.

Her smirk thickened, spreading across her face until her eyes were lined with the familiar wrinkles. "Yes, I did." She reached for my hand, and I let her grab it. "Haven't been sleeping well, and I've been working on a new sleeping draught. Don't think I've quite got it where I need it."

That explained some of the tinniness to her voice, the strangeness to her affect. My shoulders relaxed slightly. Maybe in her half-drugged state she'd left the door open and knocked a few tables over.

"Come, Max, I'll take you down to see Seamus before I see you lot off, ease your worries. Then I can sleep off the effects of this. You'll see, I'll be good as new in a few hours." She led me back to the familiar basement door, before shooting a warning glance at Darius and Wade. "Just her though, we don't need a crowd around him. He's been especially testy tonight."

Darius and Wade both opened their mouths to argue, but I shook my head. "I'll be fine." They both stood taller, shook their heads, "go check on Ellie. I'll only be a minute or two."

I'll be fine, I sent through the link again, *one of you should go explain what happened to Bishop and Charlie—someone's bound to have answered Ellie's calls by now.*

Darius shot Greta another narrowed-eye glare, the tic in his jaw working overtime as he swallowed back his disagreement.

"Hovering bunch, aren't they," Greta tapped her hand over mine, a cold, bemused look in her eyes.

I gave her a tight-lipped grin and nodded her towards the basement. "You have the keys, right?"

For a second, she looked thrown, but then she patted her hips a few times and pulled out the basement key. "I do."

I followed her down the dark staircase, finding myself oddly wishing Levi were down here. I was jumpier than usual, and his cool, sardonic presence would have been welcome.

I strained my ears, but didn't hear anything. Hopefully that meant Seamus was sleeping and not going through the pain of shifting in and out of his wolf form like before.

I stopped at the bottom of the staircase, Greta's hand still gripped in mine as she waddled after me. I pressed myself against the wall, giving her more space to work with. She dangled her keys in front of me and then worked the lock.

With a soft click, she turned the knob and pulled back ushering me forward.

When I stepped into the room, there wasn't an ounce of light. My fingers hunted along the wall, searching for a switch, but my foot caught on something and I stumbled to the floor.

Greta shuffled into the room after me and closed the door behind her, the soft click echoing as she locked us in. A little overkill, but I wouldn't fuss with her about precautions, not after the night we'd had.

I conjured a few flames of hellfire in my palm again and held them up so we could see properly. They cast dark shadows across the cracks and hollows of Greta's face. Her eyes were black pools, hard and impenetrable.

When I glanced down to see what I'd tripped on, I let out a yelp. "Vincent?"

I didn't know him particularly well, but he was one of the

people who often went on runs to bring supplies in. He was due back today.

With my other hand, I searched for a pulse, but I knew it was pointless. His eyes were open and vacant, his limbs contorted in a way that made it clear at least one of them was broken.

He was dead.

I swallowed a panicked sob and looked up at Greta.

She didn't seem entirely surprised by Vincent's condition. Her eyes were cold as they studied me, completely void of the warmth I was used to. "Oh dear, what happened to him? Seamus, do you think?"

"Greta—" the word stumbled from my lips, a quiet plea, as I studied her. What the fuck was going on? I crab-crawled backwards, away from Vincent, until my hands found something wet. A quick glance showed more blood.

A lot.

Too much.

Jaw clenched tight, I steeled myself and turned around. There were bodies. If I could even call them that. It looked more like raw meat, picked and devoured, limbs scattered around.

My vision blurred as I stifled another sob. I recognized a face in the pile. One of the patients—her eyes were dark and soft, staring back at me, lifeless in the macabre gore. I didn't remember her name, Lilith, maybe? She was a werewolf, a few years older than me. One of the demons we'd rescued from Headquarters.

Bile rose up my throat. Rescued, just for her to reach this violent end. Her head was removed from her body, and I noticed strips of skin were missing from her face.

In fact, skin was missing from most of the corpses that were stashed down here.

I scanned the remaining faces—all of them lifeless, all of

them familiar—hoping like hell I wouldn't find Seamus's in the pile.

His chains were abandoned on the floor, the metal soaked in blood and bits of fleshy-looking things I didn't want to even think about.

But no Seamus. He wasn't here.

It had been no more than a few seconds since Greta had unlocked the door, yet it felt like a lifetime as I tried to process the situation.

The room had been locked. There were no windows. What the fuck was going on? I closed my eyes, hoping like hell I was maybe caught in some strange dream, that the awful wrongness of this whole night was just another nightmare, that I'd wake curled up next to Atlas, or Declan—hell, I'd even settle for another surprise plunge wake-up call in the lake.

Something sharp punctured the back of my neck, then my back and my left thigh. I looked down and found a small dart. I ripped it from my leg, suppressing the urge to vomit, and craned my neck, my muscles growing stiff as another series of stabs hit my body.

They're dead. They're all dead. This is wrong. Something's very, very wrong.

My words were slow, stilted, as I thought them. Everything in my body felt impossibly slow, like I was swimming in a pool full of jello. I tried to speak, to turn back to Greta, to warn her away from whoever was down here, to do—something... anything. But I couldn't.

Max? What's going on? I can feel you, but we can't make out your words.

The light flickered on, the bulb dangling above me and lighting the entire scene. I almost wished the room was bathed in darkness again. I could stomach the scene in the segments and sections my hellfire lit up. Almost. But this, all at once—it was too much.

I threw up, gagging in horror when I realized that I'd emptied my stomach on someone's corpse. Part of one, anyway.

"I didn't expect to find you so quickly," Greta's voice was like a whisper. Her face morphed into something dark as she tilted her head and bent towards me. She pulled out a syringe, then crouched down next to me, grunting, "Old crickety bones, I wish he'd saved me something better to steal, selfish prick," she plunged the syringe into my neck, her face swimming before me, "they always are." My eyes slid to hers, but even that movement felt impossible. Her face carved into a grin that made her almost completely unrecognizable to me. "Should've known it'd take all I had to put you down. Now to take care of those fucking meatheads you brought. Perhaps I'll use one of their shells next."

I couldn't pull a full breath of air in, couldn't scream, couldn't even think properly.

I'd experienced this once before. In Hell. The girl who'd tried eating mine and Eli's skin had used this poison. But she hadn't used this much, and I hadn't felt the effects this quickly.

I used all of my remaining focus and strength to push my thoughts to them. They were in danger. She wanted them. I didn't understand why or how, but Greta was the enemy.

Poison. Like in hell. Greta.

What?

Who?

I heard the boys in my head, felt their panic, but I couldn't manage a response. I'd used all of my strength on those words.

"Max?" Wade yelled my name, muffled and scared as their loud, pounding footsteps took the stairs at an alarming pace. "What the fuck's going on? Are you and Greta okay?"

Greta rolled her eyes, the gesture strange and unfamiliar on her face. This wasn't Greta.

I'd sensed that something was off with her from the

moment she'd opened her door. Why hadn't I trusted my instincts?

I heard Wade ram into the door, the wood splintering and creaking at his strength.

For a moment, Greta—or the demon controlling her like a puppet—looked startled, surprised.

With quick movements, she pulled back the plunger of the syringe still poking into my neck, siphoning my blood into the small glass cylinder.

"Mine," she mumbled, her fingers manipulating the syringe in clunky movements, like she didn't quite have full control over Greta's body just yet.

I blinked, the process slow and difficult, my eyes almost refusing to reopen, whether from the paralyzed musculature due to the poison, or because I couldn't process seeing the greedy panic on Greta's face. But when my eyes finally opened again, Darius was standing there, just behind Greta, expression lethal and wild.

He'd teleported. How?

Just as Greta stuck the needle into her own chest, Darius gripped her head in his hands, his eyes cold and feral.

I tried to scream, to stop him, but my body wouldn't respond to me.

Before she could plunge my blood into her heart, he snapped her neck.

But he didn't stop there. With a sickening sound, he ripped her head from her neck, bathing the ground in even more blood.

Wade crashed through the door, brows lifting in disgust as he took in the scene before him.

"What the fuck have you done?" his voice was thunderous as he shoved Darius against the wall.

No, I tried to scream again, this time to protect Darius. The word was caught in my chest, slow and stuck like molasses.

"She's an old lady, she wasn't in her right mind." Wade gave him one more push, then abandoned him there, closing the distance between us.

His hands traced my body, looking for injuries, trying to identify the source of the problem, all while he took in the horror of the room.

I saw it settle over him, reflected in his eyes as his hands held my face.

"Fucking hell," he said, the pain in his voice cutting through my ribs like a lance.

"She was dead already," Darius muttered. He scooped me into his arms, cradling me. Like Wade, his hands and eyes roamed everywhere. "You're more powerful now," his eyes met mine, and it felt like he was convincing himself as much as me, "the venom should burn off more quickly than last time, but it looks like she used a lot."

"I don't understand." Wade grunted, his hand gripping at his hair as his focus darted between me and what was left of my favorite nurse. "Greta's been against us this whole time?"

No. No, that wasn't right.

"That wasn't Greta," Darius said. His fingers dug into my flesh as he held me to him. The fact that I could feel his grip, even if just slightly, gave me hope that he was right, that this poison was wearing off. "I think it was a shade."

I narrowed my eyes—tried to, anyway—since I couldn't formulate the question stuck on my tongue.

"They can reanimate a corpse, briefly. Legend says, if you kill them while they're possessing someone, before they can escape into a new host, they die." He glanced down at where Greta lay. For once, I was glad I couldn't move my head, that I couldn't follow his gaze with my own. His brows furrowed. "Seeing as no shadow emerged from her, I'm guessing it's true."

A sob lodged in my chest, my body unable to perform even that small feeling of release for me.

His hand caressed my cheek as his focus turned back to me. Where his eyes were filled with wild violence before, they held only softness now. "Greta was already dead. I'm sorry, Little Protector."

"A shade?" Wade asked, voice quiet as he bent over Greta. "Like from Max's cabin that day?"

Darius nodded.

A series of crashes and yells ricocheted down the hall. He spun us towards the door where Dec, Atlas, and Eli were crowding through the doorway, eyes wide with the horror of the room, all caught in the terrifying alertness that comes with being woken suddenly from a deep sleep.

They ran to me, none of them so much as taking a breath until Darius assured them that I would be fine in a few minutes —that it was the same paralysis poison some of the people found in the labs had healed from.

Charlie's calm voice sounded from above, mixed with Bishop's low grumble.

My eyes caught on Eli as he scanned the room, his expression slipping into panic once again when he didn't find what he was looking for.

"My dad?" He turned back to me, and if I were standing, I'd have been knocked to my knees from the depth of fear I saw in his eyes.

I was almost glad that I wasn't able to speak the words, to voice the grim reality into life.

Wade gripped his shoulders, squeezing softly. "He's missing."

13

ELI

"I promise," Max said, pushing me out the door.

It had been almost twenty minutes, but she still didn't have full mobility. She could speak, and had control over most of the muscles in her face and arms, but it would probably be another hour or two before she had complete control of her body back. Even so, she refused to leave the medical building. The girl, Ellie, was attached to her like velcro, and Max was devoting most of her energy towards trying to comfort her. It was a good distraction for her, because while I knew she wouldn't let herself truly sink into the grief she was feeling, I knew that Greta's loss was hitting her hard.

I hesitated, not wanting to leave her, even though she was surrounded by people and had Wade and Declan doting on her.

She grunted, in frustration. "Go. Bring him home. And be careful. He's not in his right mind."

I hesitated for another second, then pressed a chaste kiss to her lips and nodded.

It was decided that while the others fortified The Lodge, and made sure that there weren't any other shades in our midst,

Bishop, Atlas, Darius, and I would take lead on tracking down my dad.

Which, judging by the sight of things outside, wasn't going to be as difficult as I'd initially imagined tracking down a delirious werewolf would be.

The sun was up, lighting our way. Wherever Seamus had gone, he'd been in too much of a state to cover up his path. The snow was streaked with blood—though the scene looked far less gory with the sun shining on it, compared to the horrors of that basement.

I shivered at the memory of that sight. It would be burned into my brain for the rest of my life.

My stomach had dropped at the sight of all that blood—the condition of the corpses, so much death and decay. Even though I knew Max would be okay, it still felt like I'd swallowed knots of metal seeing her like that.

I turned to Darius, desperate for something to erase that sight away. "Max mentioned you teleported. Into the room?"

The vampire arched a brow, glancing briefly at Bishop, then shrugged. If we were going to get a hold on Max's powers, it was only a matter of time before the council knew we could share them. "I did."

"How?" Atlas asked, his voice even, steady. He hadn't said much, but he seemed to be doing slightly better today than he had been, more himself.

Which was odd, considering the ordeal we'd woken up to.

"Not entirely sure." He ran a hand through his hair, the silvery-blond streaked through with a few bits of dried blood. "I knew she was in trouble, that something was very, very wrong with that nurse, and I needed to get to her." He squinted slightly as he stared into the sun. "I think knowing that it was possible," he nodded to me, "you know, after the pyro here turned into a torch," I shot him a glare that he fully ignored, "knowing it was possible, that I could reach for and use her powers, made it easier to access them? It's easier to reach for something you know exists, if that makes sense? That knowledge, and the adrenaline, made it happen." He grunted. "Still felt queasy as fuck though, even though it was a short jump. Miracle I held onto my stomach, between that and the puddle of fleshy soup waiting for me on the other side of the door."

And we were back on the visuals of that room. So much for a subject change then.

I swallowed back the urge to vomit. Thank the gods I hadn't had time for breakfast this morning. Would've been a waste of resources.

"That makes sense, I guess," Atlas said, seemingly unbothered by the visuals Darius's description conjured. "We'll have to work on that more today when we get back. Faster we get a handle on using her powers, the better we'll be able to protect her."

I almost tripped at the familiar tone in his voice. He almost sounded like...himself—bossy team leader and all.

"Explain this shade shit again." Bishop shot Darius a dark glare, as if he'd been the mastermind behind the basement of gore.

He was on edge. His home had been infiltrated by a powerful demon few had even heard of, in the middle of the night, while we all slept through it. And several members of this community were now dead because of it. There was no denying the rage and guilt boiling below his skin, and the fang-hole was an easy target to aim all of that vitriol at—something I understood better than most. Still, I had to fight back the urge to swat the guy across the back of his head.

More would have been dead if Darius hadn't killed Greta—er, the demon reanimating her body, anyway.

I'd been around Bishop a lot when I was growing up, and, like his cousin, he was never really a sunshine and daisies kind of guy. Still, I didn't remember him being this easy to anger.

There must've been something in the Andrews family bloodline that turned sour after age twenty-five.

If Darius was annoyed by Bishop's displaced aggression though, he didn't say anything. "Don't know much about them, I've met exactly two shades before, and neither time offered much of an opportunity for a Q and A session. All I know is that they seem to have the ability to possess a dead body, but the duration of the stay in their fleshy hotel is largely determined by the power of the person they're reanimating. Meaning they rarely stay in one—er—place very long. I'm guessing that after Seamus demolished the crew down there, whatever corpse they'd hitched a ride in grew stale, and the nurse was the only immediately available option."

My lip curled at the thought of my dad doing that to the patients down there. It still didn't make sense to me. He wasn't himself, sure, but he was locked up. And, even if he'd gotten free, why tear up those people, bring them back to the basement where he'd been held captive, and *then* leave? "How did they get down there, though? And where'd the shade initiate? In one of the patients? Was it here all along?"

And how did we know that the shade wasn't the one who'd killed the people in the basement? Why did we assume it was my dad?

The sound of our boots crunching through snow created a strange soundtrack to the morning hike.

Darius was quiet for a while, considering, then stopped for a moment and nodded to Bishop. "The bodies—were they all patients?"

Bishop shot him a dark look. "Other than Greta, you mean?"

Darius snorted. "Obviously."

"Vincent," Bishop answered, voice clipped. "He was one of our best scouts. Came back with a fresh shipment of supplies for the med center today." He paused for a beat, then shook his head. "Between the two of them, we've taken a big loss. We have healers, but none as adept at the practice as Greta. She was special."

She was. There's always been something a little—more—about her. An omniscience that used to annoy the fuck out of me when I was a kid. She could always see through my shit better than most—and she was one of the only people capable of bossing Atlas around.

Darius shrugged before continuing on with his march. "There you have it, then."

"Meaning?" Bishop pressed.

"Meaning," Darius drew the word out, like he was growing impatient with Bishop's inability to keep up, "that your pal Vincent likely got himself killed on his scouting mission and gave the hitchhiker a nice fleshy vehicle to ride back in. Guessing he was human, because he didn't last long. And that's when the shade took over your nurse."

"And the patients?" I asked. "How'd they end up in the basement and how'd my dad get loose? And where did the poison come from? Isn't it usually from the tainted? The flesh eaters? Do shades usually work with them? Or do you think one of those creatures took my dad?"

"As brilliant as I may be, I don't have all the answers." Darius met my eyes, but looked away, like he was itchy or uncomfortable for some reason. "I'm working on a theory. I'll let you know when it's better developed."

Something about the way he said that, the flatness in his voice, convinced me that I wouldn't like whatever new theory he was shaping.

I picked up the pace, desperate to find my dad. We needed a win. Even a small one.

It took longer than I'd initially imagined to find him. It was a full hour of all-out running before we came into a small town.

The five of us stopped dead in our tracks when we got onto the main street.

"Fuck," Atlas whispered, stealing the only word I was capable of forming at the moment.

The trail we'd been following had thinned out over our hike. For the last twenty minutes it had been nothing more than a drop or two of blood every ten feet or so.

But this? This was a bloodbath. A twin to the basement scene we'd left behind for the others to clean up. Maybe even worse.

"What the hell happened?" Bishop asked. Any aggression and anger he felt towards Darius was gone, cannibalized by the horror of the sight before us.

There were at least six or seven bodies strewn about the street, all in varying levels of attachment. The only faces in sight were dead, eyes lifeless as they stared up at the sky. An abandoned arm hung awkwardly in a broken window, the meat caught on a particularly sharp shard.

Screams and cries echoed from a few of the closed-up shops, where the humans were likely bunkered down and hiding.

Gunshots rang out, coupled with grunts and clashes in a hardware store at the end of the block.

"No," I muttered, unwilling to accept that this was the handiwork of my father. This looked more like the set of a zombie movie. "This wasn't him."

I repeated the sentence to myself, over and over—half mantra, half prayer.

Please, for fuck's sake don't let this be at my dad's hands.

Darius glanced at me briefly, and the look of pity reflected in his face made me want to punch it.

Even if giving him a broken nose would only result in my own.

I shook my head and followed the sounds of commotion.

This wasn't my dad. I refused to believe that he was capable of something like this, no matter what the hell was wrong with him.

Atlas was turned into a werewolf—and Sarah. They never once did anything like...this.

Unless—could he be possessed by a shade too?

My stomach dipped at that, because I knew what that meant if he was. He was already dead.

No. I refused to let myself believe that our luck was this trash, that my father would come all this way, go through all of that pain, just for his story to end like this. The world couldn't possibly be that cruel.

My blood turned cold when I walked into the hardware store, the shelving units were shoved and knocked over, the floor littered with tools and slabs of wood. The fluorescent light in the ceiling flickered obnoxiously, like the splashes of blood and decapitated humans strewn in the aisles didn't lend enough of an ominous backdrop to the setting.

And there, in the back, was Seamus.

His teeth sank into the arm of a man fighting for control of his gun, his scream low, guttural, full of pain.

So the world really was that cruel then.

"Dad?" I approached slowly, hands raised like I was cornering a wild animal. Honestly, it wasn't far from the truth.

Seamus's eyes were dark, streaked with yellow, and wild. There was no recognition when they met mine. He pulled back, ripping a bit of flesh from the man with the gun. And then he chewed, swallowed.

I fought the urge to vomit again, but I didn't win that battle this time.

I spilled the meager contents of my stomach on the black and white tiled floor.

The man with the gun dropped it, then fell to his knees, motionless. Not a single muscle twitched; his face was frozen in horror, the shape of a scream permanently molded around his lips.

Paralyzed. Like Max.

What the fuck? Did my dad have some of that flesh-eater poison on him? Did the shade work with him?

"Fuck." Darius's eyes darted between me and my father, like he wasn't sure who to give his attention to first. "Eli, stay back."

I hadn't realized I'd been moving towards him. My body was stuck in some perverse trauma response. I was scared, fucking terrified. I wanted nothing more than to go to my dad—the pillar of wisdom and family who'd held me tall for my entire life. My body couldn't compute that that same man was now the one responsible for my fear.

"What the hell is wrong with him?" I watched in horror as my dad's hands, shaped mid-transformation into claws, peeled a thin layer of skin back from the human collapsed at his feet.

And then, dangling the flesh above his mouth, he consumed it.

I glanced at the others, hoping one of them would crack a smile, tell me this was some elaborate, ass-backwards joke. I'd punch them for it, but the relief I would feel would dispel my rage quickly.

I almost uttered the word please, begging this burgeoning fantasy to be reality.

Atlas looked gutted, his face morphed into the picture of grief—like my father was already dead before us, not this flesh-eating monster he'd become.

Bishop's skin was ashy gray, and I could see him fighting the urge to vomit.

Two shots rang out and my dad fell to his knees, the frozen human cushioning his fall slightly.

Bishop and Darius both had their dart guns poised.

Atlas's hung limp at his side.

Mine was abandoned at the entryway of the hardware store.

Seamus's eyes found mine, and for a moment, there was a flash of recognition.

"Eli."

My name sounded pained, full of torment as it pushed through his lips. Like it took all of his willpower to say.

"We know where the venom is coming from now," Darius muttered, swearing under his breath.

"Dad?" I moved towards him, hardly paying attention to the growing puddle of blood as I waded through it, slipping and sliding. I gripped his head between my hands, held his eyes with mine. "Dad? What's wrong? What happened?"

He looked confused, terrified—I saw my own horror mirrored back at me.

My stomach clenched and my fingers trembled as they held his face, my body betraying me as I fought for composure, for control.

We could fix this. I would fix this.

"Same thing that's been happening to people corrupted by shadow magic in hell," Darius said, the sentence tinny, like I was hearing it in a tunnel, "that girl that attacked you and Max in hell? That's what he is now. Or he's in the process of becoming like her anyway. Tainted one, flesh-eater, shadow-poisoned—call him what you want, but hunger controls him now."

"No." I shook my head, my vision blurring as I fought back the sob lodged in my chest. "Or if he is, we'll fix it. We'll fix him."

"I'm sorry, Eli. This isn't a thing that can be cured."

"Fuck," Bishop said, and I heard a loud series of crashes, like he'd knocked another shelving unit down.

I couldn't bring myself to look, couldn't peel my eyes from my father's for even one second.

"Are you sure?" Atlas asked, his voice low and gruff. "Maybe there's something—somewhere."

"I'm guessing the shade noticed right away," Darius said, and I could practically hear his mind whirring as he put the pieces together, like this was just some random mystery to be solved, Sherlock chasing a clue. "They—" he cleared his throat, "fed him some of the patients, harvested the venom, probably was hoping they'd join forces. Because their bodies are so transient, they must often need to outsource their work. Explains why the shade who showed up at Max's family cabin was so fine with leaving their friends once they were dead. They were business partners, a means to an end, nothing more." He paused for a moment, and I fought like hell to find holes in the story he was stringing. "I'm guessing they let Seamus free, expecting him to stick around and be grateful. The shade didn't account for the kind of ravenous hunger creatures like him experience, and he—" he cleared his throat, "I've never seen a flesh-eater quite like him. His wolf transformation was off, wrong somehow. Now we know why."

My dad started thrashing, the temporary calm thrown, as if the story was a punch in the gut, sending him back. He shook my hands loose from their hold, his teeth snarling and snapping at me as they sharpened and elongated. His claws dug into my sides, half gripping on to me, half pushing me away, like even he was at war with himself and wasn't sure which side he wanted to win the battle.

His expression morphed, flattened, until he looked like a stranger and not the man I'd spent a lifetime looking up to, trying to protect.

"Eli." Darius's tone wasn't unkind, but I knew what he was asking permission for all the same. He wanted to put him out of his misery. To put him down, like a dog.

I strained against our tug of war, slipping on the bloody spoils of my father's mid-morning snack. Bile rose in my stomach.

My dad didn't do this. He wouldn't kill those people, wouldn't do this to them. To me.

"No," I said, though I wasn't entirely sure what I was refusing. Darius's unasked question, or this new reality—maybe both.

For a moment, my father stilled, lips quivering as his gaze met mine again.

"Eli," my name burst forth like a prayer, one filled with pain, his focus waning, "please."

Whether he was asking for death or forgiveness, I couldn't tell.

I grit my teeth, swiped away a stray tear that spilled unbidden down my cheek.

"Knock him out," Bishop said, resolve clear, "don't kill him. Not yet. We'll bring him back with us." His voice was soft, filled with the quiet compassion I was used to from Bishop, back when Atlas, Dec, and I followed him around like lost puppies. "He's a good man, Eli. I can't promise we'll find a way to save him, but the least we can do is try."

Four more darts flew past me, landing dead in his chest.

14

———

DECLAN

My hand was on fire.

Well, not on fire, but very much holding it. A little ball of warm, soft light that licked up my fingers sat in the center of my palm.

"You did it!" Max smiled, her excitement zipping through me via the bond. "I knew you'd catch on quickly."

It was the first time I'd seen her smile today and the sight of it sent a river of warmth down my spine, smooth and deep like hot chocolate. I wanted to sip on it for hours.

And I'd conjure fire every minute of every day, if it would take away some of the grief and pain clawing at her chest.

Between cleaning up the mess in the medical center, treating the remaining patients, and trying to comfort Eli after he and the guys brought a knocked-out Seamus back, things had been pretty bleak.

Izzy and Ro eventually had to physically shove us out of the med center cabin, and Max's fingers nearly gouged the door frame when she fought to stay inside.

It was the first time I'd ever seen Max look stern with her best friend or brother.

But after a quick, "We've got this, go teach your boyfriends and girlfriend how to control their new tricks before we have another tragedy on our hands" from Izzy, Max finally relented.

We were all rattled by the loss of Greta.

I didn't know her on a profound personal level—didn't know her favorite color or movie—but she'd been a constant presence in my life, a figure of stability from the moment I stepped foot into Headquarters. And I knew she'd been the same for Max too.

It was a blow that would take a while to heal from.

"We've been doing this for hours." Eli stared down at his hand, face bent in concentration as he wiggled his fingers. "Why isn't it working for me?"

We were on the shoreline, away from the docks and where the cabins were planted—open ground and close enough to the water that we could train with fire without risking taking out The Lodge. Izzy was right—there'd already been enough tragedy and loss today.

Learning that Seamus was a tainted one—or on his way to becoming one—had cracked something in Eli. Whether it gave him renewed purpose or would break him down was yet to be seen.

He'd approached the training session with a rigid focus. And he hadn't so much as unclenched a single muscle since making sure Seamus was locked up and safe, that Levi understood the express orders to keep an eye on him and make sure no one harmed him.

Every time he tried to conjure the fire, his veins would practically puncture his skin from the tension lining his body.

Max bit back a small grin as she walked over to him. Massaging his hands in hers, she forced him to relax a bit.

"Don't worry, I didn't pick it up as quickly as Dec either. When I was learning," she said, her voice soft, soothing, as she closed her eyes, her chest lifting in slow, deep breaths, "it helped for me to try to visualize it. To feel the flames as if they were stemming from my blood, my skin, my bones. A part of me as much as the rest."

She cracked an eye open to make sure that Eli had his eyes closed.

He didn't.

He was watching her intently, like she was the last treasure left in the world, like he was two seconds away from licking her mouth.

Honestly, I didn't blame him.

His skin blushed slightly and he mumbled a quiet, "Sorry" as he slammed his eyes closed, doubling down on his focus.

Which apparently meant tensing back up again.

Max squeezed his hands, pushed a serene *relax, don't try so hard* through the bond and, surprisingly, he did.

"And then," she said, voice confident but soft, "when I can feel the start of the spark, I chase that warmth, until I can let it free. That's all it wants. To be free."

Her hands flared to life around his, the flames strong and powerful, a mesmerizing array of colors as his face cracked into a small smile—the first one I'd seen from him since the day's events too.

I jumped, the flames in my own hand popping into a soft, wispy smoke, before disappearing altogether.

"Interesting." Darius was leaning against the tree. While he'd managed to teleport to Max when his emotions were heightened, he'd been struggling to conjure fire or reproduce the shift since our session. "Looked like when Max conjured it, she pulled it from Declan."

Max frowned, then turned back to me, head tilted in curiosity. She held her hands before her face, the large flames effortless as she studied them. "Do you think you can conjure it again, Dec?"

"Erm, yeah, sure. Let me try." I licked my lips, then closed my eyes, trying to block out the pressure I felt from being put on the spot. I still wasn't entirely sure how I'd gotten it to work the first time.

Darius had mentioned that he'd been able to teleport because he was aware he had access to the power. That, combined with the desperate need to get to Max, had allowed him to access the ability. Deliberate intention. Need.

I tried to tap into that knowledge, to fake that sort of emotional desperation. Max was in front of me, we were, relatively speaking, quite safe on the shore here. There was no shade in our presence, and while we were all still recovering from the events of the day, the immediate threats were taken care of.

So that didn't work.

Instead, I focused on my connection to Max. Felt her inside of me, a part of me. As much me as I was. Tasted her lips. Felt her soft skin.

And through her, I felt the others too. My team.

I'd always had an awareness of them. Before Max, I devoted most of my time and energy to keeping them in line, keeping them safe, having their backs. The more I visualized that connection, the different branches that wove between us, the more I could feel them.

They were mine, all of them. And I was theirs.

The connections linking us were bright and vivid, stunning in the way bioluminescence was stunning—the kind of captivating colors and lights that took your breath away. The links also didn't feel imaginary or ephemeral. I could feel Eli's arrogance, the way it wrapped around his fears like a security blanket, Atlas's insecurities that he wasn't enough lapped against my skin, but so did his unwavering stubbornness, his strength. Wade's quiet intelligence, laced with his newfound sense of self, purpose. Darius's unwavering loyalty and reluctant compassion, braided in with a dark power that hurt to focus on too much.

And then there was Max, the crux of us all. Her determined sense of justice, her legitimate kindness, her yearning for community.

They were strong, steady, coated in warmth.

I took a deep breath, drew in that warmth, lined my veins with it, my body.

"Fucking hell," Eli whispered.

"Uh, Dec. Open your eyes." Wade's voice held a tinge of fear, of laughter. I felt it pulse through me.

I did as he said and found both of my arms engulfed in vivid, intense flames.

"Fuck." I waved my arms, panicking as the flames climbed higher, fanned by my anxiety. "I don't know how to turn these buggers off."

Max laughed, the sound enough to calm some of my unease. "Just take a deep breath, Dec. Honestly, you have far better control of them than I usually do. I could feel you harness the bonds, could feel as you pulled the flames from me." She shook her head, eyes wide in awe as she ran her hands up and down her arms, like she could still feel me there. "The bonds have never seemed so visceral to me—so clear. And you had complete control—as if you could play them like guitar strings." When I didn't relax, she laughed again—the sound a delicious melody. "Seriously, that was amazing. The fire won't hurt you. It can't. It *is* you. Just breathe."

Her dark eyes found mine, they were filled with mirth, with pride. And for a moment, I was transfixed by their depths, by the way the flames cocooning me reflected in the cool, almost-black shade of her eyes. She took a deep breath, a gentle reminder for me to do the same.

I nodded, and followed through.

But the flames didn't go down, I'd lost whatever grip on the connection I'd had, though now that I knew how to access it, how to draw from it, it would be easier next time.

A soft smirk hooked the corner of Max's mouth as I felt her—she drew the fire away from me back to herself, controlled it, and then absorbed it back into her own hands.

Darius walked over as my heartrate settled down, then swiped his arm between us like he expected to find resistance, like he could grab hold of whatever was linking Max and I.

"Fascinating." His brows furrowed in concentration. "It seems we can only borrow them. Meaning only one of us can access your power at a given time."

"How did you do that?" Wade walked up to me, grabbed my hand in his. He had that look in his eyes—the one he always wore whenever he dove into a new theory or dense textbook. He looked like he wanted to dissect me, peel me back layer by layer while he took notes. With a quill. "Can you walk me through what you were thinking about?"

"I see the incubus hasn't stolen your nerdiness." I shoved him off, laughing.

The sound bubbled up out of me, a fountain that couldn't be contained—full and demanding. Joy.

It was infectious, growing bigger and louder as the others joined in.

Even Atlas's face was split into a smile. He glanced timidly around at us all, like he felt guilty for enjoying himself, like he was still getting used to being back in his skin and figuring out how to interact with us.

Honestly, it was the same for me.

We'd all changed so much and so quickly these last few months. I was looking forward to everything being over—the war, the ritual, whatever else was inevitably thrown at us in the meantime—when we could just sit down and hang, slowly figure out how we all fit together again through all of the transformations we'd undergone.

"Makes sense you're good at this, Dec," Atlas said, his eyes meeting mine. The pride I saw there made my chest ache. He was coming back to himself. Not quite like the Atlas I'd always known, but that Atlas wasn't entirely gone either. He was growing, reshaping into something new. "This power is built on connection. You've always been our backbone, kept us in line, the strongest of the lot of us. Well," he nodded to Max, "except for Bentley of course."

Max squeezed me to her, and I could feel the rare happiness of the moment settle around us all, warm and soothing.

You're amazing, she whispered through the link, her voice and sentiment a caress that licked straight from my head down to my toes. *More powerful than you realize. You will hold this group together. Don't lose sight of that. You're connected to them all through this bond, not just me.*

There was something gentle in her tone, affection, maybe, but also something I couldn't quite name.

A spark of unease unfurled deep in my gut.

Before I could press, she turned back to the group, adding for everyone's ears, "Now, try to explain exactly how you did that. Maybe we'll get the fire chain flowing through us all before the night is up."

We worked well into the night, but we were making serious progress. Even Max—who already had amazing control over her powers—was getting stronger, more adept at conjuring.

After I explained what I saw, what I felt, the more we spoke the connections into reality, the easier it became for everyone. Wade and Darius picked it up fast, then Eli begrudgingly followed an hour after them.

Atlas took the longest, but I think that had more to do with his hesitancy around connecting. He'd made great strides with Max, had been more vulnerable with her than he'd ever been with anyone. But it would take time for him to fully open that wound for us all.

Even still, he managed it a few times.

We also quickly discovered that it was only Max's powers we could share. None of us, Max included, could mobilize Wade's power, or Darius's, or Atlas's. Just hers. And she rarely grew tired with the siphoning. She was like the sun, shining her light, her power, down on us all—freely, happily.

Well into the night, with a soft fire lighting our little work ground, casting dancing shadows around us all, we started working on teleportation. Darius and I were the only ones able to access it just yet, and we were both nauseated with every shift. It would take time, pushing through it over and over again and eventually, Max assured us, it would get easier.

Charlie and Bishop had run food out to us a couple times, bringing updates about the med center each time and occasionally sticking around for a few minutes to watch. Izzy and Ro were handling the medical ward like pros. Greta had, thankfully, left rigorous and thorough notes on each of the patients, which made their care more manageable.

Charlie suspected that the nurse had been expecting something—preparing for it. She'd always had a sort of preternatural knowing, like she could sense when something was coming before the rest of us could. And it didn't help that she'd run herself into the ground for her patients, both at The Guild and here—that kind of stamina could only last so long. We only had so much strength, so much power, and Greta had dedicated her life to giving hers to everyone she met.

It made perfect sense that she'd left behind a clear set of notes, directions to help guide us, to help us, even when she was no longer here to directly do it herself.

～

WELL AFTER MIDNIGHT, we came back to fire conjuring, all of us needing a morale boost after the rigors of teleportation before we finally hit the cabin for some much-needed rest.

The rest of The Lodge had settled down, but Bishop joined us once more to let us know there were still no new updates with Seamus, and that Levi would be crashing in the medical center tonight in case there were any issues. Levi seemed to have the best handle on Seamus—something that clearly rankled Eli, but he was doing a good job of letting those jealousies slide off his back right now.

Bishop came with two six packs of beer dangling loosely from his hands. He raised them up a few inches, brow arched. "You've been out here all day and all night. It's almost three a.m. You deserve a beer and a good sleep after today's shitshow." He paused, glancing briefly at Darius. "All of you."

Bishop didn't exactly look refreshed and revitalized himself. The dark bags under his eyes were full-on suitcases at this point.

"So do you," I said, grabbing a beer and a spot around our magical little bonfire.

He considered for a moment, indecision warring across his expression.

In the months we'd been here, Bishop had been a bit of an enigma—a phantom moving from one mission or task to the next. The brief time he'd spent watching us practice using Max's power today was maybe the closest I'd seen him to relaxing or hanging out since we got here.

Atlas nudged his shoulder, grabbing a beer. "Come on man, just one."

"Promise I won't bite," Darius said with a grin as he sat down next to Max.

Bishop shot a glare at the vampire, though it was absent the vitriol he usually reserved for Darius.

I was certain he'd refuse, that he'd make up an excuse about getting back to Charlie checking on supplies. But after a defeated grunt, he nodded, grabbed a beer, and fell back on his ass next to Wade. He propped his arms on his knees and took a long draught of the beer, his eyes watching the flames with wonder.

They were quite a sight to behold. Even I found them difficult to look away from, and I'd seen Max conjure this fire countless times over the months.

Hellfire wasn't just orange and red—it was layered with blues and purples, the colors merging and diverging in an elaborate dance that was impossible not to find beautiful—hypnotizing, even.

No one said anything for a few moments.

It had been so long since we'd been able to simply exist, to sit and enjoy each other's presence, I wasn't entirely sure how to do it anymore.

"To Greta," Max said, raising her beer. Her eyes were glazed with emotion, sadness for the loss, but there was gratitude, strength, there as well. "She was the first person to ever encourage my rule-breaking." She bumped her elbow into Darius. "And if it weren't for her slipping me her key card, I probably would never have met Darius."

"Well then," the vampire cleared his throat, raised his beer, and said, "to Greta. Apparently, I owed the woman a deeper gratitude than I ever realized."

"To Greta," echoed around the fire, a solemn peace settling around us.

"I've lost count of how many times that woman saved my life." Bishop shook his head, the shadow of a grin on his face as he took a pull of his beer. "She always had a soft spot for the rule breakers at The Guild." He shrugged, features softening slightly. "Makes sense now, of course."

"She was the best at keeping us the fuck out of trouble." Wade smirked. "I swear, the number of times she caught me spying on you all down there after your missions." He shook his head, "Alleva would have had my head before I managed to reach puberty if she knew the half of it. But Greta found ways to keep me busy, slipping me bits of information and casually looking the other way whenever I found myself hovering outside of one of your rooms after a bad sparring session."

"She let me hang around in the medical ward on weekends," Eli said, his stare distant, "when things got really bad with my mom, when my dad would disappear for days at a time—" he a blinked a few times, voice thick, before a soft smile lit his face, "she'd bring me down with her—insisted that learning basic medicine for the field was a better outlet for my anger than moping around Headquarters or shuffling through women." He took a drink, then shook his head. "Stubborn woman, but she taught me everything I know about healing."

Bishop laughed into his beer, then shook his head. "She said something similar to me, but I wasn't smart enough to take her up on the offer. Not often enough, anyway." He took a deep breath, leaned back on his hand. "She was good at that, training people without them even realizing it. I reckon most of us living in this community have more expertise in field medicine than half the medics working in The Guild. Which is good, something tells me we'll need it."

The ambiguity of the future was like a heavy veil around us all. One we could all feel, but were reluctant to focus on for too long.

But Bishop carried more than his fair share. I could almost feel the stress wrapped around him like a weighted blanket. He was gruffer, more impatient than I'd remembered him being. He'd never been a particularly warm or affectionate person, but there was a darkness about him now, an exhaustion that I felt deep in my bones just from looking at him.

How much of that was because he had an entire community here counting on him, that he was trying to keep safe? A community that we were putting in more danger simply by the nature of us existing here amongst them.

And then there was Charlie.

Neither of them had officially said anything, but it had become more than obvious that she was pregnant—the tender glances they shared, the few times I'd spotted their hands lovingly pressed to her belly.

I was pretty sure they weren't deliberately keeping it a secret —more that the pressure was high enough. I wondered if they wanted to wait, to speak the pregnancy into existence only after they were certain they were offering their child a future worth having.

"And," Darius caught my eyes, like he was reading my mind, and raised his half-empty bottle up, "to Bishop."

Bishop tensed slightly at his name in the vampire's mouth.

I still didn't fully understand the history between them, but it was clearly a loaded one. And, knowing Darius, he'd probably done quite a bit to earn that loathing Bishop seemed to reserve only for him. Still, it seemed like Bishop was warming up to him, however slowly. Darius had certainly proven himself more than once over the months.

I bit back a grin remembering how much I'd hated him for the first few weeks.

He had a habit of growing on people.

Like a fungus.

Darius's teasing expression turned unexpectedly earnest. "You, Charlie, and the others didn't have to offer us a place here, but we're grateful that you did. And we're grateful to the community here for taking in so many of us lab rats."

He took a heavy swig and we all followed suit.

"Can't believe you were really locked down there all these years." Bishop's jaw muscles shifted as he clenched and unclenched his teeth, mulling something unspoken between them. After a long, stretched moment, he met Darius's eyes and took a drink, before adding with a smug grin, "pretty sure Charlie would've sent me packing with you all if I'd refused, but we're glad to have you all the same. You've pulled your weight here, and I know that the six of you are the key to giving us the highest odds of winning this war—whatever may come of it, and whatever shape winning will take exactly."

We settled into a comfortable silence, finishing the beers, and enjoying one of the few peaceful moments we'd had together—maybe the only such moment since the Bentleys had come into our life, if I was being honest.

Max conjured a ball of fire, stared at it wistfully as it grew and then shrank again, like her own built-in fidget spinner.

After a moment, she'd worked up whatever courage she needed, before she turned to Bishop. "Do you know much about Greta's family?"

He frowned at the question, caught off guard, then shook his head. "You know, it's awful, but I really don't know almost anything about her, about her past, her family." He scrubbed a hand over his face. "Gods, that's terrible, isn't it? How had I never thought to ask?"

The last part was said more to himself.

"I don't know anything about her past either," I confessed, the shame of the admission sinking low in my gut. I'd taken her for granted. I'd taken so many people for granted. So many histories I'd never hear, just because I'd never done the work to ask for them.

Mirrored grunts and averted looks suggested the same was true for all of us.

Greta had been an enigma. Protectors usually kept to their teams, their colleagues, their families—but Greta was more of a lone wolf. Who did she confide in? Did she have a person to turn to on the particularly dark nights? Or did she carry that weight all on her own?

Max sighed, draining the last few drops of her drink before

balancing the empty bottle on her knee. "When I spoke to Evelyn—" she grunted, "gods, was that only yesterday? Feels like it was a week ago, she mentioned that Greta wasn't from The Guild line of protectors. That she might be connected to my family, or at least know something about them. With everything going on, I didn't have the chance to ask. Or, if I did, I didn't take it." She shook her head, wincing. "Fuck, and how awful am I for regretting that now, in light of everything? It seems so small compared to her loss."

The small ball of fire in Max's hand disappeared, reappearing in Atlas's palm instead. The added light danced across his features as he watched her. "You can be sad that she's gone and also sad that a well of information about your family has dried up, Bentley. Both things can be true at once."

Max studied him for a moment, swallowed, and nodded. I could tell that he said something else through the bond link, something that eased some of the bunching between her shoulders.

For a few minutes, we lazily passed the hellfire around, pulling it from whoever had it, through Max, and back again.

Childlike wonder and excitement lit Bishop's face when he watched Atlas conjure fire. Their eyes met briefly and Atlas grinned back at his cousin. For a moment, it was as if all of the shit we'd been through had fallen away. It was a brief moment, but it felt infinite, important.

Under all of the bullshit, we were still us. We'd find our way back to the core of that.

The Guild had ruined so many lives. Robbed so many of us. And now, their greed—dating back to hell's creation—could doom us all.

I'd drive myself into a fit of rage if I let myself linger on what could have been. What our lives might've looked like if we'd grown up outside of The Guild's grip. If we'd known the truth sooner.

"This is amazing," Bishop sat down, arms propped on his knees as he watched us pass the fire from person to person, like hot potato—a quick training drill Wade came up with. For once, when his eyes landed on Darius, there wasn't even the suggestion of a repressed scowl. "I've never seen anything like what you can do, Max." He shook his head. "What you can all do now, I guess."

"Well good," Darius said with a fangy grin. "Job security, I guess. For taking on The Guild."

The awe on Bishop's face turned into something else, something like...hope, maybe—sharp and useful. I could see his mind working a mile a minute as he watched us.

I understood why. If we could master these powers—and do so quickly—it would change things for us dramatically.

Even though we could only use the powers one at a time, having six of us with the capability would give us a huge leg up when we took on the council.

When I siphoned the flames from where they were with a bleary-eyed focus—from exhaustion, one beer was hardly enough to have an effect—Bishop stiffened.

"What's wrong?" As if sensing my changed focus, the fire snapped into air, until I held just my empty hand in front of my face.

He sat up taller, a light in his eyes as they caught mine. He shook his head. "Nothing's wrong. Maybe something is right." He stood up, collected the empty bottles in a hurry. "I need to think, need to mull some things over. Can you all meet me at the restaurant in the morning? I might have an idea. A wildly reckless one, but it might just be unpredictable enough to work, to give us the edge we've been needing."

"What idea?" Atlas asked, tracking Bishop's every suddenly-stilted move with the steady patience of a predator.

He shook his head. "Tomorrow. I need to think this through, if it's going to work. Don't want to get our hopes up if it's nothing." He climbed back towards the main cabins, before turning around and calling back, "and don't mention the beers to anyone. With Vincent and the shade, getting resources in is going to be more of a project than it already was. I'm supposed to save non-necessities like this for emergencies and celebratory toasts and shit. Charlie and Mer will have my head if they see the supplies dwindling before there's a proper plan in place to regenerate them."

Without another word, he was gone.

"Is he really going to leave us on that cliffhanger?" Darius asked with a snort. "What a dick."

"Yeah," Wade sighed, stood up, grabbed Max's hand, and pulled her up into a hug, "I think he is."

I stood too, suddenly feeling the effects of using Max's magic weigh on my body. Exhaustion flooded me.

"Sleep," I said, my voice practically a whimper now. "Sleep sounds very—"

A soft rustle in the nearby bush erased my sentence into air.

All of us froze, waiting to see whether this was a threat or stray animal searching for food.

Twigs cracked and icy snow crunched, alerting us to an animal far larger than a deer or a wolf.

My fingers twitched along the handle of my blade, and I saw the others reach for their own weapons from the corner of my eyes.

A tall, dark shadow loomed in the clearing about forty feet away, winding around the curve of the lake.

For a brief second, breath clogged in my throat—but then it released into a laugh.

"Ralph!" Max's voice was filled with as much lightness as I suddenly felt, as she took off towards the familiar hellhound.

"How the hell did he get here?" I asked no one in particular. Despite myself, I couldn't keep the smile from stretching across my face as I ran to greet our friendly hound.

15

MAX

I sprang awake, my breath coming out in ragged gasps as the door sprang open.

Izzy burst into Darius's room, muttering something I couldn't hear, tears streaming down her bloodshot eyes. It looked like she hadn't slept in two weeks.

"What's wrong?" I swallowed, blinking a few times as my body fought to wake up, to catch onto the urgent energy springing from Izzy in thick waves.

"I'm sorry," she said again. She was breathless and tear-streaked, her hair a mess of tangles that were falling from a precariously-perched messy bun that had shifted to just above her right ear and was holding on for dear life. "I panicked and ran here. I— I need coffee. And sleep. But right now, coffee. We need to figure out how to fix this."

"Fix what?" I asked. "Izzy, what's wrong? Are you okay?"

"I'm fine," she said, the phrase rushed and flat. She opened and closed her mouth a few times, trying to decide where to start. After a moment, she shook her head, giving up. "Coffee. My brain is fuzzy."

Darius's arm had closed around me the moment the door

opened, ready to defend and protect, but when he recognized my best friend, the strain in his arm lessened. Slightly. Until he froze and slid his intimidating glare from Izzy to the small cat curled into my side.

Shadow. She was soft and sweet, but Darius was fucking petrified of her—a realization that only seemed to enhance the cat's obsession with him.

"Love," he pressed a quick kiss to my forehead "I've accepted that you enjoy that wretched thing's company for some ungodly reason, but please keep her off the bed, I beg of you. She knows she's not allowed in here."

We both knew the cat wasn't in here for me. Cuddling with me while I cuddled with him, was the closest she could get to her true object of affection.

I lifted the cat in my arms, biting back my grin as Darius inched some space between us when Shadow purred, nodding her head into where his arm rested against me.

Shadow swiped lazily at Darius, and he hissed back, baring his fangs.

This seemed to only delight Shadow more.

Izzy hardly even noticed their interaction, which meant something was very, very wrong.

I rushed her into the small kitchenette area, giving Darius a few moments to put some, er, pants on and join us.

Thank the gods I'd begun making sure I was fully dressed when I fell asleep—made sleep-walking around the grounds and to the lake far less embarrassing.

I set Shadow down and watched as she pounced on Ralph's back, coiling herself into a small donut on his bed of fur.

Ralph let out a small huff, but slid back into his soft snores and didn't otherwise seem to mind the added few pounds of pressure.

Izzy did a double take. "Is that Ralph? Here?" She didn't wait for me to answer the obvious questions, moving straight to the one I had no response for. "How? And that cat really has no sense of danger, does she? First Darius and now Ralph? Bravest little creature in the world."

"No idea." I poured two steaming mugs of coffee, thankful that Dec had clearly already woken up and left a pot on. My brain was cloudy after what could have been only two or three hours of actual sleep. Still, I supposed I should be grateful that I was asleep for so short a time that I hadn't wound up submerged in the lake. "He showed up last night," I handed Izzy a mug and nodded for her to follow me to the couch, "alone. We have no idea how he got here or why, or what that might mean about hell."

Wade had clued us in on his dreamwalk with Serae, so we knew that things were unfurling at a rapid pace in hell, and that she didn't have contact with Lucifer, but that didn't explain how Ralph was able to travel here.

Unless Sam sent him somehow.

I drained half my cup, savoring the burn as it scorched away my conflicted thoughts about the man. He was a hellhound shifter, and hadn't bothered to tell me about it—hell, he'd used it as a way to spy on me, using the hellhound form to get in on my good graces. Fucking prick.

"Sam said that Ralph would always be able to find me if I needed him, that we are linked somehow. Maybe that got triggered or something, or maybe the shadow magic between realms is so unstable that the barrier is thinning now. Portals keep showing up, so maybe Ralph just hopped into one?"

Or, and I couldn't voice the thought because that somehow gave it life, more truth—and I wasn't ready for that possibility yet—maybe Sam was missing too.

Izzy's eyes were wide and bloodshot as she took a deep gulp of coffee, watching the unlikely animals snuggle on the worn carpet like conventional pets. "This world just keeps getting stranger by the minute, doesn't it?"

I grunted. We sat in silence for a beat before the reason for her visit and the abrupt wake-up call came rushing back.

When Izzy's eyes met mine, I knew that she could read the thoughts as soon as they unfolded on my face, as if the same realization rolled over hers in tandem.

"They both died," she whispered the words, coffee cup pressed to her bottom lip as if catching them. "She's the only one left. I'm sorry. I know how hard you've been trying to help her."

She didn't need to say more, I knew that she was referring to the two patients who'd been Sarah's bunkmates. The ones who'd also been attacked by the drude. The only ones other than Atlas and Sarah who'd survived this long. Until now.

I licked my lips, my tongue rough and dry from sleep. "How."

Izzy blinked away some of the moisture collecting in her gray eyes. "One of them succumbed the same way the others had. Their body just gave out, couldn't fight past the drude's power. Whatever stranglehold it had on them, finally won."

She let the silence settle between us for a moment, and I knew I'd regret asking my next question. "And the other one?"

A stray tear fell down her cheek, unable to be held back any longer. "She ripped her own heart out. Literally. We think that she maybe had a lucid moment, like she came back to herself for a second, but couldn't handle being pulled back into that torment again. We think—" she bit her bottom lip, "we think it was quick. I know it's no consolation, but better than the alternative, I suppose."

Bile rose up my throat at the thought. I should've checked on them, but after everything with Seamus and Greta, and training my team, Sarah and the others had slipped past. Maybe I would've seen? Would've caught something? Maybe my healing magic would have finally worked this time.

I'd given so much of it to Sarah, to Atlas. Guilt rankled,

lodged in my throat, that I hadn't made more of an effort with the others. Even though I knew that my connections to them were nonexistent, that my powers would have worked even less than they had with Sarah, who I'd at least known.

"And Sarah?" I asked, my voice little more than a cracked whisper.

"No changes, but maybe," she winced, like she was trying to soften the blow, "maybe your healing has helped hold it off some. Maybe she has more time because of you."

I swiped my cheeks with my sleeve as Izzy averted her gaze. "I should be better at this."

I didn't bother keeping the frustration and shame out of my voice.

"No," Izzy's fingers tugged my chin until I was facing her again. "You're doing everything you can, Max. We all are. We aren't responsible for their deaths, and we'll find a way to save Sarah before it's too late. I know we will."

I needed to save Sarah.

More than I needed to do anything else.

I couldn't voice the reasons why, couldn't tell Izzy that I needed Sarah to be there for my team when I wasn't. That she was the person I was counting on to lessen the blow. Not a perfect replacement, but someone they loved, someone who loved them back. And maybe, one day, the bonds between her, Atlas, and Wade would come back. We knew so little about bonds—forged or natural. It was possible they would be able to find that wholeness—that fullness—again. I had to believe that I wasn't their last opportunity at finding that kind of connection and belonging. Not when, after everything, it would be so short-lived.

And it was the one thing that would make it easier to do what I had to do. I needed to save her for them. They couldn't lose her again. I didn't want any of them to lose anyone ever again, as impossible a request as it was to make of the universe and whatever gods were listening—assuming gods even existed at all. If they did, they hardly seemed to care.

"Ro's with her," Izzy continued, her posture straightening some as she squeezed my hand in hers, like she could tell I was barely holding it together and was trying to carry some of the weight for me.

It was ridiculous considering she hadn't slept. I was the one who should've been helping her hold that burden, not the other way around.

"We're going to have her watched 24/7 from now on," she continued. "And after what happened with Greta yesterday, literally half the community here has been clamoring to volunteer in the med ward, to help." A smile brightened the curves of her face. "They're really something here, aren't they? No dead weight. Everyone really seems to want to help, to make this place a safe haven, a community." She snorted. "If I'd had any idea this place existed before, I'd have ditched The Guild ages ago.

"Happy surprise though, it turns out a lot of the people we rescued from The Guild have a pretty good knowledge about medicine too—especially when it comes to some of the supernatural beings we're less familiar with." She took a deep breath, then shook her head, as if she felt her thoughts wandering. "I'm sorry I burst in here like this, that was a shitty way to wake you up, especially when you've hardly been sleeping. I just had it in my head that I needed to tell you, and that I needed to tell you immediately. I wasn't in my right mind, wasn't thinking. You're already carrying so much. I'm sorry."

Ralph's feet started kicking, like he was chasing a rabbit—or whatever equivalent creature hellhounds chased, maybe people, who could say—until he jolted himself awake.

Shadow hopped off, light as a feather, and ran back through the cracked door to Darius's room.

I gave Izzy's hand another squeeze and shook my head. "No,

I'm glad you did. I need to meet with Bishop and the others, so I'm not sure when I'd have found my way to the med building to even learn about it all. Just keep me updated, okay? Any changes, I want to know immediately, yeah? No matter what time of day or night."

Ralph wandered over to us, his giant head nuzzling into Izzy's neck in greeting.

She giggled as she scratched behind his giant ears, her voice muffled through his fur. "Good to see you again too, you old brute."

Darius let out a sharp sound that could only be described as a squeal, followed by a barrage of curses.

Shadow came scampering back into the living room area, huddling behind Ralph and looking pleased as punch with herself.

"I can't decide if it's adorable or ridiculous that he's so terrified of an innocent little kitten," Izzy said.

I grunted in agreement as Shadow circled between my legs.

"But yes, deal. Day or night, I won't hesitate to come get you." She winked, a teasing smile cracking through some of the fatigue on her face. "Maybe next time I'll get a better peek at what your hot, creepy vampire is packing underneath those blankets. Something tells me it's glorious."

It was.

He was.

And when she poked my cheek, I could feel the heat of my blush giving that much away.

"It might be a long shot." Bishop scrubbed his hand over his face. Judging by the dark circles that had somehow grown darker than they already were yesterday, he'd gotten even less sleep than I did. In fact, I was now solidly convinced that no one in The Lodge was sleeping these days. Maybe that was a requirement or necessary condition of war, of an impending apocalypse. "But it will solve the problem of alerting them to our presence, so I think it will be worth considering."

We were back in the room that Charlie and Bishop used to host their community council meetings. My attention was rapt on Bishop, my fingers tense around the arms of the chair, waiting for him to tell us our plan. We'd been in such a standstill about how to approach the three council members that Evelyn knew how to locate.

Everyone else in the room, besides my team, was largely ignoring Bishop, even during the moments when they'd occasionally spare him a glance, trying to pretend otherwise.

Their focus kept collectively snagging on Ralph who was seated at my side.

Even though he was sitting, and I had the height boost from the conference room chair, he still towered over me.

"That's great, Bishop," Haley said. Her expression was unreadable, but it didn't escape my notice that her body was simultaneously tight and loose, like she was poised to defend at the drop of a hat if she needed to—it was a stance I'd grown used to with Darius and Atlas around, "but can we maybe first talk about the giant hellhound casually seated at our table?"

"Fucking wild, isn't it?" Jace let out a deep laugh, then leaned forward so that he could better study Ralph across the table. "I've never seen one before. Honestly, thought they'd gone extinct." He nudged Evelyn with his elbow, "not sure even The Guild has record of one in this realm, right?"

"Appears the little firecracker is full of surprises." Levi leaned against the wall, his eyes that saw too much lasered in on me with a focus I didn't want to dissect. "Daughter of Lucifer, companion to a hellhound," he let his voice trail for a moment, "any other secrets you want to share with the class?"

I didn't bother offering a response. I was too exhausted and intrigued by whatever plan Bishop had brewing to play any of Levi's games.

"Is he safe?" Charlie asked, eyes narrowed as they reluctantly swept away from Ralph to look at me. There was no fear in her voice, only concern. "We're fine with him staying here. But we need to have your word that he won't hurt anyone. Even with our rather diverse group here, none of us know much about hellhounds." Her expression flashed, briefly, with a small bit of wonder as she spared another look at Ralph. "Bishop had never even bothered mentioning them before. He's a freaking giant, isn't he?"

I couldn't help but smile. Charlie was always so in control, organizing everything around here, that I often found myself forgetting that the supernatural world was actually quite new to her. She hadn't grown up knowing that fantastical creatures from story books were real. I wondered if she always had to fight the urge when she met a new being—caught halfway between excited indulgence and the steady control she tried to mobilize for this community.

That brief glimmer warmed me towards her even more. I'd grown up on the outside too. I knew that balance well, though I was far less poised when trying to maintain it.

"He's safe." Eli, Atlas, and Dec all clipped the two words out in tandem, while Darius muttered a hushed, "far safer than that white furball you let you run rampant around this place."

Wade was seated on Ralph's other side, keeping up a steady flow of pets and scratches whenever Ralph nudged him for having the audacity to stop. "Safe and an asset."

Ralph made a friendly little chirping sound, but then growled when Evelyn reached a hand forward to pat him. She jumped and pulled her hand back to her chest, her usual stoic mask slipping for a moment, into fear.

"But he doesn't like to be touched by strangers," I added with a wince, "I should've started with that, sorry. He's good at creating those boundaries. And," I studied the hellhound, trying to see him through the lens of someone who didn't know him, who didn't see how playful and sweet and goofy he was, "I know he can be intimidating. He's very independent. And good at staying out of the way. He won't intentionally go near anyone here, and he won't harm anyone who isn't harming those he's chosen to protect."

"And he's chosen to protect you?" Levi added.

"Obviously." Eli sniffed, and I could feel him trying to pull back his annoyance with his little brother. "I mean, yes." He took a deep breath before meeting Levi's eyes. "How's my dad?"

Levi arched a brow, studying him, whatever cryptic musings passing through his head were locked away from my interpretation. "No changes."

Eli nodded, gaze now dipped to his lap as Bishop impatiently tapped his fingers on the table.

"Your idea, then?" I said, urging him to change the topic.

"Er, right." Bishop glanced briefly at Evelyn and then back to me. "As Evelyn mentioned the other day, she thinks she can locate three council members. Or at least knows where they are most likely to be found. And we know that once we attack one, we lose the element of surprise—we can basically assume that all information and intel we currently have about locations and what not will be null from that moment on. They move quickly, and if they suspect that Levi and Evelyn have been playing them the whole time, that they're still alive, they'll waste no time."

I nodded, my hands lazily running through Ralph's fur. It hadn't been super long since I'd seen him, but I'd missed him. And something about having him near soothed the chaos constantly flooding my brain. "So, we need to choose wisely—where we start, I mean. We need to determine who of the three is most likely to have or know the whereabouts of the stone.'"

Jace and Haley kept darting glances at the spot where

my hand scratched Ralph's chin, their faces twin expressions of shock and horror, like they half expected Ralph to casually snap my hand clean from my wrist at any moment.

"Or, we do a tandem strike," Bishop said, his eyes glimmering with the embers of excitement.

"But we need Max at each one." Evelyn leaned back in her chair, the picture of calm now. "She's our best hope at both sensing the stone and getting out safely with her powers. Like I said before, you all have a target on you. We need the anonymity teleportation brings, once any of you are caught on surveillance, you can't come back here. You'll risk jeopardizing this entire operation."

Bishop's face cracked into a smile—maybe the first true smile I'd seen him wear since meeting him.

And damn did it do things to his face. It was like a beacon of light, softening his usual sharp edges into something quite beautiful.

I understood why Charlie always stared at him like he was the sun now.

"That's just it. Max doesn't need to be at each confrontation. Her powers will be."

"No," Darius said, following Bishop's plan to its conclusion instantly. "Absolutely not."

The others tensed around me but said nothing, not yet.

Bishop's nostrils flared slightly, but he didn't bite back. He'd come expecting a bit of a fight, and he was settling in for the long road of winning right now.

Ignoring Darius, he focused on me, knowing I was the one who'd have to ultimately decide. "I watched you all last night. You're all incredible, making huge strides, and quickly. A few more days, maybe a week or two—they'll have your powers down. You feed on each other, you get stronger at an exponential rate when you're together. They'll be able to teleport soon, and then, they'll get strong enough to carry others with them when they do."

I sensed Haley's stare on me before I saw it. "You want them to separate. To do a tandem attack, and siphon Max's power as needed."

She sounded surprised, impressed—something I had a feeling she rarely broadcasted. And between Ralph and Bishop's plan, she'd done so twice in five minutes.

"We hit them all at once, no guess work." Jace snorted and slapped a hand down on the table. "That's bloody brilliant, Bishop."

Honestly, I agreed.

"It wouldn't be perfectly in tandem, but it'll be close. We'd need a few minutes between each mission. Only one of us can use the powers at a time. And we haven't tested their success rate with distance in mind," I said, feeling excitement—hope—for once, now that a plan was finally settling into place, "but yeah, with a bit more training, pushing the limits, this could work. Maybe even succeed."

We'd been stuck since I took down The Guild, biding our time. This could be it. We could finish this thing.

Of course, that hope was layered with the realization that getting closer to finishing this thing also meant getting closer to my own death.

I took a deep breath, pushing that wave of fear down, down, down, where the others couldn't find it.

"We are not splitting up." Wade's voice held an edge of finality, and I felt the flutter of his incubus influence push over the room—something he was clearly unaware of harnessing to such a degree. I wondered if that had grown stronger too, with the bonds solidifying.

"Look, we don't have many options." Bishop ran his hand roughly over his face, pinching the bridge of his nose. He cut his gaze to Jace, then Charlie, before meeting mine. "We've been trying to keep outside news to a minimum when you're around. We know you're under an impossible amount of pressure. But things are bad. Getting worse every day. Human news has no idea what to do with the shit that's happening, and The Guild is trying to get a hold on it, to calm them down, but they only have so much power. We're running out of time. We need to move quickly if we want there to be a world left to save. Right now, this isn't just the best option we have—it's the only one."

My stomach lurched at the statement. We had been in a bit of a bubble here—on the outskirts of the real world, in a lot of ways.

Silence settled over us all, before my team started arguing again.

"We'll try it," I said, silencing the barrage of dissents waving over me through the bonds. "If we can make this work, this is the safest and smartest option we have. We don't have time to keep picking at air, hoping some perfect solution will make itself known."

Between Lucifer's disappearance, and Ralph's sudden *appearance*, who knew how much longer we had before it was too late.

I felt everyone's eyes on me, felt the truth of my words hit my team, felt them reluctantly fight it, try to poke holes and anticipate problems, before, finally, Atlas nodded.

"There needs to be at least two of us present at each site," he said. The fire in his focus, the rigidity of his voice, it was like he was the old Atlas for a moment—donning the familiar, but dusty posture of the Team Six leader. "If we do this, we do it quickly, and we're smart about it. We get in, we find the council members, the stone, we get out. And we'll need to prepare for any contingencies. Nobody plays hero, this is going to need to be precise."

"You can't be serious?" Wade bit out, jaw tight.

"I'm going with Max," Darius said, the steel in his voice daring any of them to argue.

None of them did.

"You're the strongest, the most indestructible." Dec nodded. "I'd feel better about it knowing you were with her."

"Fucking hell," Eli grumbled, his fingers biting into the edge of the table. "We're seriously going to do this? What if there's a better option?"

"We still have a lot of training to do," Atlas said, his stare boring into Bishop's. "We train for this mission, but if we come up with a better—with a safer—option before then, we abandon this. Deal?"

Bishop considered him for a long moment before breaking their thick battle and turning his focus to me. "That's up to her, I think."

I nodded. "Deal."

～

WEEKS FLEW BY, but there was no improvement in Seamus or Sarah. Though the latter case seemed to be a good thing, because, since she wasn't getting any worse, it meant that she wasn't spiraling into the same oblivion as the others had, that my healing was helping her, if not entirely. But with Seamus, his condition seemed to only be worsening.

And Eli's mood was worsening with it, his anger hardening into an incomprehensible grief. He didn't know how to mourn a man who was still technically with us, didn't know how to fight an illness we had no rule books for, or how to hope for an outcome none of us fully understood.

Hunger seemed to rule every ounce of Seamus's focus. There were no longer those brief glimpses of the man we knew shining through. He didn't seem to recognize any of us, not even Eli. Not even Levi.

And the only way to control his screaming even slightly, was to let him peel the skin back from whatever animal the guys could hunt for him to gnaw on relentlessly.

Aside from our inability to help Seamus and Sarah, things were otherwise settling into a steady, almost comfortable routine. But that came with its own grief, its own guilt. How did one find peace, purpose, amidst others' pain?

We did our best to find a way, in the quieter moments. Now that there was a plan in place, life at The Lodge somehow both sped up and slowed down all at once.

Despite initial wariness, the community took to Ralph quickly. After a few days of scattered sidelong glances and whispers, that is.

Once Mer's son, Devin, accidentally bumped into him, everyone in the vicinity seemed to collectively hold their breath, expecting all hell to break loose. Literally. But instead, Ralph put his front paws down in that universal puppy sign for play, and took off on a leap, hopping around like an overgrown labrador with some of the older kids. He'd even lay on his back and let them climb over him.

Honestly, the hellhound was fucking loving this place, and I didn't blame him. There was a warmth here that I grew more fond of with each passing day.

And once he'd dragged out one of the younger kids who'd accidentally slipped into the lake, he won over every last skeptical heart in the place.

Now, I hardly saw him much before dusk, and once everyone realized that he wasn't going to hurt them, I think a lot of the parents actually felt safer having him around. He'd become like a giant, protective, community babysitter. One we were desperately in need of, with all of the adults stretched so thin.

Even Shadow loved him.

I found the small cat buried in a puddle of his fur most nights, whenever she couldn't sneak into Darius's room.

Of course, while everyone's fear of Ralph had dissipated, Darius's fear of Shadow remained decidedly unchanged. Not that he'd admit it was fear that he was feeling.

"That damn cat is unclean. Downright unhygienic letting her in this cabin."

"She's getting into everything."

"Mark my words, she's some secret creature we haven't heard about. One bent on killing us all. You laugh now, Little Protector, but just you wait…"

Even Bishop seemed lighter, happier, now that there was a clear mission he could pour himself into. I'd even caught a few more of those smiles on his face, though never when Charlie wasn't in the room to inspire them.

He also seemed to hate Darius less, which seemed to startle the vampire more than please him.

Darius knew how to handle people hating him, but he seemed much less sure what to do with the inevitable affection he inspired in those who took the time to get to know him—whether by choice or necessity.

Bishop's excitement, his confidence that this would work, was contagious. We all sensed it, humming beneath our skin, alive and eager.

After so many things had been hanging over us for so long, the assurance that we'd be the ones to deal with it all, despite the fact we had very little direction, had begun to feel overwhelming. Now, we had a plan. We had clear, actionable steps we could take.

We had no idea how to save the world in an abstract way, but missions we could do. They had rules, objectives. We could plan, prepare.

But the effects of the planning stages were even more noticeable in Atlas than they were in Bishop. When Atlas wasn't training with the rest of us, he was with his cousin. I often caught the two of them whispering together into the late hours, huddled up in Charlie's restaurant, picking at whatever delicious concoction she'd left for them, running through every possibility, every path.

My initial instinct had been to coddle Atlas, thinking he was pushing himself too much. Our training sessions were no walk in the park. Sparring was one thing. But manipulating magic and finding a way to siphon it through to each other? That was next level—both on the mind and the body. There hadn't been a night in weeks that I hadn't almost instantly fallen asleep the moment my head hit the pillow in whoever's room I was crashing in that night.

But Wade helped me see the truth.

As tired as Atlas was, he was also unfolding a bit. Coming back to himself. This mission, working with Bishop, it gave him a renewed sense of purpose, a space to filter all that anxiety and fear he'd been harboring close to his chest. This was an outlet, familiar. Like he'd put on a favorite pair of jeans he hadn't worn in decades, thinking they wouldn't fit, only to find that they were waiting for him, just as cozy and comfortable as he'd remembered. Maybe even more so, now that they were no longer tarnished by the fear he'd outgrown them.

As much as I resisted at first, I had to admit that Wade was right.

So, we spilled every ounce of ourselves into this mission, letting the excitement and energy fuel us even on nights when our bodies ached down to the bone from countless hours spent teleporting.

Thankfully, Wade, Darius, and I had strengths that allowed us to—ahem—heal quickly through energy exchanges of a more physical kind. Though Eli, Atlas, and Dec each assured me over and over again that they'd never not have energy for that particular activity.

Being together, skin against skin, teasing whispers in the dark of night—they were the moments I cherished most. Soaking up every second I spent with each of them, trying like hell to tattoo every touch, every feeling against my skin, reminding myself over and over again that I was doing this for them—to give them a future.

Until then, I'd let myself be greedy—indulge in every kiss, every lick, every bite that I could until the chance was inevitably robbed from me forever.

As much as I wanted this blissful bubble to last for eternity, the rush of having a plan, the luxury of spending time together with all of them, I knew that it couldn't.

And the leaps they were making in mastering my powers served as a bittersweet reminder of that.

They'd plateaued a few times, and had to build an initial callous to using my power, but slowly, they grew better at it. Within two weeks, everyone could teleport, and within a month, we could pull energy from fifty miles away from each other.

After that, their improvements came in a rush, all of us caught on the high of feeling our connection grow stronger, bolder, the feel of the power flowing through us like a sixth sense—one that had been there all along, only we'd only now just realized to look for it.

Until, eventually, there was no more stalling.

We were ready.

Every contingency to the plan had been belabored and discussed within an inch of everyone's sanity.

Eli had begun reciting different steps and locations in his sleep.

Charlie had forced Bishop to begrudgingly take a weekend off, the two of them locking themselves in their suite, for a little babymoon—the only sort that could safely take place in times like this.

Two days before we were set to leave, they finally announced the pregnancy, all smiles and excitement as everyone feigned surprise. That's when I realized that Charlie believed it too—that we were going to win. And somehow, more than Bishop's meticulous planning, and Declan's impeccable mastery of our power, that sealed my own confidence, burying the tiny sliver of doubt deep in the recesses of the lake, for good.

Charlie was like the backbone of this place, and though we were generally too busy for a casual chat, I found myself liking her more and more, the longer I was here. The community seemed to breathe alongside her—flexing and folding as she moved.

But she was busy, and taking on a lot, so I'd waited to have the conversation I needed to have with her.

That was the excuse I kept telling myself anyway.

After Greta, I knew that Charlie was the only lead I had left if I wanted to find my mother's twin.

And I was running out of time.

I was confident my powers were as strong as they were ever going to get—same with my connection to my team. Once we had the stone, that left exactly one thing: the nexus.

Saif was my best chance at finding it. I hoped so anyway.

He was also my last link to Cyrus. Cyrus's final mission, one he gave up his final months with us to see out.

The night before our planned mission, I threw back a shot of whiskey with Mer and Dec at the restaurant, took a deep breath, and went to find Charlie.

Whenever she had a spare second to breathe, she liked to sit out on the nearest dock to catch a few minutes of the sunset. It was honestly the only indulgence I ever saw her take.

Bishop was running over the plan for the millionth time with the guys, so I knew she'd be out there alone.

When I found her, I paused, suddenly unsure about what exactly I was going to say.

She sat with her feet dangling above the water, leaning back on her hands, her small stomach bump outlined in the orange and pink hues of the setting sun as they bounced back against the water.

What did I say? Where did I start? I wasn't even sure what exactly it was I was looking for here.

Shaking my head, I turned away—I'd do this after the mission, my head needed to stay focused, I didn't need to be distracted by Saif or my mother, or a family history I'd never fully know, not really—until my forehead bumped into a solid, warm mass.

"Chickening out, are we, Little Protector?"

Darius's voice sent a wave of shame through me, one that he dispelled just as quickly when he wrapped a hand around my shoulders and tugged me in close to him.

"Caught Dec at the bar, she let me know where you were. Thought you could use some moral support."

I sank against him, my chest suddenly lighter.

"Family stuff can be hard, trust me, I get it."

I nodded, walking stitched against him until we reached the end of the dock, and Charlie, and there was nowhere else to go.

We sat down next to her, me sandwiched between them both, stealing their warmth as the impossibly stunning sunset put on a show just for us.

"It's beautiful here," I whispered, the sacredness of the setting washing away any lingering anxiety, at least for a moment.

Charlie's features softened as she turned to me and nodded, that soft expression of pride that parents often get when someone compliments their children evident on her features, that pleasure at watching someone else see what they've always known.

"It is." Darius picked up a small rock, then tossed it into the lake, watching the small circles form across the surface as it hopped. "Something about this place has always pulled me here."

"I never asked," Charlie took a deep breath, studying him, "what brought you to this place, of all places, so many years ago. From what I understand, vampires usually prefer heavily-populated cities, don't they?" She ran a finger unconsciously, over a small, nearly invisible scar just above her collarbone. Darius tensed next to me, his fingers twitching over mine. "I'm sorry you lost so many years of your life imprisoned. I know it was a complicated time, but I always believed you weren't evil, even then."

In all the chaos of everything, I'd nearly forgotten that this was where The Guild had captured Darius all those years ago, that Dani had been the one to bring him in.

I knew that Bishop and Darius had a complicated relationship, and as I tried not to stare too closely at the small marks marring the smooth column of Charlie's otherwise smooth neck, pieces started to stitch themselves together.

"I was running." Darius gripped my hand tighter, threading my fingers through his, like he was worried I'd slip away. "Something about this place called to me. For a moment, I'd let myself pretend that I could live here, that I could live a regular, human life, if I simply tried hard enough. Obviously, I failed very quickly at that."

They both fell quiet, sandwiching me in their silence, their memories fading and reshaping at the edges.

Darius studied me, his stare shifting to Charlie, then back again, his curiosity and encouragement lapping against my skin like a rough tongue.

"This place." I cleared my throat, then turned to her. "You inherited it from your family, right? A protector lineage?" I took a deep breath, trying like hell not to want too badly, not to hope too hard that she had the answers I sought. "I was wondering if you could tell me—if you knew the line of protectors, your ancestors—"

"I did." Charlie's lip twitched, half in sadness, half in empathy, like she could feel the yearning stumbling in my voice. "But I'm sorry, Max. I didn't know that side of my family. My parents never mentioned—I didn't even know about the supernatural world until years after I'd started working at the restaurant, until Bishop—" she shook her head, an emotion I couldn't parse taking shape in her dark eyes, "Evelyn mentioned you were looking for your family. I wish I could help, I really do. But I'd never even met the uncle I inherited this place from. He was my mother's half brother. She was half-protector, but I don't think she even knew that. She was raised outside of the community. I don't think she'd ever even met him. And by the time I learned the truth, it was too late to ask her."

I nodded, swallowing back the lump of disappointment lodged in my throat. Even knowing this was a dead end, I felt an overwhelming kinship with Charlie. Her ties to her own history, to her family, seemed just as convoluted and difficult to trace as my own. I saw my own grief reflected in her features now. A gentle but pervasive longing, lodged in the knowledge that we'd never fully know where we came from, our stories gently erased at the beginning.

For the first time, I was almost grateful to Lucifer, for having access to the knowledge about at least some of my history, however stingy he was with sharing it. Especially so, now that I had zero access to him.

"Maybe it wasn't just this place." Darius turned, his eyes darting between us as indecision crossed his expression, like he was making sense of something beneath my skin, something I couldn't see. "That drew me here."

"What do you mean?" Charlie asked.

His bouncing stare and assessment settled on her for a

moment. "I mean, that, yes, this place drew me here. But when I met you, it became more than that. A yearning I hadn't really felt before."

My stomach clenched as Darius's words sliced through me. I knew that he'd been with many people before me, but the thought that he and Charlie had that kind of a past, that he hadn't told me—no wonder Bishop hated him so much.

"There was a rightness about you. I'd planned on killing you." He shook his head, "well, not planned per se. It usually just happened. Especially in the particular state I was in at the time. But when I bit you, something shifted slightly, coming into focus, and I knew that I couldn't kill you. That's why—"

Charlie's fingers danced over her scar again, her brows twisted in confusion as she stared at him. "That's why you saved me that day, on the ledge. Why you let them take you in?"

"The uncle," Darius nodded, leaning forward, towards us both, "the one who left you this place. What was his name?"

Charlie's eyes narrowed as she considered. "It's terrible, but I don't know that I even remember it. Like I said, I'd never met him, never even heard of him until I was told about this place."

"The name Sayty, does that ring any bells?" Darius asked, and my breath lodged in my lungs at the sound of my mother's name.

Where the hell was he going with this?"

Charlie thought for a moment, like she was rifling through an invisible filing cabinet in her mind, trying to chase the name down. "I'm sorry, it doesn't."

I exhaled, trying to understand a wave of disappointment I didn't fully understand.

"What about Saif?" Darius asked.

Charlie's expression softened, her brows raising. "That's it. Yes, Saif. That was the name on the deed. He was my uncle."

I choked on my voice as the realization struck through me.

Darius nodded, like a picture was shifting, refocusing,

coming into clarity finally. He licked his lips, lost in thought, like he was tasting a memory. "It was Max."

"Me?"

His tongue peeked out against his bottom lip again, a recognizable flare of hunger in his eyes as he watched me. "When I bit Charlie, there was something about her—something subtle, but it was there. And the first time I had you, your blood—" my cheeks warmed at that memory, and I shifted, uncomfortable with the flare of need chasing me in this entirely inappropriate moment, with Charlie right here, "so much more. I was always meant for you, Little Protector. Even before I met you, I knew your taste, hunted you."

Charlie cleared her throat, reminding us both that she was witness to the heat building between us. And when I turned back, half in a haze, there was a knowing look in her eyes, one half-teasing, half-embarrassed to be witness to the very obvious desire in Darius's stare as he watched me, unblinking.

I cleared my throat, as understanding flooded me. "My uncle," I licked my lips, trying to calm the sudden excitement expanding in my chest, "his name was Saif."

She leaned back, confusion bleeding into realization as she processed that. "We're cousins?"

"Half cousins," Darius clarified, eyes still boring into me. I could tell he was very ready to be done with this conversation now that he'd pieced everything together, and was doing everything in his power to resist the desire to pull me back to the cabin.

You have no idea, Little Protector, what just the memory of the taste of you does to me.

"Half cousins," I said, my voice pitched higher than usual with Darius's words in my thoughts.

I'm pleased that you're pleased, so I'll wait, however impatiently, for this conversation to conclude, but then I'm taking you back to my

*room and devouring you until I've had my fill. My hunger has been
—insatiable—lately...and it's been weeks since I've had you.*

It had only been two days, but my own desire matched his
all the same, and the promise of his teeth inside my neck while
our bodies coiled together sent a pang of longing through me
that I fought to push down. Not right now. Later.

Charlie's face split into a large smile, her hand reaching for
mine.

I felt my own expression mirror hers as I swallowed down
the out-of-place lust flooding my system.

I had a cousin. Family.

"Is anyone else here a relation of yours?" I asked, suddenly
greedy for more.

She shook her head, squeezed my hand. "No, not that I'm
aware of. It's why this place passed to me, a half-niece he'd
never even met, who had no knowledge of the supernatural
community that often traipsed through these woods. Saif had
no other living family." Her head tilted in apology, "except for
you, I suppose. Though given the circumstances of your life
with Cyrus, it's likely he didn't even know about you."

The lightness of finding kin faded slightly as another realization hit me.

Saif passed this place to Charlie.

Saif—just like my mother, just like Cyrus—was dead.

16

ATLAS

I woke up with a start, my skin clammy with sweat and heart racing in a panic. Max's side of my bed was empty, but I shoved my face into the pillow she usually slept on, shamelessly breathing in the smell of her.

I bit back my frustrated groan at the shadow of her, the echo I wanted so badly to be solid right now. My dick was already stiffening, and I felt the wolf settle deep in my chest as her scent engulfed us. He liked having her scent nearby.

But I wanted more than her smell right now, more than just the knowledge that she was near, that she was ours. I wanted to be buried into her wet cunt, dripping and pleading for me as I filled her.

I had half a mind to go storming through the cabin until I found her, so that I could take her before the rest of the house woke up—let them hear her moans of pleasure as their morning alarm.

I shoved my hand down my sweatpants and ran it over my shaft, the nightmare that had woken me shifting into a much more pleasant fantasy.

Fucking hell, that girl drove me wild, even when she wasn't here.

I imagined her lips wrapped around me, large eyes watching my groan of pleasure as she took me deeper into her mouth. Licked my lips at the memory of her slick heat on my tongue. I could practically hear the little moans she made when I touched her a little more roughly than she'd anticipated, her pleasure deepening in surprise, excitement as I pounded into her, teeth buried into her shoulder. The fanghole wasn't the only one who liked to bite, to mark her.

My dick throbbed, hard and demanding. There was no going back to sleep now, not until I took care of this.

My strokes grew hurried as I thought of her sleeping, naked and sated, the golden-brown expanse of her skin pebbled and shivering. Fuck, even the thought of her folded against one of my team members, grinding and finding release on a hand that wasn't mine, sent me to the very edge.

She'd gotten a lot better at closing us out in those moments, though there'd been a few times where her orgasm ripped through her with too much intensity, and she'd lost control. We didn't care anymore. Those moments quickly devolved into all of us panting at her side, passing her from one to the next in a bubble of lust that pulsed through the cabin.

The memory of a few nights ago, when the vampire took her pussy while I filled her ass, both of our teeth buried on either side of her neck as she writhed between us and screamed to oblivion, took me over the edge.

One more pump and I came into my hand, not even annoyed that I hadn't had the foresight to grab a shirt or tissue first.

I cleaned myself up with my sweatpants before tossing them over the side of the bed. I'd do laundry later. Now that my raging hard-on was taken care of, I wanted another few hours of sleep.

But the universe had a different idea.

A single, sharp ray of light pierced through the window across from me, shining right in my eye like that was its only purpose.

I groaned, trying to slide back into a more blissful dream.

Ten minutes of chasing sleep and I still couldn't catch it. Fucking hell, it was early.

I turned around, pressed my eyelids tight, praying to the gods for a few more hours of sleep. Hell, I'd be happy with twenty minutes.

Because when I woke up, it would mean that today was here. The day of our mission.

And while it had felt good, these past few weeks, to slip back into protector mode, to focus on a target, to have a purpose, I wasn't ready to admit that this was our best shot. Wasn't ready to admit that I'd failed, in all those hours spent poring over every document Evelyn and Levi had ever obtained from council, to come up with a better plan. One that would keep us all together. One that would keep her safe.

She'd stayed with the vampire last night, lucky fuck. He was the one who'd get to go with her on our mission too. But when Wade and Eli pressed him on it, presenting a logical argument as to why she should stay with one of us last night, he got that faraway look in his eyes, shrouded in darkness.

It was a look that made even me a little wary around the guy.

I'd nodded, and told them to fuck off. Darius might not be my favorite person in the world, but if there was anyone capable of bringing him back to himself, it was Max.

I would know.

Between her steady, calming presence, and Bishop's ability to keep me busy, I barely even saw the visions of my dead team-mates superimposed onto this reality anymore.

I still had nightmares every night, and still didn't quite feel like myself, but over the last few weeks, the lasting marks of the drude had started to disperse.

My jaw clenched when I thought of Sarah.

She was still locked in that agony, alone and untouchable.

Shame burned low in my gut when I thought about her locked in that room, the last surviving victim of the drude's attacks.

At first, I couldn't bring myself to visit her, couldn't stomach the sight of her pain, knowing intimately the depths of it.

Then, with the mission, I'd grown busy, letting myself get sucked back into protocols and planning.

With a sigh, I threw the blanket off of me and got ready for the day.

If my brain wasn't going to let me soak in these last few bits of sleep before the hellstorm that was coming today, then it seemed only fitting that I go visit the girl I'd been avoiding for weeks.

"Max with you?" Rowan asked, emerging from a backroom as soon as I stepped foot in the medical center. "She should be sleeping. Resting up before today."

I cocked a brow at him. He was going on the mission with her, and I knew for a fact that the guy had been sleeping fewer than two hours a night. When he wasn't with his sister, prepping for today, he was holed up in this building, taking care of as many people as he could.

He was good at it.

"Ro? Something wrong?" Arnell emerged behind him, shirtless and hair rumpled as he quickly scanned the room for obvious threat. "Atlas?"

I nodded towards the room where Sarah was kept, but didn't bother saying anything else. The one good thing about what I'd been through was that people stopped expecting small talk and niceties from me.

Not that they really ever did before either.

Ro grunted then tossed me a key before shuffling his boyfriend back into the room where they'd probably set up a cot to catch a few minutes of sleep during their vigil.

The med center had calmed down some and was unusually quiet today. Everyone was mostly asleep.

And Arnell being the resident tech genius, had been just as busy as the rest of us, trying to stay afloat and on top of information—neither of them would argue with me if it meant risking one of the rare hours they actually got to exist in the same building together.

I took a deep breath, slid the key into the lock, and then froze.

"Fucking coward," I muttered to myself.

If Sarah was locked in her nightmares, the least I could do was fucking sit there with her for a little while. I was the only one who truly knew what horrors she was going through.

With one more deep breath, I turned the handle before I had another chance to chicken out, and forced myself inside, shutting the door a little too loudly behind me.

She was alone, crouched in a corner, head ducked between her knees, her bedding largely untouched.

She looked like a shadow of the girl we'd brought back with us from hell. She'd obviously lost weight, but there was a sunkenness about her, hollowed and hunched where she'd been confident and proud before.

My throat clogged with empathy as I listened to her muttering nonsensical words to herself, no louder than a hushed whisper.

She gave no sign that she'd heard me enter or noticed me at all. Not even when I hunched down next to her, my feet less than an inch from hers.

Agony was etched into her every muscle, her every line, and my eyes clouded over at the memory of my own.

I'd made it out, thanks to Max, but Sarah had been locked inside of herself for so much longer than I had.

These last few weeks, finding out where and how I fit in my life now? It seemed so fucking selfish in comparison to what she was going through.

My hand shook as I rested it on her shoulder, my ass falling to the floor with a graceless thud as I held back the black anguish creeping through my thoughts.

"I'm so sorry, Sarah," I whispered, my voice shaky, fingers gripping into her bony shoulder blade. "I'm so fucking sorry. You shouldn't have been there. It was about me, not you. And he took it out on you. I'm so, so sorry."

My cheeks were damp now, and I sniffed as I wiped away the tears with the back of my sleeve. I didn't have a right to feel this. I was here for her, not me.

"You're strong," I said, my voice cracking. "You can get through this. You will get through this. We just got you back. We won't let you die like this. I'm sorry. I'm sorr—" I choked on my words as I fought to get the apology out. "I should have come sooner. I should have been here with you."

She'd always been there for me.

For all of us.

And I'd let her down twice now. Once when she was taken by werewolves, and now.

Something tight gripped deep in my chest as I held onto her shoulders, willing her to hear me, even though I knew that no one had been able to get a response from her.

Hell, even her mother, Declan's aunt, had tried. She'd arrived at The Lodge a few weeks ago and spent almost every waking hour trying to pull something from the daughter she'd already lost once.

The tightness grew painful, my eyes blacking out around the edges.

And Sarah's breathing changed, her chest moving in slow, tandem heaves with mine.

I felt her muscles flex beneath my palms, her lips parted in a silent gasp as she leaned into my pressure, like I was pulling her to me, tugging her through some invisible string.

I fell back, stunned, my heart racing now as I broke contact with her.

She slumped back down, her back falling into the corner, head bowed toward the ground, like I'd imagined the entire thing.

Fucking hell. How hadn't we thought of it before now?

Max hadn't taught us to heal. It was the one power that took too much from her when she used it. It had taken months of practice, and still she frequently ran herself into the ground in the early days, occasionally even flirting with a coma—or death —from pushing too hard to heal us.

That day, in the labs, even then as strong and powerful as she'd grown, I could see the toll that healing me had taken on her.

But she'd been able to because we were bonded.

I tugged at my hair as I ran from Sarah's room, pocketing the key and not even bothering to respond to Arnell's questions as I left the medical ward.

It seemed so simple now, so obvious.

Max healed us the easiest, because our ties to her were impossible to ignore. She healed Ro, because she spent a lifetime forging a connection to him.

Max hardly knew Sarah.

But we did. Wade and I were even bonded to her once.

The connection we had back then to Sarah was nothing like the one that pulled us to Max, but it wasn't nothing either. She wasn't some random girl. She'd been a part of our team. A part of us. Family.

I threw open the fanghole's bedroom and closed the distance to where Max lay draped against him.

Darius woke with a start, shoving Max behind him as his startled eyes found mine, his fangs flashing, threat clear in every line of his body.

For a moment, I thought he was going to act on the adrenaline and fear coursing through his body and attack me, the urge to protect her too strong to fight.

He'd seemed a bit off lately, more driven by raw instinct than usual.

He was often an odd, unpredictable prick, but lately it was more than that. Like he was fighting some invisible battle only he could see.

I raised my hands up in apology, and backed away, and after a tense moment, his rigid shoulders relaxed.

"What's going on?" Max grunted, her voice muffled and cracked with the edges of sleep as she fought to see around the vampire. "Darius, get off of me."

"What are you doing in here, wolf?" he asked, voice flat as he fought against his instincts, "people need to stop doing this. And you—you should know fucking better than waking me up like that. When she's here with me. When I—we're all on edge." The fight in his voice dissipated a bit as his brain recognized the absence of a threat. "Is something wrong?"

He pulled Max into his lap, his hands roving over her arms, her bare legs where the long T-shirt hit her thigh, like he was trying to convince himself that I hadn't just broken in here to report that she was hurt.

"Sarah," I said.

I heard the others' doors open, Eli swearing softly about the ungodly hour, then all of them cluttering around Darius's door frame.

Max stood up, crowding into me. Her hair was mussed and her eyes wild with fear. "Is she okay? She's not—?"

I pulled her to me, unable to resist her another moment, then pressed my nose to her neck, taking her in. This morning's solo session had nothing on the real thing, on the way she felt in my arms, the way she smelled.

"She's the same." I pulled back, then met Wade's eyes over her head. "Sort of. I think maybe I did something?"

"Did something?" Max grunted against my chest and I pulled back a little more, giving her enough room to breathe. "What do you mean?"

"I think I started to heal her a bit. Or established the connection to do it. She reacted, a little."

Her brows lifted, her eyes scanning me from head to toe, concern etched into the lines of her face. "You're okay? You didn't drain yourself, did you? Atlas, that's dangerous. Why didn't you wake me before? Khalida said that healing without training can kill you. And she was right. I've come close. You haven't had any training."

"It's okay," I squeezed her shoulders, "Bentley, I'm okay. Promise." I held her eyes until she nodded, until she believed me. "I think we can heal her though," I nodded towards Wade, "partially, I mean. Like you did with me. We were bonded to her, however briefly. Maybe we can at least buy her some more time. With your help."

It took twenty minutes of convincing her that this would work, that we'd be safe, and then twenty more minutes for everyone to fight over shower time and get ready, before I found myself back at the medical ward, this time with five more in tow.

"What's wrong?" Rowan's eyes roved over us all until he found Max, the lazy casualness from before clouding suddenly into fear. "Is it the mission? Something happen?"

Max's face split into a smile as she greeted her brother with a hug and then mussed his already out-of-control hair. "We're fine. We're going to try saving Sarah."

He exhaled his relief, then ushered us all into her room.

Sarah's position hadn't changed since I'd left her.

Max, Wade, and I circled around her, linking hands as Max talked us through how she accessed her healing magic, how it felt, how intoxicating it could become and how important it was for us to resist that, to know when to stop.

Declan stood on the sidelines, biting her nails, half-excited and half-terrified. None of us wanted to get our hopes up just for them to come collapsing down, but I could see that battle clear as day in Declan's face.

She wanted her cousin, her friend back. We all did.

The others looked on with less conflict, their concern for Max and her tendency to give too much of herself when healing at the front of all of our minds.

But maybe with more of us this time, it would be easier. Smoother.

It took a few minutes as Max patiently talked us through finding the link between me and Wade, and then both of us tracing that to Sarah. It was slippery, temporary, impossible to hold. But after a few tries, with Max's guidance, we were able to concentrate on it.

We worked, for half an hour, trying to tease Sarah out of her nightmare, to bring her back to us. Just when it seemed like we were making progress, mine or Wade's eyes would flash black, our skin growing clammy and breathing ragged, before the connection would snap altogether. And we were back at square one.

Max was patient, used to the non-linear process. She'd spent dozens of hours trying to bring Sarah back. This was only the beginning.

I felt Wade's growing frustration with himself when he lost the thread again, his fingers digging into my hand like he was trying to rip out my tendons and hold onto those instead, like his grip on me would somehow save her.

Was he inflicting the same pain on Max's hand too? I fucking hoped not.

When I went to say something, I realized I was doing the same to him. That I was clutching his hand and Sarah's shoulder like I meant them more harm than good, every vein in my arm taut with tension as I fought to chase the power and connection just out of our collective reach.

But whatever connection we had to Sarah had either weakened too much or was never strong enough to begin with. That, and our ability to access this particular power was too nascent.

Max had only barely reached me.

I'd hoped that with three of us, with our bonds as strong as they'd grown, that this would be easier. But it wasn't. In some cruel twist of fate, Max's healing strength was far more difficult to wield and control than the powers that brought destruction. My brother and I were better designed to bring the world to its knees than we were to cushion and heal it from the fall.

Max's eyes were blown pure black as she shook her head and stepped back, breaking our loop. "It's not working. There's something there, I can feel her better, through you both, but it's not enough for me to grasp onto. I don't know if—" she shook her head and took a few breaths, like she was fighting against the same frustration and anger I felt clutching my chest.

I was ready to collapse from the exertion, and a quick glance at Wade confirmed he wasn't any better off.

"No." She froze, the dark brown hues bleeding back through the black, as her eyes landed on Dec. "It's you. It should be you."

"No." Dec leaned back, confused, then shook her head. "I wasn't bonded to Sarah."

"They aren't either, not anymore anyway," Max said, an odd sadness in her voice that I didn't fully understand. Did she *want* our bonds to Sarah to be strong? I tried to ignore the petty part of me that would have preferred her jealousy in that moment.

Now wasn't the time. "But maybe it's not just about mate bonds. I healed Ro. Maybe, with healing, it's more so about connection."

"Not to mention you're the best of us at channeling Max's power." Eli nodded, coming around to the idea as he nudged her towards us. "She's right, if anyone is going to find Sarah locked in her own mind, it's going to be you."

Dec's lip quivered slightly, as she found her place between me and Sarah, her hand gripping mine.

I ignored the way her fingers trembled against mine, the way she cleared her throat, and laid a shaky hand on Sarah's head.

But then, in true Dec fashion, she stood taller and nodded, "okay, walk me through it."

Max did, and, while it wasn't an instant connection, Eli was right. Dec tapped into Max's power far more quickly than Wade and I had. After a few moments, I could feel her pull Sarah into the flow of power between the four of us, could feel her latch on with a strength that I hadn't been able to muster.

Good, you're doing really good, Dec. Max sent the words through to Dec, but connected as we were they reverberated in my thoughts just as loudly as if she'd pushed them to me. *Think about a memory, one that gets at the core of your connection to her. Ground yourself to it. Try to feel, smell, taste, until the memory turns more material. Good, good, that's it. Now locate your own essence, your power source. Good, there, you've got it. Siphon through to her, imagine your strength traveling through that connection, growing stronger, alive with energy. I've—I've never done this before, but try to pull from us all to replenish your own stores.*

I grunted under the strain as what felt like a claw dug through my chest, carving me up. My heartbeat sped up until it reached a breaking point and started to slow, too slow. Wade's hand loosened in mine as he fought to stay standing, his body trembling as he fought to keep giving.

Easy, Dec. Max's voice was strained now, farther away than it had been. Something about that sent a flare of panic through me. I could feel the wolf's energy pulse in alignment with my own, anxious and frantic. He felt cornered. The worst thing a wolf could feel when he was already more vulnerable than usual.

I dropped to my knees, and sensed more than heard Wade and Max do the same.

Fight against the pull, Dec. Max's thoughts were more like a whisper now, transparent and carried off in the wind. Away from me. Too far away. *Don't give into the euphoria of it. Too much. Dec, pull back.*

Eli and Ro started arguing, their voices tinny and difficult to parse. Darius's low, warning growl echoed the one in my own chest. Someone grabbed my shoulders, attempting to maneuver between our clasped hands as they tried to break us apart. But this wasn't a power that could be easily severed. Not until Dec was ready to let go.

Tears streamed down my face, though I didn't remember crying, didn't know why I even was. The sharp pain eased now, bleeding into a soft bliss that felt like swaying in a hammock on a warm, breezy day. I wanted to close my eyes, to lean back and rest. Just for a little while.

And then, with the power of a bomb, power pulsed hard and loud through us, my hands falling to my sides as I collapsed into the ground, my breathing ragged and rushed, like no amount of air would be enough for my lungs.

"Good," Max said, her breaths even more labored than mine as she crawled across the floor, hands searching for Dec, "good. That was good."

Fucking hell. Was this what healing typically felt like for Max? I swiped away a few strands of hair that were caked to my forehead with more sweat than I'd produce in three hours of sparring.

Those hadn't been tears running down my cheeks. My entire body was clammy and hot, my shirt sticking in wet patches as I fought to catch a breath.

Wade fell back on his ass, expression dazed and exhausted as the indigo of his irises pushed back the black abyss of his blown pupils.

Max seemed to be recovering more quickly than we were and she held her hands to Declan's cheeks. A pulse of power ran through us, like the connection between us was still just as strong, a livewire that couldn't be severed by space.

She closed her eyes, and I could feel her healing Dec, healing us too as she reached for me and then Wade.

"We shouldn't have done this today," Eli muttered, his hands running frantically over Max while he checked her for injuries. "That was super fucking reckless. Today of all days."

"Who knows how much longer Sarah would've had," she said, latching her fingers through his as they roamed over her for a second pass, "we'll be fine in a few minutes. I promise."

Darius was a silent, unmoving sentinel, eyes dark and cagey as he stood back in the shadows, like he was using his remaining will power to fight the urge to do the same. To rip Max from Declan and drag her back to his bed where he could keep her safe.

But the way his stare snagged every few seconds on Dec made it clear he was just as concerned about her. He'd clocked Dec's pallor, the way her arms still trembled slightly from the aftershocks of exertion.

"That was too much," he said, shaking his head. After a brief consideration, he came into our circle, setting one hand on Max cheek, and the other awkwardly on the top of Dec's head. "But you're okay, yes? Both of you?"

They nodded.

"We are too," Wade said with a snort, earning a smirk from the vampire, "thanks for asking."

"You're replaceable," Darius shot back, but there was no bite to his words. And I caught the way his eyes traced Wade and then me, satisfied that we were both, indeed, fine. "Though I suppose finding another incompetent incubus and arrogant werewolf this late in the game would pose an inconvenience."

"We should postpone," Eli said. "I doubt you four will be much use today after this."

After a moment, Dec's grayish-white complexion warmed up a bit, until she looked more like herself, her eyes wild and panicked as they held Max in their stare.

"We're all okay," Max said, her lips carving into a soft smile as she met his eyes, willing him to believe her. "I promise. I'll heal them, and our power will balance out better," she'd begun referring to her power like that lately—as 'ours,' "fill in the gaps and regenerate. We'll be back to fighting shape in an hour, I think. This was good," she turned back to Dec, her eyes glistening with pride, "you did good."

Max seemed lighter than she had in weeks, her cheeks flushed bright with color, her expression soft with relief. She hardly knew Sarah, but she'd dedicated almost every free moment she'd had since rescuing her to trying to save her. And after all the shit we'd been through, she'd needed a win. Maybe this would be the thing to give us an edge today, the high of this success.

I cracked my neck, my strength coming back to me with every passing moment. She was right, at this rate, I'd feel good as new before we even grabbed breakfast.

I stretched, feeling restless and jittery. It'd been weeks since I'd shifted. My wolf was growing antsy locked in my chest with all of these foreign emotions coursing through me. After our mission today, I'd let him run. Maybe see if Ralph wanted to join in.

A low moan caught all of our attention as Sarah shifted

awkwardly, like she wasn't used to moving her body, like she didn't quite feel comfortable in her own skin.

Her eyes, blue and wide, darted around the room, her breathing rushed and uneven as she processed the impossible clash of her nightmare reality with this one.

My stomach tightened at the sight. She was awake. Alive. Better.

But this was only the start of her battle.

"I'll call Jay." Ro ran a hand through his hair, the pieces sticking up in every possible direction, like he'd been incessantly tugging at it. His eyes found Max, like they always did, and held her stare for a moment, confirming that she was, indeed, okay. She couldn't speak into his head the way that she could ours, but those two had their own silent language, one just as powerful and clear. He nodded, confirming whatever he needed to. "I'll be right back. Arnell will get Charlie and the others."

Sarah's entire body shook as she watched us all. She was like a small bird, lost and far from the nest, surrounded by hungry predators. The image was so at odds with the girl we'd brought back from hell, that I didn't know how to parse the two versions of her together, to unite both halves into this new reality.

Had I looked this scared? This lost, when Max brought me back?

I'd certainly felt it. For weeks.

We all kept our distance as we watched her, none of us wanting to startle her further, to push her back into that place she'd only just escaped.

"Sarah?" Dec crouched down beside her, hands clutched around her chest like she was forcing herself not to pull her cousin to her. "It's me, Dec. Are—are you okay?" She winced, then shook her head. "Of course you're not okay."

"D-dec?" Sarah's voice was hoarse, cracked, barely discernible. Broken.

Dec's eyes brimmed with unshed tears as she nodded, swallowing back the sob she was clearly trying to keep under a tight lid.

Tears streamed silently down Max's cheeks as she watched their interaction, stilted and cold where it had been so warm before.

Sarah focused on her cousin now, her eyes raising slowly until they met hers. She took in a deep, jagged breath that broke on a sob. The sound pushed Dec over the edge and she joined her, both of the cousins collapsing into each other. Dec held her tight while Sarah wept through her pain—the scars still etched into her psyche even with her newfound freedom.

Those scars would probably never go away.

But she wouldn't feel this bad forever.

"Sarah?" Jay ran into the room, skin pale and rimmed with black under her eyes. She must've been nearby, possibly sleeping in one of the adjoining rooms. Since her arrival, she'd hardly left her daughter's side for more than a meal and few hours of sleep each night.

Sarah pulled back from Declan, eyes wide and filled with a childlike fear that I hadn't seen since we were kids. "M-mommy?"

"H-how?" Jay hiccupped a cry and found her way to her niece and daughter. She collapsed into a hug around them, like a blanket of protection, as she pulled them to her, shaking softly. "I'm here, angel, I'm here."

Jay repeated the words over and over, lips pressed to Sarah's hair as Dec pulled back a bit, giving them a moment.

I pulled Dec to her feet while she tried to discreetly wipe her tears on the back of her hand.

"I, er," Darius cleared his throat, tore the sleeve from his shirt and handed it to her with a shrug, "here, I guess."

She snorted a half laugh and took it, mopping up the salty liquid while Darius stood around awkwardly, clearly feeling out of place with the emotional turmoil in the room.

"It's true? She's awake?" Charlie's face appeared in the doorway, her face lit up with a giant smile as she watched the mother and daughter clutching each other, hovering over the spot where Sarah had crouched, restless and zombie-like since she'd arrived.

"She's awake." Max's face lit up with unfiltered joy, any vestiges of exhaustion from the healing long tucked away. "Long road ahead, but she's awake."

Charlie's eyes brimmed with tears too now, and I took a few steps back, until my shoulder bumped into Darius, suddenly understanding his discomfort with all of the emotions crowding this room. It was stifling, and I could feel my own getting lodged in my throat. I needed a breather after all of that.

I cleared my throat, thankful when Bishop appeared next to Charlie. He squeezed her to him, but his expression was just as stern and detached as it usually was, clearly either oblivious or unconcerned by the crowded, intense room.

"Glad to hear it," he said, pressing a kiss to his wife's head before turning his focus to me. "But we should give Sarah and Jay some space. It's time."

And with those two words, the emotional energy of the room shifted in an entirely new direction, just as loud, just as intense, but now laced with a fresh coating of adrenaline and fear.

17

ELI

"Be careful." Max pressed her lips to mine.

I nodded, soaking in the last few moments of her.

"We'll be fine," Dec said, crushing Max to her in a hug. "As soon as we're there, we'll send a confirmation through."

Levi sighed, clearly annoyed with the farewell processional. "For fuck's sake, we're all going to be back here in less than two hours. This doesn't exactly warrant tears and parting gifts, does it?"

I swallowed back my annoyance, not exactly pleased that I'd been saddled with him and Evelyn for this mission. But even though I didn't know him well, I recognized the waiver of uncertainty in his voice, the way his eyes kept darting about, like he was already on high alert, expecting an attack before we even left this little safe haven.

Was he going to be this jittery and prickish the whole time?

Evelyn squeezed his shoulder, a stern look on her face—both comforting and chastising him.

Fucking hell, was it too late to swap in for Wade's group?

Dec was my saving grace. I took a step closer to her, wrapping my hand around her arm as Evelyn and Levi moved in to do the same.

With a final squeeze, Max pulled back, her jaw tight as she did everything she could to swallow back the anxiety so evident in her eyes.

My eyes locked onto her, burning every sharp line and soft curve into my brain.

She'd be fine. We were all going to be fine.

The four of us in my group were up first.

According to Evelyn and Levi's intel, the council members were never all together—except for their bi-annual meetings. Safety measures apparently.

But with shit as chaotic as it was, there would be no bi-annual meeting this year. Instead, they were strictly keeping to the no-more-than-two-members-in-the-same-place rule, convening full meetings with each other via proxy and phone only.

And while they usually kept to their own homes and lives when they weren't in session, they'd spent the last year dividing their time between various Guild stations around the world.

We were heading to a small contingency satellite a few hours outside of London.

Evelyn was certain European Headquarters would be vacant, that they'd have pulled out most of their protectors after Max's pyrotechnics, fearing a repeat. Instead, they'd become even more scattered, small pockets of teams and researchers spread throughout their complex network of safehouses.

According to Evelyn, this particular campus was one of the council member's personal favorites—being only an hour's drive from their lavish home.

"Ready?" Dec's eyes met mine, sharp and clear. It would take us quite a few jumps to get all the way there, and we'd be taking turns shouldering the brunt of the work.

I wasn't too worried about it though. Outside of Max, Dec

had the strongest handle on teleportation. So if she couldn't get us there, then the mission was cracked before it could even get started. Once we were there, we'd open our mental link long enough to confirm we'd made it, then shut it down and go to work.

Get in, get out, we'd be back at The Lodge in no time. Clean, efficient, planned.

As well as something like this could be planned anyway.

After three days of arguing, we'd all decided it was best to only communicate via the link when we arrived, when the mission was done, if we'd found the source of shadow magic, or if one of us was an inch away from death and in desperate need of backup. Otherwise, it would be too much of a distraction, all of us worrying about each other. It wouldn't be good to spread our focus out across the world when we were diving into something so dangerous, so important.

We had one shot at this and if it didn't work—well, we were out of ideas.

"Ready." My focus latched onto Max again, her dark eyes the last thing my vision held onto as the world around us warped and dissolved. A swirling abyss of golden brown that I'd happily drown in.

Six jumps later, and we were lingering somewhere on the east coast. My chest tightened, but it wasn't altogether unpleasant. I'd grown so used to teleporting, our strength growing exponentially the more we worked together, pushing and pulling together, that it hardly affected me anymore.

Mostly, I was just keenly aware of the fact that this was the farthest away from the group we'd ever been, in all of our training.

I closed my eyes, feeling the warm hum of the bond, focused on the feel of it until my body was almost convinced that Max and the others were here with us now.

Dec ran her hand unconsciously over her arm, where I

knew her bond mark was etched beneath the fabric, her tight expression softening slightly, like she was making sure she could feel them all too.

Evelyn looked considerably more worse off. Her face was pinched, her hands clutching her knees as she fought to suck down a fresh breath of air.

A bolt of sympathy struck me before I could reign it in. I remembered that feeling well—the unpleasant and uncanny strangeness of your body emerging into existence from nothing. It went away, eventually. Or maybe we just built up a callus to it over time.

Levi looked mostly unphased, which annoyed me even though I knew it shouldn't.

We'd spent the last week practicing with them. Teleporting sometimes up to thirty times a day, until they had built up a near-immunity to the experience.

Ripping yourself through space had a hell of an impact on the body.

Before I could second guess it, I set my hand awkwardly on Evelyn's back, rubbing a gentle, meant-to-be soothing circle on her back as she regained her bearings.

Her muscles tensed under my touch and she froze. When she stood, finally, I saw that her eyes had glazed over a bit, as she muttered a muddled "Thanks, Eli. I'm okay."

"Er," I pulled back, cleared my throat, realizing this was the first time I'd initiated contact with her in years. I turned to Dec. "The big hop across the pond is next. You ready, or do you want a minute to psych yourself up?"

Dec pulled one of her arms across her chest, leaned into the deep stretch, then did the same with the other as she scanned the empty coastline around us. I knew the others wouldn't recognize the fear underpinning her otherwise confident expression. This was the biggest jump. We'd each tried it several times, and Dec and Max were the only ones who'd managed it without rematerializing in the middle of the ocean.

And even then, they'd only succeeded in that twice while carrying passengers.

"Another minute or two, then I'll be good." She bent at her waist, stretching her back and her legs, then sat down, eyes closed, focusing on visualizing exactly where she wanted to take us.

"Cool." I kicked at a small mound of sand, suddenly aware of the fact that while she meditated and centered herself, I was more or less left with the company of Levi and Evelyn.

For once, Levi looked as uncomfortable as I felt, his gray eyes seeming to land everywhere but in my general vicinity.

Evelyn's hands trembled softly at her sides, but other than that, she seemed one hundred percent back to the cool, confident protector persona she always channeled.

After a long, tense moment of silence though, she dropped that mask, her eyes filling with an emotion I couldn't quite decipher as they ping-ponged between me and Levi.

"I'm glad we're doing this together," she whispered, her voice taking on a soft tone I hadn't heard in years. "I can't tell you how happy—"

My spine tingled at the nostalgic familiarity of it, and I clenched my jaw, frustrated that some small sliver of my brain still missed it—still missed her. After everything.

Levi cleared his throat, muttered an embarrassed, "Mom, we'll be fine."

"I know it's just, if something happens, I don't want to leave things—" Her voice cracked, and I averted my eyes, unsure what to do with this strange version of her. We'd spent months in the same place, and she'd never once tried to crack through the armed wall I'd built up. She'd respected my wishes, and during our preparations for today, she'd kept things professional. Removed.

We hadn't been jovial with each other, exactly, but I'd grown almost used to the cold, respectful, colleague-like rapport we'd built up over the last few days.

This? This I had no fucking clue what to do with.

Levi shifted, clearly as uncomfortable as I was. "Stop worrying. It's going to go just as planned."

She set her hand against Levi's cheek, the pure love and adoration that radiated from her face as she studied him shining so brightly, I could practically feel it heating the side of my exposed face. "I know. I know. I just, I just want to make sure you know that if things don't go well, if something happens—that I love you." Her gaze turned to me. "Both of you. More than anything in this world."

She dropped her hand from Levi, took a step towards me.

My heart beat loud and hard in my chest.

I couldn't bring myself to meet her eyes, but a heated anger tore through my body. I fought it down.

I needed to focus. Why the fuck was she doing this right now? Of all times?

Did she have a death wish? Did she want to throw me off my game—the thin veneer of professionalism I'd carefully and artfully perfected to get us through this?

Of course this was happening. We were heading into what was quite possibly the most dangerous, important mission any of us would ever be on, and she wanted to do this now?

For a moment, her hand floated in my peripheral vision, like she was building the courage for something, a muscle memory that was caught halfway between remembered and forgotten. But then, ever so gently, she pressed her palm to my cheek, the warmth of her skin against mine made more noticeable by the chilly breeze wafting along the coastline.

"You need to know, Eli, that I would never have left you willingly. I never meant to hurt you. Or Seamus. But I met someone. It was a one-time thing, could never have been anything more, but I got pregnant and—" she paused, and I could hear her fighting to maintain control over her voice, "I know you might not understand, but I was protecting you both—you and your father." I tensed under her touch, but for some reason I didn't step away, didn't shove her hand from my face even though half of my brain screamed at me too. The other half remembered this warmth, this sense of safety. "You've realized by now that Levi is—" I met her eyes briefly, finding them narrowed as she searched for a word, "different. More than just a protector. I had to keep him safe. You have to know now what The Guild would have done to him if they'd known the truth. And I didn't want you and your father touched by their rage, their punishment, just by association. So I left. It was the only thing I could think to do. But I didn't leave you because I wanted to, because I chose Levi over you. You're both my sons. I love you both more than I can ever begin to explain. I thought I was saving you both. All three of you."

I couldn't bring myself to say anything. My traitorous throat was suddenly clogged, and I saw Dec's shoulders shift at my feet, an awkward bystander to this impromptu confession.

She wasn't breathing. Neither, I was pretty sure, was Levi.

I could feel how suddenly uncomfortable he was, because his shriveled posture, and diverted eyes, I knew, mirrored my own.

Evelyn dropped her hand, glanced between the three of us and shook her head, sniffling slightly as she rapidly blinked away the moisture filming her eyes. "Right, sorry. I just couldn't leave that unsaid for another moment. Not when we don't know what the events of today might bring."

"But you came back," I said, the words ripping from my lips without any permission from me. I heard the hurt in my voice and I hated myself for bleeding in front of them. Still, now that the Band-Aid had been ripped off, I could do nothing but let the wound weep. "To The Guild, I mean. If you really thought

Levi would be in danger, why did you come back? And never mention any of this to me?"

Something unrecognizable passed over her face, and Levi stiffened, fingers digging into his thighs like he could teleport himself from this spot if he just focused hard enough on it.

"I remained threaded through The Guild—occasionally taking on missions when it suited. And then, when Levi was older, I came back in a fuller capacity. He could mask his—abilities," a small, sad grin hooked the corner of his mouth, "and I told The Guild I wanted back in."

Her familiarity with Charlie and the others tugged at something in my brain. "You've been spying since then, haven't you? Working against The Guild?"

She straightened, something like pride lifting her chin as her gaze met mine. "I have. And because I'd proven myself loyal to The Guild, over the years, they allowed my discretion with respect to Levi. I told them I trained him on my own, that he operated best independently. It's why he's never been to the Academy or worked in an official capacity with any single team."

I shot a glance at him. "Any chance you're going to tell me what the fuck it is that you are?"

He grunted, shook his head.

"Didn't think so." Fuckhead. I turned back to her. "But when you rejoined, you still never told me this, never told dad —" my voice caught on that word. Watching my dad suffer from that heartbreak for so many years, why the fuck wouldn't she have just told him the truth? He would have chosen her over The Guild in less than a heartbeat. "You could have told us."

Her expression softened, jaw still tight like she was trying to keep back a wave of emotion. "Maybe. But your dad was high up in The Guild. And you—" she exhaled, "you were too, Eli. I didn't know where your loyalties lay, couldn't risk—" she glanced at Levi. Couldn't risk him. "And when I tried to establish some kind of relationship with you, you so clearly didn't want that."

"So it's my fault?" My fists were clenched so tight, I could feel my skin parting for my nails.

"No," she pinched the bridge of her nose. "No, of course not. None of this has ever been your fault. That's not what I meant. You hated me. For hurting you. For hurting your dad. It was just easier to let you. Hate can be a powerful tool, a weapon for protectors. If I couldn't have the kind of relationship with you and your father that I wanted, at least I could provide you with that. A source through which to siphon your rage and bring you two closer together. You had each other. That was all either of you really needed."

"You have no idea what I needed."

Silence fell over us all.

My chest was tight, my stomach nearly ready to retch as I parsed through all of this, reframing the last twenty years of my life through this lens. I couldn't tell if I hated her more than I did before or if I wanted to say 'fuck it' and hug her.

Either way, I was ready to vomit.

"I can't," I shook my head, taking a few steps back, "I can't deal with this shit right now." I cleared my throat, stared out at the crashing ripples of waves until I was sure I wouldn't start fucking crying right here, right now, "I need to focus. We need to focus. This," I took a deep breath, gestured aimlessly between us, "this is the past. It doesn't matter right now."

"Right," Evelyn said, her voice soft, so much more fragile than I'd ever remembered it being, "you're right. I'm sorry. This —this was. I'm being selfish. I'm sorry, Eli."

Declan stood up, cracking her neck as she moved to stand by me.

Evelyn jumped, like she'd forgotten about Dec's presence

entirely. A blush crept over her cheeks and her stare held firmly on the ground by her feet.

Dec's hand found mine and squeezed.

Warmth spread through me at her gentle, steady presence.

For most of my life, she'd been this for me.

She'd been *here*. At my side.

I squeezed back, centering myself, focusing on the bond that connected me to my team. They were the reason I was here. The reason I was freezing my ass off on some sad beach, ready to save the world.

Try to, anyway.

I'd deal with the Evelyn and Levi shit later.

If I wanted to.

But also, it was maybe okay to just—not. To just let things lay how they would. It was okay we weren't close. It didn't matter.

I'd spent so long hating my mother, letting her abandonment shape so much of how I viewed the world, my relationships—just, everything.

And I'd let that hatred overshadow the truth. I had a family. One that I loved. One that was there when I needed them, through it all. One who saw every side of me and still wanted me for their own.

Six had been there, cushioning that pain even through my angstiest years.

If I wanted to mend things with my mom, to open this cesspool of pain and swim through it, searching for anything salvageable, I could do that later. But I didn't need her. Or Levi. Not anymore. I had everything—everyone—that I deemed essential already.

I squeezed Dec's hand back, then cleared my throat, shoving any residual emotion away. "Ready?"

She winked at me, then nodded to the others. "Let's go."

Dec got us over without an issue, and after a brief rest while the other teams started their jumps, I handled the final few, significantly shorter jumps.

Turned out, aiming was a lot more difficult when we weren't trying to teleport towards Max. Visualizing was key, but it was almost impossible to visualize a place neither Dec nor I had been to before.

It had become surprisingly intuitive recognizing when Max or one of the others was pulling for power. Like a switch, or wave of energy that I could interpret once I knew to look for it.

That was good. Channeling her fire and teleportation power would be more of a breeze during this tandem attack than I'd initially thought it would be.

I bit down on the flare of excitement. This would be a success. I could feel it in my gut.

I sent through a quick confirmation to Max, then Dec and I focused on shutting down the mind link, closing that part of connection. It would make it easier for us to concentrate, and easier to focus on and pull her power when we needed to.

Once we were a mile out, according to Evelyn, who had a much better directional radar than she'd passed down to me, we stopped teleporting. It was time to wait for the others to get to their locations before we started the—hopefully relatively silent and quick—ambush.

Like Headquarters, this location was surrounded by a forest —trees and hills lined the path we carved.

As similar it was though, it smelled different here. Fresher, crisper.

How far were we from a town? From people?

Headquarters was relatively isolated, but this was next level. I could taste the brine of the sea on my tongue.

"You're sure this is the spot?" I asked. It was hard to imagine evil doings unfolding in such a beautiful place. But maybe that's what made it a smart choice.

"Positive," Evelyn said, her steps sure and steady as she led us forward. "Just a little bit longer and we're there."

The rest of the trip was spent in silence. Partially because we were aiming for stealth, but mostly because I was still reeling from her confession, as much as I'd tried to shove it away.

My relationship with Evelyn and Levi had always been a tense one—but there'd been a simplicity in that tension. I hated them and they knew it. Our interactions were uncomfortable and, in Levi's case, a little heated, but they weren't unpredictable.

This new information could change that dynamic if I let it, could complicate things I wasn't sure I wanted to complicate.

Did I want her in my life again? Beyond just as a partner in this mission?

And Levi—did I really need another brother when I already had Wade and Atlas?

I didn't need a family, but maybe forgiving them was worth it—would release something knotted and snarled inside of me. And maybe it could do the same for my dad.

"This is it," Evelyn said, her voice hushed as she ducked behind a particularly brambly tree.

I shook my spiraling thoughts away and stepped next to her. Before I could overthink it, I grabbed her hand, giving it a soft squeeze when her eyes met mine.

She exhaled, lips quivering in a hesitant smile as she squeezed my hand back.

It wasn't much, but it was all I could give her right now.

My heart hammered against my chest, calming just slightly when I felt Dec press up on my other side.

"Fucking hell," she said, her accent thick, like being back on this continent unconsciously pulled it out of her. "Of course their low-key rendezvous point would be a fucking castle."

Castle wasn't an exaggeration either.

The grounds were wild and unpolished, grasses and wild-flowers competing for space in every direction we could see. But the building was solid, sturdy.

It appeared to be made of stone, the lines not entirely perfect or symmetrical, but worn in over time, visible divots carved out that I could identify even from here.

And there were four towers attached to the behemoth structure. Or maybe turrets? I wasn't sure what the official name for the cylindrical add-ons to a castle were, but they were there, protruding and castle-like.

Dec's eyes darted briefly to Evelyn. "Do we know where she'll be?"

Our target was a council member named Amalia. If we were lucky, her co-council member and part-time fuckbuddy, Xavier, would be with her too.

Two for one, my kind of deal.

Evelyn's posture was rigid, her attention focused as she studied the grounds in front of us. Any lingering emotion from the conversation earlier had long dissolved away, leaving behind the confident, borderline arrogant persona I was much more familiar with.

Good.

As cold as she could sometimes be, I couldn't deny the fact that she was one hell of a protector. And that was not even including the extra dose of badass required to be secretly spying on the organization she'd been steadily rising in for decades.

It was the version of her that we needed today.

"They could be anywhere, but the largest suite is situated on the northwest turret." Turret. Fuck yeah, I was right. "Can't guarantee that's where she'll be now, but I'd bet my best blade that she's taken that room for herself. Amalia is," she paused for a moment, eyes narrowing as she searched for a word, "lavish."

"So how do we get up there without anyone noticing?" Declan scanned the vicinity. "I thought there'd be more people out and about."

Evelyn turned to Levi, a silent question scrunching between her brows.

"There's definitely no one outside, but let me go in first, I'll signal back if it's open."

"Why—" I started, but a sharp glare from him had me swallowing the question I knew he wouldn't answer.

The Plan.

This was part of the plan, and it was best to just go through with it as we'd prepped.

Dec and I were the ones teleporting, which meant we were necessary for getting out of this. Apparently, Levi was the expendable one.

So we waited for him, the three of us silent and tense while Levi casually strolled up to the castle and then, eventually, climbed the wall, hands and feet seamlessly finding the divots and handholds like he'd been rock climbing this wall his entire life, until he reached a black, weathered window.

Declan vibrated next to me, but she didn't look scared. Her face was focused, ready.

The waiting around was the difficult part.

I felt that too, deep in my bones.

Sometimes stillness was the most difficult part of the job.

Evelyn hadn't so much as taken a breath since Levi disappeared through the window, her anxiety practically clawing at my ribs. He might have thought of himself as expendable, the best to take risks, but she did not.

Did she ever worry so intensely about me?

I shoved away the selfish thought before it had a chance to grip me.

A pale hand dipped back through the window, waving us forward.

She exhaled, body sinking in relief.

And I found, surprisingly, that mine did the same.

As annoying as he was, I didn't want the fucker to die. And not just because his death would signal more complications than we'd anticipated.

I grabbed Dec and Evelyn's hands, and pulled them in one final jump to the room.

Precision was easier when I had a thing to visualize.

We landed, all of us still on our feet, in front of Levi.

The room was small, cluttered with long-ignored desks and random bits of furniture. Cobwebs collected along the windowsill, and the cloying, thick scent of stale air clung around us.

We said nothing, the four of us listening for the slightest sound or disturbance to suggest life on the other side of these walls.

All I could hear was the sound of our breath.

As one, we moved towards the door, walking quietly and quickly, with Levi leading the way. He apparently had heightened senses, so he'd be the first of us to recognize a protector's presence.

The hall was equally abandoned, the sconces and lamps dark and dusty from disuse.

I devoted most of my energy during our relatively peaceful scavenger hunt looking for the shadow magic source.

Not that I actually knew exactly how to do that.

Max and everyone seemed so sure that we'd 'know it when we found it' but I had my doubts. She'd described what she'd felt when she saw the stone during Atlas and Reza's bonding ceremony.

Still, it was hard to dig for a feeling I'd never felt before. I was just going off vibes.

But this was also our best and only chance at locating the fucking thing, so I didn't have a better option.

I glanced at Dec, could tell that she was focusing too. When her eyes met mine, I knew she didn't feel anything yet either. We didn't need the mindlinks to read each other.

That didn't mean it wasn't here. Could just mean we weren't close enough yet.

Either way, we weren't leaving here until we found Amalia. If we couldn't get the stone, the least we could do was take her out before she had a chance to reach out to the others and regroup. The base goal of these missions was to take out the council members, like dominoes, until we found the missing thing we were looking for.

I bumped into Levi, but swallowed the grunt of annoyance back.

His spine was rigid, unmoving. He had that sort of creepy stillness about him that Darius often invoked. The kind of stillness that no human or protector could ever believably achieve.

He nodded his head to the door on our left.

It took me a few seconds, but eventually I noticed a soft rustling. Then, voices, too quiet and far away for me to hear.

But this castle was clearly not as abandoned as it had initially seemed.

A spark of adrenaline flowed through me, from my head down through each of my limbs. Whether it was laced with anxiety or excitement, I wasn't entirely sure. It didn't matter.

We continued forward, making our way to the northwest turret, pausing inside empty rooms and closets every few minutes whenever we heard shuffled footsteps or muffled voices pass us by.

The air was thick with tension and I could practically feel

the hair on my arms lifting towards it. Waiting. Too quiet. Too quiet. Too quiet.

Levi paused at the base of a spiral staircase, the walls nothing but dark stone with a few dim lights.

Dec's eyes darted towards me, brows lifted as if to say, "This is it. Don't die."

I shot her a wink, a far too casual attempt at allaying her anxiety.

The climb was slow, with Levi at my front and Dec at my back.

My fingers flexed around the hilt of my blade, my other hand free in case I needed to call forward Max's fire.

The air in the stairwell was stale and cloying. There was an almost metallic taste to it that had my spine tingling. And not in a good way.

Something was off here, wrong.

I didn't feel the draw that Max said we would, but I could sense there was magic here, a twisted perversion of the electricity the bond to her emitted.

When we made it to a large, ornate room at the top of the narrow staircase, we filed in, slow and steady.

The room was adorned in golds and rich shades of green. The curtains around a large gold-framed bed were made of a heavy velvet-like material, and the knickknacks lining the shelves signaled a lifetime of meticulous curating and collecting.

Still, as lavish as the decor was, the air was rimmed with floating dust particles, like it hadn't been cleaned in weeks.

A small cough pulled my attention back to the bed.

The bedding was so thick, piled high with blankets and more throw pillows than one piece of furniture could reasonably hold, that I'd almost missed the frail figure sitting amongst them.

Dark clumps of muddy-brown hair were gray at the roots

and patchy, as if several sections had been ripped from the pale, blood-crusted skin of her scalp, and her blue eyes looked marled with black, as if someone had spilled a few drops of ink in their depths.

She coughed again, and sat straighter, squinting like she couldn't properly see us, her nostrils flaring slightly as if to catch our scent.

"Who the fuck is that?" I whispered out the side of my mouth, but the woman clearly heard me.

Her head turned to me and she gripped the bedding, relying on its bulk to help lift her up.

One thin, pale leg appeared around the side of the bed, then another. After a few moments, she straightened herself up and took a few steps towards us.

"Amalia?" Evelyn's expression was one of horror as she watched the frail woman move towards us. The closer she came, the more unwell she looked. Bruises and half-healed wounds covered nearly every inch of her, and dark veins bubbled against her papery skin, like every inch she moved pushed them closer to the edge of bursting. "What the hell happened to you?"

Amalia?

This was the scary council member we were here to shake down for powerful shadow magic?

She looked a breath away from passing out.

"Evelyn?" The woman winced, her voice little more than a soft croak, "You're supposed to be dead."

Levi shifted further in the room, standing between the frail woman and our mother.

I resisted the eye roll threatening to escape. This woman was not a threat.

"Well, obviously I'm not. What happened to you?" she asked again. I took a few steps forward while they shuffled awkwardly through small talk, searching amongst the cluttered shelves for anything that might possibly resemble the stone we were after. Amalia was clearly a pack rat, but of the fanciest variety. The place looked like a museum, like she'd surrounded her deathbed with a shrine—an attempt to carry the things that mattered most to her into the next life, perhaps. The result was just cluttered and gaudy. "Is this from the shadow magic?"

The woman's lip curled at that. As she shifted, a sharp metallic clang rang through the room.

When I spun back towards her, I noticed something I'd missed initially. Her small, veiny ankle was clamped tight to a large, thick chain. She tugged and shifted against it, her eyes rolling back in her head slightly as some sort of fit took over.

Spit flew from her chapped lips as she hissed and struggled against the restraints, her arms outstretched as if she could pull Evelyn to her if she just reached far enough.

The effort did nothing but leave blood trailing down her foot. The floor was littered with slivers of skin that had shed away from her ankle being rubbed raw.

My stomach tightened and I dropped a small trinket I'd picked up off a shelf onto the floor. This scene was all too familiar now, all too hopeless.

"The shadow magic," I whispered, leaning back until my eyes met Dec's. "She's been tainted by it," I swallowed back the annoying rush of bile threatening to tear through my throat, "like my dad."

"Oh Amalia," Evelyn took a step back, her face a few shades paler than usual, "you reckless, reckless woman."

The frame of the bed groaned and strained as Amalia pulled towards her.

Like Levi, I found myself inching closer to the woman, putting myself between her and Evelyn, who she so very clearly had a craving for...well, eating, probably.

I bit back my disgust and reached for Max's fire. I wouldn't use it unless I absolutely had to, because doing so meant the others wouldn't be able to. But I kept my awareness of it clear in case Amalia got loose.

The bed was sturdy, reinforced with metal and bolted to the floor.

"Who tied you here?" Levi's voice was metallic and harsh.

Amalia was beyond conversation, overcome with hunger at the temptation of so many of us. I'd watched Seamus get to this point more times than I could count. I knew we wouldn't be getting a word out of her now. Not until she'd had something to eat.

But it wasn't just the fact that we were sharing the garish room with a zombie that had me tense. The isolation of the castle, the general *offness* of this place made the hair on my arms stand up. Something was very, very wrong.

There was a strange stench that I couldn't quite name or describe.

When I took a step closer to her, it only grew stronger.

"The shadow magic," I glanced briefly at Dec, not fully willing to take my eyes off the woman desperate to eat us, "I can smell it in her blood. I think that's what I'm sensing, anyway." This was all absurdly new to me and my body was still adjusting to the boost it got from being bonded to Max. "It's twisted and rancid."

In other words, nothing like the intoxicating thrum of magic that connected us to Max that I now seemed to crave as desperately as air.

This was a perversion of it, a distortion that rearranged and snarled it into something entirely wrong.

The stone wasn't here, but it had been. I was sure of that, though I couldn't exactly explain how.

Or else Amalia had been near it. Had been infected with it, somehow.

"What—" Levi's question was cut off by a soft thud followed almost immediately by a small gasp.

I spun around, and my eyes met Evelyn's. They were wide with shock, with a desperate realization I hadn't quite grasped yet.

Time stood still as my brain caught up with the shift in the atmosphere.

A man stood behind her, a few inches taller.

"The dead," he whispered, his voice cold and hollow, "should remain dead, don't you think?"

Evelyn's black shirt grew darker in the center, wet. And then started to move, like her heart was beating outside of her ribs.

No, not her heart.

Those were—fingers.

With a loud, wet crack, the man pulled back.

Evelyn's knees fell to the ground, the shadow of surprise on her face, just a leftover ghost as she collapsed face down onto the rug.

The man held her heart in his outstretched hand. Her blood painted splatters up his wrist and seeped obscenely through his fingers as he studied us.

A dark, deep, almost soundless gasp ripped from Levi as he rushed the man, but the man merely teleported, from the bloody patch of carpet on which he stood, to the other side of Amalia's bed.

Levi's arms grasped nothing but air as he crashed into the doorway and regained his footing.

"You must be Xavier?" Declan asked. Her jaw was tight, her hands clenched into fists at her sides as she fought to keep her eyes on the man, and not on my mother's corpse at her feet.

Amalia's moans and wails grew more aggravated at Xavier's nearness, and she crawled over her bed sheets, trying to get closer to him.

His lip curled as he spared her a brief glance of disgust, then he took a few steps to the left until he was just out of the reach allowed by her invisible cage.

"And you," he glanced at Dec, scanning her from head to toe with a small grin that made my stomach turn, "you reek of power."

A flash of greed sparked in the black pools of his eyes.

Like Amalia, he'd clearly been experimenting with the shadow magic. But he seemed far more collected, in control of himself.

Levi moved towards him, ready to attack again, but Dec's arm reached out to stop him. She shot him a dark look, her order clear—stand the fuck down. We have work to do.

It was typical protector protocol. When one of us was lost on a mission, the rest were meant to go on. To buckle back the pain of that loss until the mission was complete and we'd been debriefed. Only then, in the privacy of our own cabins, in the company of our teams, did we ever dare to let that grief seep from our pores.

But Levi didn't grow up around our kind. And now that I was so far removed from The Guild, I could see how callous, how impossible that request really was.

Levi's nostrils flared as he fought the urge to fuck over the whole mission. For a moment, I thought he would. But after a few deep, sporadic breaths, he abandoned the fight altogether. He dropped to his knees next to Evelyn, searching for signs of life I knew wouldn't be there.

Still, I couldn't bring myself to look. I knew once I did, that her death would be finite.

Any hope I'd had about a possible reconciliation, gone.

"You must be her," Xavier said again, his focus on Dec and Dec alone, either oblivious to our turmoil or completely ambivalent about it. "You look a little different from how they described, but I can sense the magic in you. Strong. So much stronger than I thought it'd be. We knew you'd come to us eventually. Power is drawn to power."

Did he think she was Max? Dec caught my eyes briefly and gave me an almost imperceptible head shake.

Right. Let him think that.

"The stone," Declan stood taller, her blade still dangling from her fingers, though I knew firsthand it could be in his neck in an instant if she needed it to be, "where is it?" She tilted her head to the side, studying him, her body slipping into an almost casual stance that I knew was only for show. "I don't sense it here."

Xavier's brow arched, his mouth curving into a slimy fish hook of a smirk as he tossed Evelyn's heart on the bed—as if it was nothing. "So it's as we guessed. You can sense it, then? You're right though. It's not here."

To my absolute fucking horror, Amalia pounced on the bloody muscle, her teeth and fingers fighting for purchase over the surface area as she devoured it in a few rabid bites.

I couldn't hold back the burning surge up my throat any longer. The wet sounds of her feverishly eating a piece of my mother completely obliterated the last thread of control I had left.

I vomited a puddle at my feet, gagging and coughing until everything in my stomach was out.

Xavier groaned. "Disgusting. You're lucky I have cleaners coming tomorrow."

"Her heart? Was that fucking necessary?" Dec barked out, some of her cool mask dissolving into a rage I'd only seen a few times before.

When she shifted like she was going to walk over to me, to see if I was okay, I held up my shaky hand to stop her.

Stay on mission. We had one chance here. I wouldn't be the reason we failed it.

She fought with herself for a moment, her instinct to help me at war with our goal.

Levi was whispering something I couldn't quite hear or

understand, his hands hovering over where I was certain our mother's corpse now lay.

Xavier merely watched us, attempting to appear bored and in charge, but I could sense the pulse of excitement in his posture. He thought he had us. He thought this was it. That he finally had Max.

People grew reckless, greedy when they assumed that they'd won.

Declan was right. We could get more out of him.

We could salvage this mission, make it worth—something. It had to be. We couldn't just go back empty handed. Not after—

"The woman," I nodded towards Amalia, not entirely able to bring myself to look at her, to see the splotches of my mother's blood left on her sheets, or dribbling down her chin, "what happened to her?"

Xavier's nose curled as he watched Amalia. She preened under his gaze, momentarily satiated by the snack, though I knew from firsthand experience that her hunger was nowhere near met.

The hunger never abated. It only grew worse, compounding on itself until more and more of her time would be spent in these rabid states.

He shrugged, disgust still baked into every line of his face as he glanced down at me. He turned his attention back to Dec. Apparently she was the only one of us worthy of being spoken to. "Some are too weak to hold the kind of power we wield. Two of the lesser council members died almost instantly. Since Amalia held on, I thought she would eventually follow my fate, that she would pull through from the transfusions. Clearly," he glanced at his girlfriend, a flicker of something unreadable in his eyes as he watched her try to break through her chains with a renewed fervor, "I was mistaken. She isn't strong enough."

"The stone," Declan said again, "where is it?"

"Impatient and arrogant, just as I've heard. We've been waiting for you. If you play nicely, we can take you to it. I think you'll like what we have to offer." Xavier laughed, the bark devoid of any real humor.

He took a step closer to her and she tensed in response.

I reached for the steady flow of fire, sensing that something in the room had shifted.

"You're—" his jaw hardened as he took a deep breath, his expression melting into rage. "You're not her."

He reached for Declan and I shifted to the bed, wrapping my arms around Amalia, my blade pressed to her throat.

"Don't touch her," I bit out, trying to fight the thrashing woman in my grip. Maybe this wasn't the best idea I'd ever had.

He may have been disgusted by her, but he cared for her. He wouldn't have gone to the trouble of setting her up in this room if he'd wanted her dead.

Xavier flinched, indecision flashing across his face before he shook his head, expression a blank mask. "Kill her. She's no use to me anymore. I have no tolerance for weakness."

"This isn't strength or weakness at play," Levi's eyes were hard, his voice dull as he watched Xavier, "only greed. You've stolen power that didn't belong to you, and it will corrupt you all. She's just experiencing the consequences on a faster timeline."

Xavier's expression hardened, and I met Declan's eyes briefly. She nodded once.

This was it, we weren't getting anything more out of either of them.

The stone wasn't here. This dude wasn't going to give us anything worth dying over. We were wasting time.

Sharp pain clawed at the back of my neck, then my scalp. "What the fuck?"

When I looked down at my arms, they were covered in deep, painful scratches.

I glanced around the room, searching for the culprit, but no one had moved. Amalia thrashed in my arms, but these cuts weren't from her.

It took me a moment longer than it should have for me to get over the shock and realize what this was.

Darius.

"Fuck." If Darius was in trouble—

When my eyes found Dec, I knew she'd come to the same conclusion.

He was with Max. Was she okay? Should we go to them?

No.

This wasn't the plan. They'd stick to the plan.

I didn't have time for my own fear.

They hadn't used the bond. They were fine. Just a few scrapes. I needed to focus.

In one fluid motion, I let Amalia go, just long enough to bury my blade into her chest. She fought against me, lost in a frenzy of hunger until the light finally dimmed in her eyes. For a moment, her expression softened, her eyes almost grateful as the last vestiges of life bled out of her.

Xavier yelled, and tried to attack Dec, but as fast as he was, she'd been prepared. A flare of fire spilled through the room, catching him off guard.

"But you have traces of her power. How—"

I ripped my blade from Amalia's chest and threw it into his.

I'd nicked his heart, I was certain, but it wasn't a clean enough shot. He was still alive, still moving. With one dark look at us, hand clutching the hilt of my blade, he teleported from the room.

"Fuck! No. We have to go after him." Levi ran his hands through his hair, darkening the strands with the blood that coated his fingers. "This—this can't have all been for nothing. We'll find him."

I knew that by "this" he really meant her death.

"It isn't here," I said, unable to meet the pain reflected so clearly in his eyes. "The stone."

"We know two of them are dead at least," Declan said. "And we know that they can't control the shadow magic as well as we thought. They aren't like Max. They weren't built for it. This wasn't for nothing."

"Three, now." I shoved Amalia off of me and wiped some of her gore on the already soiled bedding.

She nodded. "That means only four left. Hopefully the others had better luck locating the stone than we did."

The fight left Levi's body, his shoulders slumping as he bent down. He lifted Evelyn's body, cradling her in his arms.

"What are—" I swallowed the question when his gray eyes met mine. I let my gaze drop briefly to her face. Her eyes were open and empty. She looked frail, almost childlike in his arms. For the first time in years, I wanted nothing more than for her to look at me again, to pull me to her in a hug, to smell her hair as she pressed a kiss to my forehead.

I sniffed, shoved down the wave of emotion, and ignored the pressure tightening around my ribs.

"We're not leaving her here." All the teasing arrogance I was used to in Levi's voice had deflated.

I studied him, seeing small pieces of her etched into his face, pieces of me, too. For the first time that I could remember, he looked almost helpless, lost. A far cry from the man who'd been barking out orders and playing hopscotch on my last nerve for months.

Now, I saw him for what he was. Just a kid. One of us. Just another pawn who'd been abused by the fucked-up rules of the power-hungry Guild.

My little brother.

And I'd spent his entire life trying as hard as I could to push him out of mine. None of it was his fault. He hadn't asked for any of it.

No wonder he was such an insufferable asshole during the few times we'd been close enough to lodge insults.

A hollow ache carved itself deep inside of me, taking shape and making itself a permanent home.

The familiar sense of loss I'd long associated with my mother grew dense, unmovable. It was sharper now, and I knew it would be permanent.

She was gone. I wouldn't get a do-over with her.

But I could have one, maybe, with Levi.

I nodded. "You're right. We're taking her home."

And then, a bolt of pain, white-hot and angry shot through my stomach.

I bent over, fighting to catch my breath, but it was impossible.

When my hand pulled away from my stomach, I saw only red.

Until even that bled to black.

18

DARIUS

With every shift away from The Lodge, I felt more like myself.

And with Max wrapped in my arms, I felt loose, giddy even. Which was maybe strange seeing as we were about to confront another building filled with protectors.

"You alright?" Max whispered. The dark knowing in her eyes always seemed to see further into the depths of my own than I often wanted her to.

"Right as rain." I cracked my face into a wide smile that had her brother Rowan taking a few steps back, whether in repulsion or fear, I wasn't sure.

He'd insisted on being part of this mission. Something Max had fought him on for days.

She wanted him safe.

He wanted to come because he wanted to help keep *her* safe.

It was all very...saccharine. Familial.

Still, I couldn't help but like him more for it. There was a warmth to their sibling connection that I'd never had with my own brother.

Claude did everything he could to keep me alive, but it was usually done while simultaneously threatening to kill me.

I grinned. I needed to check in on that fucker once all of this was through. Maybe we could pare our sibling rivalry back to something a little more tender, rather than simply beelining for each other's tender parts with barbed steel.

The thought of Claude and I embracing with affection ripped a soft bark from my lips, startling the otherwise silent surroundings.

Haley, the vampire from The Lodge's council, was also with us for this mission. She shot me a dark look, eyes narrowed and brow arched, like she could sense the shift in my mood.

She wasn't interested enough to ask. And she also didn't seem to have a death wish. Vampires knew better than to shove their way into another vampire's business. Especially where they weren't wanted.

I flashed fang at her, then licked my lips and stretched my smile further until my cheeks started to hurt.

She grunted and turned away, losing interest in my antics quickly.

I'd learned almost instantly that she had little patience for, well, much of anything or anyone outside of her work at The Lodge. Bishop was the only person she seemed to share any joviality with, and even that was measured and restrained.

Made sense, he was also a bit of a prick with a god complex.

She studied the grassy forest where we were biding our time, vigilant as ever. We'd been training with her for days, preparing for this. She never once engaged in small talk, never once showed any interest in any of us beyond the larger goals.

That served me fine. I didn't want extra eyes on me.

Not when I'd been using all of my spare energy to keep Max and the others out of my head and away from the mess growing darker and encroaching closer each day. It was like a bottle of black ink had spilled, and it was now slowly blotting away any neat lines and boundaries I'd managed to draw on the page.

As far as Haley could tell, I was just another feral vampire excited for a kill and fresh burst of blood over my tongue.

She didn't know that I had my fill of Max daily. That all other blood was like sewage water in comparison.

Which was good. I didn't want to explain myself. Didn't want to get into the fact that I was just happy to be away from The Lodge for a bit.

That place had me on the edge of cracking. It was like the ghosts of my past had hooked into my stomach, slowly tugging, tugging, tugging, until the darkness that I could usually push down, hide in the cracks and crevices of my psyche, the ones that I'd learned to cordon off, were right at the surface. Screaming into a void I couldn't escape.

I was losing time. Waking up in the middle of the night, alone and outside in patches of the overgrown landscape I didn't remember walking to.

It wasn't like the sort of sleepwalking Max was experiencing. It didn't always even happen at night. Sometimes, I'd blackout full hours of the day, my happenings and actions a mystery even to me.

There were full group conversations and inside jokes that I had no recollection of, even though the impish glances from the others suggested that I'd been there for them.

Declan had made some teasing remark before we left, the corners of her mouth sinking down into a frown when I wasn't instantly responsive to it. I feigned a laugh after a beat, because for some reason I didn't like seeing her sad, and I definitely didn't want her going off into war with anything less than fond memories of me.

But still, it was wild for others to know your memories better than you did. I'd been spending less time with the group, the few moments we weren't training, a sort of reprieve from the act.

I knew it was nothing more than The Lodge, Charlie, and Bishop—they were relics from one of the darkest periods in my life. When I was lost to the twisted, relentless consequences of abandoning my post. I didn't need a therapist to tell me that they were dredging up memories I'd long tried to forget.

Max narrowed her eyes, took a step closer. She squeezed my hands, concern clear.

I'd avoided that look, that silent question for days. Brushed it off with a joke when I could, or ignored it altogether when I couldn't.

"I'm fine." And, for the first time in a long time, it was the truth. I could breathe here. Expand my lungs. My skin no longer felt too tight for my body, my thoughts no longer felt like they weren't my own. And I didn't feel quite as much like a ticking time bomb, just on the edge of explosion. "Promise."

"Are you sure?" She took a step closer, her stare darting through me, like she could sense the darkness lurking in shadows beneath my skin, more noticeable by its sudden departure. I'd done a decent job of keeping her out of my head when I didn't want her there, but she was smart, and she read me better than anyone. She knew things had been a little...off lately, but she'd given me the space I needed, when I needed it, letting me come to her when I was ready. I would be. As soon as we finished this fucking mission and got this magic mystery rock. "If not, we can go back. Tell the others. Regroup."

"The only thing," I tilted her chin up towards me, then bent down until my lips ghosted over hers, "that I want to do more than rip this council member's spine from his skull, is take you right now up against that tree, and bury myself so far inside of you that I'm the only thing in this world you feel." I nodded to the thick tree in question, relishing the blush creeping across her neck and cheeks. "Though I don't think it's quite strong enough to withstand all the things I want to do to you"

"Fucking hell," Rowan grumbled, turning green and pale in the same places Max was pink. "I don't need to hear this shit."

I shrugged. "You signed up to be on this mission with me."

Haley rolled her eyes, giving no other sign that she was witness to this conversation.

"To be on this mission with Max," he clarified, lip curled in disgust. "Now, I'm almost hoping someone comes running out of there and decapitates me."

"Your misery isn't allowed to end today, Rowan. My girl would miss you too much. For some reason." I pressed a kiss to her soft lips, momentarily tuning the others out. "Ready to go drench another campus in fire and blood, Little Protector?"

She fought it, but I tasted her excitement in the kiss. The bloodlust.

I'd been more or less teasing about the tree fucking—I'd planned on saving that for after the mission. A little post-battle reward. Fucking her while she was coated in the blood of her enemies was incentive enough for me to stick to the rules that Bishop and the others had outlined. But now, I truly was wondering if we had time for a first round before the battle started.

Something about the feral greed in her eyes was damn near irresistible. Especially now that I was feeling more myself than I had in weeks.

I stole one more kiss, brushing my tongue against hers, until all I could focus on was the minty sweetness of her.

With a groan, I pulled back. "Right, what's the plan?"

Haley snorted. "You know the plan. We all do."

Get in, get out. As quickly as possible.

"You feel anything yet?" Rowan took a few steps closer to Max, his dramatic disgust dissipating now that I'd chained my libido to an afterparty with Max and that tree.

Max took a deep breath, closing her eyes.

I did the same, knowing she'd feel the connection to the stone far more readily than I would. Nothing. When I dug deeper, all I could feel was the impending darkness, growing restless now that it had been caged after so much free time. I opened one eye, making sure no one else—specifically, Max—could somehow see that darkness leaking out of me.

Max sighed, shaking her head. "Not yet." She opened her eyes and scanned the thick trees.

We were in southern Brazil, inside a lush, almost absurdly beautiful forest. It was a shame protectors had hidden one of The Guild Headquarters here. Always difficult to parse evil up against such a beautiful backdrop. Maybe when all of this was done, I'd take Max here sometime. A honeymoon. Or a Congratulations-For-Saving-The-World surprise-sex vacation.

I could tell she liked it here. Her shoulders were tense in anticipation of what was coming, but when she looked at the tangles of trees surrounding us, it was like she was trying to commit each one to memory. Like she was afraid she'd never see them again.

"The Guild has a way of finding beautiful places to hide their insidiousness," Rowan said, following her gaze, as if he'd plucked the thought from my head. "Suppose it was naive of us to think there was a chance you'd be able to tell if the stone was here this far out. Guess we're going in."

"And no holding back," Haley glanced between the siblings, knowing full well I didn't need telling twice. I was more than happy to spill as much blood as Max was comfortable with on this little mission. "Don't let your conscience get in the way of the bigger picture, understood?"

Ro tensed, but Max simply nodded, less openly phased by the threat of violence than I thought she might be in present company.

"You'll get no argument from me. The Guild council is quite

literally threatening to destroy the world. They tortured Darius, Atlas, Sarah, and countless others. All in the name of their own greed. Their lives are forfeit as far as I'm concerned. I'll happily paint the room with their blood before they take another thing from us. Don't worry."

She glanced sheepishly at her brother, like she expected him to fight her on this.

He studied her for a long moment, jaw hard, but not with disgust. Pride, maybe?

He nodded once to her, something passing between the two of them, then glanced south, where the campus opened through the trees less than a quarter mile away. "Lead the way," his fingers flexed over his blade, "I won't flinch away from gutting anyone who attacks us."

Blood Bath Bentleys.

Maybe they weren't so unlike my brother and I.

Haley met my eyes, confusion and surprise written across her features.

I clapped my hands together before twining my hand with Max's. "Let's go kill some council members."

THE HALLS of the main building were bustling, drenched with the stench of sweaty protectors, mobilized by their lust for blood. They clustered together in packs, their reek stifling as we split up slightly, winding between and through them, trying to blend in.

Easier said than done, perhaps, but there was no escaping it. We had to use Max's powers with discretion now, all three attacks were rolling at once and we didn't have time to waste.

Still, hiding in plain sight wasn't the worst idea. I doubted any of these protectors expected several of the bodies on their most-wanted list to voluntarily pop into their halls, ready for capture or death.

I had Max's hand grasped tightly in mine, her fingers trembling slightly with adrenaline or fear—maybe both. It was her only tell that she didn't quite belong here, that something big was brewing in these blood-stained halls, and I kept her hand protected in mine, steadying it as we moved.

If I was honest though, having her close, feeling her skin against mine, helped steady my nerves as well. There were no guarantees of success here.

And voluntarily entering a vicinity owned by the very people who'd kept me captive for years wasn't exactly my idea of a relaxing afternoon.

Rowan and Haley were a few feet behind us. The boy's fingers kept twitching toward the blade in his holster, like he was fighting every instinct in his body telling him to reach for it.

Fastest way to get found out—shoving a blade in the face of the enemy as we moved through their nest.

I clenched my teeth, hoping like hell he'd manage restraint. Truthfully though, it was kind of nice to know that I was the one most visibly in control. Not counting Haley—she never betrayed even the slightest emotion.

And it was also rather sweet to see the blood-thirsty side of Max's brother.

I was liking him more each day.

Nameless faces scattered in my peripherals as Max moved forward with purpose, her eyes open but unfocused. I knew she was searching for it, the stone. Hunting. I dug inside of myself, tried to do the same, but all I could focus on, all that I felt, was her.

She was a beacon that my body stayed constantly attuned to. It took great effort to focus on anything else.

Max took a deep breath, shook her head once, before glancing quickly behind her at her brother.

Nothing.

Did that mean it wasn't here or did that mean that it was protected, shielded somehow? Were we simply too far from wherever it was kept? I wasn't sure what the radius on Max's radar was but—

"Bentley?" A stocky, pale boy with reddish hair stopped in front of us. The only word I could think of to describe his face was punchable. "You've got to be fucking kidding me. You're here? Fucking hell, you have to have the mental capacity of an acorn to show your face here." He snorted, then pulled out a phone as he turned back to a friend, equally punchable looking, ready to sound the alarm. "Tell Jarr—"

The boys neck snapped with a smooth crack as I held his head between my hands. He dropped in a puddle of limbs at my feet, whatever warning he was preparing simply dissolved on his tongue as death took him in its grasp.

His friend screamed, the sound low and loud, alerting every passerby in the hall of our presence.

Well, fuck. There went the element of surprise. My bad.

Max took a deep breath, her fingers clutched around a dagger as she glanced from me to Rowan.

I shrugged in response. "I'm not exactly well-practiced in subtlety."

"Well, here goes," Haley muttered, trying to maintain her usual ambivalence, but I didn't miss the way the corner of her eyes pinched with excitement.

Not fear.

It would have been dull if there was no bloodshed on this mission.

And Haley was clearly itching for a fight.

"Fucking hell." Rowan took a deep breath, sighed, and positioned his back against Max's as the four of us prepared for the sudden horde of protectors preparing to descend on us.

The two of them moved together with the kind of ease and comfort that came with years of trust. Honestly, having him on our team was a fucking privilege. No one needed Max alive as badly as I did. But her brother came in a close second.

His eyes darted briefly to mine. "Some of them are young, don't know any better. Try not to kill too many of them."

A woman, eyes green and round and filled with a venom that could have made plants whither descended on us first, her blade sinking into Rowan's bicep as she clawed at his face in an effort to get to Max—more rabid than any feral wolf I'd seen.

"Never mind," Rowan grunted, shoving the girl off of him and kicking her swiftly in the stomach. "Do what you have to do. You were right. Not much room for subtlety or nuance here, is there?"

I smirked.

From there, it was bloodshed. My teeth sank deep into one man's neck, tearing and tugging—I had no interest in his blood, only his death.

The others filed in formation, the hall filled with bones snapping and dull screams as the four of us took out anyone in our way.

Some of the protectors were smart—they saw the hallway floor striped with the blood and intestines of their peers and they disappeared down random halls, through doors that closed shut with the sound of heavy bolts after them.

But there were more pouring into the hall.

I let the darkness I usually did my best to shove down float to the surface.

An arrow shot past my head, crashing into a man attempting to strangle me. He dropped, eyes wide and glassy.

I recognized the syringe in his neck, and my limbs

temporarily froze, my body recognizing the memory before my mind did.

But there it was. The rancid scent of the poison clinging to my nostrils with the etchings of a memory that wouldn't fade, no matter how deep I tried to bury it.

The protector passed out, likely dead from the strength of a poison meant to knock out demons of a much higher caliber.

They weren't trying to kill us. They were trying to capture us.

Max.

They wanted her alive.

My stomach tightened with anger that rolled all the way up my throat, until I felt one inch away from breathing fire down these halls and burning them all alive for simply being in the same vicinity as her.

"We need to get out of here." I punctuated each word with a hit, flinging the unorganized protectors into the marble walls. "Too many, this is just going to get sloppy. We don't have time."

Max nodded, grabbed Ro in front of her and tugged him deeper into the hall, away from where the thickest parts of the horde of protectors were emerging.

I spun around, searching for Haley, but she was dragging her body towards me, eyes heavy, moving far slower than she should have been.

A syringe was buried deep in her leg. It was already dead, immobilized, unable to carry her weight.

I took a deep breath, weighing our options. Better to leave her and keep going. That was the plan. That was always the plan.

One glance at Max's wide eyes as she fought to pull her brother through, and I couldn't do it.

"Keep going," I yelled to her, "we'll meet you there and then you can shift us."

Before she could argue, I charged back into the throng of

protectors descending on Haley. I wouldn't use Max's fire until I absolutely had to. That was the rule. Until we absolutely needed them, we needed to keep the lines between our bonds free—keep her magic available for when it was the last option, desperately needed.

I slammed two protectors' heads together, feeling at least one skull fracture from the pressure. A knife nicked my arm, but I was too quick for them to sink the blade in properly.

It was annoying more than anything, fighting them. They were like bees, easy to crush and relatively harmless individually, but when you had a hive dropped on you, it was more difficult to deal with. Impossible without getting stung a few times.

Another arrow, no doubt laced with a sedative whizzed close. Haley shifted in front of me slightly so that it buried in her shoulder, instead of mine. Just as I got to her.

Those were the only real threats in this fight. The best chance these assholes had at winning against us.

At the question in my eyes she only smirked. "Better one of us get hit twice than both of us taken out. Go. Help the girl."

Even with her body slowly resisting her, she'd taken no shit. Her clothes were coated in blood that I could smell didn't belong to her, her eyes bright with adrenaline, face streaked with gore and the desire for revenge.

"Yeah, yeah, I'll leave you behind later," I mumbled, sweeping her into my arms before I took off at a run none of them could match.

Didn't stop them from trying.

As soon as I turned the corner, I found Max and Rowan. She hardly waited for me to come to a halt before she wrapped her arms around us and shifted us out of the mess.

When we rematerialized, Haley was practically frozen in my arms. Her dark eyes were the only sign of life as they broadcasted her animosity through to me.

"Sorry, friend," I whispered. And I was. I wouldn't want to

miss out on the fight either. And I knew what kind of hell this particular kind of prison could be—where even your own body turned against you, trapping you.

"So much for in and out without anyone noticing." Rowan ran a hand roughly through his hair as he scanned the dark room Max had brought us to. The strands of blond stood in weird angles of chunked clumps of red. "Still in the same building, I'm guessing?"

I nodded. "I can hear the fight still, we're just a floor or two above them."

Max's hair was a wild mess of knots and waves around her blood-streaked face. Her clothes were torn, the skin revealed through the holes already healed from whatever blades had made contact.

That didn't stop me from scanning every inch of her, just to be sure.

"Do you sense the magic?" her brother studied her, but gave her space. Seemed he could sense the frustration emanating from every pore just as clearly as I could, bond or not. "Should we just leave? Go to Plan B?"

"There is no Plan B." Her eyes were on fire, electric. "Not yet. We don't leave until we take one of the council members out. This is it—this is our only—"

She let out a frustrated sigh, the rest of the sentence dissolving in the silence.

We all knew the truth. That this was our only chance. There was no going back from this mission until we took out whichever council member was here and confirmed with certainty that the stone wasn't hidden somewhere in these walls. Hopefully the others would locate it, though there hadn't been any signal suggesting they had yet.

"And her?" I glanced down at the now-immobile vampire in my arms. "Do we just ditch her or..."

Haley's eye twitched and I bit back a grin, knowing full well we weren't going to.

"Pipe down, I went after you, didn't I? Don't worry, I'm not letting that scrape I got in the process be for nothing."

Max's jaw clenched as she considered. "We leave her in this room, shift here before we shift back home."

Rowan nodded. "Adds another step, another chance for something to go wrong. But it's the best option."

I arched a brow at the girl in my arms before setting her down in a corner of the dark room. "Sit tight. You're strong, well fed. Any luck and the poison they used will be out of your system before we're back." It felt strange just leaving her there, vulnerable and out in the open. Like a betrayal. Hopefully this room stayed abandoned long enough for us to finish the job. I nodded to Max and Ro. "Let's be quick then."

With a last apologetic glance at Haley, Max led the way from the room.

The fighting downstairs had gone quiet, and I could hear the rumble of shuffling feet throughout the building as they searched for us. In an ideal world, they'd give up soon and assume we left the premises altogether—think that we'd have to be mindless to stick around once we'd been discovered once.

To be fair, we kind of were.

Only plan or not, this one wasn't panning out as hoped.

We made it less than thirty seconds before we came face-to-face with two protectors. They both looked about Max's age, and judging from the wide-eyed shock on their faces, they recognized her instantly.

Rowan charged forward, knocking the first one's head into the wall—hard enough to stun them for a minute or two, not cause any lasting damage.

Just as I reached the second one, another protector appeared around the corner.

Blonde hair, blue eyes.

I...recognized this one.

She was at Headquarters that night. Had helped us with Atlas.

"Reza?" Max moved towards the girl, hesitant and unsure. "What are you—"

The girl's features sharpened and she reached for her pocket.

Instead of a blade, she grabbed a phone.

I dropped the now unconscious protector at my feet and ran towards her, ready for her to meet the same fate.

"Wait." Max stepped forward, arms out. "We don't want to hurt you if we don't have to. Just tell us where the council member's chambers are."

"So it's true. You really were reckless enough to come back." The girl's lips twitched slightly, as she gripped the phone tighter. But she wasn't dialing. "Why the fuck are you here? Didn't get your fill of destruction just yet?"

"Because we have to be." Max's tone was matter of fact but calm as she took a step closer to the girl. "We don't have a choice. Not if we want to make things better."

The girl snorted, her blue eyes coating in a sheen of wet. "Better? You burned down the fucking Guild, Max. I took you to him, to help him. To get him out. And you ruined fucking everything. My entire life is fucked because of you." She swallowed, her jaw tight and voice wavering slightly. "I don't want to help you. I want you gone. I want the life I had before I'd ever even heard your name."

That...sounded like a threat to the Little Protector.

A low growl burrowed in my throat as I shifted in front of her. One careful move and I could have this girl's heart painting drizzles of blood over my shoes.

Max grabbed my hand, a silent warning to keep the girl alive.

Ro's shoulder brushed up against mine. "You know that the world you had before was fucked, don't you? That we're trying to right the wrongs of The Guild?" His voice was calm, steady, even though I could feel his body coiled, ready to strike if things shifted even a millimeter in the wrong direction.

"Just tell us where the council chambers are, Reza. Tell us and you can leave. Get your mom, whoever you want out of here. Leave The Guild and don't come back. Make whatever life you want on your own terms. They're the ones who've taken everything from you. Not me." Max took a deep breath. "We don't want to hurt you. We don't want to hurt anyone." She stepped towards the girl, careful and steady, like she was approaching a stray cat. "But we will if it's our only choice."

Reza swallowed, then dropped her arm until her phone hung limply at her side. "My mom is dead." She sniffed, then shook her head like she was frustrated with her body for betraying emotion. "They killed her. After that night, after what happened. I think she challenged them, wanted to leave. And they—"

Her words were punctuated by the soft crescendo of steps.

A thick, muscular boy rounded the corner, eyes hard as he took in Reza's cornered position, then the rest of us.

Before he had time to react, Reza knocked him to the ground, and after a fluid, graceful maneuver that disguised its proficiency, he was unconscious.

She stood up, turned back towards us, her eyes hard as they found Max. "His chambers are in the east wing, but he spends most of his time in a war room in the north. With the alarm of your arrival sounded, that's probably where he will be."

"Where exactly in the north wing?" Ro asked.

"I'll take you there," she took a deep breath, "but then I never want to see any of you again for as long as I live."

Traveling the halls with Reza was smooth, if smothering and uncomfortable. She knew a few passageways behind secret doors that cut our time down significantly, and we made it to the north wing without meeting another protector.

"I spent a lot of time here when I was growing up. Other side of this painting," she whispered, her voice carrying through the dark tunnel anyway. "That's the entryway. He's usually in one of the three rooms in this suite."

Max was quiet for a moment, considering this girl whose relationship to her I didn't fully understand. Both times I'd seen them interact, they seemed to hate each other. Though Max's dislike appeared more reactionary to the girl's clear hostility than anything else. "You can come back with us. If you want. You have more information now, about the truth. You're allowed to change your mind based on that. You can join us, start over there."

Even in the dark, I could see the shadows of the girl's face drop in surprise. She considered for a moment as she studied Max, but then her jaw sharpened and she straightened her posture. "I meant what I said. I want nothing to do with you. With any of this, or any of you."

Without another word, she turned and started walking back the way we'd come.

"Where are you going?" Ro whispered, clearly as conflicted as I was about letting her just...leave.

"Getting out of here before she burns this place down. You should too, if you know what's good for you. Death and destruction cling to her like shadows." Her words snapped harsh, with finality.

Without another glance back, she took off at a run.

I tensed, tempted to go after her, snap her neck, tie up any loose ends. I was grateful for her help, but I didn't like the idea of leaving a potential vulnerability festering in the wind.

"Don't." Max rested her hand on my forearm, her warmth fighting back any chill I felt with being back in protector territory. "Let her go. She's right."

"Bit dramatic, isn't she?" Ro said with a half-hearted smirk, a wry attempt to lighten the mood. "Far as I know, you've only burned down one campus. That's hardly a pattern."

"So far," I added. "Let's see where her penchant for pyrotechnics gets her by the end of the night."

Max snorted. With a quick look at us both, she shoved the painting forward, drawing a thick wash of bright light into the tunnel as the room opened before us.

Like a portal into a strange realm, dark into light, we emerged. Only the room wasn't empty, as we'd anticipated.

There were at least thirty people crowded together, their chaotic and erratic mutterings hushed into silence as they turned towards us.

"Fuck," Ro whispered, "it can never be easy, can it?"

"Ah," a soft, disembodied voice called from within the crowd, "you're here. Good. Now I don't have to do the tedious work of searching for you in this labyrinth of a monstrosity they deign to call a castle."

19

MAX

The sea of people parted, revealing a man—bald, white, and dressed in heavy velvet robes like he was cosplaying for some wizard convention.

I recognized him immediately.

He'd been there that night, at Headquarters. He was the council member who'd teleported away, right before I'd burned everything to the ground.

The one who'd infused his veins with shadow magic he'd stolen from the demons The Guild held captive, from the stone.

"Much preferred the other site. Simpler, more...pragmatic." He scrunched his nose, scanning the walls with distaste, an artist unimpressed with the current exhibit. "But I suppose it has served its purpose after you turned the other branch to ash." HIs brow arched. "Impressive display, if a bit excessive."

My fingers tingled, flooding with a desire to pull my fire up as a shield between us and them.

I scanned the people quickly, trying to assess who they were. A few of them looked vaguely familiar, like I'd seen them in passing while living at The Guild, but I couldn't recall any names. Most I was certain I'd never laid eyes on before.

A woman walked forward, the angles of her pale face severe and shadowed. She moved slowly, but with a grace that I could never muster, until she was shoulder-to-shoulder with the man.

Her robes looked more modern than his. They'd clearly been tailored to fit her like a glove. But it was the insignia at her collar that had my pulse thumping quickly.

Another council member. We were standing before two of them.

"This is Elizabeth," he said, arching a brow that was all muscle and no hair, "one of my colleagues."

She made no response to the acknowledgment. Like him, there was something off about her. There was no sheen of shadow magic glimmering in her eyes, but there was something unmistakably wrong—like her skin was an ill-fitting costume over a magic that had contorted her from within. It no longer fit quite the same as it perhaps once did.

To a human, or even a protector, she probably looked no different than she had before the magic. Dark hair was pinned in a tight bun at the nape of her neck, and makeup was impeccably applied to highlight and add color to her features.

It was the shadow magic. It clawed and licked against my skin, until the hair on my arms stood at end. The tune in the air was sharp and out of key, the static electricity of the atmosphere pricked and fizzled along my body.

"And my name is Jarrod." He took a step closer and Darius shifted forward until his arm pressed against mine. "It's time we were properly introduced. I've been waiting to speak with you."

I made no response, not offering him anything.

I could get Ro and Darius out of here—a thing I reminded myself of on a careful, constant loop. I wasn't certain that I could take on two council members. We didn't know the extent of their power, or whether mine matched theirs in strength or ability.

I knew that between me and Darius, we could handle the rest in the room. And Ro wasn't a slouch either.

But they were all clearly armed, and we were cornered into a tiny hole in the wall. Every advantage was theirs.

Except for the fact that we could run. Back through the tunnel, back to Haley. I could teleport, get us out of here.

If it came to that.

Until it did, we needed to use this moment for what it was—an opportunity.

Jarrod was clearly full of himself. The smug lines of his face made it clear that he thought he was in control, that he had something to offer.

And he had the one thing I was after—information.

It wouldn't be impossible to use his arrogance, his flare for the dramatic to our benefit.

I stepped down from the portrait ledge and walked into the room, ignoring Ro and Darius's blistering glares behind me as they moved to stand on either side. Tension radiated from them both—somehow stifling and comforting me in equal measure.

I nodded to the stiff protectors in the room, noting the collection of blades, dart guns—and even a few regular guns—clutched in their hands, many of which were pointed in our direction. "This the reception committee you typically reserve for conversations?"

Jarrod's lips thinned into a smirk, one that didn't quite work with the musculature of his face. Forced. Brittle.

He was trying to keep things contained, but he wasn't very good at it. Eagerness lined every twitch of his thin fingers.

"I don't often hold meetings with people who have the power to burn down the room I'm standing in with one snap of their fingers." That slimy grin quivered slightly, like it was fighting to hold the unfamiliar stretch. "And I've been told that you and your—" he nodded towards Darius and then Ro, "friends—have slaughtered many innocent protectors just moments ago, under this very roof. I'd say that warrants a bit of a protective detail, wouldn't you?"

Ro straightened. "We didn't initiate that fight."

"Perhaps not." Jarrod's eyes narrowed briefly, then he turned to his guard, hands raised. "But in the spirit of goodwill, so long as Miss Bentley agrees not to use her powers, we can all put our weapons down. I believe that we can all stand to benefit from a brief conversation. A temporary truce that will perhaps last an eternity, if you like what I have to say."

Elizabeth hadn't shifted an inch, her eyes, unblinking, drove through me like a laser—sharp, but like she was looking beyond me.

The others, after a few cursory glances and grunts, lowered their weapons to their sides.

It was a meaningless gesture, as we all knew. It would take half a breath for them to be back and pointing at us, but I was faster than they were. And so was Darius.

We'd get ourselves and Ro out of here if needed.

"You see, Miss Bentley," Jarrod spread his arms, pausing, "is it okay to call you that? I know of course that you aren't truly Cyrus's child." Cy's name on his lips landed like a barbed arrow in my chest. "I'm very sorry for your loss by the way. Tarren has always been rather—over-eager and careless when emotions are high. But from what I understand, you've taken your revenge." I swallowed the pain, a scorching metal knot in my throat; did my best to ignore the current of rage washing over me. He let out a breathy laugh, his hands coming together. "No worries girl, we hold no bad blood where that is concerned. A life for a life, no one could fault you for that. But past events aside, I've been waiting for you to reach out again. You've been rather difficult to track down, you see. But I believe we can help each other."

Still, I said nothing.

His right eye twitched and I could tell he was growing frustrated with my stubbornness and doing his best to hide it. "As you've no doubt deduced, we've been experimenting with magic."

"Stealing it, you mean," Darius bit out.

"Our connection to this magic goes back millennia." Jarrod's jaw clenched. "We are just attempting to harness and control it so that we might protect the world from what's to come. We will need power to survive it, order." With a quick, frantic movement, he pulled up Elizabeth's shirt sleeve, revealing dark, angry-looking bruises bubbling under her skin from her veins, like an ink spill, the spread slow and webbed. Then, with a small cringe, he revealed the same under his own cloak. "But you see, we aren't exactly perfectly equipped as hosts. At least not yet." He sighed, dramatic and low, as if this was a performance that he'd practiced several days in front of the mirror. "Two of ours have died and while the rest of us have survived the transfusions, we haven't metabolized as successfully as we'd hoped. But you," he shifted his chin up, eyes meeting mine dramatically, as his band of protectors hung on every word of his sermon, "you, I believe, are the key to our success. To everything. To saving humanity and protectors alike. A conduit, it seems, perfectly made for this magic to flow through. Aren't you, girl?"

Darius grunted. "Magic isn't something to control and shape into your liking. How have you not learned that yet? What's happening right now?" He shook his head, frustration and disdain mapped out on his eyes. "It's because protectors have warped this power. Time has stripped your people of it because you did not respect it as you should have. Your greed has made the magic hungry, chaotic, violent."

On the surface, what Jarrod was spouting sounded almost in line with what Lucifer had told me. But I knew enough of this Guild council's greed to not believe benevolence was their goal. No matter how they framed it.

"I can't speak for the past." Jarrod's nostrils flared slightly, but he otherwise made no sign that he'd heard Darius, his dark eyes not moving from mine as he continued. "You see, with your power, we can seal off hell for good," he continued, oblivious to the tension lining every muscle in my body, "destroy it and everything within it, even. If you let us wield your power, link your power with ours, we can accomplish the original goal of our ancestors. Rid the world of demons forever. Save this world and all the people in it. For good. Protectors would be free—to live and exist in harmony with humanity. No more forced bonds. No more fighting. Just peace. We want the same thing, Miss Bentley. A life worth living, one unencumbered by evil or the duty to destroy it."

My jaw was stiff with how tightly my teeth were grinding together. But I couldn't hold back my disgust. "You mean that you want to use me to kill *everyone* in hell? They're people, not things. No less worthy than anyone in this realm."

"You know little about what exists in the depths of hell, Miss Bentley. Of what even the creatures who live there have tried to keep locked, buried." He steepled his fingers and brought them to his lips, nodding and eyes shut, the gesture performative and dramatic. "Nevertheless, you have compassion, empathy. Again, I can't fault you for that, however misguided it may be. I was warned that your sympathies have," his gaze landed briefly on Darius before meeting mine again, "expanded. Matters are serious enough that we are willing to work with you, to put these differences of ours aside. They are small, in the grand scheme of things. We've been diligently working on a compromise these last months. And my researchers believe we've found a way, perhaps, to simply close the realms. Forever. It's more complicated, and will put you more at risk. It will require all of your power—and ours. You must bond yourself to us—fortify the line of anchors for centuries to come." He held his arms wide in front of himself, an invisible offering. "And, in the spirit of laying it all out there, even then, I can't promise it will work."

"Bond?" Darius's voice was a low rumble, one that I felt reverberate through my chest with menace. "Over my dead body. And yours."

"Your friends may stay in this realm of course," Jarrod continued, oblivious to Darius's brewing, dangerous rage, "as a thank you for your part in this mission. But it is possible that we've found a way for the hell realm to go on existing, eternally severed from ours. Perhaps everyone can win, Miss Bentley, don't you see? A world without demons plaguing our kind—it's the protector dream manifesting before our very eyes. How very lucky you are, to be the one to grant it."

"You want us to damn everyone who's been shoved into that prison your people created, you mean?" Darius's tone was light, casual to the unpracticed observer, but I could feel the disgust lacing every syllable. When I glanced at him, I saw the familiar restraint buckling and bending as he tried to contain it. Darius had been so on edge, so close to snapping these last few weeks. And now, I could see him tap dancing erratically on the last millimeters of that cliff. "So that you can maintain your position unchallenged as the most powerful creatures in this world. Curious, it's the council specifically who needs to bond with her." He shook his head then turned to me. "He's lying, Max. That's not how the magic between realms works. It's powered by balance, feeding from both sides. Hell cannot exist if that connection is forever severed. He can't possibly know otherwise."

"Protectors *are* demons," Ro added, his voice unwavering, "just weaker. This has always been about protectors wanting more power. Even if you could manage it, Darius is right. You just want to secure a future in which you remain at the top of the food chain. And this time," he nodded to me, "you want to use her power to amplify and fortify your own. You're too weak for it without her. The magic you siphoned is clearly destroying —" he grunted, disgusted, "*rejecting*—you. You're insufficient hosts. Unworthy."

Jarrod's facade of ease and magnanimity slipped instantly from his expression. His jaw was tight, eyes narrowed and heated, as he lowered his arms, clenching his hands into fists at his side. I could tell he was resisting the urge to reach for this blade, which I took as a good sign. It meant that he was more comfortable using that in a fight than he was his magic. That bode well for us.

Several of the protectors who'd been quiet and obedient so far, lifted their weapons, preparing for the moment this farce of a truce broke into the inevitable war it was always going to be.

"Curious," he said, nostrils flaring slightly as his eyes darted between the three of us, "that the people who are supposed to care for this girl above all else are so quick to hold onto their own prejudice," He grinned, dark and malicious, "and condemn her to an early grave in the process."

I froze, my lungs emptying.

Please no.

Not here.

Not right now.

Not like this.

Ro shifted his weight. "What?"

"Enough," I choked out as soon as I could find the barest sliver of my voice. "This isn't—" I shook my head. "The stone. Where are you keeping the stone?"

This was the only piece of information worth ripping from the man before me. Everything else was lies and propaganda. He didn't care for the survival of this world or humanity, only his own.

A cold, harsh bark of a laugh ripped from his lips as he focused on Darius, on Ro—ignoring me entirely for once.

"So she hasn't told you?" He tilted his head, meeting my

eyes again. "Or perhaps you don't even know yourself." He read the truth, which I knew was now etched clear as glass on my face, no matter how hard I tried to disguise it. "No, the former. Well," he clapped his hands together in glee, the crash of the sound echoing through the room, "perhaps this will help persuade your companions to my side. You see," he took a step closer to Ro, identifying him as the safer target apparently, "the ritual your sister is planning requires several things—most expensive among them, her life."

Turn around.

Grab them both, teleport the fuck out of here.

Now.

But, for some reason, I couldn't move. Couldn't breathe. Black dots swam in my vision, blurring the scene before me, until it felt like I was watching the realization unfold from above—outside of my body, a passive observer no different than the army of protectors lining the room. My fingers battled between tingling and numbness, and I couldn't convince my muscles to move.

Do something. Do fucking *anything*, Max. Come on.

All I could do was stand there, watch this scene play out with Jarrod in complete control.

"You didn't really think any one person could survive it, did you?" Jarrod's tone was taunting now, and I could feel the conflict burrowing through Ro on my right, the struggle not to believe the words this asshat of a man was uttering. "No one person could survive pulling that much power through herself —the very power used to create and stabilize the realms for centuries? Come now, boy—" he shook his head, made an infantilizing tsking noise as he moved closer, "I'm certain Cyrus raised you to be smarter than that."

"It's not true." Ro's body was coiled, every muscle begging to spring into action and attack this man. But he reigned it in and turned to me. "Max, tell him."

Darius was silent, an impossible stillness and blankness that terrified me more than any of the people in this room could.

A hot tear spilled down my cheek, anger I couldn't swallow back—but also guilt. I fought to take a breath, but my lungs refused to work.

"No." Ro took a step back like I'd slapped him.

I felt something shift in the room, something dangerous and all-consuming.

It called to me, both familiar and not.

But it wasn't coming from Jarrod, or Elizabeth, or the anxious hum of protectors who were not-so-discreetly lifting their weapons and preparing to attack at the drop of a hat.

It was Darius.

His eyes were daggers, unfamiliar and unseeing as I tried to make contact.

His breathing was labored, like he was fighting some heavy battle I couldn't see. The veins along his forearms were defined and bulging, the grip of his fists so tight that blood was streaming through his fingers and pooling onto the floor.

"What are you doing to him?" I turned to Jarrod, then back to my vampire, scanning for the signs of a wound—just, something. But he was untouched.

Elizabeth's focus shifted to Darius, looking for the first time since I laid eyes on her like she wasn't utterly bored.

"I—" Jarrod looked confused, then took a step back, shaking his head.

He hadn't done anything.

The confused stares pulsing with concern and apprehension from the other protectors suggested it wasn't any of them either.

Fuck.

My fear for Darius helped break through my paralysis.

I reached through my bond, desperately trying to feel

Darius, to communicate, to see what was going on, but it was clogged. Blocked. I mentally screamed to him, but my voice withered into nothing, swallowed by a void.

I reached for his arm, tentative and slow. "Dariu—"

He erupted in flames—hot and angry. They spread through the room, taking out the protectors on his side of the room in a single breath.

Jarrod's eyes widened, his face somehow growing even paler as he backed away from us. With a quick glance in my direction, he muttered a hurried "until we meet again, Miss Bentley," before he teleported from the room, leaving the others to fend for themselves.

The dozen or so protectors who'd survived the first wave scrambled and clamored over each other as fire spread through the room. Everything caught, until the entire suite was engulfed.

Screams echoed through the room, a harmony from hell.

"Go!" I shoved Ro back through the tunnel as heat licked at my face.

Stubborn as always, he resisted. "I'm not leaving you."

"This is my power. I'm immune to it," I gritted out, as heat flared along my back, both a caress and scorch. Smoke curled through the air and the crackle of flames was punctuated by the loud coughing coming from those still alive, their voices no longer capable of screaming. "You're not. Go back to Haley."

"No. Max—"

I knew that stubborn set of his jaw, that particular angle of his eyes.

Ro, please. Just this once. Just go.

"I'll come to you. As soon as—" I glanced at Darius. Pure, unadulterated rage emanated from every last inch of him, unlike anything I'd ever seen before. Truthfully, even if I could protect Ro from the fire, something told me he wasn't safe from the man standing next to me. None of us were. "Please go. Please just go."

Ro hesitated another moment, his mouth tight as he witnessed the destruction behind me—destruction I was trying like hell not to look back at right now. With a frustrated groan, his eyes met mine. "Five minutes, Max. That's all you have before I come back."

And then he left.

Satisfied, I exhaled, choking on smoke when I took another breath.

Once I was certain Ro was far enough back, that he was safe from Darius's inferno, I turned around.

Every last protector was gone, nothing more than bones and ash on a floor that was disintegrating and collapsing to the room below us.

Still, the fire only blazed harder, catching through the suite, to whatever lay beyond that, leaving destruction and pain in its wake.

Elizabeth was the only one still standing.

Rather than run, she simply watched me, expression vacant.

Without uttering a word, she walked into the fresh wave of hellfire ripping from Darius—silent and stoic until the last beat of her heart.

And then we were alone.

Why didn't she go after Jarrod? Why didn't she teleport?

"Darius," I yelled, trying to reach him through the chaos.

My foot caught on a crack in the floor that opened into a huge hole. I heaved myself up before I fell through completely.

"Darius," I tried again.

He either didn't hear me or didn't want to respond.

Fire snaked through the tunnel now, the walls crumbling with a fresh blast of flames.

I tried to call it back, to pull the fire from him like we'd practiced so many times, but I couldn't.

He'd cut me off. I had no idea how, but I couldn't reach him.

A loud crash sounded on the other side of the wall and screams pierced through the hall.

We needed to get out of here. Now.

Jumping over a particularly gnarly wall of flames, I reached him.

When I grabbed his face between my hands, his eyes finally met mine. But they were cold and hard, the usual warmth nowhere to be seen.

But he didn't hurt me. Didn't attack.

That was something.

"It's okay," I whispered, temporarily lost in his dark stare. "It's okay. Breathe. You're safe. I'm safe. We need to leave this place."

He didn't respond, but he wasn't pulling up fresh waves of fire either.

"Darius, come back to me."

Something flickered in his stare, but I still couldn't quite reach him.

"We need to get out of here." Not bothering to explain my plan, I held onto him and teleported to the room where we'd left Haley.

Ro had her cradled in his arms, his eyes hard when they met mine.

Without a word, I grabbed his arm and shifted us outside.

Protectors swarmed the grounds. The wing we'd been in was completely swallowed by a fire that only seemed to be gaining momentum. The top floors had collapsed, leaving nothing but rubble.

I took in the sight for one breath before I shifted us again, pausing no more than a second between each jump until my feet finally planted on the familiar rocky shore of the lake.

Ro dropped Haley and fell to his knees as he spilled the contents of his stomach on the ground.

Even I felt a little queasy, my strength completely drained. I'd never pushed the limit quite that far before without breaking for at least a few minutes between the longer jumps.

Haley was still out from the poison, but her fingers twitched like she was slowly regaining feeling and control.

"You're back!" A voice called behind us.

I spun around, still struggling to catch my breath, for my brain and body to catch up to what had just happened.

Charlie came running, a warm smile tugging her lips, though it slowly melted, her expression etching with lines of concern as her eyes shifted beyond me.

Darius.

When I turned to find him, he'd moved at lightning speed.

He pinned Charlie to a thick tree and sank his teeth deep into the side of her neck. No preamble, no warning.

Her scream reverberated through the woods, slicing through me like a blade.

"No." My stomach dropped.

No.

No, no, no.

I ran to them and used all of my remaining strength to pull him off of her, trying like hell not to let his teeth tear her up too badly in the process.

I succeeded, eventually, but it was one of those moments that felt like a lifetime.

Blood coated her shirt and neck, but it didn't appear like he'd hit an artery.

One small fucking win, at least.

Ro was at her side almost as quickly as I was and caught her as she started to fall.

She was pregnant. And part protector. I had no fucking clue what his bite would do to her. Or her unborn child.

Darius had moved back. He was twenty feet or so away from us now, pounding his fists into a large boulder that stood in the middle of the shallow part of the lakeshore.

"Darius—" I stepped towards him, then looked back at the mess of gore staining Charlie's shirt, stuck between helping her and stopping him. I froze for a moment, trying to decide where I was of the most use.

"I have her. She's alive," Ro said, shooing me forward. "Go. Stop him. Before he attacks her or someone else again."

I nodded, unable to find words, as I ran towards Darius.

Water bit at my ankles and calves but I hardly noticed it as I reached him.

"Darius—"

He punched his fist into the boulder again. His bones cracked as bits of stone and dirt rained down into the lake, chipped and pulverized.

Blood was everywhere—his and Charlie's.

"Darius stop!"

He didn't.

He wouldn't look at me.

He was punishing himself, trying to keep from hurting anyone—fighting whatever spell or magic had control of him right now.

There'd been moments, since I met him, when I watched him sink into himself. I knew he fought darker impulses. Knew from his brother Claude, that his role as a portal guardian—and the subsequent abandonment of his post—had infected him with shadow magic. The power was hungry and alive, requiring a balance that Darius constantly resisted, warped and dangerous as it was.

I'd never seen it get this much of a hold over him though. Not even close.

I stepped between Darius and the rock, preparing to fend off any sudden attacks if I had to.

But he froze, blinking. Fear shone like a beacon from his stare, gutting me with the war of guilt and bloodlust that tore through him.

"She's okay. She'll be okay. You didn't mean it. I know you didn't mean it. Breathe, Darius. Breathe."

His eyes met mine again, brief and piercing, and I could see a world of emotions reflected back at me.

One was strong, clear as day. Betrayal.

I'd lied to him. Had been planning to see this war to my grave for months. And now he knew it.

He shook his head, took a few steps back, until the water licked at his waist. Blood-coated fingers threaded through his platinum locks and he tugged, letting out a bellowing scream that sang equal parts rage and pain.

He tore at his scalp, the back of his neck, his arms, his shoulders, lines of red etched in every bit of skin he touched, painting his misery across the smooth expanse of his skin.

"No, Darius—" I waded over to him and grabbed him in my arms as he shook and thrashed and resisted.

For a fraction of a second, something rippled through him and he stilled briefly.

I thought, for a moment that he was breaking through, that he was fighting his darker impulses back.

Just as a wave of relief flooded my belly, his teeth pierced the flesh at the base of my neck.

I stiffened for a moment, shocked. Then I tried like hell to shove him away, but his grip was a vice, pulling me closer, tighter against him.

He'd fed from me many times, but he'd never pulled so much, so deeply—so violently.

Blood streamed down my shirt, raining droplets over the lake surrounding us.

I clawed my fingers into his back, caught between stopping

him and letting him take his fill. Maybe he needed to feed, maybe that would help whatever—this—was?

"Darius," I whispered against his chest, where only scraps of his shirt remained. I tasted salt and iron on his skin.

My vision blurred, blotting out at the edges as I fought for control, for consciousness.

Darius

I felt the bond, the link between us, reached and grabbed for it like the lifeline I knew it to be—but it was difficult, as tenuous as threading rope through an impossibly small needle.

He stiffened, his hand snaking down the side of my body, stopping at my thigh.

With a gasp, he ripped his teeth from my flesh, then threw me back with enough force that I landed on my ass a few feet closer to shore.

Cold waves lapped against my skin, cooling the wound there that would be closed by nightfall.

My dagger hung loosely at his side. With stiff, hurried force, he gripped the sheath in both hands and buried it deep into his stomach.

He leaned back, face lifted to the sky and yelled.

The sound was deep and heart wrenching. It tore through the sky.

A ripple in the air separated us and a flash of light, the scene shifting slightly, like transparent photographs set on top of each other.

A heavy sound pulsed around us—low but palpable, like a raucous crack of thunder. The aftershocks shook the lakeshore, rattling the trees and everything in sight.

A thick wave thrashed over me, pulling me under. When I emerged back to the surface, there were two of him.

I blinked a few times, fighting the waves as I stood back up. I walked towards the two Dariuses, my mind fighting like hell to make sense of this.

"Claude?"

Another figure stood suddenly beside him—a man I recognized from hell.

Nash.

In his arms was a girl. Her body was draped and still, though whether she was dead or had simply passed out, I wasn't sure.

Darius's twin allowed confusion to take him over for exactly three seconds as he glanced at the new arrivals, but not a moment longer.

His jaw set in a hard line as his eyes found his brother.

The rippling air between us transformed back to stillness.

"Fucking hell," Claude muttered, "you're a mess."

With a resounding crack, he snapped Darius's neck—not bothering to catch him as he collapsed and the water swallowed him whole.

20

ATLAS

Bishop turned to Tex, who he'd tapped to join our arm of the mission. "You can shift now if you want."

Without a word, Tex mechanically kicked off his shoes, tugged off his clothes, cracked his neck in one direction and then the other, before the transformation took over.

His wolf form seemed to come so naturally to him, and I bit back my jealousy.

It was strange, missing the tenuous connection I'd been developing with my wolf. My time in The Guild labs sent me back so far in the process that I couldn't even be mad that Bishop wanted to tap another wolf for our prong of the attack.

Tex would be in wolf form, which he honestly seemed to prefer.

In all of my time at The Lodge, during all of our training together for today, I'd never heard Tex utter more than a grunt in acknowledgement.

I knew he was with Charlie's friend, Mer, but that was the extent of my knowledge.

Tex's wolf was deep shades of red and brown, as bulky and muscular as the man he shared a body with.

He shook out his thick fur, and sank low to the ground, nose pressed to the dirt and grime, assessing the small abandoned barn we'd chosen for our holding pattern. Our mark was less than fifty feet away, so once we left these dilapidated walls, there'd be no more element of surprise, no going back.

In his wolf form, Tex's senses would be stronger than ours, so he'd be the first to notice if we had company. That eased some of my anxiety.

But only some. The majority of my fear was thousands of miles away with Max.

I hated that we were all separated. Bishop's plan was a good one, but I honestly would have preferred if it hadn't been.

We were in the Midwest, somewhere between Cleveland and Detroit, where one of the satellite branches of The Guild operated. I'd been here before, as had Bishop and Wade, so we were the ideal candidates to take on this location.

Finding our way through the place wouldn't be the difficult part though.

"Never thought I'd get to go on a mission with you two after all," Bishop said, his mouth curving into a small grin, no longer looking quite as nauseous as he had when we'd finished our journey. "Kind of exciting, isn't it?"

"When I was a kid, I always hoped Atlas and I would end up on a team with you." Wade snorted. "Never imagined that our first mission together would involve infiltrating The Guild and offing a member of the council."

Bishop's smile widened and he clapped a hand down on Wade's shoulder the way he used to when he was half his size. "Kind of exciting though. Charlie almost always has me busy at The Lodge. I rarely get out into the world, a taste of the action and all that."

I smiled in spite of myself, recalling the list of 'make sures' and 'be carefuls' that Charlie had saddled him—and then the rest of us—with, before giving him an awkwardly long kiss that had made me feel like a voyeur to witness.

"You've made a good life for yourself, Bishop." I nodded towards the door, ready to go. We'd been the last group in the procession, so we didn't have the luxury of waiting around too long. Which, honestly, was ideal. Adrenaline had me bouncing on my feet, raring to go. "Let's get in, get out, and get you home to your family before Charlie sends a search party.

He laughed, his eyes lighting up at the mention of her.

I meant it. Apocalypse and chaos of The Lodge and all that came with it aside, I was happy for Bishop. He'd found a community, a home. I'd missed him, and grieving his loss was tough, but it warmed me now to know that this kind of life was possible—-that people who'd grown up in our family, with fathers like Tarren, had a chance at working through all the bullshit.

At finding tenderness.

It gave me hope for whatever possible future I might carve out with Max. Like maybe I wasn't as much of a lost cause as I'd told myself I was.

"You think the lab is the best starting place?" Wade asked, eyes darting around as we shuffled towards the large warehouse-like building in front of us.

The grounds were quiet, and Tex guided our path around the couple of protectors who'd been out patrolling.

He was good. Quick, quiet, and oddly adept at communicating in his wolf form.

Bishop and I both nodded.

Their lab was less sophisticated than the one back at Headquarters had been, but I had a feeling they'd used some of their time in the last months fortifying and strengthening it.

It was the second-largest Guild campus in the States, so it made sense that Evelyn clocked Rebecca, one of the oldest council members, here.

The entry hall was quiet, nothing but the dull, cobwebbed lights casting over the worn, red carpet and a few scattered chairs.

Bishop glanced at me, nodded, and we moved in, following Tex deeper into the building.

This structure was only two floors and a basement, and I knew that the second floor was almost exclusively living quarters.

If Rebecca wasn't in the conference area that team leaders frequently used to debrief, then she'd almost certainly be in the basement.

That's where the most security was, and where the inner workings of this station usually went down.

It was also where I'd spent the majority of my time during my brief stays at this branch.

Tex froze, a low growl emanating from him—a growl my own wolf felt and responded to.

I grabbed my blade and nodded to Wade and Bishop to be on alert.

We weren't as alone as we thought we were.

Rather than stay and find out, or get caught by whoever was close by, we took off at a run. Better to find what we came for as quickly as possible—fewer chances for fucking up or getting caught off guard that way.

But when we turned into the hall, we met two people. Both looked to be in their late twenties and both were clearly not expecting us.

"Who are you?" The shorter one asked, his curiosity melting almost instantly to terror when his gaze snagged on Tex. "Fuck."

His friend took off in the opposite direction, running as fast as he could.

Tex glanced back at Bishop, whose lips were pressed in a

grim line, and at his nod, eclipsed the distance to the runner, until he overtook him completely.

The attack was quick and brutal, and the protector's corpse lay mangled on the floor, the red carpet beneath him turning a darker shade as it absorbed his blood.

Wade knocked the other guy out, who'd let surprise cannibalize any chance at responding forcefully to our presence.

Unconscious, not dead. Probably. I didn't much care either way, if I was being honest. Not anymore.

But when I looked back, I saw three sets of eyes disappear around the corner.

Fuck. More of them.

Before I could take off after them, a sharp, loud alarm reverberated through the building, echoing through the hall in tandem with a blaring red light that flashed in the ceiling.

Wade exhaled. "Guess there goes the element of surprise."

"Check the room, quick," I yelled to Tex, my voice competing with the siren.

The debriefing room was a few feet away from him and he'd shoved the door open by the time the rest of us caught up to him.

"Empty," Bishop muttered, turning back to me with a sardonic smirk, "suppose it wouldn't have been fun if it had been that easy. Lead the way to the labs."

Loud footsteps sounded above as protectors swarmed from their rooms. Ignoring them entirely, I rushed us down two more halls, through a back room, and down the stairs to the labs and medical ward.

We were only challenged by four more protectors who had the sense to notice we were running in the opposite direction from everyone else and therefore not friendly. But we took them down quickly and discreetly.

"It's locked." Wade cursed. "Suppose that we should have

expected that." He turned to me, eyes narrowed. "One quick jump shouldn't hurt, right?"

We were only to use Max's powers in desperate need, to help preserve them for whichever team needed them most, but we both knew we had no other option here.

"Might as well shift us to the center of the lab if we're using it anyway, give us the best advantage," I said. "You remember where it is?"

Wade nodded then held a tentative hand out to Tex, not entirely sure how he'd respond to being pushed through space in his wolf form. There'd been a reason he'd waited until the barn to transform.

"Please don't bite me," he gritted as he grabbed the wolf, then clasped me and Bishop into an awkward hug, before teleporting.

One of the main control rooms was usually situated where we landed. But clearly, they'd made some changes since the last time I'd been here.

"Fuck." I got my bearings as quickly as possible, but then did my best not to move. We were surrounded by cells, the glass walls encasing them the only thing separating us from the demons thrashing around on the other side.

Tex was growling, and stiffly put as much distance between us as he could, clearly responding poorly to his first shift in this form.

"Um, Atlas," Wade muttered, at my back, "isn't that her?"

I spun around, not exactly sure which 'her' I expected to find.

One glass wall was wider than the others and revealed ten faces on the other side.

The farthest one on the left, a short woman with streaks of gray woven through her blonde hair, watched us with the promise of pain in her eyes.

"Rebecca, I assume." Bishop's jaw was clenched as he

watched the panel of protectors. "Never seen her in person before, but no mistaking those dark lines down her neck."

The series of faces watching us weren't demons. They were in an observation room. And we were in the center of some weird arena they'd boxed in for some reason.

Behind them were a series of security screens revealing various rooms from the building. All of them revealed still and calm loops, where I knew there was really panic and chaos above.

Rebecca followed my focus, brows arched.

"I see Arnell has disrupted our feeds again. Truly seamless work." Her voice filtered in above us, grainy and voluminous through a speaker. She shook her head. "Shame we lost that boy's skills, though I do hope we'll welcome him back soon. I thought after the last time, we'd tightened up our security. I'd been assured that hacking in again would be an impossible feat. Clearly not. Thankfully, we've been expecting some kind of breach, so the alarms gave us enough time to collect ourselves. Just barely." Her eyes narrowed, head tilted to the side. "I must say, I wasn't expecting your teleportation abilities. Interesting, truly."

All four of us remained silent, with Tex prowling the perimeter of the cages, hardly reacting as the people inside pounded and screamed against their barriers.

"A shame the girl isn't with you." The lines of her face were etched with disappointment, and the other protectors clustered around her seemed to all be alternating between either a strained, anticipated excitement, and fear. "I've been hoping to meet her, to speak to her. Another time, perhaps."

"I don't sense anything here," Wade muttered to me, ignoring her and the other protectors entirely.

His focus darted briefly to Tex and back to me and I knew he feared the same thing I did. Wolves didn't like being contained. And we'd effectively brought Tex into a cage through one of the most disorienting ways of travel conceivable.

If we weren't careful, it was entirely possible he'd attack one of us.

I didn't blame him. My lungs were struggling to pull in full breaths of air as I fought my panic. All I could smell was the medicinal cocktail of chemicals they pumped into the demons they kept here. Well, that, mixed with blood.

I knew that they often injected demons with things to suppress their power, but it felt like that shit was in the air here. My wolf was uneasy too and I could feel myself on the verge of transforming.

My flesh stung at the mere memory of living locked up in these cells, even if this wasn't the branch where I'd been kept.

All cages were the same in the end.

"Do you?" Wade asked.

I swallowed back my fear, trying like hell to ignore the panic flooding my brain at the memories of being one of The Guild's prisoners. My thoughts had already started cycling back to the terror that the Drude had played in my mind on loop.

Closing my eyes, I took a deep breath, then tried to sense the shadow magic. But I knew if Wade didn't feel anything, then chances were I didn't stand a chance. He had a much closer connection to shadow magic than I did.

Nothing.

Until all I saw were flashes of visions I hadn't suffered in weeks: *Max dead at my feet. Wade with his head lying four feet from the rest of his body.*

My eyes sprang open and I swallowed back the hot bile bubbling up in the back of my throat.

I took a deep breath, pressed the images down as far as they would go. Fuck this.

The shadow magic wasn't here. We needed to kill this woman and get the fuck out. A wrongness hung in the air, and I could feel myself on the edge of losing the small facade of composure I'd built up these last few months.

"The stone," I said, my voice loud and echoing off the walls. "Where are you keeping it?"

If I were a council member, I wouldn't bother answering such a question.

Which was why it was shocking as hell when she did.

"Now Atlas," she made a tsking noise that crackled through the speakers above us, her pedantic disdain raining down on us all, "you didn't really believe that we'd keep the thing you could use to control us somewhere you'd think to look, did you? The thing you want most? Tarren had his faults, but I thought he taught you boys better than that."

Wade stiffened at my side. A careful glance down revealed his fingers clutching the handle of his blade with far more force than would be useful in a fight.

He was just as on edge as I was, and I wasn't sure if it was because there really was something in the air—something that messed with our minds, or just because she was fucking with us. An entirely different kind of psychological warfare.

"And you." Rebecca's eyes narrowed as she studied Bishop. "Your face, it's familiar. I've seen you in reports." She tilted her head to the side, considering. "Not as dead as we thought, are you?" Her lips spread into a gummy smile that looked uncannily like a wolf preparing to snap. "We'll rectify that today." Then, turning to a man at her side, she added, "The girl's not here, I'm done with this. Release them so we can finish up our work for the day. I'm famished."

For a moment, I thought she meant to release us, which didn't make sense. We weren't trapped here. She was the one who'd need releasing.

But just as quickly as the confusion arrived, it dispersed.

The tandem puffs of airlocks released in cadence around us, followed by the heavy click of bolts I couldn't see.

And then, the thick glass windows separating us from the locked-up demons surrounding us were gone.

"Fuck." Wade shifted so that he was at my back as the demons poured into what was now very clearly going to be used as an arena for the sick fucks on the other side of the observation deck. The room filled with snarls and screams as the creatures fought for their freedom, for resources—most of them probably so drugged they had no conception of what they were doing. Tex was across the room locked in a fight with another wolf, and Bishop was fending off attacks left and right as he struggled to get closer to him. "We need to kill her and then get the fuck out of here."

But we couldn't leave Tex and we couldn't leave Bishop. I wouldn't return to The Lodge without them.

"Kill her, quickly," I muttered from the side of my mouth, hoping she wouldn't hear me, "she won't expect you shifting to her while the rest of us are fighting. Attack her from behind, go straight for the heart. I'll get them," I bit out.

Wade cursed, then nodded. "Don't die."

I didn't wait for him to dematerialize, instead I took off at a run towards the far end of the room, where Tex was locked in a fight against two wolves now.

One of the prisoners latched onto me, claws digging through the muscle of my shoulder, but I shoved them off without too much effort.

Bishop reached them almost as soon as I did.

In tandem we raised our blades, ready to join in the fray, but then I froze.

The larger of the two wolves, with fur a shade of black that looked almost blue, caught the attention of my wolf. It took me a second to realize why, but my stomach dropped when I did.

"Mavis."

Bishop froze. "The kid who used to hang around you guys all the time?"

I nodded.

I knew from Sarah that Mavis had turned, that he was feral, and that The Guild had been torturing him with their experiments. Neither of us had been in a position to find him when Max and Darius broke us out of that place, and by the time I'd come to, it was clear that he hadn't made the trip with us to Bishop and Charlie's set up. He must have been transferred before that night, to this facility. That, or he'd run, as had several other captive demons, and found himself in Guild control again somewhere down the line.

His yellow eyes snagged on mine briefly as he sank his teeth into Tex's shoulder, but there was no recognition there.

"Fuck." Bishop ran a hand through his hair in frustration, then fell to the side as a battle between what looked like two vampires shoved too close. "We can't kill him, Atlas. I can't kill him."

I nodded, frozen with indecision for a moment, but then I grabbed the other wolf attacking Tex—the one I had no connection with—and threw him a few feet away.

He snapped and snarled, then crouched low in preparation to attack again. This time I had no doubt I would be on the receiving end of his temper, but another creature jostled him, drawing his ire instead.

Bishop wrestled with Mavis, trying like hell to get between him and Tex. It was a dangerous, reckless thing to do. If Mavis didn't attack him, it was entirely possible Tex would.

Before I could intervene, I went crashing into the nearest wall, across from the observation deck..I strained my eyes through the throng of demons, trying to get a look at Wade.

Rebeccca was dead, her body collapsed like a doll in a chair, a hole in her chest where her heart used to be, and Wade was fighting the only four protectors who remained in the booth. The rest had either fled at his dramatic arrival or were dead.

A vampire snapped at my neck and I knocked him to the

ground, only to get attacked by two more creatures I couldn't identify.

From the corner of my eye, I saw Bishop holding Mavis, pulling him away from the onslaught, his skin caked in blood.

Mavis bit Bishop's hand, but he didn't let him go. Raw determination lined my cousin's brows as he tried like hell to get Mavis back to safety.

Tex was preoccupied, locked in a fight with the werewolf I'd torn off him.

Two more demons were behind Bishop, preparing to attack. Fuck.

This counted as an emergency.

I focused on my bond with Max, on conjuring her fire, but no matter how hard I tried, I couldn't get it to materialize. Was it because of whatever shit they had pumping in this room? The distance?

No. We'd been able to teleport.

Or was Max or someone else using it? Were they in as much danger right now as we were?

With a grunt, I knocked one of the demons back as I slid my blade into the chest of the other.

Not waiting for the others to react or respond, I ran back towards Bishop and Tex, trying like hell to get to them.

"Behind yo—" I screamed, the sound half grunt as a wolf knocked into me. I shoved him away and stood back up. "Drop Mavis, he can handle himself. Bishop, your six."

Wade rematerialized in front of me, his eyes wide as he momentarily tried to decide who to help. He shoved a blade into a demon on his right, his face caked in sweat. "Took me a second to teleport. Someone else must have been."

I tried to pull fire again, but couldn't. "Can you access her hellfire?"

Wade reached Tex, dodged a blow from a vampire who was attacking the wolf. He shook his head. "I can't."

Fuck.

I shoved another demon away, but the crowd between me and Bishop was even thicker now.

I teleported to him, just as a vampire sank his fangs into Bishop's neck.

He let Mavis's thrashing body go at the shock of it, and I slammed my blade into the vamp's back, between two ribs, with enough force to pierce his heart.

He collapsed, taking Bishop down with him.

"Get Tex and bring him here," I yelled to Wade. They were about fifteen feet away, their fight taking them further and further from us. "We need to get the fuck out of here, now."

Bishop stood, shaking his head. "We aren't leaving Mavis here to die. That kid deserves better. We're bringing him home with us."

Before I could stop him, he took off after him.

"He's feral, Bishop, you can't get to him while he's like that." I tried to follow and froze.

Darkness swirled around the edges of my vision and a figure stood before me.

Unlike everyone else in the room, there wasn't a speck of blood or gore on her. She had dark hair that fell across her face, and when her eyes met mine, I lost the ability to breathe.

A drude.

No.

I took a few steps back, tripped on a body, and completely ignored the jolt of another falling into me.

"I won't go back there, I won't go back," I whispered.

Grab your blade, Atlas. Come on.

My hands were stiff, my fingers frozen in a claw-like grip that I couldn't budge.

Suddenly, I didn't see the white room, splashed in shades of red, crowded with demons just fighting for a chance at survival.

All that I saw was my team.

Max was in front of me, her throat sliced, blood trickling to the ground around her. She gasped, eyes wide with fear as they found me.

"Atlas," my name was a blood-laced gurgle on her lips. "Help me."

I crawled towards her, pressed my hands to her throat as I tried like hell to stem the bleeding. My vision blurred and my heart beat so rapidly that I was half-convinced it would bruise my ribs.

"No. Not again. Not again."

Her body stilled beneath me. Gone.

Wade was next to me, indigo eyes leaking tears of red as he crouched over her. A blade was submerged in his chest as he sank down around her.

We were losing. It was over.

I screamed until my throat went hoarse from the force of it.

Wade stood up, the dagger gone, his eyes dry. "Atlas."

I blinked. The two scenes smashed together as I watched the drude collapse in front of me, her neck snapped at a bad angle as Wade's mouth moved.

The ringing and echo of my scream dissolved into the chaos of the room. "Wade?"

"Atlas!" He was crouching over me now, Tex at his side, snarling a warning at a demon who got too close. "Where's Bishop?"

Bishop.

Shaking my head, I stood. I dug my fingers into my palm, focusing on the pain to ground me.

Bishop was across the room, surrounded by two wolves, neither of which was familiar.

"No." My chest gripped at the sight of the wolf at his feet. Mavis. Still. Too still.

The wolves lunged at Bishop, just as Wade grabbed me and teleported the three of us to him.

When we rematerialized, the larger of the two wolves had Bishop's throat in his mouth.

I grabbed onto Bishop with one hand, and buried my hand into Mavis's fur in the other. We'd bring his body home, at least. Mavis deserved that much. For a moment, I thought I felt the soft pulse of the wolf's heart.

A tendril of hope spurred in my chest.

Was he somehow still alive?

In another breath, Wade pulled us out.

I fought for breath, my lungs tight as our new surroundings came into focus. We were back in the barn, but we'd brought the other wolf with us too.

In one fluid movement, I pulled him away from Bishop and snapped his neck. He wasn't dead, but he wouldn't be able to attack us for a while. Maybe when he woke up, he'd stand a chance at a new life, away from the fucked-up depravity of Guild imprisonment.

Tex began to shift back, the loud cracks and pops of his bones a painful soundtrack.

"Atlas," Wade's voice was low, laced with panic. "Atlas!"

When I turned around, Wade was clutching Bishop's throat, trying to stem the blood from where the wolf had hitched a ride.

For a moment, I was disoriented by the similarities of this scene to the one I saw conjured in the drude's nightmare.

Like Max's had been, Bishop's eyes were wide open.

Only Bishop's eyes were empty.

Wade shook his head, eyes glazing over slightly as his jaw clenched in an attempt to swallow back his emotion.

My own throat tightened with grief.

Bishop was dead.

21

MAX

Claude tossed Darius's body over his shoulder and carried him to shore, with far less care and tenderness than Nash employed with the woman in his arms.

"Claude?" Nash's voice was harsh and deep.

The woman cradled in his arms was breathing, so not dead. And now that I was up close, I had a better look at her. Light skin, made more stark by the jet black of her hair, and a grayish tinge to her lips, though I had a feeling that had more to do with the chill than anything else.

Her nose, the curve of her mouth, the high cheekbones, the almost ethereal beauty...

"She's related to you," I said, looking up at Nash.

"How the fuck are you here?" Claude studied the man, his eyes darting between Nash and the woman he held. "Is that—" for maybe the first time since I met him, Claude looked lost for words, "I thought she was dead?"

Nash pulled the woman closer, his expression stiffening slightly. "Where are we?"

"I didn't know you two could teleport," I blurted out.

"We can't," they responded in unison.

Claude shrugged Darius off his shoulder until he dropped to the ground with a loud thud.

I bent down next to him, turning him face up so that I could get a good look at him.

"Seems you can," I muttered, as I pressed my fingers to his pulse. I knew he wasn't dead, but I needed to feel it for myself. I relaxed slightly as the steady thump tapped its slow, familiar rhythm.

"He'll be fine." Claude shook his head, considering. "He'll wake up, anyway." He shrugged, as if not sure. "I think."

"Can someone please tell me where I am?" Nash's jaw was tight, his nostrils flaring slightly as he studied us. "I've never been to this particular pocket of hell." He turned to Claude. "And what the fuck are you two doing here?"

"You're not in hell," I said. Though I had no fucking clue how that happened.

Satisfied that Darius was alive, and that whatever he'd been battling was at least quieted down for now, I turned back to Ro and Charlie.

She was the immediate concern. I'd deal with the brooding vampires once I was certain Charlie and the baby were okay.

I still couldn't wrap my mind around the fact that Darius had attacked her. That he'd attacked me. What the hell was going on?

"What do you mean we're not in hell? How? How is any of this possible?"

I felt Nash and Claude follow as I ran to her.

"What—" Ro eyed the newcomers with suspicion, "Who—"

"How is she?" I asked, cutting him off.

For a moment, he looked like he might press the issue, but then his gaze dropped back down to Charlie and he let it slide.

Her eyes were open, and Ro had a piece of his shirt pressed to the wound at her neck.

"Stable, I think. But I can't know for sure how his bite will affect them."

Protectors rarely survived vampire venom unharmed, especially not when the bite was to the neck.

Normally, I'd panic, but Charlie had already survived Darius's bite once before, and she only had a little bit of protector blood running through her veins. I figured that meant she had better odds than most at making it through this with minimal long-term effects.

"I'll be okay." Charlie's voice was weak, and I could hear the waiver of fear lacing it. "But my baby. Make sure—"

I placed one hand on her forehead, it was clammy with sweat, despite the chill in the air, and pulled Ro's makeshift bandage back to get a better look at the wound.

"Sorry," I muttered as she winced. It didn't look too bad, but the outer appearance was rarely indicative of the damage these bites could do.

"Can you heal her?" Ro asked, keeping his focus split between me and the men at my back.

"I can try."

"You know, last time this happened, I fell in love with my nursemaid," Charlie said through a grin that was punctured with a wince.

"Bishop?" I tried to picture the gruff man I'd come to know being tender towards anyone. "Well, since that's not an option, I'll settle for you naming your baby after me."

She chuckled, then groaned.

"Deep breaths," I said, regretting my shitty attempt at humor.

Nash and Claude's impatience chafed at my skin, but even they seemed to see that Charlie was the priority right now.

Closing my eyes, I focused all of my attention on shoving them out of my mind. Instead, I searched for Charlie. Healing my team had become like second nature, but it was always more difficult to heal others.

Still, I'd had a lot of practice in the medical wards and it helped that I'd gotten to know Charlie over the last few months. Not to mention I was hoping the fact that we shared blood would help the success rate too.

The world shifted as I tuned everything out, until all I could think about, all I could feel was the slippery thread of Charlie—her life force or energy supply, I didn't really understand the mechanics of it.

I exhaled in relief when I realized that I could feel her, that the blood connection, however small, did seem to strengthen my ability, at least a bit.

As I focused, I realized that I sensed Darius too—his venom slipping into her bloodstream.

I pushed as much power and strength into mending the wound, into drawing it out. The familiar tingling heat burrowed beneath my skin, coating my hands.

I didn't have much experience with healing pregnant people, or babies in general, but I felt a rush as the second life-force made itself known, strong but tenuous at the same time.

The baby was okay. I was fairly certain anyway, though I couldn't make any predictions about long-term effects. It wasn't often that pregnant human-protectors were bitten by a shadow-touched vampire and survived.

This was new territory.

Then again, it was probably equally likely that the world would end before the child was even born and we learned of the effects.

Vaguely, I was aware that there were more people joining us, that there were voices echoing in the breeze, though I couldn't make out any of the words. My vision blurred, and I waivered slightly, dizzy, drunk on the feel of letting my strength flow into them.

"Max." A hand grabbed my shoulder, gentle at first, but it grew more firm. "Max, stop."

Light filled my chest and I wanted so badly to sink into it. To pour more of myself into the heat, to just rest for a while. Letting go meant I'd have to deal with the clusterfuck waiting for me on the beach, with Darius.

"Max."

I resisted the temptation and fell back on my ass, my lungs pumping overtime as I caught my breath.

Ro's face was in front of me, his eyes searching, concerned.

I cleared my throat, blinking as my focus recalibrated to the scene surrounding us. "I'm okay."

Healing was a difficult art, and the element of my power I still struggled with most. It was so easy—going over the edge, giving too much.

He studied me for a moment longer, like he wasn't fully convinced, but then he nodded and sat back down. "You need to work on holding back a little."

"I'll add it to my list of things to get to eventually." I took a deep breath. "Is Charlie—"

"Right as rain." She came into view as Ro shifted out of the way, her smile wide as she ran a hand over neck. There was still a mark, but it was small and looked months healed. And not at all like a supernatural wound should. "Doesn't even hurt anymore." She pressed a hand over her belly as her eyes found mine. "Thank you. Truly. I owe you."

"We're family," I smiled, "but if either of us owes the other anything, it's me."

Charlie had given me so much—a home, comfort, community. And, though I knew it would take time to foster the bond between us, she was the only link to my family that I had left. Not counting Ro, of course.

Mer was there now, and she crouched down to help Charlie up. When she was satisfied that her friend was indeed okay, she scanned the rest of us. "Well, glad to see you guys made it back safely, but it seems you've multiplied your numbers. I don't remember that being an option in any of the possible outcomes Bishop had planned for."

I jumped, reminded suddenly that Claude and Nash were here.

"We didn't bring them," I said, noticing a few more familiar faces scattered nearby, eyeing the newcomers warily. "They just —oof" The words were swallowed as Izzy dove into me, crushing me in a hug violent enough that it would have left bruises on a human.

"You're okay." She pulled back, grinning in acknowledgment to Ro, who was also suddenly swept up in a much more tender welcome back with Arnell.

She did a double take, her focus darting between Darius at my feet and his angrier-looking brother.

"Max, not to alarm you or anything," she took a step closer to Claude, studying him, "but did you know that there's currently two of your vampire?"

Claude eyed her with vacant amusement, which was a considerably kinder expression than he reserved for most interactions.

"This is Darius's twin," I said, the resemblance between them obvious, even though their personalities and the way they carried themselves shaded in some differences. "And their friend, Nash."

"Friend is not a word I would use," Nash said, still cradling the girl in his arms while his eyes scanned everyone, like he was waiting for someone to attack.

"And who's she?" Izzy asked, either unaware of Nash's general tension, or unconcerned by it.

For a moment, I didn't think he'd answer.

In fact, I was beginning to wonder if he might attack.

Clearly Claude thought so too, because he shifted his

weight slightly, putting himself between Nash and the rest of us.

"My sister," he said, "Nika."

Nika.

The name sparked recognition in my chest. "Darius's friend? I thought she was dead?"

Nash arched a brow. "Darius has an odd definition of friendship, considering he ruined her life."

"The girl has a point," Claude studied the pair of them, "I was under the impression that Nika had died as well."

"Your brother drew his own conclusions," Nash clutched her closer to his chest, as if he was afraid Claude might try ripping her from him, "I simply let him."

"How are the three of you here?" I asked, sensing that things between the two vampires were veering towards issues and technicalities I had no interest in entertaining. They had shit to work through, but now wasn't the time. I turned to Mer. "And have any of the others arrived?"

She shook her head and I swallowed the anxiety threatening to boil in my chest.

One thing at a time.

If I let myself focus on all the potential lines of fear threading through my bones right now, I'd never stand a chance at surviving the rest of the day.

They'd be okay. And they'd use the bond to reach out if they weren't.

Claude furrowed his brows. "I have no idea." Something told me he rarely didn't know what was going on, and judging by the stiffness in his posture, he wasn't a particularly big fan of the feeling. "One moment I was at the bar, then I," he gestured around, lip curling in disgust, "then I was in the middle of a lake, where my brother was thrashing about like an enraged toddler."

I took a step closer to Darius, a wave of protectiveness washing over me.

"Do you know what was wrong with him?" My voice was quiet, small. "Why he—"

Claude reached his hand to my chin, his touch more gentle than I'd have anticipated as he tilted my head to the side. "He attacked you."

"And then himself." Defensiveness wrapped around me like a snake and I brushed his hand away. "I'm fine. He was fighting himself, I just don't understand why. One moment he was himself, the next he was—" I gestured to the water, not quite sure how to put into words what had come over Darius, "you know. It—it was like a switch had flipped."

Claude crouched next to his brother, his designer pants somehow still looking suave and tailored perfectly to him, despite the fact that they were soaked. "Do you have any idea what could have triggered such a sudden switch? What happened immediately before?"

Ro grunted.

"I," I glanced at him, guilt curling under my ribs at the hardness in his eyes, the set of his jaw. Now that we knew Charlie was okay and Darius wasn't an immediate threat, it was clear that Ro's anger was beginning to simmer again. I'd have to talk to him soon—to all of them—about what Darius and Ro learned today. "I have an idea."

Claude looked up at me, brow arching, but he didn't press the matter further. "And what about before this," he cleared his throat, "trigger. Was he normal—" he stood up, "normal for Darius, I mean?"

My mouth went dry, because the truth was that Darius hadn't quite been himself for a while now.

I'd given him space, knowing he didn't want to talk about it. I'd figured it had something to do with his history with Charlie and the others here, with all the shit we were dealing with.

But maybe I was wrong. Maybe I should have pushed.

"He's been a little distant," I said, "sort of tucked inside of himself, lost in his thoughts. If that makes sense? I've seen him like that a few times before. Once—" I licked my lips, "once at your house. After the two of you fought. The way he sank into himself after?"

Claude and Nash shared a dark look, and the sight of it sent my heart raging inside of its cage.

"He'll be okay though, right?" I hated how weak I sounded, but I needed to know. I couldn't do this without him. Couldn't — "When he wakes up, he'll come back to himself?"

Any of the frostiness that Claude usually reserved when speaking about Darius dissolved, until I saw my own fear written in the lines of his face.

"I don't—" he shook his head. "I don't know, Max. My brother has been fighting his demons for many years. When he abandoned his post, he upset the balance. Portal guardians are always consumed by the shadow magic they intersect with, eventually. And he's—" he took a deep breath, his familiar eyes more tender than I'd ever seen them as they met mine, "I did try to warn you."

"He brought us here," Nash said, his voice distant, like it was filtering through a tunnel as I processed Claude's words. "We are two sets of the same. I don't know how he did it, but his power brought us here—an attempt to recalibrate, perhaps."

"It shouldn't be possible," Claude said, though I could see from the set of his face that he didn't disagree with Nash's assessment.

"Your sister," Izzy started after a few moments of silence, her gaze darting between me and the two men, "Nika. Is she okay?"

Claude jolted, like he'd forgotten about her entirely.

"She's unwell, but she'll be fine." Nash's grip tightened around his sister and he took a few steps back, towards the water. "She's been unwell for years. Since Darius abandoned his post."

"Unwell in the way that he's unwell?" I asked.

Nash nodded. His jaw strained, and I could tell that he was priming himself to tear off at a run the second one of us so much as twitched in a way that threatened her. "She could not keep the dark hold of shadow magic at bay for as long as Darius could. Once he upset the balance, and with things as difficult as they were in hell—it took her over."

"Do you mean to tell me that Nika has been living like—" Claude stumbled over the words as he motioned to his brother, but we all knew what he meant. Had she been as lost to herself as Darius had been just now—for years?

Nash was silent.

"You just kept her like that?" Claude asked. "You should have—"

"Should have what?" Nash's nostrils flared as he tried to contain whatever storm of emotions was struggling to fight its way to the surface. "Should have reached out? How? I couldn't get in contact with either of you. You just left us there." He snorted, the sound devoid of humor." Or do you mean that I should have killed her?" He shook his head, took a few steps back, until the water lapped at his shoes. "Things are off balance already. I don't know what will happen if one of us dies. It's not ideal, but I kept her safe, alive, did what I had to do. I've been trying to find a way to cure her, to sever her from her post, to get a replacement, to restore her—anything." He swallowed as his eyes found his old friend. "It's Nika, Claude. What the fuck was I supposed to do? She's my family. She's all I have."

"Years?" Claude cursed, then ran a hand through his hair, ruffling up the characteristically perfect style. "Is she ever awake? Ever herself?"

I held my breath waiting for Nash's answer.

Years? Could Darius really lose himself to that kind of darkness for years?

"I broke her neck when I landed here, after I realized she'd been pulled with me too. It's better if she's unconscious, she's easier to monitor." Nash took a deep breath. "I keep her locked up. There's a warehouse that's been abandoned for years. She has space. But here—I can't handle her when she's conscious and loose, can't know what she'll do. Sometimes, pieces of the old her push through and I get little glimpses. Those moments are rare, and they've only been growing more so. I thought with things shifting, maybe—" he exhaled, "she's not like the flesh-eaters, the other shadow-tainted. The magic hasn't warped her in quite the same way that it has them, I think because she's a vessel for it. That's what we are as guardians. Though her hunger for blood, for violence, has become insatiable. She's become a more amplified version of herself, but one that's controlled by a power she's constantly at war with, one she can't fight back against on her own."

Izzy's arm snaked around me, pulling me tight against her, but I barely felt her. I couldn't peel my eyes from Darius's sleeping form.

A damp curl of silvery-blond hair curved over his brow. I bent down and swept it away, my skin tingling where it touched his.

"He brought you here," I whispered, my fingers tracing the familiar line of his jaw, his bottom lip. "Why did he bring all three of you here? How?" Neither of them answered, though I sensed their prickly stares on me. "What happens when the two halves of a set are in one place, one realm?"

"I don't know," Claude said, his frustration with the phrase leaking into his voice. "Once our roles were assumed, it wasn't supposed to be possible. Darius came the closest—when he traveled to hell with you, but that was after he'd already rescinded his role. I've never really been able to pass through our portal."

"Lucifer." I stood up, walked towards Nash. "Have you heard from him? Seen him? He might have some idea—maybe,"

Nash shook his head. "No one's seen him in months."

"Sam?" I asked, desperation choking me.

Nash and Sam knew each other. Nash had been the one to open the portal in the hell realm last time we were there. He knew Sam well enough to know that he was a hellhound.

Nash shook his head again, and I had to fight back the urge to strangle him at the uselessness of that gesture, at what it signified.

"I think that Sam went looking for Lucifer, but that was weeks ago. Neither of them has been seen or heard from in ages." His eyes narrowed at my expression. "Long distance communication isn't exactly easy in hell. Current predicament aside, most of us can't simply teleport when we'd like to get somewhere. And neither Lucifer nor Samael are exactly forthcoming with their whereabouts. Or information. I'm merely an acquaintance, they don't keep me apprised of their comings and goings."

"Max?" The familiar sound of Declan's voice cut through me, puncturing the tension and reshaping the scene into something new.

Relief flooded me. They were back.

I spun around, and saw her figure appear through the trees, not far from our cabin. They must have landed there.

I broke out into a run, ignoring our new guests as I took off towards her, not slowing until she met me halfway, the two of us colliding at a speed that would no doubt bruise us both temporarily.

Her lips found mine, brief and firm, before she pulled back to look at me, her hands pressed to either side of my face. "You're okay?"

I nodded, scanning her for injuries. There was blood on her shirt, but I didn't see any wounds. Thank fucking gods.

"And you? Where's Eli?" My hands traced over her as I looked behind her, searching for him.

Levi emerged, with Eli draped over his shoulders.

He wasn't moving.

Bile rose up my chest as I groped angrily for the bond, but the panic only eased briefly when I found it.

"He's alive." Declan twined my fingers through hers as she searched towards the beach. "Just unconscious. Took us longer than expected to get back without his help. I'm fucking knackered. Not sure what happened to him, but I think it's the fanghole. Where is he?" Her grip tightened around my hand. "Is that Claude? What the hell's going on?"

I didn't give Levi more than a quick nod before I enlisted his help in setting Eli down at my feet.

His skin was deathly pale and tinged with gray. And the front of his shirt was caked in blood.

As gently as possible, I lifted it up, searching for his injuries. His torso was marred in what looked like scratches, but not the kind that came from claws—and there was a deep wound in the center of his diaphragm that mirrored the exact spot Darius had stabbed himself.

"The blood bond," I whispered, "he'll be okay."

We didn't know the limits of their bond, but in the past, it seemed to be focused on mirroring wounds specifically. If one of them was asleep or knocked out, it didn't seem to affect the other.

Healing Eli took far less time and energy than healing Charlie had. He came to slowly at first, then all at once. He shot up, eyes wild and searching until they landed on me. "Max?"

I nodded, unable to keep the grin off my face. They were alive. They were okay.

"Atlas and Wade?" Dec asked, her voice flooded with

concern and impatience as she studied the others down the way.

"Not yet," I responded, though it came out more as a grunt.

Eli pulled me to him, burying his face in my neck.

It took me a moment before I realized they were missing someone.

"Where's Evelyn?" I asked, the question drying up when I noticed Levi's expression over Eli's shoulder. I knew that look with an intimacy that shook me to my core. Pain, rage, and fear, all boiled together into grief.

I squeezed Eli tighter as he stifled a broken sob.

It didn't take long for them to fill me in, and when they got to the end, we were interrupted by another arrival.

Atlas, Wade, and Tex materialized a few paces from us, dressed in blood and the remaining tatters of their clothing.

I ran to them, both relieved to see them finally back, but terrified by the empty expression stretched on all three of their faces.

Without a word, Atas set a wolf down at his feet—one I'd never seen before, though I didn't have time to ask before my heart sank.

Charlie shifted next to me, her arm on my shoulder, excitement and worry vibrating through her grip.

Tex took a few steps forward, his shoulders sagging under the weight of Bishop cradled in his arms.

He wasn't moving. He wasn't breathing.

Charlie's scream tore through my chest, echoing through the trees, as I kept her from falling.

The rest of the world was silent, cloaked in her pain.

22

WADE

The afternoon bled into evening, as the entire community came together to lay rest to Evelyn and Bishop.

I couldn't even look at Charlie without choking up.

He was alive and well this morning—excited, even for his first mission in ages.

And now he was gone, leaving his wife and unborn child behind without him.

The world had never felt so cruel.

Worse, it had all been for fucking nothing.

Three missions, two deaths, and not a single fucking clue as to where the stone was.

Instead, all we had were a bunch of dead ends, some extra vampires to deal with, and Darius lost to his own darkness.

Max spent most of the evening trying her damndest to be helpful, serving everyone food, watching the kids, preparing rooms for Claude, Nika, and Nash. When she wasn't running from chore to chore, trying to keep busy, she was sidled next to Eli, me, Atlas—a soothing presence as we all processed the gaping, constraining feeling of loss.

Now that we'd all retired back to the cabin though, she hadn't left Darius's room. He'd woken, briefly, but Claude had been there at the time. He snapped his brother's neck again before he could fully rouse, with the same nonchalance one might crack an egg.

"You should rest." I leaned against the door frame, watching her.

"I will." Her hand was twined with Darius's. She looked back at me over her shoulder, forcing a small smile across her face. The sight of it was like a blade to the gut—so much fear, so much pain braided into her features. "You should too. It's been a difficult day."

I was exhausted, but I couldn't bring my body to leave her right now, not like this.

I stepped into the fanghole's room and closed the door behind me. I'd wait up with her a bit, until she was ready to sleep.

Plus, if I was being honest, I didn't want to be alone with my thoughts right now. Didn't want to see Bishop's death playing on repeat in my mind.

"He'll be okay." I drew her to my side and pressed a kiss to the side of her forehead. My throat tightened when she stifled a sob. "We'll figure out how to get him back."

"He's always been terrified of this," her face pressed into me, and I could feel my shirt soaking with the tears she was trying to hide, "of the darkness pulling him under. He tried to hide it, and I should have—" her breath hitched, "I thought it would be better to give him space, but I was wrong. And now I don't know how to reach him."

"I know—" I paused, latching onto that word—darkness. She was right. Darius had been off for weeks. At the time, I'd assumed it had been the state of things generally, the chaos and planning of prepping for this mission. But what if this was the darkness Serae had referenced? What if it really hadn't been about Atlas, but Darius?

I pulled back a few inches, cupped Max's face in my hands as I wiped a few stray tears away with my thumb. "What if we can?"

Her dark eyes glistened, narrowing in confusion.

"What if we can reach him?"

For the first time since we'd gotten back, I felt the embers of hope ignite. I'd all but forgotten that dream-walk with my aunt, especially considering I'd woken up from it to find Max nearly drowning. Not wasting a breath, I relayed my dream with Serae, the details coming back with some clarity the more I focused on remembering.

Max and I had a power that no one else in our bond group had—we could siphon and feed off emotions. Lust was only one of them, the easiest for us to access. But it was only an entry point, a catalyst for tapping into our prey's lifeforce.

If my aunt was right about our strengths, then there was a possibility that we could feed off the darkness consuming Darius, or at least distribute its hold evenly across us all, until it was no longer debilitating with its weight.

Once the plan was set, the hardest part was falling asleep. Both of us were wired as we lay there together, smashed into Darius's bed, just waiting for the adrenaline of having a plan to drain into exhaustion. But in the way that sleep always seemed to eventually work, I slid from awake and anxious to dreaming the exact moment I stopped fighting it.

Neither of us spared much energy on crafting a particularly glamorous dreamscape. Just a room, dark and earthy.

The moment Darius stepped foot into the space, he sprang at me like a bullet, crashing us both to the ground with a calamity of grunts and groans.

His fangs pierced my neck, and I was surprised by the fact that it didn't hurt as he pulled a mouthful of blood. It almost felt—good. For the first time, I could feel what Max felt when he fed on her, a blissful sort of power and control.

Before my own whims grew too pliant here, I ripped my head away from him and pinned him to the ground, a feral writhing mess as he tried to fight me.

I slammed his head to the ground, earning a fresh snarl. "I'm stronger than you here, you fuck."

The fanghole didn't respond, just continued thrashing about, trying like hell to attack as I held him down.

Cuffs appeared around his wrists, attached to heavy, metal links. The soft clink and strain echoed through the room as his arms pulled taut above his head, until he started to rise above me.

Max had fashioned restraints and she used her magic to thread them through the ceiling, until Darius stood, his toes dangling over the edge of the wooden floor, fighting to find purchase.

She grinned a wicked grin, her eyes hard as she strode closer to him, eyebrow arched. "Familiar position, no?"

I wasn't sure what she was referring to, but a flash of recognition broke through Darius's vicious growl as she prowled around him.

Good. This was working.

I brought out the fanghole's worst, and she, his best. Together we stood a chance of cracking him, siphoning out the darkness gripping him.

She traced a finger over the long smooth expanse of his chest, his muscles stretched to the edge of pain.

He gasped at her touch, the crash of chains providing a dark soundtrack to the scene.

The fanghole's stare met mine, briefly, annoyance and aggression etched across his face.

I crafted a sturdy black chair for myself, planting it a few feet in front of him, then sat down to watch whatever show she had planned, waiting until she required me.

The featherlight touches along his torso turned sharp and antagonizing. Her nails drew blood, and she met his stare with a taunt.

"You took," her voice was stern, filled with a thick control that was woven with lust, "without asking."

She traced her tongue over the cuts, and Darius's breathing shifted suddenly from aggressive to, well, still aggressive, but turned the fuck on.

And fuck if I wasn't too.

"Is this what you want?" Max tilted her neck to the side, watching Darius with sultry eyes that had my dick straining against my pants. A dark grin hooked the curves of her lips as she took a step back from him. "Too bad."

A dagger appeared in her hand and she sliced into her palm.

Darius watched the blood pool there, until it began dripping through her fingers.

Without a word she smeared it over his face, then walked away from him, not turning to look at me until she reached my chair.

Darius thrashed feverishly where he hung, his erection the only indication that it was more than rage coursing through his brain.

This would work, she knew how to tease and read him, to draw out every—

I closed my eyes and hissed as her hand slid down my pants.

Without me even feeling it, she'd transitioned the chair into a long chaise lounge, and pushed me back on it as she worked her hands over my cock, her fingers tracing the veins and rim of the head like it was a musical instrument only she knew how to tune.

When I opened my eyes again, I was naked below her, and she was wearing a lacy bra and crotchless panties, held up by a garter. The shade was red, but so dark the lace shifted to black in some places, like the deepest pools of blood.

The vampire thrashed harder against his restraints as Max lowered her lips to my dick, her dark eyes darting between the two of us as she took me into her mouth.

I bucked against her as the bolt that held his chains strained against his fury. If this world, and everything in it, weren't crafted through us, I had no doubt that he'd have ripped holes through the ceiling by now.

As it was, Max controlled it all.

I gladly relinquished all of my control to her.

She crawled over me, her eyes light with power, putting on a show for us both—and damn if I wasn't grateful for my front row seat.

Her fingers wrapped around my throat, pulling me to a seated position as she sank down on me, tugging the back of my hair so that my neck was exposed to her.

My eyes met hers, the question clear, and I groaned in response, a new, unfamiliar need surging through me.

Yes. Yes. *Whatever the fuck you want.*

She bared her teeth and I saw fangs, white and sharp, and then she buried them in my neck, drawing blood as she rode me, the pace both too slow and then too fast as she edged me.

Lights blurred my vision as I filled her, until all that was left was the ecstasy of being consumed by her.

Darius's rage echoed around the room as he watched us.

When she pulled back, my blood dripped down her chin, painting her with my lust. She pressed her lips to mine, and as my tongue tangled with hers, I felt fangs of my own descend.

I bit her lip, licking away the blood as she gasped, tightening around my dick.

Neither of us were vampires, and I didn't have any interest

in drinking blood in the waking world—but here, we became whatever the fuck we wanted. Right now, I wanted nothing more than to feel the warmth of her blood pooling on my tongue.

So I took it.

Darius let out a growl that sounded more wolf than vampire as I sank my teeth into the side of her neck.

She tasted decadent and deep, like the richest dark chocolate, a sumptuous dessert.

One mouthful and I was intoxicated.

She clenched around me as I spun her around so that her back was on the chaise and I was above her.

I drove my dick into her, harder—faster, as I drank my fill.

Her nails, longer and sharper than they were in waking life, clawed into my back as she chased her orgasm. Her screams echoed around the walls, amplifying with each pump as she reached the edge and I poured into her, both of us falling over it.

Stars swam through my vision as pleasure rolled through us. We had a habit of feeding on each other's powers in these dreams, making every touch electric, every breath fire.

After a few breathless moments, both of us in a boneless tangle, Darius's loud clanging broke through my reverie.

The fucker was even more pissed now.

Good.

I shot him a smug smirk as Max climbed off of me and sauntered over to him, her neck and chest dripping with her blood.

The vamp eyed her, unblinking, the desperation of his hunger and desire hitting me like a molten wave.

"Fuck." I bit my lip, trying to reign my own desire in.

But that was the thing about these dreams, about Max. I got off just watching her too, even if I wasn't the focus of her attention.

In a slow, languid tug, she released some of the tension in Darius's restraints, until his feet met the cold floor, his arms hanging only loosely above him now.

He leaned forward, his body inching toward her, fangs extended as he licked his lips.

Power from the two of them bolted through me as she pressed a chaste kiss to his lips.

"You want to play nice, now?" She asked, voice coy.

He didn't blink, didn't look away—but I heard the low growl building in his chest, a predator desperate for his prey.

I knew what he wanted, could feel it in my body as if the desires were my own.

To chase.

To fuck.

To taste.

Her.

He wanted her, nothing more, wanted to consume her completely until there was nothing left.

There was lust, obviously, and beneath that, love and obsession. Those things were always there, for all of us, when Max was around.

But there was anger too, pain—woven tightly through the darkness riding at the surface.

With a simple snap of her fingers, the cuffs released him.

He didn't move at first, just let his arms drop to his sides as he stared her down.

If this weren't a dream, I'd be between them in an instant.

But she was stronger than he was here. Her control of the situation, her desire, increased as he watched her, flooding her with a renewed sense of need.

He stalked forward, one step, then another, until his chest brushed against her.

It was a tenuous game of control that Max was weaving here —taking it, then sharing it. Dominating him, then letting him dominate. I could feel the cracks it created through his shield, could sense the fanghole I knew and loathed beneath the surface, fighting for breath.

She struck first, baiting him as she tore off at a run.

He went after her, growling in frustration when she disappeared from his grasp, only to be standing where she'd just started.

This time, when he ran, she didn't move. She stayed there, smug, excited, filled with an anticipation that had my own dick hardening again.

She pounced on him before he reached her, and then they went down, the two of them a pile of limbs, teeth, and lust as they fought for control, for dominance.

In one smooth shift, he pressed her back into the ground, his arm around her throat as he sank into her—dick and teeth.

Their fucking was rough, feral, filled with equal parts fear and need—the anger I'd sensed before louder now, until it was the only thing I felt, like it was ballooning in his chest.

She wrapped her legs around his waist, twisting until she was on top, controlling the devastating pace he'd tried to set— pushing him harder, faster, as her teeth pierced his neck.

Her claws raked down his back as they took their fill of each other.

"Darius," she moaned, her lips tracing up to his, where they clashed together, each stealing the other's breath as their movements turned more fluid, more tender.

"Don't." His voice cracked, half whisper, half beg, and the shadow magic gripping him flooded through our bonds. "Max."

The wave of energy was heavy and angry, clutching my chest with pure force until all I saw was red, all that I felt was rage.

I choked on it, losing myself in its embrace as I tried to carry the weight of it. But it was crushing, suffocating.

He'd held this for years?

All of it? On his own?

My eyes swam, but when I turned back to Max, she seemed only strengthened by the power, like it called to her—shaping and sharpening, molding within her as she softened the edges of the magic's need to take.

She pulled it from him, then pulled it from me, slowly at first, and then all at once—until my lungs remembered how to fill with air again.

Her eyes were luminous, glowing briefly, as she siphoned it through her, settling and sculpting it.

There was a flash of light, like lightning through the room, the floor rumbled and shifted for a moment, then everything went still.

"Don't." Darius clutched Max, his face pressed into her neck as he held her in his arms, shaking quietly. "Please. I'm sorry, I'm sorry, I'm—"

"Shh," she pressed her lips to his head and held him to her, legs wrapped around his back as the two of them rocked. "It's okay. It'll be okay."

"Please, you have to promise," he whispered, his body racked with sobs now, clutching at her like she couldn't get close enough, no matter how tightly they held onto each other. "You can't leave me."

She stilled at his words, her eyes searching, until they met mine. Power still radiated from her, but the glow was diluted with tears now.

"I can't lose you."

23

MAX

I slept for a few more hours, curled in between them both, sinking into their warmth, the simple rightness of feeling their skin against mine.

It took some finesse, but I shifted the shadow magic across the bonds, letting it fortify and strengthen them, rather than linger inside of any one of us.

The bonds were somehow stronger now, like the magic Darius had held always belonged to us, was always meant to draw us closer.

He was never meant to hold it on his own, I understood that now.

Even in sleep, I could feel that Darius was lighter, breathing easier than he had since we'd stepped foot in this place.

But I dreaded the morning, because I knew that I'd have to talk to him today—knew what had triggered the upset in the tenuous balancing act he walked every day. Eventually, I'd have to talk to the others too, but hopefully that could wait a few more days, until after they'd had a chance to process everything that had happened on the mission. We still needed to debrief, to figure out what we were going to do next.

The truth was, I didn't have any ideas. And the person who'd been the brains of this operation, who'd put this meticulous plan together, was gone.

I curled into Darius, breathing in the scent of his skin.

Terror gripped beneath my ribs as I thought about what Charlie was going through right now.

More than terror though, in the parts of myself I hated, there was also gratitude—that I hadn't lost any members of my team.

Losing Bishop and Evelyn was painful, but I couldn't imagine losing one of my own team.

It felt selfish and horrible, to be excited by the fact that Darius was himself again now, that we'd been able to use our bond to keep that darkness at bay, at least for a little longer.

The sun had hardly crept through the window, when he shifted next to me.

His eyes met mine, his jaw tight. I watched the maelstrom of emotions play out across his eyes.

There was so much that I wanted to say to him, but I couldn't find the words; didn't know how to heal the wound between us, because there was no solution to the problem that had carved it there.

"I—" I whispered, searching for something to say, to ease his pain, but I couldn't. "I'm glad you're back."

Slowly, the anger and grief there bled into a hard determination.

Wordlessly, he slid his hand into his pocket, pulling out a phone I didn't recognize. He swung his legs over the bed and dialed a number while he stretched, his lean muscles glistening in the soft light of the window.

"When did you get a phone?" I asked, already missing his warmth. He'd lost every phone he'd been given, and had stuck to borrowing Dec's more often than not when he needed one. It was a habit that she hated, because he always made sure to change her background photo to a ridiculously up-close selfie of his face—the kind of proportions only a well-intentioned boomer could manifest.

Secretly though, I knew she loved it, that she loved him. We all did.

Shadow ran into the room, then nudged her head along his calf in greeting.

I froze, not entirely sure Darius was fully back to himself. I was fairly certain Wade's siphoning plan had worked, but it was also a very real possibility that Shadow was unknowingly walking towards her death.

We hadn't had a chance to test the theory in action, to make sure that the hunger had abated.

But Darius simply looked down at her, scrunched his nose, then tossed a pillow to Wade. "Wake up, you prick." Then he picked Shadow up and set her carefully in my lap, before wiping his hands on his pants like the transfer had left him contaminated.

Wade grunted, blinking awake. "What the hell? What time is it?"

"Get here now," Darius said into the phone, ignoring us both. "And bring the girl too." He paused, grunted. "No." Another pause, he opened the door and walked out. "Yeah, that one. She deserves to know, so make sure she's here too. Family meeting. One minute."

There was the muffled sound of a voice on the other end, but Darius hung up on whoever he'd called without so much as a goodbye.

Wade mouthed, "family meeting?" then looked at me, confused, but I could only shrug.

"Well, he seems fine," he said, his words muddy with sleep. "Back to his old confusing-as-hell self anyway."

"Where'd you get that phone?" I whisper-shouted, not wanting to wake the others up. They needed sleep. We all did.

"Swiped it from Haley," he yelled back, clearly unconcerned about noise control, "when we left her in the room. She wasn't using it, so I didn't think she'd miss it. I'll return it today, she's probably up and moving again." His volume didn't change, but his voice sounded farther away as we moved through the cabin. "Though come to think of it, not entirely sure how many of those darts she got hit with. Might be a few days."

Loud banging proceeded down the hall as doors slammed open and a cacophony of groggy curses filled the small cabin.

Ralph added loud, chirping barks, clearly amused by the ruckus and wanting to participate.

"Fucking hell." Wade fell back on the bed, then pressed his pillow over his face and groaned. "It's not even 6 a.m., what a shitty way to thank us for saving his life."

It took only five minutes for all of us to assemble in the main room, and Izzy arrived dressed in bright purple sleep pants, smelling like toothpaste.

Ro stood next to Darius, the two of them communicating wordlessly in a way that had me worried, while Ralph wove from person to person, accepting good morning pats from everyone—and demanding two from Izzy, a demand she happily obliged.

"Max is determined to die," Darius barked out, no preamble. "So I called this family meeting so that we can put our brains, brawn, and beauty together to come up with a plan to stop her."

My stomach sank.

Fuck.

I clutched onto Ralph for support as I fell back onto the couch, between Izzy and Eli.

"What are you talking about?" Eli asked, then he shook his head, confused. "Also, how are you awake and...normal again? For you, I mean."

Darius sighed, like this was the most tiresome question in

the world. "We'll get to that later. My me-ness doesn't really matter right now," he shot a glance to me, then Wade, "though I am deeply grateful for it. What matters is that Max will not survive Lucifer's mystical little ritual, and she had no intention of letting any of you know that, so I'm telling you now. Because I'd like your help with stopping her."

My mouth went dry.

Wade snorted, the joke melting when his eyes found mine. "What's he talking about?"

Atlas was unreadable, and Declan had frozen mid coffee pour. The steaming liquid overflowed onto the counter, but she didn't seem to care or notice.

Izzy's hand found its way around my arm and she gave a tight squeeze of support. She studied me for a moment, eyes wide and filled with so much love that I nearly vomited. I could read her like a book in that moment, the pages spilled open.

This is what you've been hiding, her eyes screamed. *This* is what you've avoided talking to me about.

My throat tightened at the lines of pity and grief on her face as she read mine just as easily.

"That's not true, right?" Eli turned to me, eyes searching. His skin paled as I fought to find something to say. "Fucking hell."

Darius shoved his arm forward. "Yes, true. See. It's all over her face. Guilt." He crossed his arms. "So now we need to put together a plan to stop it."

"I—" my voice cracked.

"Were you ever planning on telling us?" Declan asked, hissing as coffee spilled onto her feet from her overpour. "Or was this just going to be a valiant sail off into the horizon, leave-us-all-to-pick-up-the-fucking-pieces-without-you kind of thing." The gentle lilt of her accent was thicker than usual. "Not even a goodbye or even a silly attempt at finding another option with us?"

"I was going to tell you." My voice sounded weak to my own ears, filled with guilt, and I hated myself for it. "I just—I didn't know how or when. And it was just easier to focus on other things."

If I didn't talk about it, maybe it wouldn't feel quite so real. Quite so fucking terrifying.

"Other things?" Wade's voice was devoid of its usual warmth. "There are no *other things* when it comes to your survival, Max. It's the *only* thing."

"Doesn't matter," Darius grabbed a coffee from Dec, blowing on it as his eyes landed on me. He didn't even drink coffee. "It's not happening. We need to come up with some back-up plans, that's why we're here. It's," he paused, silently scanning the room, "seven against one."

Ralph barked.

"Right, sorry, eight. Eight against one. And I'm sure if the miserable cat were around, she'd be on our side too. We win the vote either way."

"There—" I shook my head and paused, digging for my resolve, "there isn't a back-up plan. It's not something to vote on. I'm the catalyst. If we don't complete the ritual, that potentially endangers everyone in this realm and everyone in hell. Including me. I'm dead either way. At least this way, my death can mean something. I can potentially save you all."

"Potentially," Darius said, dragging the word out, like he'd discovered a clue. "There's no guarantee that will happen. Just what Lucifer says." He snorted. "And who the fuck trusts that asshole anyway? He's got slimy, maleficent vibes about him. I've personally never liked him and I'm very well known for my discerning taste." He winked at me. "Obviously."

"It's not a chance we can take." I looked at them all, my gaze landing on Ro last, begging him to see reason. We grew up as protectors. We knew our lives were likely going to be cut short. It was the norm for people who dove headfirst into danger. This was no different—a sacrifice that needed to be made. The greater good. We were designed for this. "Ro, it's the whole world. I mean, you have to understand—"

He scoffed, his arms crossed over his chest as he stood taller. "Don't look at me like that, Max. You honestly thought I'd understand this? That I'd just nod along and let you do it? *Help* you do it? Do you know me at all? Do you know how un-fucking-fair that is—" his voice hitched, and I watched him swallow back tears that so rarely found themselves close to the surface. "Fuck that and fuck you for thinking it."

"Explain," Atlas said. The sharp hollowness of the word cut through my anxiety, curdling it in my stomach like expired milk.

"I—" I sighed, my tongue tied up as I fought to maintain composure, but I was one push away from breaking down in tears. "I don't know the details, just that the ritual requires my full strength, the stone, and the nexus. Lucifer doesn't think I will survive it. No person could survive it."

"You learned this when?" Atlas's voice was cool, detached, but his eyes were almost pure yellow and I could see him struggling to maintain composure, to control his anger.

I blinked back tears, knowing that this was his biggest fear. Letting me in, letting me close, loving me—just to lose me.

And I'd allowed him to love me anyway, knowing that I'd eventually have to break him.

"The first night," I swallowed, my throat tight, "that I woke up in the lake. I had a dream-walk with Lucifer, and he—he confirmed it then."

"Months?" Ro sniffed, his jaw clenching so tightly that I could hear his teeth grind. "You've been keeping this from us for fucking months, Max?"

"Yes, much time has been wasted," Darius narrowed his eyes, considering, "which is why we can't waste anymore. Hence, the family meeting. Who has ideas?"

"There aren't—" I started, but Darius cut me off.

"You know, I really should have known better. I was so caught up in the whole," he raised his hands in exaggerated finger quotes, "being the good guy thing," he scoffed, took a sip of coffee and cringed at the bitterness, "that I started seeing the best in things, hoping for a bright and sunshiny future. Hell," he turned to me, brows scrunched in disbelief, "I was even willing to live with a cat. But obviously sex and blood and love and what not have made me gullible and—" he waved his hand searching for the word before clearly give up, "you know, rose-colored glasses and what not, content to go with the flow, follow the will of the other good guys in their perfect world of nonsense. Because when I really think about it, *of course* you can't survive that. A literal realm's worth of power flowing through you? Get fucking real. How the fuck could anyone fucking survive that?" He shook his head, pointing his finger at me while he paced back and forth. "You see, this is why sometimes murder is good. Sometimes being greedy and cruel lets you see the world with more clarity, the images sharper, more true. See things for what they really are—all the shitty and evil and whatnot bits of it. If I hadn't been so...so fucking *reformed*, maybe I would have figured this out months ago—maybe before Lucifer even confirmed it. Could have taken you away, and hidden you somewhere—like I've been wanting to do since you broke me out of that damn lab."

"Lucifer's been looking for other options." I sank back into the couch, hyper aware of everyone's eyes on me. "That's what he's been doing since the first time we left hell. He just hasn't found whatever it was that he was looking for."

"And now he's missing," Ro's voice was even, too steady.

Yes. Now he was missing. As was Samael. We had no next option, no clue where to fucking go from here. For the first time, the utter helplessness and hopelessness of the situation clung to my bones, weighing them down.

"I just wanted the rest of my time here with you all to be good memories. I know I should have said something, but I didn't want you all to look at me like," I gestured around the room to them all, "like that."

Izzy squeezed my arm again, quiet solidarity. Her anger and frustration lapped at my skin, but I could also feel her pushing that away for now. She knew I needed someone in my corner on this, and she'd do her best to be that person, even though I could tell she disagreed with me.

That realization—the simple depth of her friendship—made my vision blur.

"No," Darius's eyes widened and he took a step towards me, hand outstretched, before he paused, pulling it back, "no tears. This isn't the end of things. It can't be. I refuse for us to go through everything we went through just for," he scoffed, "for *this* to be reward."

"We still have time." Eli bent forward, elbows on his knees as he scratched the back of his neck. "We don't have the stone, or any leads on it. We don't know where the nexus is." He grunted, "also no leads. Kind of weird to be pleased with the fact that we're missing these things, but at least it buys us more time—to plan for another path, another option."

"There isn't—" I licked my lips, "the blood oath."

"The what?" Ro asked.

I jumped at the sound of a loud crash. Darius's coffee mug was now shattered on the floor across the room, a watery-brown stain dripping on the wall above it.

"Fuck!" he ran his hands roughly through his hair, and for a moment, I froze, convinced that last night's dream-walk hadn't worked, that the magic would overtake him again, upsetting the delicate balance we'd created. "I fucking knew that goddamn oath would bite us in the end."

"Explain." Declan leaned against the kitchen counter, her arms crossed over her chest. "Now."

"When I made that blood oath with Lucifer, and then broke it," I said, ignoring Darius's scoff, "it means that Lucifer has ultimate say over my will, until he chooses to relinquish it."

"Meaning?" Izzy asked.

"Meaning that he can make me go through with the ritual, even if I didn't want to. If I refuse his demand, I'll die. My life will be forfeited either way."

The flash of hope that Darius had been broadcasting dimmed all at once, until there was just panic and anger etched into his eyes.

"There isn't another option," I said, "I'm sorry. I really am. I didn't want to do this to you all. Seeing your pain—your grief—before I'm even gone, that's the only difficult part of this decision for me."

"There is." Ro's gaze latched on mine, before he turned to Darius. "There is another option." Darius stood taller, soaking in every word Ro uttered, like he was bestowing the elixir of life. "Jarrod, that council member—he seemed to think that Max could survive if she shared her power with them, if they helped with the ritual."

"Then we do that," Wade said, pacing, "obviously. How? How do we find them?"

"There's still the problem of the oath," Darius said, "Lucifer won't agree to working with the council."

"Then we don't tell him," Ro snorted, "obviously."

"Or we tell a partial lie," Dec added, "don't tell him until it's too late for him to stop her, to invoke the oath."

I shook my head. "The Guild doesn't want to save the hell realm. Their offer was to destroy hell, and everyone stuck there, for good, or *potentially*—" and I stretched this word out, because I didn't trust Jarrod or the remaining council members —of which there were now only two—as far as I could throw them, "just reseal it—repeat the ritual used that created hell in the first place. No more portals, no more barriers, no more realms. Just two separate worlds, bolstering protectors in this one. I think they think this would help infuse the protector line with the power they've lost through the generations. A do-over of sorts."

"Great," Dec said, brows lifted, "we do that. Go back to the status quo."

The others murmured their assent, but Darius just watched me, his expression grim.

"No," I whispered. "I don't believe the council really thinks that's an option. And if it were, I still wouldn't do it."

"No?" Eli grunted, "what do you mean no? It's an option, Max. Maybe our only one. And if we work with the council, we'll get the stone. They might even know where the nexus is. They don't have a death wish. They want to survive," he said the last part under his breath, like I didn't also want that, "it's in everyone's best interest if we protect the realms from collapsing. Maybe, just this once, we can actually work with them to keep as many people alive as possible. And then, once this is done, we can figure out a way to help people there, to create portals, to get them out—whatever you want."

"And then what, The Guild is just in control of everything, forever?" I added, shaking my head. "That's *why* they would help. Their own greed. Maybe we should want more than the status quo. The only ones who stand to benefit from a return to where we started are the people who held all the power then— protectors. I don't want this to end at the beginning. We've learned too much. What does the status quo look like, exactly? Let's say it works? We seal the realm, and maybe—*maybe* the people stuck in hell survive. Then what? Demons are just stuck there? Forever? Hell is fucking miserable, we've been there. It's a prison that slowly drains the lives of the people stuck there. And *here*, what's here? The council, The Guild, they just get to keep their power, their control? Just because you want to keep me alive for a few more years?"

As if The Guild wouldn't kill me the first chance they got, after they drained every last thing they needed from me.

They didn't keep promises, they had no honor.

Had we learned nothing?

I stood up, begging them to understand. I'd thought about this, I'd already run this through my head, walked every possible path. "I don't want to return to the status quo. I don't want to be the reason the world is stuck in that toxic sludge forever. I want the possibility of something better. A world that people can remake however they collectively see fit—one that isn't built on a lust for power. There's no guarantee that it will be better than what we have now, but there's at least the possibility—and that's everything. Don't you see that?"

"So what the fuck was the point in all of this then?" Ro yelled, his eyes rimmed with red. "Why did you bring us all here? I thought this was supposed to be your big army—that we were going to wage war against the council? What the fuck is this ridiculous Defiance for then, if you're just going to throw us all away to become a martyr?"

"The council is nothing in the grand scheme of things. They are one small pawn in an infinitely bigger battle. And we've succeeded to the best of our abilities in that battle. There are only two of them left, The Guild's power is crumbling." My chest squeezed, and I wanted nothing more than to hug him, to erase the pain I could feel from here, as if it was my own. "I think maybe I didn't bring an army here. I think that this place, the people we've brought together, the people who were here before us—they'll be needed after the ritual, not before."

"To fight?" Izzy asked, her eyes narrowed as she watched me. "For what comes after you're gone, you mean? The council? Demons? Humans? What?"

"I don't know," I said, "maybe. But maybe the thing that will be needed most isn't war. Maybe it's community. Maybe that's the point. Charlie and Bishop helped build a place that meets the needs of everyone who is willing to be a part of it. There's something magical about that, isn't there? There's hope here, the possibility of something better for everyone—a future worth fighting for. Maybe this community's job isn't to tear things down, but to build things back up."

Atlas's eyes met mine, sheer stubbornness and hurt battling in their depths. "There's no future worth fighting for that doesn't include you, Bentley."

Ignoring him, and the way my breath hitched at his words, I walked over to Ro. I grabbed his hand, silently begging him to understand—begging him to see what I saw. "All we ever wanted was to feel like we belonged somewhere, to be part of something we believed in. To feel like part of a community. I thought when we went to The Guild, that maybe there we'd find it. And we did," I gestured around the room, to the people who'd become my family, "but it wasn't The Guild that fostered that. We did. This place," I squeezed his hand, "the Lodge—it's home. *This* is that community." I turned around the room, looking at them all. "You can't ask me to betray that. You have to let me make this choice."

And this place, the people here, they would be here for him —for them all—when I was gone. They'd be here for each other. A family just as strong, just as sturdy, even if I wasn't here with them. That, more than anything, gave me a sense of peace.

"I can't—" A tear fell down Ro's cheek, and I watched his chin dimple, his lips strain as he fought to keep more back. "I can't lose you too, Max."

The pain in his voice cracked my chest in half, and I fought to keep my own sob from following his.

"You have to let us try." Atlas stood next to me now, his eyes searching, begging. "We have time. We don't have any of the things we need for the ritual. That means that there's time for us to find another way. We'll talk to Charlie, we'll talk to everyone. We'll all put our heads together, research, consolidate our resources, and find—something."

I opened my mouth to tell him it was pointless, that it would just be a waste of the remaining time we had left together.

If Lucifer couldn't find a loophole, I had no idea how anyone else could.

But Atlas shook his head. "You have to give us this one thing, Max. We can't just give up. We can't just walk you to your death without a fight. I won't do it. If we have to accept your decisions as yours, then you owe us this. You said it yourself— that there's hope here, the possibility of something better, right? That's what you love about this place—the community? Let us work with them, then. Let us try to find another path, another option. Please."

24

ATLAS

"Please tell me we're not really thinking about letting her go through with this shit, right?" Darius narrowed his eyes as he approached the table.

I was sitting in the restaurant, at the far back table, where I'd asked them to meet me.

Max was with Rowan, Izzy, and everyone else who was trying to reorganize and hold things down while everyone processed the shit show that those ridiculous tandem missions had been.

Charlie and Bishop's immense presence in this place only became more obvious by the struggle to fill their roles.

I clutched my coffee mug, shoving thoughts of Bishop away.

Charlie's scream still reverberated through my skull whenever I let myself linger on that moment, on the sheer despair of it.

I was supposed to bring him back to her.

To their child.

Instead, he was just gone.

Wade and Eli made their way over, both of them looking as exhausted and burdened as I felt.

Darius grinned as he studied me. "No, you won't let her do it. You have a plan."

Wade's brows raised at that, some of the weight he was carrying temporary lifting. "You do?"

Eli spun the chair next to me around and sat down, his head resting on his arms. His eyes were dark, lined with shadowy bags, devoid of the spark and arrogance I was used to.

He glanced at me, and straightened up, like he could feel my pity. "Where's Dec?"

"Here," she yelled, rushing through the door. "Sorry, lost track of time getting Mavis settled in."

Right, Mavis.

Fucking hell, what a mess that kid was.

Whatever The Guild had done to him made my early relationship with my wolf look like a healthy, co-beneficial partnership. I had no idea if he'd ever come out of it—if even an echo of the man I knew still existed in there at all.

If Bishop sacrificed himself for a ghost.

I took a sip of my coffee, cringing at the tepid temperature. I must've been sitting here, lost in my thoughts, for longer than I'd realized.

"I've been thinking," I cleared my throat, blinking the memory of Bishop's final breaths back, "about the fact that there are only two council members left."

The four of them studied me, a panoramic of equal parts hope and impatience.

I focused on Wade. "Whenever a council member dies, what's the first thing that happens?"

"Another is anointed," he said, not missing a beat. "So what?"

"So, if what we learned was true," Dec's brows pinched, and I could see her already putting together the puzzle pieces of my plan, "two had already died before our mission. From their fucked magic infusions. Likely a while ago."

"So what?" Eli echoed Wade's question, but with a far more cynical tone. "Good fucking riddance."

"They didn't name any replacements." Wade sat straighter, the tremor of interest tugging at a muscle in his cheek, below his right eye. "And they probably won't be in a rush to fill the three other seats we left newly-vacant either."

I nodded. "Exactly. Why?"

Eli sighed. "Why the fuck does it matter?"

"They want the power for themselves," Wade continued, a spark of something lighting his expression. The kid always loved puzzles. And while Dec was better at reading me, often following my thoughts down to their logical conclusions before even I'd reached them, Wade was the real problem-solver of the group. "They're going to use this as a chance to move the seven-person council down to two—" he grunted, "or, better yet, probably a one-person dictatorship. More power centralized, less arguing about how things are run."

I nodded. "Which means that those who would likely otherwise be in the running, might be disappointed by this new shift in protocol, this abandonment of tradition."

Eli grunted. "So what? The council is greedy, let them kill each other off. They're hardly our biggest issue at the moment."

"You want to sew discord and chaos." The corner of Darius's mouth curved into a hook. "Turn them against each other. Fantastic."

"We don't know where the final two council members are right now." I scanned around the room, but we were alone. The restaurant wasn't open today. Charlie was usually the one cooking and running it. Everyone was giving her some space to grieve, but this place was like a cold shell compared to the usual warmth and conversation that flowed over lunchtime. "And we don't know how to get in touch with them, or where they're keeping the stone. But—"

"But those who are feeling shafted, might know the answer

to both of those locations," Declan finished for me, her nose twitching as she tried to hold in her excitement. I understood. It felt wrong being excited about anything right now. "And unlike the untraceable council members, Arnell can get us a line to them. They're reachable, less protected." She arched her brow. "And if we can spark that discontent into a flame, perhaps we can convince them to give the remaining council members up. A trade."

"Not a trade. A coup." Eli ran a hand roughly through his hair as he considered, his expression softening some. He nodded. "We offer to get rid of them, do their dirty work. They can't do it. But with Max and her power, we're stronger than they are. Not a terrible idea."

"Sorry, but how exactly does this save Max?" Darius asked with a shrug. "I'm all for fucking with The Guild, and this isn't the worst plan I can think of for getting the stone and killing those last two dingleberries, but it seems this plan just pushes us closer to the ritual. Closer to—" he swallowed, not finishing the thought.

We all felt the heaviness of it anyway.

"I've been thinking," I glanced at him, "about what they said to you. Promising to bond to her, to use her power—that if she bonded to a full council, she might survive somehow."

"She'll never do that," Eli groaned, "didn't you listen to her? She's determined to just throw the fucking towel in rather than give them any more power—"

I raised my hand, nodding. "I know, I know. What I'm saying is, what if *we* become that council. What if *we* find a way to anchor her?" I glanced at Wade, gesturing between him and Darius. "Like what you just did, spreading the weight of his magic through the bond, letting Max reshape it? What if we did that for her, but on a larger scale. If giving her power to shadow-tainted council members might save her, why can't we do that instead? The five of us? Get them to tell us how they were planning to save her, to use her power to keep them all alive. But instead of destroying the hell realm or sealing it back up, we bring down the barrier for good."

"We kill them and use our bond to save her instead." Eli's brows lifted, impressed.

I turned to Darius. "You said that one person could never survive that amount of magic coursing through them. We share a link with her—a true bond. That has to be better than whatever bullshit the council would try to forge with her."

Eli grinned. "One person couldn't survive it, but maybe the six of us could, together."

"Exactly," I said. "We spread it through all of us, carry it alongside her—maybe she doesn't die?"

"Or maybe we all do," Declan added, though there wasn't any resistance in her tone, just a simple acceptance of the fact. "Two council members died from just their miniscule injections of magic that wasn't theirs, and one of them ended up a flesh-eater who was as good as de—" she paused, her eyes darting briefly to Eli, and I knew, like mine, her thoughts had shifted to Seamus. "We might die too. That kind of magic, we don't know what it'll do to us. How it might change us." She shrugged, "but if that's our best option, I'm in."

"I'd rather die alongside her than watch her shift into the afterlife without me," Darius sat back and sighed, looking oddly calm and collected for someone potentially forfeiting their life, "far more tolerable than being left in this world without her anyway."

"She'll never agree to it," Wade shook his head, "there's not a chance. Not if she thinks any of us might die."

"That's not her choice to make," I said, my voice more clipped than I'd intended. "She kept her plan from us. For months. And if she expects us to respect her decisions, her autonomy, then we're owed the same."

Dec took a deep breath, exhaling on a sigh. She considered for a moment, then nodded. "Agreed."

"We keep it from her until the end then," Eli met each of our eyes, as we nodded. "Which means she can't come with us when we shake down the council's underlings. She's smart. She'll figure out what we're up to, and there won't be a way to talk around the details we need from them."

"Someone will stay here, distract her," Darius agreed.

"And once we have what we need from the council's former minions, we leave no witnesses," Dec added, her face unreadable but for the unflinching flare of violence in her eyes.

"Not just a coup of the remaining council members, but we cut out those excited to take their places too." Eli considered for a beat, clearly surprised and impressed with her ruthlessness. He nodded. "I like it."

"And we do it soon, before they have time to regroup," Wade added, the wheels in his mind spinning on full throttle now. "We ask Arnell to get us in touch with them immediately."

Darius cleared his throat. "When it's time, I may know of some back up that we can enlist in the fun."

25

DARIUS

My fist sat an inch from the thick wooden door of Mer's cabin, but I couldn't bring myself to knock.

"Fuck it." I'd come back later.

When I turned around, the tight knot in my stomach loosened a bit. But when the sharp creak of the door opening sounded, any looseness disappeared.

"I've been watching you pace in front of my house for the last twenty minutes."

Busted.

Squinting, I turned around to find Mer leaning against the frame, her eyes sparkling with equal parts amusement and anger.

"I'm famously bad at apology tours, I fear," I said, trying to keep my tone light, teasing. That was always familiar ground for me, but it felt flat this time.

She grunted, disgust lining the set of her mouth. "Clearly. Didn't think you were going to actually knock, so figured I'd save you the trouble." She lifted her eyebrows. "Now that I have, give me one reason why I shouldn't kill you for nearly killing my best friend."

"You're human," I supplied automatically. "You wouldn't be able to."

Mer was tough, but she had nothing on a vampire. I winced at the look on her face, knowing as soon as the words left my mouth that they were the wrong ones to say.

"I'm sure it wouldn't be difficult for me to convince Tex to hold you down while I carved your heart out of your chest." She grunted. "Come to think of it, it'd probably be more difficult for me to convince him to keep you alive than to help me kill you."

I nodded, knowing I deserved it.

I ran my hand over my face, massaging the throbbing ache in my temple.

When I woke up, my memories of returning from our trip came back, but only fragments and hard-to-decipher blurs.

One that stood out—nearly killing Charlie.

"What do you want, Darius?"

"Is she okay?"

Mer took a step closer to me, shutting the door behind me. "Her husband—and the father of her soon-to-be-born baby just died. What do you think?"

I nodded. "Right."

Bishop wasn't my favorite person in the world, but I knew that Charlie loved him—and over the last few weeks, I'd even found myself not entirely despising my time spent in his company.

"I went by her apartment—"

"She didn't want to stay there." Mer dropped her eyes, some of her animosity towards me draining. "Can't say I blame her. Every inch of that place reminds her of him." Her eyes met mine. "She's staying with me, for as long as she wants."

"Makes sense. You're a good friend."

A heavy silence fell between us.

I felt Mer's eyes on me, but I couldn't bring myself to meet her gaze. Shame hung like a heavy boulder in my throat, and it took me a few minutes to work my voice around it.

"Max healed her though, right. She's—" Clearing my throat, I glanced at her briefly before setting my focus back down on the weather-worn basketball that sat on her small porch. "She's okay? Alive, I mean?"

"She'll survive, yes. No lasting effects." She grunted, "physically, I mean. I imagine that being attacked by someone you considered a friend takes a toll on your mental and emotional wellbeing."

"Right." I swallowed. "I'm glad she's alive. Thanks."

I turned around and took a few steps away from her, my heart thumping loud and heavy in my chest.

I could have killed her.

I could have killed Max—

Panic clouded my vision as the memory of their blood mingled on my tongue, a ghost of the almost-massacre.

My fists clenched at my side, and I fought with all of my willpower not to claw my heart out myself, save Mer the trouble. The power existed inside of me, infecting me—a darkness that could take over in the blink of an eye.

It had happened before, but I hadn't cared as much when I'd finally returned to myself. I hadn't had people that I cared about then, people I loved.

My chest was tight, resisting every breath of air I tried to squeeze into it.

"That's it?" Mer called after me. Her feet crunched through the gravel as she walked towards me. "You're not going to see her? You're not going to apologize?"

I shook my head. "Not right now."

"Why?"

"Because I don't deserve her forgiveness until I've earned it. And I know Charlie. I don't want to burden her with feeling like she needs to give it to me. Not now, not when she's already going through so much—" I spun around and jumped, finding Mer only a few inches away from me, her wide, doll-like eyes sharp on my face as she studied me, "pain."

I knew when people were afraid of me, I could usually smell the tangy scent of their fear with a single inhale.

Mer wasn't.

I wasn't sure if that made her brave or reckless.

"I never understood why she always vouched for you." She tilted her head, her arms crossed over her chest. "Over the years, they'd occasionally fight about you—Bishop and her, I mean. Dani too, whenever she was around for a visit and that night came up in conversation. But Charlie always swore you were good, that you saved her that day. Sacrificed your freedom for her life."

My throat tightened, and as much as I wanted to walk away from this conversation, as much as I wanted to sink myself into a problem that I could actually solve, I couldn't. It was like my body had suddenly decided it wasn't mine to control.

"Is it true what your friends said—Max, your brother, the others?" When I didn't respond, she continued. "That there's a power inside of you that you sometimes can't control? One that comes from the barrier between realms that are fracturing. The same magic that everyone is terrified will one day destroy us all?"

My tongue was sandpaper in my mouth, dry and rough, incapable of creating speech.

"And that instead of letting it consume you, instead of letting it out to hurt people, you devote all of your strength to fighting it back, to keeping it locked in?" She narrowed her eyes. "That you've done this for years? Even while in captivity? When sinking into it might have provided you some semblance of reprieve or protection?"

"It's hardly so noble—" my jaw was stiff as I spoke.

"Hardly." She arched a brow, her sharp stare sinking into

me, like she could see and understand things about me even I had no grasp of. "You're right. Charlie would accept your apology and try to ease your guilt if you saw her right now. She already doesn't blame you, hasn't even thought of the bite since the moment he—" for the first time, her voice wavered, "since they brought him back. But I think giving her time to grieve Bishop's loss is wise right now, it's the right move. Besides, while Charlie might be ready to forgive you now, I'm not sure you're ready to hear it."

I swallowed, then turned around, annoyed by this human girl's shrewdness. I felt naked under her perusal, and not in a good way.

"Darius," she called, when I'd made it only a few steps away from her. I didn't turn back around, but I didn't keep moving either. Once again, my body seemed to have a mind of its own, one that didn't belong to me. "While you're on this apology tour of yours, might I add a suggested stop?" I said nothing in her pause, waiting—and hating myself for this girl's strange power over me. "You. I'm no expert in vampire psychology, but even to me—years and years of holding that in, of holding it together and hating yourself for the brief occasions you couldn't," her voice trailed through the wind around me. "I don't know, seems like a good enough penance, doesn't it?"

Claude stood, his feet clothed in shoes that looked obnoxiously expensive, pressed boldly into the shore less than an inch from where the water curled against the rocks. He was still, staring out at the place where he'd materialized when I brought them here.

"Have you seen the ripple again?"

When I'd spoken to him earlier, he mentioned seeing the gentle ripple of a portal, like an iridescent flap over the skyline, a few times. Each time he'd approached, his hand would go straight through. Almost like a permanent tear, but one that didn't seem to lead anywhere.

He didn't turn back to answer, but I noticed the tension in his shoulders. I bit back my smug grin, knowing that I'd snuck up on him—a rare thing to do to a vampire, especially one as powerful as he was.

"Once or twice," he answered, whatever daze his thoughts had wrapped him in, coming slowly undone at my approach. "There's something strange about this place, unsettling. I can't put my finger on it."

I shrugged, staring out into the deceptively calm water.

"That, or it's just the unbalance of having all four of us here," he said, more to himself than to me.

"Speaking of, where's Nash?" I scanned the grounds, half expecting him to jump out and decapitate me at any moment. "Maybe I didn't close the portal properly."

Not that I exactly understood how I opened it up in the first place.

He turned to me, considering for a moment. "You're doing better."

I didn't say anything to that. There was nothing to add. I was better.

As the day bled into night, I felt more like myself than I could remember feeling in years. The burden I'd carried for so many years had lost most of its weight overnight.

I'd carry it all again, tenfold, if it meant that I could keep Max safe.

As usual, whenever I thought I was saving her, she was the one saving me.

Maybe I needed to stop chronically underestimating her strength.

Or overestimating mine.

"Nash is in the medical building." Claude's eyes narrowed

slightly as he turned back to the lake. He was stiff here, somehow even more uptight than usual. He wasn't used to not being the one in control of things, and he didn't do well with trusting strangers. "He's looking over the notes here, apparently one of the boys," his face scrunched in thought, "Arnell, I think his name was?" At my nod, he continued. "Right, well apparently a recent security breach has helped him break into some database. He's pulled up a ton of Guild research on those tainted with shadow magic, on their experiments. Nash doesn't understand much of it—"

"But he's hoping that he might find something to help Nika?" I finished for him. My chest tightened at my friend's name. I hadn't been to see her yet, not that it would make much of a difference. She was unconscious, and every time she came to, she had to be knocked out again. She was much stronger than Eli's father, the werewolf, so Nash was in charge of keeping her under control here so that she didn't lash out and kill anyone.

Claude nodded. "While he isn't versed in the way of medicine or machinery in this realm, apparently he's been fighting for a way to cure her for years. Perhaps combining both sets of knowledge will point to a lead." He shrugged. "That's his hope anyway. Not much else for him to do here in the meantime. We're both just sort of—" he paused, searching for the word, "waiting. Nash has it in his head that the four of us here together might somehow help balance her out, restore her. He swears he's noticed an improvement in her temperament since being here. Can't imagine what that says about her temperament before." He exhaled, exhaustion evident in every line of his expression. "But you pulled us here for a reason. Maybe there's something to his theory about balance. He's clinging to that possibility anyway, and I agreed to stay for a little while longer, to satisfy my own curiosities."

"You don't think it will work?"

"What?" He grunted. "Do I think that existing in the same space will just magically heal her somehow after years of being trapped in her own mind? No." His fists were clenched at his sides. "You weren't there, when the magic tore her apart. It's not something that can just be—undone."

I knew that the 'her' he was referring to wasn't Nika.

He meant our sister. Nessa.

The sister I'd effectively killed when I abandoned my post.

But Nika and Nessa were not the same.

Nika survived because she was a true mirror—a twin and appointed portal guardian.

Maybe she could be saved, restored—like I'd been.

Of course, it was equally likely that Claude was right. The prick did have an obnoxious habit of rarely being wrong. Perhaps, like Nessa, Nika was simply too far gone. For all we knew, the four of us together in the same spot could push her faster towards her doom.

"Then again," he said, pulling me from my thought spiral, "you've come back from that very edge—a thing I would have said was impossible yesterday. Maybe it's possible that Nash really will find a way to get her back. Who am I to destroy his pipe dreams, particularly when the world might very well be collapsing around us as we speak?"

We were quiet for a moment, the silence heavy and uncomfortable.

"Odds he'll trust me enough to work with me?"

"Work with?" Claude snorted, but in a way that was somehow still dignified. "No. But I think he'll be okay with using you."

I sniffed, staring aimlessly at the water, resisting the urge to glance at my brother, to read if the grudge he held against me was as strong as Nash's.

"You abandoned them both in hell, when they thought they'd found a ticket out. Instead, our freedom led to their imprisonment." Claude's lip curled, though his stare didn't waiver from the lake. "It was never quite that neat. You and I merely traded one prison for another, I suppose. Of course, then you abandoned your post here, which directly led to his twin's demise."

The truth screamed against my lips, but I wasn't ready to release it. To tell him why I left. That at the time, I thought I was saving Ness. I thought I was saving him.

"Sometimes I let myself wonder what our lives would have been if we were never given our posts. If we'd simply stayed in hell and found another way to protect her—if we weren't attached to a magic that is slowly eating us alive, beholden to its volatile greed and violent whims. Perhaps she'd be alive. Perhaps we'd—" he shook his head, abandoning the thought. "Of course, what ifs are useless in the grand scheme of things, especially now."

Silence fell between us, thick with all of the unsaid bullshit.

Claude sighed. "No, brother, if you want to procure Nash's help with anything, I think you'll have to offer him something too tempting for him to resist."

Claude spoke for more than just Nash, and we both knew it.

I owed them both apologies. But I also knew I owed them more than that, that right now, apologies were meaningless. My brief tour was going on hiatus.

"How about revenge?"

26

MAX

"Go." Declan handed me a ball that had the hellhound trotting up to us, tongue lolling out the side of his mouth as he wagged his tail. "Get out of here, take a few hours to relax. You need it. We'll be fine."

"But—"

"Max, we'll be okay for a few hours." A small grin tugged at the corner of her mouth, but something about it felt flat and she dropped her eyes when they met mine. She was just as exhausted and drained as we all were.

"Do you want to join me?" I twined her fingers through mine.

For a moment, she wrestled with the offer, a tension I couldn't place. "Not this time, I'm going to stay back and keep an eye on things, maybe catch a nap."

"Alright." I swallowed my disappointment. They'd all been so strange this morning. "I won't be long."

She straightened. "Take as long as you need, Max. Go recharge, take Ralph. This is a marathon, not a sprint. We need you strong and rested for the long haul if we're going to have any hope of—you know, figuring this all out."

Finding a way for me to not die, she meant.

I pulled away, feeling uncomfortable, though I couldn't place why, exactly. Maybe she was right. The pent-up energy of everything.

Tensions were high and I still felt the fumes of our 'family meeting' coat every interaction I had with my team.

"Just, you know," I tapped my head, "reach out if you need anything."

She shook her head. "Give them the space and privacy to process everything. They need it."

Her eyes screamed the truth. She needed it too.

I sniffed, staring at my shoes. "Right."

Ralph nudged my left hand, nosing the cartoonishly small ball that he was obsessed with.

Dec squeezed my shoulder. "It was quite a bomb, Max. We just need some time to figure this all out. And so do you. To say the last few days have been chaotic and gut-wrenching would be the world's biggest understatement, yeah?"

I nodded, suddenly feeling the weight of the cabin press in on me. "You're right."

It wasn't just our cabin either, the unspoken (and very loudly spoken, thank you, Darius) anger and fear, the planning, the grief. The grounds of the Lodge itself were suffocating, the grief unavoidable—attacking us from all directions. Both the loss we were all trying to process and the future loss I was trying like hell to make tomorrow's problem.

"Alright." I fought the desire to leave for another moment, sensing something that Declan wasn't telling me. Maybe she was right though. That was why I needed to leave. To give them space. To think through some things myself for a few hours.

To just go—exist—for a few hours, without the weight of everything suffocating me.

Resisting the urge to press anymore, I kissed the corner of her mouth. "I'll see you in a bit, I guess."

I tasted it in the atmosphere, the heavy sadness that cloaked the community here—metallic and cold and impossible to ignore. I felt Evelyn and Bishop's absence like a heavy stone in the base of my lungs. Saw pain in every pair of eyes I met as I walked through the now-familiar buildings and paths of the grounds. Could feel my own clogging my throat every time I tried to take a breath.

Dec was right. I really was close to burning out. Not just from the last few days, but from the last few months.

I couldn't argue with my team anymore. Couldn't stand to see the hurt and betrayal etched across their features after our talk. I didn't want the remainder of our time together to be filled with so much fear, so much hurt.

As much as they fought me, I knew they were trying their best to understand, to let me go. I needed to find a way to mend things, while giving them the space to express and process what they needed to.

It helped some that they were mobilized by Atlas's request. Since our talk, whenever I entered a room, I'd often find them huddled together, whispering and conspiring, going over options and possibilities that I knew were pointless.

I didn't fight them though. He was right. I did owe them this. I couldn't tell them how to grieve, how to make this okay for them.

But I also couldn't sit there and just...watch them pour over options that I knew would prove futile. So, I sank all of my time and energy into helping out around The Lodge. I did my best to take over some of Charlie's duties, while Mer and some of the others kept watch over her.

I'd kept myself so busy that I'd hardly even had time to catch up with Claude and Nash, but I knew that Darius was keeping an eye on them. Between chores and checking on everyone, I caught glimpses of the three of them a few times. They were always bickering, but even after everything they'd been through, it was clear there was still a healthy layer of affection and love underneath all the muck—they just needed time to dig it up.

I spent last night curled up with Eli, holding him while he tried to process shit with his mom on top of everything else. I hated that he was offered my death on a platter so soon after losing his mom. His complicated emotions about her, about everything, were tangled and gnarled, and my chest ached whenever I lingered on his pain for too long.

I'd tried checking on Levi too a few times when things calmed down, but no one had seen him since their return.

Stopping where the path closed into the woods, I bent over, the heaviness of everything suddenly loud and undeniable when faced with the stillness of the morning.

Maybe Dec was right. I'd been throwing myself into tackling so many issues, helping as many people as I could after our missions, that it was all just building up—becoming overwhelming.

I pressed my palm into my sternum and took a deep breath, reaching for the bonds, grateful that I could feel them all there —even though it hurt, even though it brought back the edges of my own grief I'd only just managed to fold into myself—a quiet, but ever-present echo.

Go. Declan's voice filtered into my thoughts, pulling them back from the dark cliff they balanced on. *I promise we'll be okay here for a few hours. That hellhound needs a run and he won't leave your side. Eli's okay. Wade and Atlas are okay. Darius is...well, Darius—which I never thought I'd say is a fucking relief. I'll hold things down while you're away and I'll be here when you get back.*

I took a deep breath, nodding to myself, then pushed the connection away, as she'd asked.

She was right. We all just needed some space.

This afternoon, we were going to regroup, go over mission debriefs and make a plan for next steps. There were two council members left, and while I had no fucking clue where they'd be hiding, I knew that they were the key to getting the stone—so that's where we'd start.

Ralph's paws crunched in the sparse patches of snow as he slowed his stride to match mine.

I buried my hand in his thick fur, drawing strength from his steady presence. She wasn't wrong. He hadn't stopped patrolling our cabin, herding us all together throughout the chaos of the last few days. We didn't really have the space for six adults and a giant hellhound in the cabin, but none of us would turn him away. He brought a warmth to our team, made the space feel more homey and lived in.

He'd been a silent companion, a beacon of comfort and warmth I hadn't realized how much we'd all needed.

Hell, Darius had even stopped threatening to toss Shadow out into the snow once he realized that Ralph now considered her part of his pack.

The cold dawn breeze fluttered through his fur and turned his breaths into soft clouds of smoke, making him appear more hellhound-like than usual.

We stood there for a while, the two of us taking in the sights of the lake from the periphery.

Charlie was on the dock, leaning into Mer as her shoulders shook with soft sobs.

My vision went hazy from witnessing her pain.

Since our return I couldn't bring myself to speak more than a few words to her, to comfort her. I wasn't sure what my place was with a cousin I'd only just learned was family and I didn't know how to ease a hurt that I knew only too well couldn't be eased.

Partially because I knew that it was my fault, at least to some degree. Charlie and Bishop's child would grow up father-less because of a mission I'd helped orchestrate.

But also because her grief was the sort that hollowed out

my chest in an unfamiliar way, one that made me feel nauseated if I let myself linger in it too long.

She'd lost her partner.

I couldn't even begin to imagine what it would feel like
losing one of mine.

I'd be putting them all through the same agony one day.

The realization lodged heavy and icy in my gut, curling its
blade-like fingers over my ribs and squeezing tight. Looking at
her was like looking at a premonition of what they'd go
through.

Soon, probably.

Though not as soon as we'd planned. I was both grateful
and ashamed of that.

All this pain, and it was all for nothing. We'd lost two
members of this community and we were no closer to finding
the stone.

The only thread we had to hold onto was the fact that there
were only two council members left.

Of course, without Evelyn's intel, we had no way of finding
them, no way of tracking down where they might be hiding the
stone.

It was a thought spiral I slid down on an infinite loop whenever the grief bled into rage.

Ralph's head nudged me as a small whisper-bark brought
me back from the edge.

"Right," I muttered, "air."

I forced my lips into the closest thing to a smile I could
manage right now and patted him. "Let's go for a run, boy."

When his tail wagged, his entire back end followed suit.

I took off, and he kept pace next to me, slowing his stride to
match mine, both of us adding considerable speed once our
legs were warmed up.

Before I realized it, the forced smile shifted into a sincere one, as the crisp air chilled my cheeks and the strain of exercise lifted the vice that had been tightening around my chest.

We ran hard and fast, suffocating the ruminating thoughts until they had no energy of their own to churn.

We were maybe eight or nine miles into it when we paused in a clearing, Ralph demanding some water and a quick game of fetch.

He dropped the red ball at my feet. One of the kids at camp had given it to him and I rarely saw him without it anymore. It was a bit absurd—the small size of the ball compared to the large size of the dog—but he loved it.

I tossed the ball as far as I could throw it, wiping the excessive slobber coating it against my thigh.

He took off, pouncing and prancing through the brush more like a deer or giant rabbit than a dog, and disappeared from sight, his playful soft barks echoing through the trees and forcing the sleeping birds from their perches.

I stood in the small clearing, catching my breath and enjoying the small reprieve while he dug through snow and piles of sticks, trying to find his prize.

It was a bright, crisp morning, and even in the thick of the forest, I felt the gentle heat of the sun kiss my skin. I closed my eyes for a moment, basking in the feel of it, letting some of the heaviness that had been weighing me down evaporate from my pores.

A twig snapped behind me, disturbing the brief peace I'd fought so hard to find.

My blade was already clutched at my side, my muscle memory faster than my fear, as I spun around to meet the intruder.

I expected a rabbit or a wolf, some animal startled from rest by Ralph's rambunctious play.

Instead, there was a man.

He stood tall and lean, the few visible patches of his brown skin marred with scars and inked markings. Dark, wavy hair fell over his brows and down to his shoulders, meeting a thick, curly black beard that held a few stray twigs hostage in their strands.

He was dressed for the weather, in hiking boots and a down jacket, a large pack hitched high on his back. If it weren't for the blade dangling from his right hand, I'd have thought him just a human man who'd wandered off a hiking path.

But he didn't seem lost, and his glare was just as sharp as the weapon his fingers tightened around.

They were dark as coal and pinned narrowly on me, like he'd been searching for something and I'd come up lacking.

There was something familiar in the lines of his face, though I couldn't pin down what exactly it was.

I didn't know every person who lived at The Lodge by name, but I was certain I'd never seen this man around before. He had the sort of presence that couldn't easily be forgotten. Strong, foreboding. Dangerous.

"Hi. Are you lost?" I'd give him the benefit of the doubt, but my feet shifted anyway, years of Cy's training preparing my body for a spar, even though teleporting would probably be the safest thing to do out here if it came to blows.

His shoulders relaxed as he studied me, a small grin hooking the corner of his mouth, though I couldn't entirely tell if the smirk was malicious or not. "No. I don't think that I am."

Ralph came bulldozing back, the red ball dropping at my feet with a liquid flop, as he put himself between me and the strange man. A low, soft growl rippled from his chest, vibrating the ground at my feet.

From the brief flashes I could see of him around Ralph, the man looked startled.

He dropped the blade at his feet and took a few steps back.

"Easy," he said, his voice a low, deep rumble, "I mean no harm."

Ralph took a step closer, then another, his loud sniffs echoing through the clearing as he pressed his nose to the ground, then to the man's feet.

I stepped around for a better look and found the mysterious man craning his neck back, eyes shut and trying not to panic as Ralph's nose pressed to his chest.

He looked rightfully hesitant, but not nearly surprised enough by the presence of a giant supernatural hound as he would be if he were human.

Ralph let out a strange whine I'd never heard before, then spun in a circle, his tail wagging with a vengeance.

Then he jumped towards the man, but instead of attacking, he licked the man's face, from his chin to his temple.

The man's lip curled in disgust, but he didn't dare push the hellhound away. Instead, he stood there, his face slick with saliva, a curl of his hair protruding at an awkward angle, caked in slime.

Unbothered by the man's ambivalence, Ralph nuzzled the red ball over until it hit his mud-coated shoe, waiting patiently for him to throw it.

I held my breath, confusion fighting for shock as I watched the scene unfold before me.

The man glanced briefly from me to Ralph, and I could see that he was just as conflicted, every muscle frozen, like he wasn't entirely sure if the hound wanted to play or was simply tasting out his next meal. With a heavy sigh, he bent down slowly, picked up the ball and tossed it far into the woods.

Ralph took off with a happy leap, not even sparing me a glance as he ran off after his prize. Traitor.

The man relaxed, watching the hellhound pounce through the snow like a puppy. "Friend of yours, I take it?"

I'd never seen Ralph take so quickly to a stranger, and he'd always been a good judge of character. Still, I couldn't bring myself to trust this man just yet.

I arched a brow, not wanting to give an inch. "Who are you? How did you find this place?"

He dropped the pack from his back with a soft thud, then took a few steps closer to me.

I held my dagger up between us, stopping him before he got any closer. "My patience isn't exactly elastic these days."

"Neither was hers," he said, that small half-smile again, though this time it quivered just slightly. "Ever. And I know this place because it's mine."

I didn't drop the blade, but I didn't push forward to break his skin either. "The Lodge?"

"And my name," in a move too fast for me to predict or react to, he disarmed my dagger and held it to my throat, "is Saif. Judging by that familiar, stubborn expression on your face, that must make you my niece."

27

____

DARIUS

"Fucking hell that's awful." Nash's face was nearly green as his knees started to buckle. He didn't fall down or vomit though, so that was something. He was still getting his earth-side sea legs, so teleporting was probably extra fucking awful for him right about now. The moment he caught his balance, he was bent next to Nika, calming her. Attempting to, anyway.

"You're welcome for the free ride," I muttered. They were rare. Wait until he got a load of how much plane tickets cost.

I turned to Eli, Atlas, and Wade, who'd brought Claude and Nika, making sure nothing catastrophic had happened to them on the trip over.

Nika didn't appear to have eaten any of them during the shift here, so I was counting that as a win.

Arnell set up the meeting and we'd left as soon as Dec was certain Max made it to the woods, that she'd be gone for a few hours.

She was staying behind, begrudgingly, as was Ro. It was a precaution in case shit went down and we needed help getting out of here—or keeping Max distracted.

Nika snapped when Nash touched her, and for a moment I thought she was going to go full evil dead and try to kill us all. Do The Guild a favor.

Instead, her eyes darted to each of us, lingering longer on me and Claude, like she recognized us. Almost.

Thick chains cuffed her hands and legs, a brace around her neck to keep her from attacking—but she hadn't yet.

Nash raised his hands, approaching her slowly this time, like she was a wounded puppy and not a feral, overpowered vampire who wanted to drain every ounce of blood from his veins.

Love was a veil sometimes.

Still, when he caught her gaze in his, some of the tension eased from her shoulders. Maybe he was right, maybe she was getting a little better, the balance righting itself—if only just slightly.

"I still don't see why we needed to bring her," Wade mumbled, quiet enough that only me and Atlas heard him. "Seems like an unnecessary liability in what is already a tense, risky situation."

"She deserves revenge on the people who did this to us, who did this to her," I said, keeping my voice even. I owed her this. We all did.

I held my breath as Nash unlocked her chains, unsure whether the odds were higher that she'd bolt out of here or attack her twin. Or me.

She did none of the above, thankfully, choosing instead to continue watching us all like hawks—a scavenger selecting its next meal with care.

I shrugged. It was the best-case scenario, though I'd be lying if I said it didn't sting, seeing her like this.

Growing up, she was the loudest, gentlest, happiest of us all. Now, she was a shell of the girl I knew, frightened and cornered into a wild violence that would have broken her heart.

It broke mine now. Fucking cruel what this world had done to her. What I'd done to her, however unintentionally.

"We're meeting them at the site, it'll take us a few minutes to walk there, can she make it?" Atlas asked, tone matter-of-fact. He was in mission-mode, as Max liked to call it.

Still, as collected as he sounded, I saw the threads of yellow in his eyes.

The wolf was at the surface. Good. We needed him.

Nash shot him a look, voice tense. "She'll make it."

He whispered something in her ear as Eli and Wade led us forward, blades hanging loose in their hands. Their steps were quiet and sure, like they walked these grounds in their sleep.

When Nika started to follow, I let go of the breath I'd been holding.

It was a risk, bringing her, but it felt right. Including her in this. She deserved revenge as much as we did for what The Guild had done to us all, for what they'd forced us to become.

When her dark eyes met mine, my stomach tightened at what I saw. It was brief, but it was there—a flash of my best friend.

That small flash disappeared quickly though, as she let loose a low, guttural growl, her teeth bared as she lunged towards me.

I didn't flinch, didn't back away. I let her fingers grip onto me, so tight that she'd have snapped bone if I were a human.

"Easy, Nik," Nash cooed, calm and steady, like she was a toddler. "That's Darius. He's a prick, but he was your friend."

My brain latched onto that word—was—but I didn't fight him on it. Instead, I held her gaze, as we kept walking, like nothing out of the ordinary was happening. Eventually, she loosened her grip. Her muscles rippled and tensed as she resisted the deep urge to feed on me. She didn't.

"Good." Nash's face lit up with a smile as he caught my eye —a shared recognition in her progress.

It took him a minute to realize he was sharing that moment with, well, me, and he dropped his gaze when he did.

He was right not to abandon her, to hold onto hope. She was still in there, buried deep under the blood lust.

She had better control than I had when hunger took over.

Eli whistled when the forest opened into a clearing. "She really did a number on this place."

He grinned, brows raised, impressed.

Wade grunted. "Damn right she did."

The council's underlings asked for a meeting spot. I suggested their old headquarters. A bit of a petty power move on my part, perhaps, bringing them to the scene of a battle they'd clearly lost.

The grounds were covered in the charred remains of the cabins, and I could smell the softest tinge of smoke damage in the air, even months later. The building I'd spent years in was burnt to a crisp, looking more like the site of ancient ruins than like the state-of-the-art 'research' center that it was. Good riddance.

It wasn't just a site of destruction though.

The woods had started to reclaim the grounds as their own.

There were new patches of grass, wildflowers budding in the cracked, fractured concrete, and more than a few nests of refuge built by the local wildlife.

It was beautiful in its own way. I much preferred it like this at least.

There were seven large vans about a hundred feet away, untouched by the brutal scorch of Max's fire.

In a succession of unnecessarily loud slams, protectors poured out of them, most in full riot gear.

I stiffened, even though I'd known they would be here.

I felt Claude do the same at my side.

It was against our nature to willingly meet protectors, especially when we were deeply outnumbered.

They'd agreed to the terms Arnell had conveyed. Seven of us would meet here, but they were bringing fifty of their own.

If I had my way, that would leave the grounds anointed with the blood and entrails of fifty bodies when I was through. I didn't trust a single one of them.

Honestly, I was just impressed they'd all managed to pack themselves like sardines in those seven vans and keep it to the number they promised.

"Here we go," Eli muttered under his breath, fingers flexing over the handle of his dagger. He looked at me from the corner of his eyes, his mouth twisted into an arrogant grin. "Try not to lose your shit too quickly, eh vamp? Just remember if you get cut, I get cut."

I winked. "Like I'm not deeply aware—at all times—of how often your recklessness has resulted in getting me injured."

Truthfully, I forgot all the time, and was more than a little thankful for the reminder. Max didn't like it when we were hurt.

"Serves you right, binding yourself to a fucking protector," Claude muttered.

"Was the full patrol really necessary?" Wade's lip curled in disgust as the protectors made their way towards us, many of them carrying dart guns likely filled with cartridges of the poison I was only too familiar with.

But it was the last arrival that had my pulse beating a bit faster than I'd have liked.

It was a frail-looking girl, her ankles and arms bound. Even from here, I could see that her eyes were pitch black, the reddish curls framing her face kept waving into a smokey-shadow.

I swore. "They brought a fucking drude. Where the hell do they keep getting them from?" They were supposed to be nearly extinct. I'd never even come across one in my particular pocket of hell, yet these assholes kept trotting them out like they were as common as bad opinions.

Atlas stiffened beside me, and I was filled with a renewed anger on his behalf.

"A drude wasn't part of the deal," I said, my voice tight.

The girl's expression was drawn, half dazed, and there was an unhealthy grayish tinge to her skin that made her look half-dead, translucent. She didn't have a good hold on the human form she was in, but she was being forced to embody it anyway. Caged in flesh. Starving.

She'd feed the first chance she was given. I couldn't even blame her.

That's how the council was controlling the druden they'd captured. Starvation. Desperation. The druden were so in need of feeding on nightmares, on pain, that when given the chance, they didn't think twice—there were no options, other than killing whoever was within reach.

"Drude?" A thin white man, dressed in a standard, poorly-fitted suit took a few steps towards us, distinguishing himself in the crowd.

Claude bristled, but I had a feeling it was more so because he was offended by the man's fashion taste than anything else.

The man arched his brow, and followed my line of sight. "Is that what you call them?" He shrugged, his gaze swinging back to Atlas. "Apologies, Mr. Andrews, I hear you are intimately familiar with their powers. One can never be too safe these days and we're not exactly evenly matched. Consider its presence an incentive to keep the peace today. If it's any consolation, the creature's keeper assures me that it can't attack until unbound. Our restrictive technology has improved exponentially in the last year—truly marvelous discoveries are made when the stakes are high." His lips narrowed as he parted his hands in a peace offering. "Let's just make sure it remains unnecessary, shall we?"

Nika vibrated with barely-constrained tension.

Nash insisted she was gaining better control over herself, but I wasn't so sure.

I shot Nash a look, imploring him to keep her from pouncing. We needed to get what we came here for first, then she could have her fill—a buffet of asshole if she wanted.

He grabbed her wrist and whispered to her. She didn't calm completely, but I could tell she was implementing more restraint.

"So," the man clapped his hands together, as his lackeys filed around him in some super-agent formation I was certain they'd practiced for hours. "Arnell told us you were finally ready to negotiate—to give up the girl."

A low growl emanated from Atlas, one I felt mirrored in my own chest.

The man's thin lips stretched into a slimy, greedy smile, and I had the sudden urge to make sure Nika didn't drain him dry when the time came for it. Sometimes you could just tell when a dude had rotten blood.

His focus was reserved completely for Atlas, Eli, and Wade —his entourage busy with throwing tentative, fearful looks at the rest of us.

I flashed fang, just for the fuck of it, grinning when two of them flinched.

"Then you misunderstood. We're not giving her up." Wade took a step forward. "We want to discuss the Council's future goals—or, rather, what they should be."

Of all of us, Wade was the most level-headed, the best at keeping his emotions in check. We'd decided early on that he'd handle most of the conversation. Incubi were always useful to keep around for social and political manipulations.

I heard the gentle suggestion of power in his words. The kid was getting good at controlling his new magic tricks.

The man's smile twitched before re-fixing itself to his face.

"It's good to see you boys again. I haven't set eyes on you myself since you were," he gestured to waist-height, "about this tall."

"I'm assuming," Wade pressed, ignoring the man's awkward attempt to relate, "that you agreed to meet with us because, like us," Wade's focus shifted, his gaze cutting to a few of the other protectors in the assembly, like he could sense which ones truly held the power here, "you know that the council doesn't have The Guild's true interests at heart."

"And tell me, Mr. Andrews," a tall, muscular woman took a few steps forward until she stood shoulder-to-shoulder next to Sir Slimeball. "Whose interests are you committed to these days?"

'You may not have noticed, but the world is quite literally hanging on the precipice of collapse." Wade grinned, a reserved, political sort of grin, though I knew him well enough now to see the hatred packed behind it, to feel the pulse of his power fighting for restraint. It was rare for lust demons to have much power in the waking world, especially when they weren't in hell. Since we'd strengthened the bonds to Max, all of our strengths had been slowly enhancing. "We are invested in keeping as many people alive as possible. As are you, I'm sure."

"Of course, of course," Slimeball cooed. The woman next to him merely nodded, expression tight.

"Good," Wade's eyes narrowed, just a fraction, "I'm glad we are agreed on that at least. Especially given that the current council seems to only be focused on power. Not for The Guild, not for humanity. For themselves."

Several of the protectors bristled and tensed, a few of them darting glances at each other.

"We don't agree with everything The Guild stands for," Wade continued, "especially not with how things have been handled lately. But our own values and beliefs aren't important right now. We're willing to work with you, for the sake of survival, but we are not willing to work with those who put their own thirst for power ahead of the safety of others."

"Are you suggesting a coup, Mr. Andrews?" The woman's brow arched, and she exchanged a look with another weasel in their ranks, her lips betraying the small start of a smile. She was interested. Very. "That you'd work with a different council—one more aligned with your values, perhaps?"

"We've noticed that you only have two council members left," Eli said, his voice deep and devoid of its usual snark and arrogance. So he *could* turn it off when he wanted to. "That no others have been appointed to the vacant slots. It seems they are invested in keeping the power they've—found," he stalled on the word. Stolen. The power they've stolen. "For themselves. And so long as they keep that power, you aren't strong enough to take them out. Not alone, anyway."

"And you are?" Some faceless dickhole in the crowd yelled out.

I ignored the urge to march over and disembowel him immediately. Instead, I played out the fantasy over and over on a loop in my mind.

Max would be proud of my restraint.

"We are," Wade said, somehow maintaining his smoothness, despite how fucking obnoxious these raging dildos were.

"What do you suggest, exactly?" Another one of their minions asked, finding the courage to speak. "What's in it for us?"

I bit back a groan. This was going to take forever to get them slowly to our side of things. My brain was going to rot with how slow and vapid they were.

"We'll take out your council problem," I took a step forward, delighted when a few of the protectors closest to me flinched back, hands instinctively flexing over their weapons. Try me. Please. I'd love an excuse to feed one of them to my dear friend Nika. "If you tell us where to find them, and where to find the stone they are keeping. Then, you're all free to fight over however many council spots you want. Hell," I shrugged, "make yourselves kings and queens for all we care. Divvy up your internal power however suits your fancy. We give—and I truly cannot stress this enough—precisely zero fucks."

"Darius," Eli mumbled, "what the fuck are you doing?"

"Speeding things along," I whispered back. "We only have so long to make this happen, and they're being offensively obtuse. I'm simply stating things in a way they'll understand. You know, keeping things under three syllables, removing all metaphors."

"I do admire your directness." The creepy dude coughed out a laugh that was so fake it made my stomach turn. "And while we *might* be able to point you to the council members, the stone must remain with us. It's a sacred relic of our people. We were charged with protecting it and must remain so."

I snorted. Protecting my ass.

"That's not going to work for us." Atlas's voice was soft, but it carried through the field, even and cold, and laced with a growl that ushered no question whether the man was a were-wolf. "The stone is necessary to stabilize the realms."

"Ah, but we can help with that process, can't we?" The man turned to the woman, to the rest of his peers in question. "We can help the girl—take her burden."

Take her power, they meant. Greedy fucks.

They nodded in assent, avarice etched into every last one of them, like a virus. It had become an epidemic, something those high up in The Guild could never escape—the thirst for more power.

Even if we did let them live, it was clear their fight for those new sparkly council positions would be a battle of death and deceit. The only one who didn't look excited was the drude, and that was because she was half dead *and* their prisoner.

"And how would you do that, exactly?" I asked. "Take her burden, I mean?"

The two proto-leaders shared a glance, silently assessing each other's thoughts.

The woman took a step forward, still choosing to speak to Atlas, Wade, and Eli, and ignoring the rest of us like we were nothing but used gum on the underside of a desk. Pricks. "She is a siphon, but she does not need to remain one. We can use the stone to bind her to us—to forge bonds just as we have between protectors for years. She is still one of us after all, this is no different." My teeth ground together as I bit back my retort. "Then, once we have access to her power, we can remove it from her, and thus her role in this. Once we are strong enough, once we've survived the injections of shadow magic—"

"How exactly are you injecting magic you've stolen into protectors?" I asked.

His nostrils flared "That's none of your concern, and it's not stolen."

Several of his lackeys eyed the drude with discomfort.

Ah. So it was through their recent acquisition of druden. That explained why they'd grown to rely on them so heavily.

"Once we are closer to her level," she continued, "our power will grow when connected to hers, she need simply relinquish it to us. Then, the seven of us who are anointed can act as siphons. We will repair the barrier between worlds, as has always been ordained. If we're careful, between the seven of us, it should be enough to stabilize and stitch the realms closed. With our presence, our expertise, the notes from our elders detailing the original ritual—we can mend the rift. We can keep her alive."

Claude grumbled. "And keep everyone trapped in hell, until the magic of the realm destroys them all, you mean."

The hell realm wouldn't be the only place to suffer. Giving them access to Max's power would put the whole world in even more danger than it already was. These fuckheads cared for nothing but themselves.

"We were told there was a way to simply pull down the veil separating the realms, remove the shadow magic barrier altogether," I said, though my instincts had been screaming at me that this was a crock of steaming shit from the moment I'd heard it.

"And let demons roam freely in this world?" Slimeball let out a sound somewhere between a wheeze and a gasp. "No, that's not possible. It's against everything we stand for. Our ancestors would never have created such a provision."

Bingo. The Guild, surprising exactly no one, never had honor.

I ground my teeth together, but kept my urges to kill, maim, and decapitate at bay when Eli shot me a warning look.

"If you were told otherwise," he continued, "I apologize. it was merely an attempt by Jarrod or Xavier to pacify you and secure your chances of working with them. A lie, nothing more. But if you work with us, we can save the girl. And you have our word we will harm none of you. You may live your lives in this world, as if you were human."

How mag-fucking-nanimous.

Of course the council had been lying. About everything. From day one.

All they cared about was obtaining more power, even if it killed them. It had *already* killed two of them.

They were addicted to the mere promise of it, the possibility. And, council members or not, these dickholes were no different.

I would deeply enjoy watching Nika have her fill of them, now that I was confident in the truth: they needed us, we didn't need them.

The only thing they had to offer in return was death and destruction—greed could lead to nothing else.

Hell, their greed caused this whole mess, it wouldn't fix it.

"We were wrong." I whispered, quiet enough that only our side could pick it up. "They were never going to even do the ritual. Temporarily stabilize the barrier, maybe. Buy some more time for their brutal reign to regroup. This was always just about stealing her power, even if it kills them in the process. They can't help her. Not really. But I think we can. When the time comes."

Atlas's theory that six was better than one when it came to the ritual was promising. It would either save her, or take us all out too.

Either way, when it came down to it, she wouldn't be alone.

And our way of attempting to save her wouldn't kill off or condemn an entire realm of people.

We just had to figure out how to do it.

Wade studied me, his jaw clenched tight, expression unreadable. For a second I thought he might push back, fight me on this. Instead, he nodded, almost imperceptibly, before turning back to them.

"Deal," he lied, voice loud and clear. "You can take her power, if that will save her. I suppose we have no other option."

I grinned. Translation: we did, we just weren't letting these fucktwats in on it.

"Tell us where to find the stone and the council members and we'll bring you Max," he added, lips pressed into a firm line as he tried to contain his cool for a few more minutes.

A rancid smile carved its way across the creep's face, one that was mirrored on several of his cronies as well. They were so consumed with greed, with the promise of dipping their toes in pools of stolen power, that they weren't thinking straight.

He pulled a small piece of paper and a pen from his pocket. Silently, he scratched a few lines onto it, before stepping midway between his group and ours. "These are the coordinates. You'll find the stone and Jarrod's hideout there. But we'll need something in return, collateral to guarantee you won't betray us."

Wade stiffened, narrowing his eyes. "What kind of collateral?"

The woman tilted her chin forward, her posture straightening. "We require that three of the girl's current bonds come with us, and agree to take power dampeners. Just until your end of the bargain is upheld and we have inherited the girl's burden."

Yeah, so not fucking happening. On any level.

"Just to clarify," Eli's hand flexed around his dagger, "the world's literal survival is at stake here, and your number one concern is still maintaining the upper hand?"

The woman's eyes narrowed, just a touch, but her fake-ass smile remained plastered to her face. "We have no reason to trust you, Mr. Bentley, this merely gives you a reason to hold up your end of the bargain. We are doing this for the greater good."

The greater good of her pockets, maybe.

So, basically, if I understood this right, the TLDR of their 'greater good' plan: steal Max's power, kill off every creature in hell, be the strongest beings in the world, and reap congratulations for saving humanity.

And that was assuming they managed to do all of the above without accidentally killing everyone off in the process. Something I had no faith in.

I fought back the tremendous urge to roll my eyes.

Instead, my focus locked on that small square of paper, gripped in the man's greasy fingers. He'd given us the coordinates, we just had to trust that they were accurate, that they weren't fucking with us on this one thing at least.

Which meant that all we needed to do here was remove it from his grasp...or remove his hand from his wrist. I didn't much care either way, though one certainly sounded more exciting.

A small flutter of noise, both loud and soft at once stole the attention of a few of their minions. They bristled and gasped, fear rippling over them like a wave.

A man had materialized at the edge of the forest, his expression grim.

"Councilmember Xavier," the woman said, her voice wavering with fear, despite her attempt to contain it. "We weren't expecting you here."

"Clearly," he said, "but I see you've done one useful thing and drawn most of the girl's bonds to one place. How convenient."

28

———

MAX

My breath caught in my lungs, shock rolling over me that had nothing to do with the fact that he pressed the edge of my blade to the sensitive flesh of my neck.

"Saif? As in Sayty's twin?" The blade dented further into my skin when I spoke, but I didn't fight him off, didn't back away.

It was easier to study him now that his face was barely even a foot from mine. There was a layer of grime covering the visible patches of his face, and his hair was knotted with matts, like dried blood had fused bits of the wild waves to his scalp. His full lips were chapped, and there appeared to be a small piece of one ear missing—an almost impossible feat for a partial demon.

He smelled of dried sweat and musk and there was something almost wild about him that I couldn't quite pinpoint, but that fit perfectly in these woods. I wondered when the last time he'd even been indoors had been.

There was an otherworldliness in the dark abyss of his eyes, an intelligence that was almost terrifying to look directly at for more than a moment or two.

But after taking him in, I found myself searching for fragments of myself too. Pulling apart Lucifer's features that had braided with my own, trying to fill in the missing bits, crafting an image of my mother from the man who stood in front of me, using myself as part of the blueprint.

He dropped his wrist and pressed the handle of my blade into my palm, our fingers brushing as I closed mine around the familiar hilt.

A shot of warmth sparked down my spine, easing any of the remaining tension still cradled in my body. There was a kinship I felt suddenly, thrumming through my veins.

His stare burned into my skin, like he was studying me with just as much curiosity, just as much disbelief.

"As in my uncle?" I whispered, afraid to speak it too loudly, like putting voice to the hope would give the universe a chance to seize it away from me, to blot it out before I could be sure.

His jaw worked subtly at the word, the only indication he'd heard me.

For a moment that felt far longer than it probably was, he said nothing, just held my gaze in his, considering. Then, with a heavy exhale, he took a step back.

"Forgive me." He shook his head, eyes now taking in our surroundings, landing everywhere but back on me, like he'd already used up all of his capacity to take me in. "It's been a long time since I've seen her. And you share so—"

He took a few steps back, then sat down next to his pack, shoulders slumping slightly like the heaviness of whatever he'd been through had finally come to collect.

"I thought you were dead." Hadn't that been what Charlie had said? That she'd inherited her restaurant at The Lodge from an uncle she'd never known? From Saif?

"Good as." He nodded, then began digging roughly through his pack until he pulled out a pouch of water and then immediately drained it into his mouth. "That was intended."

My legs, of their own volition, buckled, until the rest of my body followed suit and I found myself suddenly sitting on the cold, wet forest floor a few feet away from my resurrected uncle.

Ralph pranced back over to us, oblivious to my shock. He dropped the ball in my lap before he circled a few times and curled into my side, his warmth a welcome presence as I leaned into him.

A ridiculous smile carved across my face. This was our first win in so long. And we so desperately needed one. "My fa— Cyrus. He adopted me. He tried finding you. But Charlie said you'd died. You left The Lodge to her and the others—to The Defiance."

"The Defiance, eh?" His nose curled slightly. "That's what they went with? Has a bit of unnecessary drama to it, doesn't it?" He tilted his head, considering. "Cyrus. She mentioned him before. A good man, she said. He raised you, yes?" I nodded. "Then I'll be happy to meet him."

The joy ripped from my stomach like a knife. "He—" I took a deep breath, trying to dislodge the sudden weight in my chest. "He's gone."

Saif's expression softened slightly. "I see. I'm sorry. That appears to be the case for far too many who deserved a longer chance at happiness." As if sensing my discomfort, he rifled through his bag once more and pulled out an orange, peeling as he tackled the rest of my unanswered questions. "I needed people to think I was dead, and so I made it so. But, as you can see," he tossed the cured peel back in his pack as he broke the fruit into two, tossing me half. "I am not. Not yet, anyway."

"Where have you been?" An edge of accusation slipped into my tone before I could correct it. If her twin survived, why did Sayty give me to Cyrus? Not that I would give up a single moment I'd had with him, with Ro—but could I have had this uncle in my life too? Another tether to family?

"Hunting."

"For what?"

"At first, for my troublemaker of a sister. She had a knack for hiding that not even I could ever quite crack. Then, after I realized how futile that was, for Michael."

"Sayty? My mom, you mean? Or a different sister?"

"Your mother." His stare snagged on my face again, as if he was parsing her out in me the way I had been moments before in him. "But I didn't find her."

I choked on the small chunk of orange. Did he not know?

I suddenly hated myself, that I'd have to be the one to shatter that hope.

"She's gone too."

He considered me for a moment, popped a slice of orange into his mouth, chewed, and swallowed it, before responding. "Maybe. I didn't believe that for many years. You see, for protectors, twins are rare." He offered a slice of orange to Ralph, grinning when the hellhound inspected it for a moment before swallowing it whole. "And your mother and I—we are the anchors. At least we were. I'm not entirely sure if your birth negated that."

"Anchors?" It was the same word that Lucifer had used about me. An anchor which the shadow magic could sift through. A catalyst.

"Do you know the history of the realms?"

"Some of it." I tossed the rest of my orange to Ralph. The adrenaline coursing through my body made it impossible to stomach anything right now. "Cyrus told me that Sayty's line— your line too, I suppose—had a hand in creating hell. That your ancestors split ties with The Guild after, attempting to restore the balance of power The Guild had misaligned."

He nodded. "That's part of it. Our ancestors were tricked into using magic they didn't understand—manipulated and used by those who went on to formulate the so-called Guild." He took a deep breath, letting it out in a heavy sigh. "But creating an entire realm is no simple thing and they had no idea what they were really getting into. They imagined it to be a truce, one that would bring peace to different factions of demons, while creating a shield to protect humans from our world. And to keep our world protected from humans. That kind of ritual, that kind of binding, required very key, very rare ingredients. Anchors. Not a place, but a person. Two people, mirrored selves. Doppelgangers. Twins." His brow arched as he glanced at me, meeting my eyes only briefly, "I don't know if you are aware of this, but our family is prone to twins. They skip generations, always at least one, but more often two or three in one of our descendant lines."

"And twins are powerful." I hated myself as soon as the statement slipped through. Obviously he knew that already. I found myself desperately wanting to please this uncle, to impress him with the half-formed scraps of knowledge I'd been handed through Lucifer, Cyrus, and the others.

He grinned, pushing past the embarrassment I was sure was legible on my cheeks. "Very. But do you know why they are so powerful?"

I shook my head, wanting the explanation to come from him.

"Because they are in perfect unity, perfect balance. When supernatural twins are born, they represent a magical sync that isn't often found, one that cannot simply be created. A way to siphon and control power through a constant ebb and flow— mirrors that refract and reflect in perfect harmony. Like a breath—an inhaling and exhaling in equal measure. It's a fragile power, but an impossibly important one."

"Which is why twins are so often portal guardians." I thought of Nash, and what had become of his sister Nika, what had happened to Darius and his younger sister—both harsh, painful examples of what could come from disruptions to that delicate balance.

He ran his fingers through his long beard, nodding. "Portal guardians are twins because the realms were created by twins. They are a fragmented mirror of that power, an attempt to harness and use it. But it is always an imperfect system—they are not of the original lines. According to our stories, when the realms were created, power was siphoned through two pairs, one on this side and one on the other."

"And so our family," the phrase tasted strange on my tongue, "was one of those sets?"

"Yes. But that power cannot die. With it, the realms collapse. So every other generation or two, twins would be born from that ancestral line, the power and connection to the magic inherited by the new generation."

"You and my mom, you mean—you are the most recent twins? The anchors?"

"Yes, we were. Or are," he grunted, "I hardly know anymore."

"What do you mean?"

"The connection to the realms, to the magic, only works as a set. When that set is fractured or broken, it has nowhere to go, the balance is twisted. Things began to change, morph, when Sayty disappeared into hell many years ago."

"You weren't with her?" It was only one of a thousand questions I wanted the answer to.

I knew of course that she'd been to hell. Where else would she have met Lucifer? Though it was still shocking to consider. The Guild had never been able to access the hell realm—it was one of the reasons they told us they kept their prisoners. To pull the location from them, to find a way to close the realms for good—to protect humanity.

A weird spark of pride licked up my spine at my mother defying them—at her doing the one thing they could not.

He shook his head. "Sayty and I were almost never in the same place at the same time. From the moment we were born, we've been in the same room as each other only a handful of times. The anchors' power is more volatile when we are together. It becomes too unpredictable, an infinite echo that grows too strong—too easy to manipulate, too tempting for others to try and harness. And the power only holds if we continue our lines and stay alive until we do. The odds are better if we are not together."

Like the council. They were certainly more difficult to find and kill when we had to track them down across the world.

"When your mother returned, she was pregnant with you. She visited me here, very briefly, though I remember only one thing from that meeting—" seeing the question form on my lips, he grinned then pressed on before I could interrupt, "You have her patience, I see. She was with a man, one who had the ability to mind warp. I remembered only what he wanted me to remember. Probably for your safety as well as mine."

"Do you know who he was?"

He shook his head. "I remember almost nothing about him, just that he was there, that he apologized for his mental intrusion." He snorted. "Which was thoughtful, I suppose."

"The one thing?" I dug my hands into Ralph's fur to keep from grabbing Saif's head and shaking the answers from it. I'd been fed so few truths about my family, about my mother's history—I was greedy for every morsel he'd give me.

"He told me to find Michael. That if I could locate him, I could potentially save my life—and yours."

"You know about the realm's collapsing, then? That I will need to prevent it?"

His nostrils flared slightly, like he was sniffing the magic in the air. "Even the humans are beginning to sense that something is off, Max. And I am more closely tied to the magic between realms than almost anyone." He tilted his head, studying me again. "Or at least I was, before you."

"Who is Michael?" I asked, not entirely sure if I should apologize for that.

"The missing half to the other set." At my look of confusion, he grunted. "You are the daughter of Lucifer, are you not?"

I exhaled. "As in Michael, Michael? Like the angel?"

"He's no more angel than Lucifer or our ancestors, or any of the other ancients from before. Whatever word we attach to them, he and Lucifer are the only pair. Through them on one side, and our ancestors on the other, the realms were created—worlds mirrored to each other, at first. But protectors grew greedy. And it became clear very quickly to our ancestors that crafting the new realm had nothing to do with creating more space, with protecting humanity from the power we wield. It had only to do with some people's incessant thirst for power. Because it was born of greed, the magic through the years grew only more demanding, ever-hungry. It fed and thrived on a thirst for violence, power, and chaos, distorting the energy into something it was never meant to be."

"Lucifer has a twin," I repeated, my brain stuck on that thought. "He never mentioned it."

"So you've met him?" Saif asked, his eyes hard and the subtle curve of his mouth flattening out into a line. He clearly had no love for the man.

I nodded, not entirely sure what else to say. My feelings where Lucifer was concerned were a tangled mess that I had no intention of sifting through any time soon. "Did you find him? Michael, I mean?"

Saif's jaw worked as he studied his calloused hands. "I spent over a decade searching for Sayty. I was certain that she was alive, that if she wasn't, I would know somehow—that I'd feel it. We usually die together, when it happens. When the new generation of anchors takes our power. I think my connection to the magic disappeared when she did. But I remained. And though I felt different, I thought she might be out there still, that she'd simply found a way to bind the power—a difficult art that very few have perfected." His eyes met mine before they dropped again, a sheepishness in his stare, a guilt. "I admit that I wanted it back. That kind of power, the connection to the world, it could be intoxicating at times. Very few people are born into this world with such a clear purpose—and it was all the more unsettling to have it ripped away. It was there, and then it wasn't. But if she was dead, it shouldn't have disappeared—it would have gone to the next line. And since she gave birth to only one child, it shouldn't have passed to you."

He grunted. "It took me many years to realize that you were likely the daughter of not one line, but two. That my sister likely carried Lucifer's child. That maybe, because you are the daughter of the two lines, I don't know—maybe it makes sense for it all to end with you. A singularity. The workings of our world are never as predictable or tidy as we often think, but in some ways, there is a kind of beautiful symmetry to your existence. To the world we've broken, collapsing around us." His lips thinned into a rigid line. "It's unfair, perhaps—that those who had no hand in destroying it must inherit the disaster. But such is the way of this world."

"And now," I cleared my throat, my mouth had gone bone dry. He'd stopped searching for her, she'd been missing far longer than the ten years he'd looked. I felt the small tendril of hope dissolve on my tongue. That could only mean— "and now you believe that she's dead?"

Saif toyed with the empty bag that held his water for a moment before he nodded. He swallowed, studied a patch of the ground to his left before his glassy eyes met mine. "I'm sorry I did not heed her wishes sooner. I thought if I found her —" he pinched the bridge of his nose, took a deep breath, "but my apologies give you nothing. I've spent the last years of my life trying to find Michael. And with Sayty gone, it was more imperative than ever that the world think me either dead or missing. I couldn't have anyone after me, after the power in our line, after you. The best hope was that they blame the fluctuations in the realms on the anchor power dying out—a natural end.

"So, to keep them from looking for me or my power, better that they think me dead. It offered a freedom I'd never had before. And I used it to fulfill her last wish." He licked his lips, a frustrated bark of a laugh pulling from them. "But of course, I failed in that too. And now it is too late, and it is you who will pay that price. Perhaps we all will. If I had found him, if we could have reversed the spell cast in the creation of the realms with all four mirrors, the chances of you surviving such a ritual would be slightly less bleak.

"Lucifer, Michael, me, you—it would be an imperfect mirror, an echo, really—but a chance. The original set survived, and though our side of the power has weakened over the years, it's not impossible to hope that we could too, in the undoing of the ritual. I searched for years, through pockets of shadow magic and portals, but I could not find him. I wasted years held captive in some offshoot of hell, but even when I escaped, I could not find anyone who'd seen or heard from him in centuries. He seems to have disappeared shortly after the realms were created."

He slipped a hand in his jacket and tugged, pulling away a worn rope with a large stone dangling from the middle.

As if of its own accord, my hand reached for it, my eyes locked on the strange stone, the rest of the world falling into background particles. I held my breath at the sight of it.

Power, both familiar and not, washed over me, coating my skin, diving deep into the marrow of my bones, infiltrating all of my senses until it was all I could see. All I could feel.

"Shadow magic," I said, feeling the almost familiar pull to it. With great difficulty, I tore my eyes from it to look at Saif. "But different, somehow."

Saif nodded, his eyes unblinking as they bore into me. "Greta got word that you were here. That your power was growing. Things have sped impossibly in the last year—things that once put in motion, we can't return from. The fabric of our reality is collapsing —and the choices of greedy men many years ago could spell death for every living being in this realm and all others. A bit ridiculous then, that with such high stakes, and all my time searching, this is the only thing I have to give. A pendant that belonged to Michael. A family heirloom I only just recently came by. All other trails to the man himself have dried up. It is said that his blood, a piece of his power, is infused in the heart of it. Perhaps you can make use of it, perhaps it will be enough to prevent the world's undoing."

"Greta?" her name came out as nothing more than a pathetic croak.

A wistful expression flitted briefly across his face, but melted as he studied me for a moment. "She's gone too, isn't she?"

I nodded.

He sighed, then cursed under his breath. "She was the only one I was in contact with, and even then, only very minimally. She didn't know who I was, not fully. But she sensed the urgency, and agreed to become my eyes on you. Though I'm told you did not always make that easy," his mouth bent into that fish-hook grin again, "like your mother in that way too, I suppose."

Silence settled around us like a cold fog.

The euphoria at seeing him slowly dissolved into dark, echoless understanding. I couldn't deny the flutter in my chest at the possibility he'd found a way to save me. A Hail Mary in the final seconds of the game. Instead, he brought a crushing certainty that the worlds were collapsing. That I would die. That even then, the ritual might only just keep things together —a fragile possibility.

Strangely, that mere whiff of hope had made the unsettling reality only more difficult to face. There might have been a way —a way to stay with Darius, Eli, Atlas, Wade, and Declan—but it was now gone.

"So that's it then," I said, closing my fingers around the stone, comforted, if slightly by the steady weight.

Saif took a deep breath, watching me again, though I couldn't tell what he saw, what he was trying to read. "Are you very scared?"

The question was a deep, aching blow to the chest, but it also held relief, a balloon of tension popping its release.

Was I scared?

I hadn't really let myself linger on this specific fear. I'd been close to death so many times, that adrenaline and fear were impossible threads for me to unwind.

But this was different than all those times before.

I'd be willingly going to my death—I would be my own cause of destruction.

I wouldn't fight it, not knowing what I knew now, what could become of the world if I did.

And, honestly? I was fucking terrified.

As much as I wanted to be the kind of heroic figure who could just go into the darkest night, wearing a badge of bravery and honor, with no selfishness and fear braided into it, I wasn't. I wasn't some forged, selfless hero.

I was just a girl who'd been born into a specific past, just the end of a story and lineage of pain and sacrifice I only barely understood.

In comparison to what came before me, and what lay ahead of me, I felt weak—clumsy and incompetent.

I nodded, swallowing back the rush of emotion that washed over me, thick and hurried, now that I finally dared to look at it.

"Me too," he whispered. Some strange kinship floated between us, a tether of acknowledgment, of sameness. The power that flowed through me flowed through him too, but when I looked into his eyes, I saw the same fear, the same sense of incompetence against what we were up against. We were just two people, each holding only a fraction of the power of our ancestors, the original anchors. And we were all that stood between the realm and a power that had grown only stronger with a hunger to devour it.

Though we'd had radically different experiences, the loneliness of our roles in this world was mirrored in each other.

Saif wouldn't try to stop me. He wouldn't fight me on my decision like my team had, wouldn't tell me it was the wrong choice.

Because it wasn't.

The blood of our ancestors flowed through us—that power, that connection was a sacred promise that had to be fulfilled. Put right.

He stood up, closed the few feet between us, and dropped next to me, awkwardly patting Ralph on the head as the hound adjusted to the added presence.

Saif's shoulder pressed against mine, his side leaning into me—a strange, unexpected comfort, steady and true even though I'd only just met him.

Silence fell over us for a long stretch, but it wasn't uncomfortable. If anything, it was just surreal.

My mother's twin was alive. My uncle. And he was sitting next to me.

Something about his presence gave me a new kind of strength—an acceptance of what was to come. Maybe even a sense of pride in feeling connected to this long line of ancestors I'd been deprived of knowing. I wasn't alone in this task. I didn't know him, but Saif was here now, he was part of this with me.

An idea started to form, ephemeral and transparent at first, but growing solid with hope.

"Do you know where we're from?" I asked, trying to keep the excitement from my voice. I'd been denied my own history for so long that I was starved for even the barest taste of it, the smallest morsel. But it was bigger than that, bigger than my own desires. "The ritual requires a nexus. Lucifer thinks it might be where the original ritual took place, though he has no memory of it."

"Our ancestors are from a region in Southwest Asia, near modern day Lebanon." He paused, considering for a moment, while I lingered on that word—*our*. "Though that doesn't necessarily mean that was where this all began. The ancients could shift through space, they moved through the world with a different kind of ease than most understand. The spot where they landed—it could be anywhere."

I slumped back against Ralph, wrestling with the impossible scope of *anywhere*.

Lucifer was supposedly there in some capacity—maybe we had a better chance of jostling his memory, with magic, or a trick of some sort.

"Is he certain that it must be the literal place of origin?"

I shrugged, unsure.

We settled back into silence, the temporary lightness growing heavier with each passing moment.

"I'm sorry," he said, breaking the fragile silence, "I wish that I'd done more, that I hadn't spent so much time trying to avoid what couldn't be avoided. I'm sorry that I've left you to face this alone."

"I know." I wasn't alone. My fear slowly started to ebb, making way for not quite the calm of acceptance, but something much closer to it than I'd felt before. "I understand. I wouldn't have been able to let go of that hope either, if I thought she might still be alive, out there somewhere."

His jaw clenched, expression unreadable. He took a deep, steadying breath, then turned to me. His rough hands grabbed mine, peeling my fingers back until he revealed the stone.

His gaze dropped to it, focused and unsure. After a heavy sigh, he nodded, then he picked the stone up, sliced the sharp edge into the tender flesh of my palm, and carved a rune into my skin that I couldn't make sense of.

"Hey," I pulled my arm back, staring at the small pool of blood cradled in my hand. "What the hell?"

Without explanation, he sliced a similar wound into his own flesh, then grasped my hand with his, our blood mingling as one.

His eyes held mine, unblinking, and I found myself unable to move, unable to look away. He spoke in a language I didn't recognize, but it resonated deep in my chest like a rumbling drum, and moved up my throat until his low and melodic voice harmonized with mine. I didn't breathe as an unfamiliar tightness wrapped around me, a vise I couldn't break from.

Panic bled through every atom in my body, but I couldn't bring myself to stand up or push him away. It was like he'd cast a trance over me, one my body was determined to wait out, no matter the consequences.

The black of his eyes bled, until no white remained, the swirling smoke there calling to me in its strangeness.

Then, as quick and firm as the trance had held, it loosened.

He fell back, breaths harsh and unsteady. The color quickly drained from his face, the light from his stare, until he looked thirty years older than he was, almost sickly.

Michael's pendant dangled from his hand as he fell back against Ralph, his eyes open and unfocused as they searched aimlessly before finally landing on me.

"It isn't much, my niece. But it is, unfortunately, the only thing left for me to give you—an unbinding spell, my blood to yours. Any remnants of my power are yours. Any lingering blocks placed on you in infancy are gone. It's not enough for you to survive the ritual, but it will hopefully be enough for you to see it through."

And with that, his eyes closed, and the tension in his body fell slack.

29

DARIUS

Well, this certainly wasn't on the roster, but I also wasn't going to balk at the opportunity to kill another one of the infamous Guild council members.

Two of the protectors broke rank at the sight of him and took off running towards the vans.

Xavier disappeared, rematerializing in front of one of the runners, just as she reached the first van. In one smooth motion, he snapped her neck, doing the same to her friend before her body even stilled on the ground.

"Imagine my surprise," his face twisted into a cruel, dangerous smile, "when I found myself in your labs, Peter," Sir Slimeball, apparently Peter, flinched, shoving the small piece of paper discreetly into his pocket, "only to learn that you'd not only stolen one of our most protected creatures, but set up a rather significant meeting without alerting me."

This wasn't the council member I'd encountered, but I could feel his power flaring from here.

At least this made one less prick we'd have to track down. Maybe this little tête-a-tête was more productive than I'd anticipated. And maybe Max would be less pissed about us handling this behind her back if we brought her Xavier's head on a platter in apology.

I was all for a little bloody groveling.

"W-we," Peter swallowed, shaking visibly, though he was clearly trying to buckle down his fear, "we were hoping to surprise you. We've just been brokering a deal."

"A deal?" he arched his brow, whether impressed or unconvinced, I couldn't tell. "And what kind of deal did you think you had the authority to broker without my presence?"

"We need to take him out and get that paper from Slimeball before he teleports out of here," I mumbled to the others. "Last thing we need is him alerting his friend in time to relocate the stone."

Claude's jaw was rigid. "I can feel his power from here. How the fuck does a protector have that much?"

"You've missed a lot recently." I grunted. "They're getting stronger too. Like now that there's only two of them, the power is concentrating in the bodies that remain. They must've all been linked somehow, bonded or whatever."

Would the same happen for Max? If we were all out of the picture, would she grow stronger?

I shook the thought off almost immediately—she'd grown stronger through connection, through building the bonds. Not fracturing them.

Why then did the council seem stronger as individuals?

"Then let's give him a taste of the power he covets so much," Nash said, for once looking at someone with more hatred than he did me.

I could get used to not being the number one enemy in this group.

I grinned, meeting his eyes.

I fucking loved when revenge came with a poetic flare.

Xavier and Peter were talking, and while I didn't bother

parsing out the details, it was clear that good old Peter was doing what he did best—riding both sides, but ultimately selling us out on the off chance Xavier had more strength than the rest of us. Fucking twatwaffle.

The other protectors were restless and already dividing amongst themselves—most moving closer to Xavier, as if they'd arrived with the council member and not Peter. But there were also a few brave souls hedging their bets with us and closing ranks around the woman who'd been negotiating with us. They were likely counting on the possibility that their loyalty now would mean a chance at a new council seat later.

"Who goes for the paper?" Eli asked.

The situation was rapidly dissolving, we needed to be quick.

"You and Wade." Atlas's eyes were locked on the drude, "I've got something else to take care of."

Ominous, but whatever.

"Count of three?" I whispered, sliding closer to Claude and Nash. I stopped, glancing back at the others. "Oh, and Nika gets to eat whoever she wants, but no one leaves here alive—can't give them an opportunity to move their base before we ransack it. Deal?"

They grunted their assent and I beamed.

To think, a few short months ago and they'd all been so squeamish about murder.

Now, they were hungry for it. They were coming along so nicely.

"One, two," I grabbed Claude's arm in one hand, and Nash's in the other. He kept hold of Nika. "Three."

I shifted the four of us across the grounds until we were two feet behind Xavier.

Claude sliced a thick line through his palm the moment he was steady enough to do it, before grabbing my hand and stabbing it with more force than was probably necessary.

Probably should've warned Eli about that.

Nash did the same, wincing when Nika lashed out from the pain.

It took less than a breath, but Xavier spun around, face contorted with rage. The moment he noticed Claude and Nash whispering—all of our palms held together a few inches from him, our blood somehow smearing and staining the air, a transparent and macabre painting—that rage morphed into the slightest twinge of fear.

"Oh no you don't," I tackled him to the ground just as he shifted, contorting and moving through space with him.

But while he was bloated with power that didn't belong to him, he was less practiced in teleportation than I was, and clearly unaccustomed to having a passenger.

We flickered from location to location around Guild grounds, like a lightning bug visible only every few feet.

The shifts were uncomfortable and straining, and I struggled to catch a breath. The moment I started to feel my body again, we were off to somewhere new.

It didn't take long before I wrestled him back to where we started, where a portal flickered in the air, an invisible flag in the wind.

"We've never made one like this before." Claude studied it, the portal flaring and swirling now like a tornado was caught inside. "Not exactly sure where it will take him, what it will do to him."

"Don't care," I grunted.

Before I could shove him forward, Nika sank her teeth into his neck, draining deep, thick pulls of his tainted blood.

The three of us tried to wrestle him from her grasp, but we were fighting her—in the middle of a feeding frenzy—in addition to Xavier's erratic, desperate strains to get away from us all.

His face paled, the dark threads that had blown out his

pupils, slowly dispersing, until all that I saw was the unguarded, feral fear. He was dying.

I had no idea what his blood would do to Nika, but she was ravenous over it, and no matter how much we fought to extricate her fangs, we couldn't.

When she finally let go, he grew limp and heavy, like she'd drained more than just his blood.

Before he had a chance to heal or react, I shoved my hand deep into his chest cavity, savoring the feel of warm blood drenching my skin as my fingers closed over his heart. I ripped my arm back and maneuvered him towards the hungry portal. "He'll be dead regardless, let the shadows decide his fate—they're owed their own revenge for his crimes."

Xavier's eyes were wide and unseeing as he fell back, lips rounded in a noiseless scream as his stiff fingers tried to hold onto me now instead of push me away. Claude pulled back his hands, carelessly breaking several fingers in the process. In a single blink, he was gone, his limbs swallowed into the hole at angles that made me wince.

I held the steaming heart in my hand for a moment longer, before tossing it in after him.

The portal rippled with an iridescent flare, like the veil was extending its own form of gratitude for the sacrifice.

Nash and Claude were already working to close it, their brows caked in sweat from the effort.

"Go have fun, Nika" I said, moving to help them. My eyes locked on hers. "But the ones we came with are off limits."

Her mouth hooked into a grin, her eyes narrowed with a different kind of thirst than I'd seen in their depths before now —she was hungry for revenge, no longer clouded by the feral bloodlust that had been controlling her. As if the council member's blood had sated what couldn't before be sated.

Huh. I'd unpack it later. No use getting Nash's hopes up now if it was only a temporary reprieve.

She nodded to me once, clear understanding etched into her expression as her gaze shifted to the crowd of scrambling protectors. Not needing to be told twice, she took off, tearing into the one closest to her.

"Go," Claude grunted, nudging his head towards the action. "We've got this."

I narrowed my eyes. "You sure?"

Nash snorted. "Trust me, we're more practiced at this than you are."

There wasn't much animosity in his tone though, just a stiff teasing, like he had to exercise the now-unfamiliar muscle.

I nodded, suppressing a grin as I ran back into the action.

I'd torn through four protectors before the woman, Peter's companion, stood before me, trembling.

Her face contorted in fear and disgust as I bared my teeth.

"We had a deal," she barked, voice raspy and trembling as she took a few steps back, vulnerable now that Peter lay in a crumpled heap at her feet, and the majority of her entourage had abandoned her for death. "Where's your sense of honor?"

"My honor?" I gripped her by the neck, languishing the feel of her trembling in my hands. I nodded in the vague direction of where The Guild labs once stood and smiled. "I must have left it buried in my cage."

I snapped her neck, savoring the sound.

Eli and Wade were finishing off the last scavengers.

When I scanned for the wolf, I saw him standing with the drude. He'd pulled the key from the demon's handler, and rather than kill either of them, he...let the Nightmare go.

The girl's body flickered between shadow and form as she studied him, her eyes rounded in surprise.

The handler at her side bent over, crumbling in on himself, hands clutched to his temple as a dark, ominous scream echoed around us.

Slowly, the drude looked more solid, less frail. And then,

with a last glance at Atlas, she dispersed into a black shadow and fled from the scene.

Atlas studied the handler for a long moment—the last protector alive on the grounds.

"Should we—uh," Wade studied the pair of them, "finish this off?"

"No." Atlas met his brother's eyes, something unreadable in his expression, though he looked less burdened than before. "He won't be able to fight her power for long. He will be dead soon. She deserved to finish him off."

"And, er," Eli scanned the gruesome scene, hardly even flinching as Nika made her way over to us, drenched in blood and entrails, "Do we go after the drude?"

Atlas shook his head. "No, she had no control over her power in those cells. Let her go, she won't get in our way. No one deserves to die in a cage."

"This was certainly a much more dramatic meeting than I'd anticipated. But we're one more council member down," Eli said, nodding to Claude and Nash as they made their way over to us looking haggard and exhausted. "All good?"

Claude nodded, but Nash didn't move his focus from Nika.

She was...relatively calm, minus the gorefest she was wearing. And while she was silent and standoffish, there was something different about her general affect, like she was more herself than I'd seen her.

I watched tempered hope sprout in her brother's expression, hoping again, for his sake as much as hers, that this was not just a temporary reprieve.

Eli studied her with just as much hesitant interest.

Maybe it was the four of us together again, uniting through a portal, maybe Xavier's power-infused blood had cured her, maybe it was nothing—just a passing calm from gorging on all that blood, a high from our success today. Only time would tell.

"You think it will actually work?" Claude cleared his throat, then turned to me. "That using your connection to Max will help you save her?"

The flutter of excitement in my stomach turned sour as I glanced at the others. I had no fucking idea. We'd either developed a plan that had the potential to save Max, or we'd all just effectively signed our death warrants along with hers.

Claude gripped my shoulder, lightly squeezing at my silence. For some reason, my throat tightened, like there was a metal ball stuck there.

His expression softened when I glanced at him.

"I hope it works," he muttered.

I found myself believing that he did too. "Max is hard not to root for, isn't she? Hard not to love."

"Not just for her sake, brother." He squeezed my shoulder again, and that obnoxious metal ball doubled in size.

Wade bent down over Slimeball's slim form, and fished through his pocket. He pulled out the crumbled piece of paper, flattening it out as the sun beat down on us.

I took a deep breath. "Please tell me there are actual coordinates on that thing and that this wasn't all for nothing."

Wade pressed the sheet into my chest with a smug grin. "Let's go home, get cleaned up, and then we can tell Max the good news."

30

MAX

Ralph carried Saif to the medical ward, and while my uncle was most certainly not dead, I also had no idea if he would wake up again.

It was another mystery to add to the list of fifty that I already had to figure out.

The excitement and shock of encountering him had bled into heartache and a strange sense of acceptance.

But now, I was just numb.

"He just passed out?" Izzy asked again, her eyes narrowed in focus as she hooked his limp form up to several of the machines Greta had managed to scavenge. "You don't know how or why?"

I curled my fingers into fists, a strange new buzz tingling through them that I wasn't ready to dissect yet. "I think he whispered some spell."

"A spell?"

I blinked a few times at her question. I'd somehow known the spell too, had chanted it alongside him, but the memory was like a shadowy wisp, one I couldn't quite curl my fingers around. "Something about unblocking my—"

"Max?" A deep voice called, cutting through my anxiety about Saif and whatever power transfer he'd initiated, only to make room for a new panic when I turned to meet it.

"Arnell?"

He ran into the room, his chest heaving in deep breaths, eyes blown wide with concern.

My stomach flipped at the sight, at the concern drenching every tense muscle in his body. Arnell was almost always collected, calm—even during some of the most dangerous missions.

He only got like this when—

"Ro." I latched on to Ralph, using him to keep myself upright. "My team? What's wrong? What happened?" On instinct, I took a deep breath, searching for the tethers connecting me to them.

I exhaled. They were alive. Safe. But still shutting me out. Declan's new project of giving me time to destress.

"I'm sorry—" he shook his head, "they said I couldn't tell you."

Any relief I felt disappeared. "Couldn't tell me what?"

"They had a meeting," he swallowed, his eyes not meeting mine, "with some people from The Guild." He wet his lips. "With some high-up people in The Guild, just below the council."

My mouth went dry.

"Dec stayed behind," he continued, his voice higher than usual, his fingers trembling. "And I got a new message after the others left, about twenty minutes ago. From Jarrod. H-he must have found out about the meeting, about their attempted coup. He said something about a massacre for a massacre, the people he grew up with for yours." He licked his lips. "We weren't sure what that meant, but then Ro started panicking about the town you grew up in. They went to check, said they'd be back in five minutes once they verified things were okay. I—" he took a deep breath that did nothing to dispel the anxiety radiating from him. If they left twenty minutes ago, that five-minute time limit was more than up. "I tried to stop them, but Dec just disappeared. And then I wanted to go after them, but I realized that I have no fucking clue where you grew up. Whenever we talked about his childhood, Ro never gave me specifics about the location, just the people."

Arnell continued talking, but his words melted into the air, indecipherable to me. I licked my lips, trying to bring moisture back to my mouth, to form words. I shook my head, trying to process what the hell had happened in my few hours away. Half of my family went off on one dangerous mission, while the other half went on another. Without me.

I swallowed the betrayal, now wasn't the time for that.

I cut my eyes to Izzy, she shook her head, hands up in surrender. She had no idea.

That did nothing to soften the fear unfurling in my chest though.

"Are any of them back? Have you heard anything?" I fought to keep the tremor of terror from my voice, but it just came out sounding robotic, metallic and distant. How long could I compartmentalize my emotions away until I lost all ability to control them? I had a feeling I'd find out soon.

Arnell shook his head, his fingers and hands twisting in a knot as he tried to calm his own panic. That softened something in me and I reached my hand for his, squeezing his trembling fingers in mine.

I wasn't the only one worried about Ro—and I was eased by a strong sense of gratitude that Ro had found someone else to love him as fiercely as I did. Maybe that would make leaving him behind without me a little bit easier. "I'll get him back, Arnell. I promise."

"I'll go—" he started to say, but I let go of his hands and disappeared before he had a chance.

It was broad daylight, and in any other situation, I'd aim to be more subtle, to avoid human eyes. Right now, I didn't give a fuck if any of them in our town saw me.

When the world reshaped itself, I was in the middle of a familiar street, right outside the very post office where Ro and I had picked up Seamus's letter begging Cy to come help train at The Guild.

But it looked nothing like I'd remembered.

Smoke billowed around me, the heavy heat of thick flames crisping the hair on my arms.

A loud crack, and a roaring wave of noise pulled my attention.

The diner.

It had collapsed, swallowed almost entirely by flames now.

My breath lodged in my chest, clogged and unwavering as visions of sitting in there every Saturday night with Ro tugged at my memory.

"Max?" the voice was soft, drowning in the angry clatter of the fire. The whole town was burning. The smell of charred meat and smoke all I could breathe in. A body was on the ground, outside of the diner, all recognizable features burnt away.

I bent over, vomiting when I saw another arm lying still under the rubble. A familiar gold bracelet circled the wrist.

Darlene.

Darlene who served at the diner.

Darlene who'd played a feature role in every birthday, who made this town I lived on the outskirts of feel like home whenever she could.

Darlene who greeted us with a smile that took up her whole face whenever we walked in.

Darlene who was one of the only people I'd met who was brave enough to tease Cyrus.

Darlene who was dead.

Not just Darlene. They were all dead.

Michael, the boy I'd kissed, Jason, his brother—Jarrod had killed them all.

I wasn't sure how I knew, but I felt it in my bones, an unwavering certainty that made it impossible to breathe. They wouldn't have stood a chance against his power, against his rage.

Which meant that they weren't just all dead—they were dead because of me. Because I left them all here to fend for themselves.

Why didn't I plan for something like this? Could I have saved them somehow?

My hands were numb and stiff at the same time, my ears ringing with a low, droning buzz.

"Max?" The voice was louder now, and it sliced through my racing thoughts long enough to pull my focus.

"Declan?"

She pulled me to her in a tight hug. "I'm sorry. I'm so, so sorry. We didn't get here in time—we tried, it was—"

"Ro?" I croaked out, my voice raw from the force of vomiting. I pulled out of Dec's hold, frantic now as I searched for him. I didn't want to be comforted, didn't want her to make this better, to make things okay in the way only Dec knew how to do. "Ro? Where is he?"

I screamed his name over and over again. My vision blurring as I fought back tears.

Not him. Not Ro. He couldn't be gone.

Declan grabbed me, her hold firm but still somehow gentle. She was speaking, trying to calm me, but I couldn't form meaning from her words.

"Ro!" I yelled, my voice puncturing through the roar of the fire as my lungs filled with smoke. I coughed, scratching against Dec's hold, as I fought to push through, to find him.

"Max!"

I sobbed out a breath of relief as familiar blue eyes formed in front of me, blurry through my tears, but impossible not to recognize.

"I'm here, I'm here." Ro pulled me to him, and I sank against his familiar form, clutching his shirt as I fought to hold myself up. "I'm okay."

A loud crash echoed around us, the ground rumbling from the force of it. Ro ducked, tried redirecting us away. I was vaguely aware of another building collapsing, but I couldn't bring myself to move away from his hug, to spring into action.

I'd almost lost him. For a brief, terrifying moment, I was convinced that I had—that he'd been lost to this town, like the rest of them.

Dec grabbed hold of us both and the familiar sensation of shifting from one spot to another rolled through me.

We didn't go far, just a few feet away from the bulk of the damage—far enough that we weren't in immediate danger from the fire, only the smoke.

"We checked," she whispered, her voice trembling with regret as she pressed a soft kiss to my hair, "they're all gone. I'm so, so sorry. We shouldn't have—"

I shook my head, finally pulling back from Ro, from them both.

"What—what did you do?"

"We were trying to find a way, to get to Xavier and Jarrod, the stone—" her breathing was stilted as she fought back tears. "It was reckless, we should have known that they'd find out, that they'd take revenge—but I never thought something like this—I'm sorry. I'm so, fucking sorry, Max."

I fell to my knees as the horror of the town spread out before us—the image more hellish than anything I'd experienced in the deepest depths of hell. The fire had been roaring hard and long—it had already started ripping through the forest, the branches and dried leaves providing fresh kindling. I knew it would take hours—maybe days—to get it under control. How much more destruction, death, would the council be responsible for? Would I be responsible for?

Buildings crumbled and charred, and when I turned to the right, I saw a pile of bodies—most of them familiar.

Their necks had been slashed and they'd been stacked in a pile, as if they were haphazardly discarded, unimportant.

A hand, too small, curled around a plush toy.

A patch of familiar blonde hair, but I refused to let myself linger on it, to determine with any certainty if it belonged to Michael. If I didn't verify, if I didn't confirm it with absolute certainty, maybe I could live in the fairytale that they'd gotten away, that some of them had survived.

I choked on a sob, retching again, but there was nothing left in my stomach, only the bitter taste of bile.

The three of us sat there, clogged in the utter terror of the scene for what could have been five minutes or five hours—time had become meaningless.

Tears streaked Ro's face, carving clean lines through the ash. His hands were covered in bloody cuts and burns, and when I looked down at Declan's, I noticed hers were too.

Their clothes were singed and cut, with small holes burned through the fabric where fire had eaten it away.

They'd been digging through the rubble, fighting to find someone—anyone. That's why they hadn't returned right away, why Arnell hadn't heard back from them. They were trying to salvage something, to save the people here.

My chest squeezed at the thought.

But one more glance at the pile of bodies Jarrod left for me made it abundantly clear that he'd sucked the life out of this town before he'd burned whatever remained.

He would leave no survivors. To someone like him, that kind of humanity would be a marker of weakness.

If those were the rules he wanted to play by, I'd gladly do my part.

"I'll kill him," I said, my hands shaking with anger I no longer had the strength to repress.

I'd kill him, and I'd make him suffer before I did, make him feel every ounce of pain and fear he'd put this town through—tenfold.

There was no redemption for someone like him, someone who stole power and used it to torture and destroy those who had none.

"I—" I paused, swallowing whatever else I was going to say, as my stomach bottomed out, even though I didn't think there were any lower depths for it to go. I looked up, meeting Ro's eyes. "The cabin."

WE SHIFTED THERE TOGETHER, but as soon as the familiar landscape filtered into focus, I almost wished it hadn't.

Jarrod stood near the entrance of what used to be our home, surrounded by what had to be at least a hundred of his lackeys.

So he hadn't committed all of that slaughter alone.

But I couldn't focus on any of them.

The image of our cabin, eaten alive by flames and curls of smoke would be imprinted on my brain for the rest of my life.

"It's gone," I mouthed, unable to find my voice through the grief, "it's all gone."

The journal.

A wave of grief knocked me to my knees when I realized that the last bit of Cyrus I had, the words he'd etched into the pages while we grew up—I'd left it in the cabin months ago.

It was gone too.

Ro grunted, the sound angry and deep, almost animalistic, before he charged towards Jarrod and his army.

Declan had her shit together enough to grab him and pull back, using all of her strength to contain him while he used all of his in a desperate attempt to shake her off.

I stood there, frozen—unable to muster the strength for anger, for anything other than the deep, suffocating pain of grief.

"This is all rather unfortunate," Jarrod said, pulling my attention back to him. "If you had simply agreed to my terms when they were originally offered to you, we wouldn't have had to sink to such levels." He made a soft clicking sound with his tongue. "All those people, dead when they had nothing to do with this." He shook his head. "Such a shame. A terrible price for an important lesson."

"Why?" My voice cracked, and I clutched my chest, fighting like hell to suck in a breath. "I—"

"Because I can't kill you." Jarrod's mouth spread into a sneer as he glanced around at his followers. They stood, unmoving, the traces of the massacre they'd taken part in cloaked their clothes, stained their skin. "I need you. We all do." He spread his arms open wide, like it was the most obvious thing in the world, "I need your power. With it comes the only chance we have at surviving. Yet you remain stubborn, and stubborn children need to be broken. Only then can you be of use to me."

"You killed them. You killed them all." Ro spat, his voice filled with a venom I'd never heard. He renewed his attempts to rush towards Jarrod, hatred etched in every line of his face, but Dec's hold remained strong.

"Well," Jarrod tilted his head to the side as he studied me, eyes narrowed, "if I couldn't kill you, and our conversation got us nowhere, what options did I have? Like most insolent children, I can punish you. Take things from you—the things you love most."

"They're people," Declan said, "not fucking toys. You're a monster." She shook her head, eyes wide in disbelief. "You're all fucking monsters. There were children—" her voice broke. "You killed children."

"Humans die every day." Jarrod shrugged, as if the distinction bore no scrutiny. "You are running out of time, Miss Bentley. Consider this a little push, urging you to reconsider your stance on things. You're a smart girl, a quick learner—I think you'll see things my way soon. And when you do, have your little techy friend send us word—he's clearly figured out how to reach us."

He nodded to the sea of his minions, and without a word they parted.

I screamed at what I saw, the sound so deep and feral that I hardly recognized it as my own.

The tree where we'd scattered Cy's ashes, and the ground surrounding it, were burnt to a crisp.

"Consider this town, this cabin, just old, empty graves of your past." Jarrod spoke as if the dozens of humans they'd killed were no more important than specs of dust—as if I'd needed any more convincing that he cared nothing for protecting humanity, only for power. "But we can dig fresh graves, Miss Bentley. And we can fill them with those you love most." He shifted back into my line of sight, Cy's resting place lifting in plumes of smoke behind him. "My intel has identified a small little resort—one not too far from here—that has experienced a large uptick in activity, despite all suggestions that it closed several years ago. Work with us, and maybe I won't investigate this particular anomaly for myself. Work with us, and no one else you love has to die."

The Lodge.

Bile crawled up my throat, hot and stinging.

No.

He could not do this to them.

He needed to die.

Now.

It didn't matter if his death meant that we'd never find the stone. We'd find another way to get to it, to complete the ritual.

He wasn't touching them.

Something inside of me broke and all that I saw was red.

I screamed, rushing forward, my own flames licking along my arms and braiding with those around the cabin. I let my pain out, unthinking, as I killed every protector I reached.

There was no hesitation, no regret, only pain. Only rage.

When I spun around, ready for him, hungry for the prey I was really hunting, a series of darts hit me square in the chest.

Jarrod's face, complete with that nauseating smirk of his, was the last thing I saw before the flames, and everything they consumed, turned to black.

31

MAX

The fresh scent of briney water clouded my senses, the taste of the air salty and sweet on my tongue.

"I thought we'd meet sooner than this," a deep voice sounded behind me, "it's been a long time."

I spun around, my head dizzy with confusion, my thoughts slower than usual, like they were carving their way through molasses.

"Lucifer?" I blinked several times, taking in his appearance. He looked worse than I'd ever seen him, his hair a mussed mess, his beard an uneven shadow, his eyes rimmed with red and colored in the soft bruising colors that came from weeks—maybe even months—of little to no sleep. There was a greenness to his pallor that made him look sickly, and his frame was more skeletal than I remembered.

If I didn't know better, I'd think he was seriously ill, maybe even dying.

The starkness of his appearance was so not Lucifer-like that I found myself holding my breath, a renewed sense of fear licking against my neck.

The still, iridescent surface of The Styx framed the landscape, and with a few deep breaths, I realized this was a dream. This was where we'd met the one and only other time I'd pulled him into a dream-walk.

I cleared my throat, feeling more disoriented than I usually did in one of my dreams. "What are we doing here?"

"You tell me." He arched a thick, dark brow, somehow looking just as menacing and in control as ever, despite his appearance suggesting otherwise. "You brought me here. I have no control over this realm, it is all you."

I nodded, then licked my lips, feeling suddenly parched. For a moment, I considered scooping up a handful of the mesmerizing water, sipping from it in deep gulps—but I knew this was no ordinary river, and I had no clue what kind of power it could wield over me, even in a dream.

"It's peaceful here," he said, his face relaxing a bit. "Things in my realm have not been this...soft in a long time."

The tension in his shoulders deflated, his posture looking almost human in its ease.

"It's getting worse?" I asked, even though I knew the answer, could feel it in my bones, in the strange static in the air that enveloped us all when I let myself linger on it for too long.

We were running out of time. I knew this was true in the same way I knew the lines and curves of my own hands.

He didn't answer, but I read the depths of his confirmation, of his fear, in his silence.

I needed to work faster, to fight harder. A cloying feeling in my gut told me that we had days until it was too late, not weeks, not months.

My jaw tightened, teeth grinding together as I tried to swallow my frustration. We'd been flitting away time, pushing off the inevitable. All this loss, all this pain—it would be for nothing if we didn't even get a chance to fix things. To set things right.

We'd been sequestered at The Lodge, playing house for

months in this perfect little snow globe of peace. It allowed me to gloss over reality—to not see the way the realms were crumbling around us.

Even the clueless humans on the news knew that something big was coming—stores had been depleted in preparation for some climate catastrophe, an unknown apocalypse that everyone could sense, even those without supernatural power.

The world was crafted almost entirely of fear now, and that was a dangerous thing.

People did terrible things when they were afraid.

I studied him as he moved closer to me, my brain rapidly filling in the gaps and pieces as I quickly oriented myself to this reality. "You've been missing."

"Not missing." An arrogant look eclipsed his expression—apparently, he lost none of his confidence, even when unwell. "I've known where I was all this time. I've been missing, perhaps, to those by whom I didn't want to be found."

I bit back the snarky retort clawing at my tongue. "We're getting close," I said instead, even though I had no idea if it was really the truth, "most of the council is dead. I expect we'll have the stone soon."

For a moment, he said nothing, his dark, unreadable eyes studying me in that way of his. It took all of my willpower to meet his stare, unblinking. Lucifer had a habit of looking at me that felt like I was being sliced through with a blade. He carved and probed, shaping me into bits that he seemed far more able to interpret and dissect than even I was. It was uncomfortable at the best of times, downright painful at the worst.

"You're ready," he whispered, and a flash of something, disappointment maybe, or regret, flashed across his face—there and then gone. "Your power, I can feel it, even here where my own is weakened."

My hand curled into a fist, my fingers tracing over the cut

Saif had made—the cut that had somehow still not fully healed.

I took a deep breath, and nodded. "My Uncle—Sayty's twin," Lucifer stilled at the sound of her name, "he found me, performed some kind of spell. I think he transferred some of his power to me, or broke whatever binding spell my mother had put on me when I was born. He said it would hopefully be enough," I cleared my throat, my mouth dry, "to complete the ritual, I mean, not to keep me alive."

Lucifer didn't move, he wasn't even breathing, but I could feel his fragile desire for me to continue.

The meeting with Saif came back slowly at first, then all at once, until I couldn't get the name off my tongue fast enough. "Michael."

Whatever Lucifer was expecting me to say, it wasn't that— the name of his brother dripping with accusation.

He took a step back, lips parting slightly as if the breath had been stolen from his lungs.

"You never told me you were a twin, that you had a brother, that the two of you were part of the original ritual—the one that," I gestured absently at the oddly serene setting around us. As dangerous as hell was, it was often still painfully beautiful. "Created this place."

"I—" he dropped his gaze, angling his body towards the river, "I haven't heard that name in many years. My connection to him was severed for as long as I can remember. For a while, I searched for him. But I've long assumed that he was dead. I'm not even sure he survived the original ritual."

"He might be," I said, "Saif couldn't find him, just an amulet."

His eyes narrowed at that, considering. "An amulet?"

I nodded, not having much more to offer him. I hadn't had time to really study it, and Saif was still—well, I wasn't sure if he was alive or dead, or if he'd be stuck in whatever coma he was in forever. The thought of losing another member of my family as soon as I'd found them was too bleak to linger on right now.

"As for my place in the creation of this realm," Lucifer started, "you have to understand that I was not myself for a very long time—my memories, my power, they were all corrupted, fed to the magic that requires us to bleed for it. To survive. I only know what I've been able to piece together over the last few years—it's truly not much more than you know yourself." A sad grin tugged at his mouth. "I suppose we are alike in that way—both strangers to ourselves."

I wasn't entirely sure what he meant, but I also wasn't sure that it mattered, not anymore.

He was lost in his own thoughts for a few moments, until it almost seemed like he'd forgotten I was standing here with him entirely.

"Where have you been?"

He flinched, as if startled by my presence or the question. "I was looking for someone, for something."

"And you couldn't tell Samael or Serae or me?" I didn't bother disguising the frustration in my voice. I'd done nothing but fight for this man and his ritual, for the chance to die, in order to save the realms. I was done acting like he was my superior, like someone who's good opinion I valued. I knew what I was to him—a lamb he was diligently preparing for slaughter. "Do you need to keep the secrets that you keep, or is it just part of the whole," I gestured absently, "mysterious devil persona you're trying to protect?"

His brow twitched before he flattened his expression again. Always in control. "Serae didn't need to know, and Samael had business of his own to attend to. We've been busy, and revealing our whereabouts and plans is very often the fastest way to negate them in this realm."

"Business that's bigger than preventing the literal death of everyone across the realms, you mean?"

Lucifer's jaw grew more rigid, if that was possible. It was the only revelation that he was growing frustrated with my insolence. "We all have different roles to fill, Max. Sam and I—" he cleared his throat, suddenly looking uncomfortable, "we're limited here, but we've been trying to find other options, another way."

"Did you find one?" I had to ask, but I was far beyond expecting some last-minute plan to save me. Any vestiges of hope I had for that died during my meeting with Saif.

His eyes met mine again, and I softened slightly. I wasn't the best at reading this man—I wasn't sure that anyone had ever found it possible to read him—but there was regret there, hesitation.

"I—" he sniffed, his posture stiff and uncertain, "I've been trying to find Azrael. I'd settle even for his scythe at this point. I thought I could wait, that I'd have a better chance when I could move more freely through the realms, that dissolving the barrier might force him out of hiding. But his power would be of greater use to me now."

He'd mentioned that name to me before. Azrael was the guardian of The Styx, and he'd been missing for a long time.

I was getting fucking sick and tired of these missing ancient old dudes.

"Did you find him?" I asked, reading the answer already in the sharp edges of his demeanor.

He shook his head, his lips twitching into a barely-perceptible frown.

"What do you need him for?"

Michael, Azrael, the stone, the nexus—we were all just chasing ghosts, it seemed.

Everything felt like echoes of "what ifs" and rituals, all of us grasping at straws, desperately hoping to clutch something or someone that might save us as we were inevitably shoved off this impending cliff.

There were no heroes though. My stomach sank with the weight of that realization.

That was the truth of it, wasn't it? We were all just equally lost—children playing at a game of gods.

"Azrael is connected to the realm of the dead, I was hoping that if I could find him, he might—" Lucifer let the words trail off, sinking between us.

"Sayty," I said, my chest tightening at the thought. "You want to find him so that you might reach out to my mother."

He loved her. Or at least he had long ago. As much as someone like him was capable of an emotion so big.

"I'd give anything to see your mother, yes, even just for a moment," there was a gravel in his voice, a slip of emotion that was rare for him, and I was reminded of our last dream-walk, of the ways this world ate at the edges of his shields. His eyes met mine. "But I was hoping to find him sooner." He paused, shoulders sinking slightly. "For you."

"For me?"

"I thought he might be able to intervene somehow—that after the ritual, when you're in the in-between, that he—it," he shook his head, hands in tight fists at his side, like he was angry at himself for betraying the fact that he cared, like compassion was a weakness, "it was a foolish hope, but I—" his gaze cut to me again, furtive, apologetic, "I had to try."

Emotion tightened my throat, making it impossible for me to swallow, to speak for a few minutes.

"It's okay." I reached for his hand. He flinched at first, shocked by the touch, but he didn't pull away as I held onto him. "It means a lot that you tried, but it'll be okay. I'll be okay. I won't fight you on the ritual, you won't need to even use the blood oath. I'll do it. Gladly, if it means saving everyone I care about. There is no choice, I know what needs to be done."

His eyes narrowed slightly at the mention of the blood oath, like he'd forgotten that last power chip altogether.

Odd, considering my assessment of him had been that he devoted all of his energy to stockpiling his power over others, no different than The Guild in that way.

But maybe that thirst for power had less to do with him than I thought.

He wanted power over death, but his reasons were born of something more pure, something that had nothing to do with control.

His fingers tightened around mine, his skin surprisingly cool and soft to the touch.

Then, he shook his head, something inside of him snapping. He dropped my hand and took a step back.

"No."

"No? No, what?"

"I thought I would be able to. But I can't. I won't let you do it. I—" his brows furrowed, like he was genuinely surprised or confused by whatever thoughts were flashing through his mind, "I can't. I won't lose you too. It was foolish of me to think that when it came time for it, that I could just sacrifice you to combat a greed you had no part in feeding. I've never been that strong. If I lose you both, and now, with no way to get you back, what even is the point?"

"I—" Warmth flooded through me, and I resisted the sudden urge to pull him into a hug, to soothe the flood of thoughts that were so clearly ripping and tearing through his peace. "I don't think there's a choice. I appreciate your hesitancy, I really do." It was nice realizing, for the first time, that I was more than just a pawn to the man who donated half of my DNA. "But there are no other options."

"You don't deserve this world, this life." He straightened, darkness clouding his expression before it became inaccessible to me again. "It should be me who carries this burden, not you."

We were silent for a few moments, lost in our own thoughts.

"I can stop you," he said, the words mumbled so softly I barely caught them, as if he was formulating a new plan he'd only just considered. "The oath. I could keep you from going through with it. I could order it."

I snorted. "I'd likely die anyway. And so would you and everyone else."

He startled again, like the words had slipped out without his knowledge. He turned to me, the lines of his face hard. "You could stop, before it gets to be too much—restabilize the barrier between realms, don't dissolve it. It could work, buy us some more time to forge another plan. Or maybe my power. If I find one of the ancients who can somehow transfer it to you— or my lifeforce. Maybe—maybe I can help. Or if I find—"

He continued rambling, but I stopped listening to his brainstorm. I knew it was futile. We were out of time.

A small tendril of affection unfurled in my chest, releasing some of the unease and fear that I'd been unconsciously bottling for months.

I hadn't been certain that we could trust Lucifer, that his path forward was the right one for the world—both his realm and mine. I'd been expecting something darker, more selfish, in his motivations. A plan to kill all protectors, or to level all of humanity, perhaps.

I saw now that as prickly as he usually was, I was ultimately wrong about him. He was an asshole most of the time, and I didn't agree with most of his methods. But I saw now how much his decisions were ruled by his own loneliness.

This had never been about my power—about him gaining more, just for the sake of it. This wasn't even about revenge, about taking out The Guild.

He wasn't some pure beacon of good, but he wasn't evil either.

He was willing to lay down his life, to give up his power—while The Guild fought only to steal more.

I reached for his hand again, threading his fingers through mine, and squeezed, cutting off his desperate ramblings. I bit back a grin. Perhaps I'd inherited my proclivity for rambling from him.

The edges of the dream world grew blurry, and I wasn't sure how I knew, but I felt somewhere, deep down, that this would be our last time together—that I wouldn't see him again before the ritual.

"Tell me about her," I said, staring out at the rippling stillness of the river.

His hand tensed in mine, and I was certain that the strange magic of this dream world that softened and opened him up had finally dispersed—but then he relaxed.

"She was naively kind," he started, his voice soft, but betraying no emotion, "deeply compassionate. But she was also no pushover. Strong. Wild. Ambitious." I chanced a glimpse of him out of the corner of my eyes and saw that his own were sparkling as he allowed himself, for once, to get lost in the memory of her. "She was stubborn, maybe even more stubborn than me—something I wouldn't have thought possible before knowing her. Intelligent. Beautiful, obviously, but it was so much more than just beauty, in the way I've always understood and used the term. She redefined it for me—filled it with light. The first time I saw her smile, really smile, I forgot how to breathe. Before her I—I wasn't myself.

"It was like meeting her shaped me into existence somehow, lifted me from a cave I'd been locked in for centuries. When she left," he cleared his throat and paused, collecting himself, "I was certain I wouldn't survive it. The only thing that kept me going was the possibility that I'd escape here one day, that I'd find her. That I'd make things right."

There it was—the true reason he wanted the realms dissolved, his innate power returned. So that he could find her, reunite. Try again.

I hoped he would. I hoped, in the depth of my chest, that she was alive, somewhere out there. That when this was all over, they'd be reunited. Find peace at least, even if the love that once existed between them was no more than a memory for her.

A steady release eased over me as his words cloaked me, peculiarly warm and filling me with soft rays of hope.

I wanted the people I loved to find happiness, to find love and joy in the messiness of the world—and regular messiness, not the kind crumbling at the edges from The Guild's greed. I wanted that for them all, even if I couldn't be there to witness it.

He'd stopped talking, I wasn't sure when, and we both simply existed next to each other for a while, watching the serene landscape of The Styx.

It had a way of drawing me in. It always had.

My heartrate picked up, my body chasing an idea, a recognition that my mind was slowly catching up to.

I knew these lines of the shore, the rocky landscape, the taste of the air. This feeling of connectedness, I felt it every time I was near this shore, but it wasn't the only one that made me feel this way.

My dreams with Lucifer—they should have been impossible, he'd said so himself. And every time I had them, we met here.

For weeks—no, months—I'd found myself waking from a restless sleep, floating in the depths of Lake Cadaver.

A shocked chortle ripped from my lips at that name.

Of course.

Of course that was the name.

It was where Darius had pulled Claude, Nash, Nika—where he'd ripped a portal with an ease that he shouldn't have been able to master.

Our time at The Lodge had drawn out the shadow magic he fought so hard to repress for years.

Hell, he'd been drawn to the lake long before he even met me.

I didn't breathe as the pieces slowly knit themselves together.

The edges of the dream fractured and tore.

I was vaguely aware of Lucifer yelling my name, of him reaching for me.

It was a futile, panicked gesture, and too late for me to say goodbye.

I woke up, blinking, my head doused in an icy cool, familiar pool of water.

I fought back the urge to laugh, kicking my way to the surface as the waves kissed my skin.

When I broke it, I took a deep breath, lying back in the lake and floating for a few moments.

Erratic splashing pulled me from my reverie.

"Max!" Wade's arms wrapped around me as he pulled us both to the shore. "I went to check on you in the clinic and you were gone."

I blinked as the ephemeral haze between sleep and waking melted slowly from the edges of my mind. "The clinic?"

He hugged me to him, his warmth seeping against me, my skin humming with the sensation of his nearness.

"Ralph brought you back, you were knocked out." He cursed. "We've been waiting for the sedatives to wear off. They were working through your system quickly, you weren't out that long, considering how many darts those assholes hit you with."

Jarrod.

The town.

Our cabin.

Cy.

The threads of what had happened came flooding back, stealing the breath I'd only just found as they stitched together.

I'd kill him.

Rip his soul from his body and tear it to shreds, if such a thing as a soul even existed—if someone as foul as him could even possess one.

I pushed back from Wade, locking my eyes on his. "Dec, Ro—"

Had Ralph carried us all?

He clenched his jaw, his fingers digging deeper into me as he held onto me.

I knew what he was going to say before the words left his mouth, saw the truth, the fury, etched into the indigo wells of his eyes.

"They took them."

My mind went temporarily blank. Then the silence was eclipsed by a dark, unfamiliar rage that boiled low and steady in my gut.

No.

He couldn't have them. He couldn't take them from me too.

"We shouldn't have left. I'm sorry. It was reckless, and we fucked up, Max." Wade studied me, expression filled with an anger that was a mirror to my own. "But it wasn't for nothing. And now we think we might know where they are. We can get a team together in an hour, maybe two, prepare—"

I shook my head, not letting him finish.

No.

No planning, no waiting. I was done waiting.

This was a desperate, poorly crafted trap that Jarrod had set for me, but it would work as effectively as he'd hoped. Of course it would.

If Jarrod wanted me to come to him, that's what he would

get. And he would watch me tear him—and any followers power-hungry enough to get in my way—to shreds.

No more negotiating, no more pretending this ended in anything but death.

I was going after them. Now.

And after I brought them back, we were going to end this once and for all, before anyone had the chance to stop us again. Before there was a chance for second guessing anything.

No more hesitation. The stakes were too high.

I took one last look at the lake, frustrated with myself that it had taken me so long to realize the truth. It seemed so impossibly obvious now.

A perfect mirror to The River Styx.

The nexus.

Power flooded my veins, my body pulsing with it, now that I was finally letting myself embrace it—giving myself over to it.

I was a vessel, if I allowed myself to be. Nothing more.

The puzzle shifted into place.

Now, it was time to collect the final piece.

32

DECLAN

The first thing I felt was pain.

The second, a strange, uncomfortable stiffness in my arms. Like they were made of some kind of thick metal, and not flesh and bones.

I blinked, or at least I tried to. My eyelids were impossibly heavy and though I'd just woken up, my body was already begging me to fall back into the painless depths of sleep.

Only, it was a ruse, because my sleep had been anything but painless. Nightmares, more real than any dream I'd ever experienced, had plagued every corner of my sleep.

I whimpered at the brief flashes of them licking at the peripherals of my memory.

Flashes of gore painted my eyelids, and my head pounded with the echo of horror-stricken screams—some of them mine, but not all of them.

I forced my eyes open, desperately fighting my body's demand for rest. My skin ached, the touch of fabric from my shirt pure agony where it lay against my torso, every nerve rubbed raw.

There were thick tubes shoved into my arms, liquid apparently streaming both in and out of my veins.

What the fuck. Where was I? What happened?

The lighting was abrasive, that awful bright white that should be illegal to use in any room that wasn't a hospital. It did nothing to help the pounding drum in my skull.

"Declan?" A soft voice whispered to my right, but I couldn't quite move my neck around to see. "Are you awake? Are you okay?"

I blinked back the stark light, trying to get a feel for my surroundings. I was in a small room, the walls and ceiling a white as obnoxiously loud as the light bouncing off their surfaces. From my position, I couldn't see a door—or much of anything.

I twisted, just slightly, wincing as pain shot up my spine. I followed the winding tubes from my arms. They led through a small hole in what looked like a glass wall, though I'd bet all the money in my bank account that it was shatterproof—impenetrable.

Familiar whirring blotted out the dull buzzing in my ears and the echoes of screams I was doing my best to ignore. I clocked a few machines just outside of my cage. I focused on them, trying like hell to ground myself in the present—anything to get away from the possibility of more sleep.

"Wh-" it was the only thing I could manage—a sound that would have to function as a question for now.

My head felt like it weighed two thousand pounds, my body like it had been buried under an avalanche.

Were we back in the lab?

No.

Max had burned it down.

A different lab, then?

The sterile coldness of this place had The Guild written all over it. Sterile-white was practically their branding package.

What happened?

My memories were sand, slipping through my fingers as I tried to collect them, coming to me in disjointed patches.

I reached for Max, chancing closing my eyes for a few moments in an attempt to feel her, to speak through our link. Only I couldn't. All I saw when my eyes closed was death, all I felt a breath-stealing panic.

"Jarrod knocked Max out," the voice whispered again, the sound more familiar this time. I held onto it, used the gentle warmth as a rope to pull me out of my spiral. Rowan. "Us too, though he hit you with the same number of tranqs as Max, so it'll probably take you a while to feel like yourself. I've only been awake and cognizant for an hour or two," a pause, "I think. You—" he sighed, "you were screaming. What was he doing to you? You were yelling, and then it was just silent, I thought—" his voice caught, "I thought you were gone for a moment there."

"Is—" the word was more grunt than anything, my throat raw. I didn't want to think about why—if I had been screaming, I didn't want to linger on the reasons, didn't want to revisit those dreams.

"She's not here," he said, picking up on the question I couldn't voice. "Think they left her." He grunted. Left her? The cabin. The town. My stomach threatened to empty itself at the memory of the massacre I'd been too late to stop. All of those innocent people, gone. And for no reason other than their proximity to Max, and Jarrod's insatiable greed. "I think he's keeping us for collateral, to ensure that she comes around to his plan. Force her into some kind of negotiation."

"That," a new voice—sharp, loud, and abrasive this time, "and we're running a little experiment. If it goes well, I may not even need her at all."

Jarrod appeared on the other side of my cage, his beady

eyes assessing every inch of my body, his mouth twisted in a greedy little grin that grated like nails on a chalkboard.

"What're you doing to her?" There was a series of loud, dull thumps that rumbled my wall, and I knew Rowan was likely ramming against it in an effort to get to me or attack Jarrod. Maybe both. "Leave her alone. O-or take me—use me instead."

"You're all but useless to me, unfortunately." Jared glanced in the direction of Ro's voice, his nose scrunched in disgust. "You see, I had a thought." He lifted a small vial, dark with blood, but there was an almost iridescent shadow to it when he held it up to the light. He turned to me, fully stepping into his supervillain era, no longer bothered with trying to pretend he was anything else. "You see, Xavier noted that when you found him, with Evelyn and the others, *you* were particularly strong. He told me that you were able to easily pull and use Ms. Bentley's powers, and with impressive ease." His smile brightened.

My stomach lurched at the barely-constrained excitement in his voice.

"And I perhaps am uniquely positioned to understand just how impressive that is," he continued. "I know firsthand how difficult these powers can be to master." He tilted his head. "I can't be sure that draining you will give me access to her powers too, at least not to the extent that you are tuned into them, but it's a risk I'm willing to take. If I can move things along without the girl's direct compliance, well," he grunted out a half-hearted chuckle, "that would certainly make things smoother for me—for us all, really—wouldn't it?"

He emptied the vial into his mouth, cringing slightly at the taste. He licked his lip then shrugged. "Remarkable isn't it, the depths one must sink to when trying to save our kind. I'm practically a vampire now." His forehead lined as he studied the empty vial, blood still staining the glass. "Not quite to my preferences, but assuming I survive the sample, I'll be ready for transfusions in a few hours. Those are less...revolting to suffer through."

The banging from Rowan's side of the wall grew more erratic, more desperate—but I knew it was futile. The Guild designed these cells to hold the strongest, most dangerous supernatural creatures they could catch. We stood no chance of getting out with attempts at using brute force. Especially not as weakened as we were.

Hell, I could barely even lift my head more than a few inches without wincing.

I took a deep breath and closed my eyes again, this time ignoring the flashes of violence that seemed to be permanently etched into my brain's memory.

The bond. I needed to fight past whatever they'd done to me.

What *had* they done to me? Was it a drude?

My chest hollowed at that possibility. If it had been—if I'd been this affected from one brief encounter with one of those creatures, how had Atlas survived months locked with one? How had Sarah?

The bond still hummed inside of me, its normal glow and strength dampened, but it was still there. That meant Max was okay. Or at least alive. Maybe that was the best I could hope for right now. I wasn't sure any of us would ever be okay again.

If I could get some of my strength back, I could reach her, warn her—keep her from coming here.

"On the chance that I'm wrong," Jarrod continued, oblivious to my attempts, "I wanted to have options, collateral here that might influence Ms. Bentley to see things my way. She's young, troubled. But I'm sure that with the right amount of...suggestion, even she can be convinced to see reason." Jarrod's gaze drifted over to where I assumed Rowan was glaring daggers at him, his expression bored and a little annoyed. "But if you continue that racket, I might be convinced I only need one of your lives to trade in exchange for her cooperation. Tell me," his expression curled into a dark smile, "who do you think she cares more for? A brother who doesn't even share her blood? Or a mate?" His eyes glistened, bloated with cruelty. "Of course she has four others, so perhaps it's the illusion of family she'd prefer to save—the only remnant of childhood she has left. She does strike me as the sentimental type."

"Where are we?" I barked out, sitting up, despite the wave of nausea and pain the miniscule movement sent through me. I needed to keep his focus off of Rowan. There was no way in hell I was letting his bloodthirsty thoughts anywhere near reality.

Max had lost too much.

I refused, after everything, to deliver her a dead brother.

He studied me, surprise raising his brows. "You don't feel it, then? I was told you might."

I swallowed, my mouth drier than sandpaper. "Feel what?"

His eyes narrowed, confusion and anger battling out across his features. "The stone."

The stone.

It was here?

I glanced around the room again, or whatever small slice of it I could see from my cage, but nothing about this dungeon stood out. It looked like a miniature version of Headquarters' lab, though unfamiliar enough that I knew I'd never been here.

"Perhaps that creature took too much from you." Jarrod shrugged, then walked out of my sight line. "Oh well, not necessary that you sense it, but I must say I'm disappointed all the same. The scientist in me is truly so curious to test the limitations of this bond of yours. Perhaps we should have started there. If things were less," his eyes narrowed in thought, "urgent, we would have."

Metal clanked against metal, the sound echoing harsh and abrasive in the sterile room.

I shivered at the possibility of which tools he was gathering. Somehow not seeing them made it all the worse.

We're almost there. Hang on.

The words were a whisper at first—a gentle breeze given form. And then, I'd half-convinced myself they'd been nothing more than my imagination, my subconscious desperately clinging to some possibility of survival, creating hope where there was none.

But then I heard them again, louder this time.

"Don't worry though, I'll put you under again. I'm not a monster." A soft chuckle, like he'd made a joke. "I don't believe in pain for pain's sake, despite what you might think of me."

"Tell that to the town you cremated," I spat out, bile coating my tongue. How many people had died at this man's hands? Or, if not his hands, at his orders?

"A tragedy, to be sure. But one that was meant to prevent a much larger one, in the end," he mused, still fussing with tools I couldn't see.

"Your job is to protect people," Rowan said, his voice dark and on the edge of breaking. "To save them."

"I'm trying," Jarrod barked. He dropped whatever he was doing and walked back over to us, his posture rigid, expression unhinged. "To save us all. Don't you get that? These deaths, however tragic, are nothing compared to what will come, if we don't destroy hell." His eyes locked on mine. "You used to believe in our work, Ms. Connolly, our mission. I've read your files. You were a fierce hunter, rising through the ranks. Who knows?" he shook his head, eyes wide, incredulous, "another decade or two and you could have been appointed a seat on the council. Instead," disgust ate away at his expression, "you've thrown it all away. And for what? A girl? A vampire who's convinced you he's not evil? Teammates come back from the dead as a werewolf and whatever the hell the younger Andrews boy is now. Tell me, Ms. Connolly—how many lives have they taken since you've turned your back on us?" His lip curled as his gaze cut to Rowan, then back to me. "You're no different than me. You act all holier than thou, but look at the trail of violence you've left in your wake since abandoning your post. Since abandoning the mission passed down to you from your ancestors. You had potential, but you were too weak to see it through."

"I believed in The Guild, yes," I fought to keep my words even, to distill the rage boiling in my blood down to something more usable. "I thought I was part of something important, that we were working towards the greater good. Then," I sat up straighter, ignoring the sharp bolts of pain shooting through my spine, "I got more information. And I changed my opinions and actions accordingly. That's not weakness, that's critical thinking."

A shadow fell across his features, but before he could respond, a crash echoed through the room, explosive and thundering.

Jarrod flinched, the little color he had in his face dissipating quickly.

I couldn't see beyond the boundaries of my cell window, but I could feel them all.

They were here.

Jarrod dropped the small blade he'd been gripping, the sharp, tinny clank as it hit the floor almost comedically soft compared to the sound of my team's entrance.

"You've come." His voice was higher than normal, his lips quivering slightly at the corner. He was afraid. "That's good. Though perhaps a bit sooner than I'd planned for." He winced. "Tell me, have you considered my offer?"

There was another loud crash, and then a soft scream that was cut off almost as quickly as it started. Jarrod's fingers trembled at his sides, his eyes shifting from side to side, as he watched whatever was unfolding unfold.

He licked his lips, glanced quickly at me, then raised his hands up in surrender as he took a step back. "Now, Ms. Bentley, you have to understand." He stumbled, his breathing erratic as he tried to create more distance between them. "I'm trying to serve the greater good—to help humanity. We can work tog—"

He was going to run. Teleport. I read the decision on his face the moment he made it.

Apparently, so did Max, because she came into view in a flash, her hand wrapping around his neck.

To outside observers, it would be a strange sight—this short, lean girl, hardly half the size of this man bulked with muscle, holding his life in the palm of her hands. But I knew the depths of her power, felt it make a home in my own marrow.

Jarrod's eyes widened as he read his death in her eyes.

"Wait." Darius came into sight, eyes shifting briefly to me with a small nod of acknowledgment.

Max only tightened her grip as her other hand shot deep in Jarrod's chest, where I knew his heart would be pumping a panicked rhythm against her knuckles.

"Yes," Darius said, voice soft like he was speaking to a frightened animal, "kill him. But I have an idea before we leave his body."

Picking up the small blade Jarrod had dropped, Darius sliced a deep line into the man's arm, collecting his blood in a small jar.

It was a strange sight, watching the room suddenly still and quiet as Darius stole the council member's blood.

"There," he said, fastening a lid on the container, eyes sparkling with delight. "Kill away, my dear."

I grunted in disbelief. Was he really focused on his own stomach right now?

Max said nothing. She merely withdrew her hand, Jarrod's heart along with it.

He collapsed at her feet, his death surprisingly anti-climactic.

When she took a step towards me, her gaze cutting to her brother, then back again, I realized that she was covered in blood. Her dark clothes were soaked with it, her arms painted red.

Jarrod wasn't the only person they'd encountered then, on their way into this hell hole.

I failed to conjure much pity for those who died at her hands. Not after what they'd done.

Her eyes were black, pupils blown wide, her expression flat, like she was only partially here with us.

She got that way sometimes, when she used too much power—like she gave a little of herself over to it, in exchange for more strength.

"You're okay," she said, her jaw rigid, like she was fighting desperately to contain the storm of fury etched into her bones. She turned to her brother again. "Both of you?"

I nodded, my body still stiff and sore from whatever Jarrod and the drude had done to me while I was asleep.

Her eyes fell to the tubes dangling from my arms, nostrils flaring at the sight, her anger almost palpable in the air. The tips of her fingers sparked when she twitched them, like the hellfire was aching for a chance to scorch this place to the ground.

Wade, Atlas, and Eli came into view, the five of them huddled together so that they could get a good look at me and Ro.

They were all covered in gore, all wearing identical masks of fury that were slowly melting with relief.

It was done. The council was dead.

I took a deep breath, and when I exhaled, it felt like I'd shed an entire boulder's worth of weight from my chest.

Max glanced down at Jarrod, sparing him only a momentary glance. "His death was too quick. I should have made him suffer."

"No amount of torment would have been enough." Darius nudged the corpse with his foot, mouth dipping into a frown. "At least it's done."

"Get them out," she said, her words stiff, filled with gravel. She tensed, head tilting to the side. "It's here. The stone. I'll retrieve it." She took a deep breath, shivering slightly. The dark edges of her irises started slowly bleeding through with familiar threads of brown. She reached her hand forward, the tips of her fingers gliding gently against the wall. "So much death, so much torment within these walls."

"Well, we didn't leave much standing upstairs. Might as well finish the job with style." Darius grinned. "What do you say, Little Protector? Are you in the mood for one final Guild-worthy bonfire?"

33

MAX

The stone sat on our kitchen table. It was larger than I remembered, and far heavier than I'd anticipated.

The stone itself was tall and jagged, encased in a large basin that seemed to be made of the same iridescent material that Lucifer's blade was composed of. The base of the stone was submerged in a shimmery, thick liquid that seemed to swirl and move of its own accord, the colors shifting and metallic, almost like an oil slick.

In some ways, it reminded me of The River Styx, which made sense—everything seemed to go back to that river.

"So this is it?" Izzy arched her brow, bending over to study the mesmerizing liquid in the basin, but making sure she didn't get close enough to touch it.

It was early, the sun only just rising, but The Lodge had a stillness today that was unusual. I'd gone for a walk earlier and the place felt like a ghost town.

When I realized that the lake was going to be the center of the ritual, I had Charlie clear out everyone staying too close to the shoreline. I had no idea what kind of recoil there'd be with power this uncharted and unpredictable.

I didn't want to have any more blood on my hands than I already did.

She was hesitant at first when I told her my plan, but with The Guild taken care of, there was less reason for us all to remain packed so tightly together. The community had spent the months we'd devoted to training building more lodging further out into the woods. It would be enough to house everyone. At least until things were handled here on my end.

Most people had already begun avoiding the lake after Darius ripped open the portal—something I was belatedly grateful for.

Izzy was one of the few who hadn't been able to resist walking along the water's edge. Like Charlie, I often found her out there in the mornings watching the sunrise, either oblivious to, or unafraid of the portal that occasionally shimmered on the skyline.

Izzy had been working odd hours in the med ward, which meant that her sleep schedule was as unbalanced as mine. She'd found me wandering out there early this morning and brought me some fresh coffee—a gesture that had clogged my throat with gratitude.

I wish I'd spent more time with her, that the time we did spend together hadn't been so bogged down in planning out missions and chores.

"This is it," I whispered, trying not to wake the others.

I couldn't pull my eyes from it, the urge to run my fingers over the stone almost impossible to resist.

Last night, after healing Dec and filling Charlie and the others in on what had happened, I fell asleep, exhausted, sandwiched between Dec and Eli.

But I only slept for a few hours. Between the remnants of anger and power flooding through my veins, and the constant urge to keep checking on the stone, sleep had proven nearly impossible for me, no matter how tired I was.

Every breath I waited felt too long, every second a lifetime of *too late, too late, too late* echoing through my mind.

I'd crawled out from Eli's limbs several times, just to come look at the stone, to make sure it was here, that we'd really found it.

It was mesmerizing, the way the moonlight pouring through the window highlighted the strange, swirling colors that seemed to be in constant motion. And then, from some angles, it would look entirely ordinary—so ordinary that I was almost convinced we had the wrong thing, that this rock couldn't possibly be the key to saving so many lives.

As if it heard me, the stone answered my doubts by sending a gentle thrum against my skin, like livewire.

Around midnight, I overheard Wade, Darius, and Atlas whispering together in one of the other bedrooms.

They were too quiet for me to catch more than a stray word here and there, but I knew they were up to something, that they were going to try to stop me from going through with it altogether. Finding the stone and identifying the nexus changed everything—moved things along far more quickly than they'd been hoping for.

But they didn't feel the same urgency that I did, they didn't taste the sour twist of magic in the air, didn't feel the plane between realms pulsing with breath.

They were out of time.

I was out of time.

Izzy shivered and stepped back from the rock. "Can't believe this is what they've been using to forge bonds. So surreal." She turned to me, her hand unconsciously hovering a few inches above one of the jagged ridges of the stone. When she noticed, she flinched, and pulled her arm back, folding it over her chest. "And you're sure it will work for the ritual too?"

I bit my lip, remembering the first time I saw the stone—the bonding ritual between Atlas and Reza.

The air flared with the memory, growing hot and angry.

When I glanced back at the stone, it seemed to almost glow —there one moment, then gone the next, almost like it felt my memory, and the pain laced within it.

I knew the limits of what this stone could achieve were beyond our comprehension. Something about its proximity created a buzz in the air, and late, in the darkest parts of the night, I was almost certain I could hear a voice calling to me from it, begging me to reunite it with the lake outside.

"Yes, it'll work."

In one of the brief reprieves of sleep I'd managed to steal, I'd dreamt of the ritual, watching it play out like an old movie. I knew what I had to do, how I had to do it. I wasn't sure if the stone was sentient, if it sent me the dream itself somehow, or if the dream was some latent memory passed down in my blood, risen to the surface now that it was time.

I supposed it didn't matter either way.

Izzy grabbed my hand, squeezing softly, her voice barely even a whisper. "When?"

I cleared my throat, studying her. When I saw her eyes glaze over with grief, her throat bobbing as she fought desperately to contain it, I squeezed her hand back. She knew what this ritual meant, knew that I would go through with it. Unlike the others, she wouldn't argue with me, wouldn't convince me to wait.

We were out of time—a truth I felt so viscerally that it might as well have been tattooed into my bones.

"Now."

She tensed next to me, her head shooting to the doors down the hall, before she dropped my hand and grabbed me by the shoulders instead, turning me towards her until her eyes were all I saw. "You're not waking them? You're not saying goodbye?"

My throat tightened. I slid my hand into my pocket and pulled out a small, tattered notebook. I'd spent the first part of my morning writing them letters, each of them—inking in my wishes and hopes for their futures, telling them how much I loved them, thanking them for giving me so much joy, so much love since meeting them. There would never be enough words to give them, never enough time, but it would have to do.

"Can you give them this wh—" my voice broke, and I took a moment to collect myself before handing her the pages, "when it's done? There's a letter for you too." I licked my lips, sniffing as I tried to hold it together. "And Ro."

My chest squeezed at the thought of my brother, at the thought of leaving him behind—the last remnant of a family I'd taken for granted too many times.

I squeezed my eyes closed, reminding myself over and over again that he wouldn't be alone. He had Arnell, he had Izzy, he had this entire community he'd helped build. He'd be okay.

I hadn't planned on telling Izzy beforehand. I hadn't planned on telling anyone. They knew it was coming, but prolonging the inevitable, the goodbyes, just seemed impossibly cruel to us all.

Mostly because I wasn't sure how to say goodbye. Wasn't sure I could go through with it after lingering in that pain with them all. Wasn't sure if I'd have the strength to leave them when they begged me to stay.

So, I'd written them letters.

This would be better, I'd told myself. I'd save them from witnessing it. They'd simply wake up in a few hours to a new world—a better one, hopefully.

They'd be angry, devastated, but they'd be alive. They'd realize that we succeeded. And they'd have each other.

They'd be okay.

They could build a new life, a new world.

I pressed the notebook into Izzy's hands, and she dropped it, like it had burned her, the soft thud echoing in the silence around us.

"Max, no." She shook her head, tears carving silent and

angry tracks down her cheeks. "You can't do that. It isn't right. You can't just do this on your own. It's not fair to them, and it's not fair to you either. And Ro, he doesn't deserve this—"

"I can't say goodbye to them," I whispered, unable to meet her stare. "I won't be able to do it. I know it's not fair, trust me. None of this is fair." My voice broke on a tremor. "But I have to do it alone. It's the only way I can go through with it."

I squeezed my hands into fists to cover up how badly they were shaking. I wanted to be brave, to face the ritual with pride and purpose. But I was fucking terrified. And if they gave me an out, which I knew they'd try to do, it would be only more difficult for me to resist—for me to see my own heartbreak mirrored on their faces and not do everything I could to repair it.

"Well, you won't be alone." Izzy grabbed my hands, unfolding my fists and threading my fingers through hers. I could tell she wanted to argue, to say more, but her face softened, relenting. "I'll stay with you," she squeezed my hands, "until the end."

My lips trembled, the word 'no' stuck on my tongue.

I swallowed it back and nodded.

I'd allow myself this one comfort.

I sniffed. "If things get shaky, or something dangerous happens, promise me you'll go? I have Charlie, Haley, and the others on alert."

"Promise."

THE LAKE WAS FREEZING, but I welcomed the chill as I stepped in.

It helped ground me, tuning out the soft buzzing in my ears, the stiffness in my hands. It was like my mind was fighting to separate from my body, like I was watching myself from above —here but also not.

I blinked, the soft glow of the sun warm against my cheek, forcing myself to focus on the bitter chill against my skin. I couldn't dissociate from this, I needed to be here, to focus.

Izzy stood close to the rocky shore, the closest I'd let her get, arms wrapped around herself as she shook with silent tears. Ralph was next to her, ready to rush her away if needed.

He'd followed us out, despite my panicked attempts to lull him back to sleep in the cabin.

I couldn't hide from Ralph though. There was a magic about him that I didn't understand, that I couldn't fight. He'd sensed the truth of the situation without me uttering a word.

Izzy and I'd agreed, no goodbyes. But pulling out of her bone-crushing hug for the last time had almost broken me, especially when it was punctured by Ralph's soft whine.

I gave them a soft smile before I trudged deeper into the lake, the stone and basin oddly floating in front of me, the fixture somehow abandoning its bulky weight in the water.

The basin zipped with an electric energy the moment the water touched it, shooting lightning zaps from where my skin guided it, all the way through my spine.

I'd closed the bond links as best as I could when I'd woken up this morning. I didn't want them to feel what I felt, to know my plans before I had a chance to execute them, to feel when— when I was gone.

It was a betrayal, one that would haunt me in whatever world I crossed over into.

I let myself feel the soft hum of my team one more time, let the warmth there, strengthened by love, wash over me.

They'd be okay.

Everything would be okay.

I visualized the tethers between us that had become so clear in my mind the last few months. All of our work strengthening, nurturing them had made them feel psychically physical in a way they hadn't before.

I took a deep breath, basking in their rightness, their strength.

And then, I visualized severing them, swallowing my scream at the sudden hollowness, the stabbing pain.

I let myself mourn the loss for one moment, and then, I waded further, squeezing the amulet that dangled from my neck just below the locket Cy had given me.

Michael's amulet was warm to the touch, and surprisingly helped ease the new ache in my chest. I didn't understand it, didn't know if it would be useful. There'd been no amulet in the strange dream-walk I had. But it reminded me of Saif, of Sayty. And if I had to do this alone, bringing these small ties to family helped me feel less lonely.

The stone sparked and shimmered when we reached the strange portal Darius had torn open. It hadn't remained permanently open, but there'd been moments, when the breeze fluttered just right, that I could see the tear between worlds.

This was where it would happen.

Holding my hand up to the shimmering sky, I let my fingers trace along the edges of the portal. It felt different than the others I'd been through, and seemed to almost welcome my presence, like it was guiding me home, my skin tingling in the places where I traced it.

Taking a deep breath, I shoved the lingering fears deep into the recesses of my mind, letting my body guide me through a ritual it had memorized long before it belonged to me.

I pulled my hand back then, with a fluid motion, sliced the flesh of my palm against the sharp ridge of the stone. I watched as my blood washed over the side, collecting in the shimmering pool of liquid.

My movements were mechanical, transfixed as the scene

played out just as it had in my dream, the directions easy to follow as if there were no way to mess this up.

The pool of liquid changed colors as it mixed with my blood, and I waited until there was enough of it, enough of my power swirling in the depths—until it turned the milky-white it had in my dream.

My heartbeat raged against my ribs, the wind picking up with urgency, until my hair whipped against my face in thick ropes of black.

Though the water had been still when I entered, waves crashed around me now, tumultuous and thirsty, the water spilling into the basin and joining the murky mixture there.

With a deep, panicked breath, I brought my lips to the ridge of the bowl and took deep sips of the liquid until it was drained to the bottom.

The iridescence of the stone was gone now, but it glowed a gentle blue.

When I looked down at my arms, I saw the glow mirrored in my veins.

The mixture was bitter, repulsive and I fought to keep it down as my body fought just as hard to reject it.

My throat burned with fire and I clutched my stomach as sharp pangs shot through me.

Breathing became impossible, my lungs suddenly raw and tight.

I ignored the pain, my lips and tongue seamlessly shaping the words of the ritual. It was a language I didn't know or understand, but my mouth formed the lilting phrases with precision and ease, a familiarity and mastery that was etched in my body, deep in my roots, my voice a sister song to another that had long been unanswered.

My arms stretched out, like they were preparing for a hug, and my body began to lift towards the portal seam, held there in mid-air, floating above the water, weightless. My mouth stretched wide in a scream, though the sound that emerged matched the cadence of the spell.

Tears streamed down my face as every atom in my body opened raw and wide, magic and power slicing through me, the pain deep and unrelenting, but still, I welcomed it.

My thoughts were slower than usual, like they were fighting their way to form through a viscous liquid.

Not tears, I realized. I was crying blood. I watched it drip a crimson pool into the lake at my waist, a dark, thick river.

Blood that I tasted on my tongue as it spilled from the seam of my lips.

This, this was it. It was almost done.

My trembling body eased at the promise that it would fall into rest soon.

Thunder sounded around me, a perfect base to the song ripping from my lungs, shocks of lightning bolting through the sky—now dark and angry, no sun in sight.

There was rustling behind me, yelling, but I ignored it. I couldn't turn my head, couldn't remove my focus from the stone as the portal stretched and widened, shaping into something new—not a shape at all.

My vision blurred as the portal cut through me, and I knew it was almost over. I felt my feeble flesh wither against it, no match for the power that pulsed in the air—a one-use vessel that would melt with the barrier it sifted, one and the same.

The rustling around me grew louder, closer—and then there was a new pain, one that I wasn't prepared for.

A hand grabbed mine, pulling my body back down to the water, grounding me.

The bonds I'd fought so hard to seal off, the lines of connection I thought I'd permanently severed, burst open with a new flare of power.

I turned my head, finding a pair of familiar brown eyes, threaded with gold, pupils blown wide.

Atlas.

His stare locked on mine, and while I saw a brief flash of anger at my betrayal, it was overshadowed by affection, by determination.

Darius grabbed my other hand, and as I shifted, I saw them all. I *felt* them all—Wade, Eli, and Declan too, connected to me with a strength I was too weak to fight against no matter how hard I tried.

No.

I knew their intentions as if they were my own. They were going to stay, even if it meant they died with me.

They'd waited until the exact moment I was too physically drained to fight them.

I tried to tug my hands away, panic gripping me, choking me. No. No. No.

But their hold only grew tighter, enforced with a power and magic I couldn't fend off.

We're with you, Declan's voice echoed in my head, soft and sure and so filled with love that my body ached with it. *Until the end.*

Darius's stare found mine, and I saw my own pain mirrored in him, mirrored in them all. Their bodies were nothing against this power. The ritual would destroy them all.

Didn't they see that this was hopeless? Wasteful?

No getting rid of us, Little Protector. We'll follow you in this life and in the next.

Their decision, their confirmation rippled through them all.

Never much cared for the singular chosen-one-martyr trope, Eli's voice still held humor alongside the pain.

Community, right? Wade echoed. *We're in this together.*

They huddled closer, until their warmth pressed against me from all sides, cocooning me as the waves of power shot through us all. Our breaths became one, then slowed to a halt.

I fought desperately to pull the magic through me, to protect them from the worst of it, but they fought me in turn, greedily pulling it through the bonds the moment I had hold of it.

And then, as the connection between us pulled tight and fractured, began to wither from the duress, the strangest thing happened.

It somehow grew stronger, angrier—fortified.

I blinked, my heart beating a new rhythm, a warm, familiar presence growing stronger in my bones.

"Ro?" His name was a rasp on my lips as he grabbed my shoulder.

His expression was rigid, his eyes fierce as I felt his own strength infuse mine.

And then another wave of power, strengthening us again.

"Izzy."

Her gray eyes locked on mine, determined and hard as she pushed her strength into me.

Her friendship raked against my skin, burrowing deep— her love, as solid and intentional as my team's and my brother's.

"We're not leaving you," Ro said, his jaw rigid as he fought to get the words out, the force pressing down on me, on us, crushing. "You are a part of us all, Max."

Emotion clutched at my throat, thick and hot, as my vision blurred.

Then, the small trickle of strength that they lent grew into a flood.

When I turned, my neck craning back beyond the clutch of my team, I saw Charlie alongside Ralph, her face set in determination.

Next to them, Mer, Haley, and Jace. Then Claude, Nash, and Nika. And beyond them, Arnell, Sharla—the entire community housed at The Lodge. There had to be over a hundred of them.

Ropes of power tethered me to them, their strength reinforcing my own as they lent me as much as they could.

No.

Fear lashed through me.

What were they doing? What were they thinking?

I'd be the death of them all.

"NO." I pushed the word out, fought with every fiber of my being to free myself from their clutches. Their compassion would kill them all. "No."

This wasn't how this was supposed to happen, this wasn't what was planned. No more death. Just mine. It was supposed to end with me.

This was always your army, Max, Atlas's voice filtered through my panic. *This is what it means to be a community, the kind worth being a part of anyway.*

Besides, you can't have all the glory, Little Protector. I quite like the idea of going out a hero—no one would ever expect it.

As if the others had heard Darius's words, the lines of connection grew more urgent, forceful, carving into me with a ferocity that matched that of the shadow magic lining the realms.

The world shimmered and shifted, the ground shaking and fracturing at our feet.

Still, they held steady, their strength infusing my own as power, unlike anything I'd felt before, flooded through me.

The portal tore open, until I saw The Styx shimmering through it, and beyond it, Lucifer, Sam, and Serae—their expressions hard and unyielding.

When they saw me, Lucifer and Sam tore into the water, eyes wide and urgent when they saw the others there too. Serae's eyes gleamed from the shoreline, and when they met mine, she nodded once.

But The Styx would kill them, wouldn't it?

Their power pulsed through me as the distance between us closed.

The amulet vibrated against my chest, emitting a soft glow—a warmth that seeped into my skin like lava.

A sharp light eclipsed my vision, bright and unyielding, until I could see nothing else.

Still, I felt them all, the threads of their power braiding together with mine. They multiplied and pulsed, nearly as bright and fortified as the bonds that tied me to my team. Different, but just as strong.

And then a new thread, this one unfamiliar and unseen, but I could taste it as it flooded through me. It was similar to mine, but also not, and it barreled into me with purpose.

I clung to it desperately as all feeling and senses blurred at the edges into nothingness, my body no longer mine.

There was an ear-shattering crack, and then the absence of sound, one sharp tether of pain, gripping taut at my chest—and then it was cut, undone, the worlds slipping away into nothing.

34

WADE

1 **4 Days After the Ritual**

"Fucking finally." I exhaled in relief when I saw Max.

She was asleep, her brows pinched slightly and her skin, paler than usual, was covered in a soft sheen. Every few minutes, her muscles would spasm, limbs contorting awkwardly, like she was battling something—or someone—in sleep. While her expression in the physical realm was one of peace, here she seemed almost pained, like she was fighting off some sort of psychic pain. A final boss that only she could see.

For some reason, I couldn't seem to do anything. I hovered over her, unable to move, unable to wield my usual dream-walking powers.

It was fucking tormenting. To do nothing but watch her.

I reached towards her, desperate to ease the furrow in her brow or press her hair, slicked with sweat across her forehead, back behind her ear. But I was limbless here. I might as well not have a body at all. I just observed, awkwardly, uselessly.

As annoying as it was, I was just glad to actually reach her, however limited that reach was.

After the ritual, we'd all been knocked out—all of us who'd linked to her, anyway, which was almost everyone nearby. Some of us were out longer than others.

The rest of Six and I woke up after about a week, from what we were able to gather. And we'd been slowly recovering since.

My body ached in a way I'd never felt before, and none of us had been able to access or use Max's powers. We couldn't even feel the bond, an absence that fucking terrified me every time I tried to reach for the familiar warmth—a terror that could only be quelled by pressing my fingers to her pulse, feeling the slow beat.

She was alive, but it was like she'd been locked off from us all, a protective cocoon around her as her body healed.

Because she would heal.

She'd wake up.

Eventually.

She had to.

It took me several days just to work up enough strength to dream-walk, which was strange, because dream-walking was how I often regenerated my power. But even then, I couldn't reach her right away. I wasn't sure why. Reaching for her was like trying to reach across the ocean, with only my arms to stretch. Instead, I'd focused on dream-walking to Dec, then Eli, but I could only hold the dreamscape for a few minutes at a time, like trying to hold water in the palm of my hand, the tenuous threads slipping through the cracks of my fingers.

Until today.

She was here.

And while I'd never experienced a dreamscape quite like

this one, unable to control a damn thing—including my own body—it was a start.

17 Days After the Ritual

I pushed the disappointment away at being stuck to the ceiling again, a frozen blob that just had to float here and watch the girl I loved contort in pain, unable to rescue her from it.

She was never one to be rescued though, always the one to do the rescuing.

My last dream-walk to her had cost me. I'd woken up drained, more tired than I'd been before, and unable to reach for her again immediately. I was determined to get stronger, to stay longer, to bring her back or lend her my energy—whatever it took to have her awake and with us again.

She whimpered, and my stomach flipped at the noise.

I fought again to reach for her, but I didn't achieve anything. It was like she was in a glass case—a mental version of The Guild's cells—and I didn't have the necessary skills or tools to break through.

Yet.

"It worked," I said, my pulse thrumming against my skin when she twitched at the sound of my voice. It was slight, maybe even a figment of my imagination, but I clung to that small response with everything I had. "We think it worked anyway, we aren't really sure."

There wasn't any way to really verify if we'd dissolved the realms or stabilized them or what. Surviving the apocalypse hadn't come with an instruction manual, unfortunately. And when the ritual was completed, we'd all been unconscious. There weren't any buzzing neon signs hovering above The Lodge declaring the world saved, the final boss defeated.

"Your uncle," I said, excitement flooding me at the prospect of delivering good news for once, on the off chance she could hear and understand me, "he woke up. He was actually the first one. I think something you did unlocked whatever hold the anchor magic had on him." Saif didn't look exactly refreshed. He was weak, and seemed to have aged during his slumber, like the power had drained some of his youth. But he was alive, and seemed unbothered by the cost his body had paid. "He's actually the one who helped get us all inside—after, well, whatever happened, happened. Everyone else is awake now—"

I let the rest of the sentence drift off.

Everyone else except for her.

The edges of the dream blurred, and as hard as I fought to stay here with her, the world dissolved around me.

19 Days After the Ritual

"Some more good news. I think Seamus is better. We're trying not to get ahead of ourselves and call it a cure just yet, but the blood that Darius collected—not sure if you remember, you were kind of—" possessed by a boiling rage that I'd never seen the likes of before, "out of it that day, but he had an idea. A good one. He collected some of Jarrod's blood on a hunch, after—"

I held my breath, waiting with desperation for some kind of reaction, for the flutter behind her eyelids to grow strong enough to part them. Each day that passed when she didn't wake up was like living through a never-ending nightmare.

It wasn't fair that she wasn't there to celebrate with us. And we couldn't bring ourselves to enjoy the win without her.

All I could do in the meantime was talk to her as if she were awake, will it strong enough into reality that one day soon, it would be.

"Well, I guess we never filled you in on all the details of that meeting," I winced, remembering the flare of anger that seemed to pulse from her every pore, amplified by her fear about what might happen to Dec and Rowan in Jarrod's custody. "Sorry about that again, by the way. We shouldn't have gone behind your back, we shouldn't have met with The Guild. If we hadn't, maybe Dec, your home—" I shook my head, my mouth going dry at the thought of all those people, that entire town, dead, because of Jarrod's power complex. "But then, at the same time, that's the whole reason we knew where to find Dec, where to find Jarrod, and the stone."

I sighed, then pinched the bridge of my nose. "Sorry, I'm really shit at this one-sided conversation thing. I miss talking to you." I missed closing my eyes each night and creating entire worlds in our dreams together. It was our place, our thing. It was lonely now, confusing without her here with me. *Really* here.

"Anyway, where was I?" I lingered in silence for a moment, trying to collect my thoughts. I didn't have full control of them, it was like this dream was only partially lucid, the world not entirely my own. I was simply a traveler here, stopping by.

"Right, the blood. Nika—do you remember Nika?" I shook my head, grunting. "Of course you do, she's maybe the first vampire we've met who's even more unhinged than Darius."

I pictured Max rolling her eyes at that, a smirk tugging at the corner of her mouth in reluctant amusement.

Fuck, I missed her.

"Well, I guess not anymore. That day, she attacked Xavier, drained him. And she's been better. More like herself. According to Nash and Claude, I mean. I obviously had nothing to compare it to. Anyway, Darius had a hunch and it paid off, for once."

I grunted at the memory of his smug face when he realized it.

Nash was too shocked, too excited to have his sister back—well, mostly back—that he didn't even give Darius shit for his arrogance.

The animosity between them had been slowly dissolving since, not entirely gone, but I was no longer concerned that Nash would try and covertly kill our vampire in the middle of the night.

Dec still locked the door as an added caution, just in case. Not that a locked door would keep a vampire out if he wanted inside. Love made people irrational though.

"Darius collected Jarrod's blood," I continued, "and now Seamus is...not entirely back to his old self, but he's close. He's better. He doesn't even need to be chained up anymore."

I laughed, but it sounded flat, even to me. "Darius even has a board that he's keeping track of his progress on. Right now it says something like '18 days since Seamus has tried to eat someone.' So, yeah, your vampire is still as ridiculous as always. He misses you too. We all do."

In truth, I was fairly certain that Darius would start killing everyone around the site, just because they had the audacity to wake up before Max, if she didn't come to soon.

He wasn't exactly well known for his restraint.

Max's head tilted slightly, a loose strand of hair sliding off her cheek.

Was there more color there than I'd remembered? Her skin was still tacky with sweat, but her body didn't seem quite as tense as it had on that first day.

Was I imagining it? Was I so desperate to see improvement that my brain had started fabricating its own reality altogether?

Eager that this was working, I pushed on. "Seamus and Darius have taken an antagonistic liking to each other. I think

Darius is just milking the fact that someone other than him has experienced blood lust in the family."

22 Days After the Ritual

"Max, you have to wake up. Please."

She looked more at peace now, like she did in the real world. Like this sleep was nothing but a typical rest, even though it had been almost a month.

There'd been no improvements, no changes in her awareness. But physically, she seemed fine.

Izzy, Ro, and the others in the med ward couldn't figure out why she wasn't waking up.

Something about her peaceful expression here scared me though. Before, it seemed like she was fighting something.

Had she just given up?

What would happen to her if she had?

Would she be resigned to this sleeping world forever, until her body withered away?

"We miss you. I miss you—" my voice hitched, my eyes blurring her slightly out of focus as I fought the wave of grief back. "Things are different. We don't have much access to information out here to confirm anything, but electricity has been out for the most part, phone service is fucked, and the world just feels...strange. Claude, and some of the others left a few days ago. They wanted to get back home, to check on things. See if this is happening everywhere or just—here. There've been a few earthquakes, some weird weather. Charlie is pushing for us to head somewhere else, to find another location and set up a space there, in case the ritual upset some tenuous balance here. We need to get a better grasp of what's going on."

But we didn't want to leave. Didn't want to move her. Taking her from this place felt wrong somehow, like she was tied to it in some fundamental way. Like the power in the atmosphere might help push her back to us.

I swallowed, unsure how much to reveal. I didn't know much, had no clue what the world would look like when she opened her eyes again. Maybe it was better to focus on the positives, in case she could understand me?

"Izzy and Ro are doing well. Ralph too." I knew she'd want to know about the others, about Samael and Lucifer. But when we awoke, they were gone. We had no idea if they were dead or alive.

Same with Levi. No one had seen him.

Eli swore that he wasn't worried about his brother, insisted that he'd probably woken up and left to get a fresh start, away from this mess. But I knew him well enough to know that it was bullshit. He just couldn't split his concern right now, his sanity wouldn't allow him.

Right now, Max was the only thing we could collectively focus on.

"I'm going to try dream-walking with one of the others next time, see if I can bring them here. I'm getting stronger, slowly. I think I might be able to. Darius and Atlas seem to have a secret battle going on between them. It's called 'who can be the biggest prick.'"

Honestly, they were pretty evenly matched.

"They lash out at anyone who goes near your door." I grinned. "You should've heard Izzy cuss them out though. Pretty sure she would've attacked them both, but Ro grabbed her and held her back in time. They eventually let her in to see you. Ralph too. The hellhound hasn't left the floor next to your bed. Dec tried to coax him into a game of fetch a few days ago, but he wouldn't even acknowledge that red ball of his that he's always carrying around."

We were getting kind of worried about him, truth be told. I had no idea what hellhounds required to survive, but he hadn't been eating or drinking or showing much interest in anything.

"And Dec and Eli," I sighed, "they haven't left the cabin for more than a few minutes at a time either. We've just been taking turns, lying next to you. Darius and Rowan dragged in some extra mattresses so that none of us have to sleep anywhere else.

"We're all here with you. I hope that you can feel us. That you don't feel alone, wherever you are." I closed my eyes, wanting so desperately to hold her, to see the familiar spark in her eyes when she looked at me. "Please, Max. Please wake up."

Two Months **After the Ritual**

MY HEAD WAS on a familiar pillow. Max's chest rose in slow breaths before descending again.

I pressed my hand against her skin, basking in the warmth.

Usually, in dream-walks, I pulled energy from Max. We always had a balanced relationship of give and take in these dreams, but now I fought desperately to drain my power, for her to pull as much as she needed.

Even if it killed me.

Sometimes, I swore I felt her draw from me, especially when I held her hand, her fingers curling around mine once or twice, but it was always too subtle for me to know whether it really happened or if I just wanted it so badly that I simply thought it did. While I woke up exhausted every day, I had no way of knowing if that had more to do with the fact that I hadn't used my incubus powers to feed in months or if she really was pulling some of my energy.

The bed she was on now was large, comfortable; the room bright and warm, but small, a near copy of her bedroom from the cabin. I figured if she could choose any place in the world to sleep, it would be there. Bouquets of impossibly large flowers were arranged in every nook and corner, her favorite books in haphazard stacks, just like she preferred them, all of them just waiting to be read. The walls were covered with posters and messages the others had begged me to transcribe and surround her with.

I had no idea if she could sense the warmth and love encasing her while she slept, but it made them feel a little better at least when I described it each morning, took their input, and made the dreamscape better the next night. It gave them a sense of purpose, maybe, when they spent most of their days feeling useless.

To me, it mostly felt like I was visiting the inside of a shrine every time I went to sleep.

Despite trying almost every night, I couldn't bring any of them with me in the dream-walk. All it did was drain me too much to reach her at all. Traveling with others was something that always worked best when I was with Max anyway, with her power, her strength amplifying my own.

Two weeks ago, I woke up next to her, no longer hovering above like an observer of the dream. I could shape the room into whatever I wanted, like I was usually able to do. And so I'd shaped it into this.

But she was still always asleep and, save for the few times when I could have sworn she'd sensed my presence, my voice, she remained largely unresponsive.

At first, I'd taken my new agency in the dream as a sign of improvement, that she was getting stronger, but as time went on, I worried it was more so a sign of my own strength returning than hers.

We'd moved out of The Lodge a month ago in an attempt to avoid the chaos and uncertainty around the grounds. Things had grown more dire, more unpredictable. What had once been a place of comfort was now drained of all the things that made it home.

Instead, we hoped that finding Max somewhere quiet and safe to rest would help speed along the process.

None of us would lend voice to the fear that we all felt.

That Max would be lost in her dream world forever.

That what she'd been through was too much to recover from, just as Lucifer thought it would be.

That we'd collectively lent her just enough power to keep her alive, but not enough to live.

That by interfering with the ritual, we'd unintentionally trapped her inside of herself, a fate worse, maybe, than even death.

Aside from me, no one else really slept much these days. The only reason I did was because I knew I could see her in my dreams, that each time I closed my eyes, there'd be a chance she'd be awake on the other side, waiting for me.

Exhaustion was destroying us though. Instead of sleeping, the team oscillated between finding random projects to keep them busy and bickering with each other, picking fights whenever one of us sank too far into grief or began to lose hope. Usually, it worked well enough to distract us back from that cliff, but not always.

Ro and Izzy helped when they could, neither interested in letting us leave their sights until Max was awake.

I'd merely suggested *once* that they go meet up with Arnell and the others, promising that we'd find them when she woke up.

They nearly took my head off before the suggestion fully left my lips.

I hadn't mentioned abandoning our weird little purgatory again after that.

A few weeks ago, Ro and Dec came up with a plan for a new project, one that breathed new life into the group, kept us busy most of the time, all of us trading between watching over our girl and helping out.

Honestly, having somewhere to filter all of this fear and anxious energy had been a fucking godsend.

It required that we move again, but we didn't have to go too far this time, and we didn't run into too many other people in the process.

The ritual seemed to have worked, we were growing more certain of it every day.

But the world was transforming around us as a result, uncertainty at every corner.

We weren't willing to risk exploring things properly until Max was safe and herself again.

Darius created a new sign with "X amount of days since Atlas has threatened to murder someone," a few weeks ago, and we'd finally made it to a record we were all proud of—two.

But like most temporary reprieves, that burst of hope and possibility slowly began to sizzle out.

Most nights now, I didn't say too much when I dream-walked here. There wasn't exactly a surplus of good news to share. There wasn't much news at all, really, and I didn't want to fill her unconscious thoughts with our concerns for her, with the depths of our grief.

Instead, I just held her, savoring the feel of her skin against mine, the gentle thrum of her pulse, my lips pressed to the side of her head, whispering over and over again how much I loved her.

How much we all loved her.

. . .

3 Months **After the Ritual**

We abandoned the project. We'd finished it first, but it grew too painful to think about not getting to share it with her.

And without Max there to enjoy the final product, it was pointless.

About a week ago, we collectively decided that the best thing we could do was go find the others. That when Max woke up, she'd want to be surrounded by the community she'd sacrificed so much for—the community that sacrificed so much for her in return.

We still couldn't teleport, and I was beginning to wonder if we'd ever have access to Max's powers again, even when she did wake up.

When I let myself think about why we couldn't reach them, what that might mean, I'd lose myself to a dark place I devoted most of my waking hours to staying out of.

Phone service was spotty these days, but luckily, Arnell knew where we'd been living and came by to check on Ro.

That night, we decided to go back with him, since we were no longer hopeful about the idea of staying in a current spot. We found a couple of vans that were working reliably enough nearby and made the trip to a small campsite they'd been living in, only an hour drive or so from The Lodge.

They'd built it out quite a bit during their time here, and while it didn't have the same charm or inspire the same feeling of home that the original Lodge always had, it was nice enough. Impressive, really, considering everything.

Seeing everyone infused my team with a renewed sense of purpose, of hope, too, which was a nice bonus.

Our friends were alive and, all things considered, thriving as best as could be expected.

While Saif and Seamus weren't happy about the fact that

we'd taken off in the middle of the night, instead of following everyone here in the first place or bringing them with us, they were so glad to have us back that any lingering anger dissolved into relief almost instantly.

They'd also developed a strange friendship, equal parts bickering and stubborn silence, and I rarely found one without the other.

I wanted so desperately for Max to see this new location they'd carved out in our absence.

It was different from The Lodge, sure, but with everyone here, together, it was almost as good as before.

Almost.

3 Months, Five Days After the Ritual

When I woke up in the now-nightly dream-walk, I pressed my face into the curve of her neck, breathing her in.

It was silly, maybe, since she didn't feel or smell any different in this world than she did in the waking one, but here, Max was just mine, and any lingering anxieties I had during the daylight hours quieted, at least partially.

I took a deep breath, hugging her to me, then exhaled slowly, like each breath out risked pushing her further away from me.

She shifted in my arms and I froze.

I was too afraid to break the moment, convinced suddenly that this wasn't our usual dream-walk but just a general, run-of-the-mill dream—one that existed in my head and nowhere else.

This time when I exhaled, she squirmed, as if my breath tickled her, the movement too obvious now to be only in my imagination.

Hesitantly, reluctantly, I pulled my face away from her.

This was the exact room of our dream-walk. I'd carefully arranged all of the usual things on the walls. No regular, run-of-the-mill dream, then. I had agency here.

Max shifted slightly, then turned her face towards mine.

Her lips parted into a soft smile as she stretched, her arms shifting until they wrapped around my neck.

I didn't move, didn't breathe, terrified I'd break the spell.

Slowly, as if she thought the room might be brighter than she was ready for, she fluttered her eyelids open, her smile widening as her eyes found mine. "Wade."

My name was raspy and warm on her tongue.

I stared at her, lost for words.

Her brows pinched and she laughed. The sound, soft and cracking with sleep, stole the breath from my lungs. "You look like you've seen a ghost."

My fingers tightened around her, pulling her closer to me, like they too needed confirmation that I hadn't.

Still, I couldn't say anything.

Her hand slid to my cheek, where I knew there was more stubble than she was used to seeing on me, her thumb stroking in soft, slow circles that skimmed the corner of my lips.

Her touch was featherlight and I groaned at the sensation, like my body had forgotten how good it felt to be under her touch, how desperately perfect she was.

"New look?" she asked, brow arching as she studied me for a long, drawn moment. "I like it. Suits you." She pressed her thumb into the furrow of my brows, gently rubbing it out. "Though a bit serious."

She closed her eyes for a moment, and a flare of panic flooded me—that I'd imagined it all, that she was asleep again, that the last few seconds had been nothing but the ruminations of a desperate man clawing onto the last vestiges of his sanity.

But then she opened them again, and when she did, the

comfortable cotton pajama set she'd been wearing was replaced with my favorite black silk shorts and bra.

"Better?" She asked, eyes sparkling with a teasing glow. As if this were just a simple game, one of our usual dream-walks.

We'd often spend the first few minutes of these dreams crafting new scenes, new clothes, each trying to outlast the other in the budding tension that became impossible to resist whenever we were together here.

I opened my mouth, fighting to find words, but none came.

Unconcerned, she pressed her lips to mine and kissed me, her leg sliding between mine until we were tangled and close.

My heart beat ragged and hopeful against my chest, desperately trying to get to hers.

Her power flared against me, a hunger and need I hadn't experienced in months pumping through my veins, hot and impatient.

She slid her tongue between my lips, and I was hard the moment it touched mine, deepening the kiss.

I pressed her to me, a satisfied groan building in my chest when she gasped, her hips rolling so that she could feel the already-rigid outline of my dick.

Heat flooded me as she dug her nails into my back, riding against me.

Her energy flared against mine, and mine responded in kind—ravenous, desperate.

It took everything I had to keep from pulling energy from her, to resist as it plowed against me, demanding entrance and our usual play, our usual exchange.

I froze, fought as hard as I could not to kiss her, not to take this any further. She'd been gone for months, I didn't want to steal whatever strength she'd managed to conjure in that time.

Sensing something was off, she pulled back, her expression hurt, like she'd taken my reticence as rejection. "What's wrong?"

My throat ached at the sight of her.

Here. Awake. Alive.

"You've been asleep."

"Well," the corner of her mouth twitched into a grin, "yeah. That *is* the nature of a dream-walk. The one requirement, some might say."

"No," I held her face in my palms, my eyes devouring the sight of her. "You've been asleep since the ritual. It's been months."

Confusion painted across her face. "Months?"

I nodded, the pad of my thumb pressing against her full bottom lip of its own accord, until her mouth parted for me.

I couldn't resist her here. I never could.

As if pulled by the same thread, she sucked the tip of my thumb between her lips, tasting me, her eyes closed in ecstasy.

Her power grew stronger, and I felt it lick against my skin, my body half-convinced it was my dick she had in her mouth, not my finger.

"Everyone's okay?" she asked, her tongue sweeping over my finger, drawing it fully into her mouth again.

A strangled sound pulled from my throat, as I nodded. "Yes. Mostly."

"Good. In that case," her breathing was ragged now as she kissed the palm of my hand, nipped the pulse point at my wrist, her thigh rubbing seductively against my dick, "let's discuss the details later, if that works for you? I feel like I'm going to explode if I resist you for another second."

Resist? This was what she called resisting? I was on the edge of coming just from the feel of her leg against me.

That desperate, strangled sound again was the only response I had for her.

She understood though, and pressed her mouth to mine, teeth and tongues tangling as she slid her hand down my pants.

Her thumb pressed over the bead of pre-cum as she rubbed it into the ridge of my dick.

"Fuck," she whimpered, into my mouth, her breath hot and addictive, "I'm drenched. Now, Wade. I need you now."

Her words nearly undid me, and I used all of my strength to keep from busting in my pants.

With hurried hands, far less graceful than I was used to in these dreams, I shoved my sweatpants and boxers down. But I didn't have the restraint necessary to do the same for her.

Instead, sliding the loose, flimsy silk of her absurdly short shorts to the side, I shoved inside of her, choking on a gasp as her warmth enveloped me.

She moaned into my mouth, her kiss growing more urgent and fired as her hips met mine, thrust for thrust.

"Gods, I love you," she whispered, letting me swallow the words whole as she climbed towards her edge and I fought desperately not to fall over it first.

Delicious tension lined every muscle of my body as she pulled from me, my power clumsy and straining in its desperation to feed her own.

"Love isn't a strong enough word for how I feel about you." I pressed my tongue, my teeth, to the spots I'd memorized along her neck, knowing exactly where, and how, to pull those intoxicating sounds from her throat.

She clenched around me, her teeth and nails digging into my flesh, piercing my skin in a way that only amplified my pleasure.

"I'm close," I warned, as I pumped into her, fighting to hold back.

"Good," she said, the word more gasp than anything as she rode me. "Come for me, Wade."

I rutted into her, one more thrust, and exploded, relishing the sound of her own orgasm as her body tightened around mine, the evidence of our lust wet along her thighs.

My breathing was erratic, my heart pumping frantically, as I held her to me, feeling whole for the first time in months.

Unable to form words, I pressed a kiss to her forehead, my head buzzing and vision blurring from the force of my orgasm.

She smiled against me before playfully biting my chest. The jolt of ecstasy had me vowing right then and there to tattoo the imprints of her teeth there the moment I woke up. "Don't go sleepy on me now, Wade, that was only round one."

35

MAX

The light was harsh and abrasive against my eyelids, and I wanted nothing more than to sink back into my dream with Wade, to restage the fourth and fifth orgasm he'd given me, to feel the intoxicating flare of his power as it braided with my own.

But no matter how hard I fought it, my body refused to stay asleep for another moment.

Something shifted against me, warm and familiar, then a cold, wet nudge pressed against my hand, jolting me.

Reluctantly, I opened my eyes, squinting against the rays of light pouring through the part in the curtain.

Ralph nudged my hand again, until my fingers were behind his right ear, primed and ready to scratch his favorite spot.

Smiling, I acquiesced to the not-so-subtle request, and he yipped with excitement before jumping up and slathering my face with too-wet licks.

"Ralph," I laughed, half-heartedly shoving him off me as I sat up.

The room had been silent before, but it was now filled with

the sort of silence that was preternatural, on the edge of breaking.

When he finally settled down, head in my lap, I could see more than just giant tufts of black hair.

There were mattresses strewn about the crowded room, familiar faces staring back at me, eyes wide, jolted from sleep, and frozen—Darius, Atlas, Dec, Wade, Eli, Ro, and Izzy.

"Um," grinning, I shook my head in confusion, patting Ralph again when a gentle nudge reminded me he wasn't done receiving scratches "good morning."

As if my voice had pierced the strange bubble of silence, they all moved at once, climbing over each other and the mattresses to get to me, until we were one giant tangle of limbs and bodies.

I couldn't see who was hugging me where, and I could hardly breathe with the weight of them all on top of me, arguing with each other about giving me space, but no one seemed willing or able to move away.

Somehow, I still managed to laugh, warmth filling me from head to toe.

36

MAX

A COUPLE OF WEEKS LATER…

Warm breath kissed the side of my neck and I curled into it, not bothering to hide the delighted smile spreading across my face.

Atlas pulled me closer, pressing his lips against the spot where my neck met my shoulder.

I squirmed in his grip until I could see his face properly.

He groaned, eyes still closed, before burrowing closer to me again—a cat reluctant to leave the warmth.

I would never get tired of seeing him like this—hair mussed with sleep, words abandoned for a groggy rasp, cheek indented with the lacy pattern lining my camisole.

Atlas hated mornings.

Or, rather, he hated getting out of bed on mornings when I was sleeping next to him. Even more so since the ritual.

They hadn't let me out of their sight since the moment I woke up, doting on me at all times while my strength came back.

No one allowed me to help around the town, despite the fact that Charlie was due any minute and was being equally monitored and bed-ridden.

Still, situational clinginess aside, I never would've guessed that the perfectly cold, arrogant leader of Six who I'd met my first day at The Guild was a complete cuddle bug.

Sun streamed through his window. It had to be late morning, maybe even noon, but he didn't seem to mind.

Normally, I wouldn't either, but we were leaving today.

Not that anyone would tell me where we were going beyond, "it's a surprise."

"Atlas," I whispered, burrowing down under the covers until my nose met his, only mildly self-conscious about my morning breath. "I think we're late."

One eye popped open, the familiar sight of gold and brown shadowed by a few loose strands of dark hair. My stomach flipped at the sight, and I was now fully convinced that my body would be forever shocked by the effortless effect they all had on it.

One look—hell, one eye—and I was a puddle of goo.

"We're not late. They won't leave without us." His voice was raspy and heated, like hot chocolate syrup, and he roped his arms around me, pulling me so close that my leg had nowhere to go but between his. "I'm not ready to leave this spot yet."

I bit my lip, a poor attempt to hide my smile.

He inched closer, his teeth lightly tugging on my lip until my own released it. He soothed the soft indentations with his tongue.

"Atlas," I said again, this time far less convincingly.

He swallowed whatever else was going to follow that with his tongue sliding against mine, until the only sound I could make was a needy, aching moan.

Fuck it, I was now thoroughly convinced. They could wait another few minutes before we got on the road.

I was suddenly grateful we'd said our temporary goodbyes to the group last night, especially if it had given me an excuse to linger in Atlas's arms for a little longer.

He pressed me closer, a feverish need suddenly taking over him as he pulled me onto his lap. HIs fingers combed through my hair, the pads rough and soothing as he tugged at the loose bun hanging at the base of my skull. He tilted my head and went deeper.

"I haven't brushed my teeth," I said, gasping as he kissed my jaw, down my neck.

"I don't care."

He was hard as a rock, and my head felt dizzy with heat as I shifted forward, sliding against him—slow, teasing.

He hissed as I ground myself against him, giving him just short of what he was really hunting for.

With an arched brow, he gripped me, shifting us around until my head fell back on his pillow and he hovered over me.

Slowly, torturously, he slid his hand down the front of my pants, my skin aching at every inch of his touch. I soaked his fingers as he ran them over me, his thumb circling my clit, which was already throbbing.

I hummed in assent, shifting forward, desperate for more pressure, but he pulled back slightly, teasing and pinching me as I gasped and started spinning out of control.

Every inch of my skin tingled, my body impossibly sensitive as pleasure raked through me.

His eyes, wild with barely-contained restraint, told me all I needed to know—he was on the edge too, my pleasure his. Each of us starving for the other in a game we'd both lose— only to both win. Massively, massively win.

"Tell me what you want."

"I want you to make me forget my own name," I said, crying out when he slid two fingers into me.

They'd all been so careful with me since I'd woken up, but this was the exception. Sex was one of the ways I grew stronger, and they'd all been so very willing to help with those...training exercises.

Atlas pulled his hand out of my underwear, stare filled with challenge, unflinching from mine as he tasted my arousal on his fingers.

"Unless," I teased, heart pounding wildly, "you want me to just go take care of things myself."

When I turned away slightly, like I was off to do just that, he snapped.

He flipped me until I was on all fours, arm bracing me as he ripped off my underwear leaving me bare to him.

One, firm slap echoed through the room as the sting of his palm shot through my body.

In one fluid motion, he sheathed himself inside of me from behind, arm still firm on my hips as he set the pace.

I was grateful for his steady hold as my body melted against him, waves of pleasure shooting through me at his rough, possessive pace.

His free hand traced up my thigh, inching forward until he found my clit.

I hissed, my vision blurring at the edges as I chased a climax I had no control over.

"You're mine, Bentley," Atlas whispered in my ear, voice ragged and demanding.

"Mm," I agreed, unable to form words as the orgasm washed over me, my body turning boneless in his arms as he finished too.

He held me to him, shifting until my head rested on his chest.

"Okay," he said after a minute or two of peace that had me halfway back to sleep again, "I guess we should get ready now."

"Ready for what?"

"Did you forget?" he asked. His chuckle rumbled against my cheek where it pressed against his chest. "We were already late before we started."

Fuck. My eyes widened and I shot up, frantically tossing one of his shirts over my head.

His eyes latched on the hem of it where it kissed my thighs, no underwear in sight.

He grabbed me, pressing a kiss against my hair, his dick stiffening again.

"It feels good, doesn't it?" I asked, filled suddenly with a renewed giddiness at what life could shape up to now.

"What feels good?" he trailed a hand up my thigh, under the hem of the shirt, drawing tantalizing, teasing circles that traveled closer and closer to where I craved them. "This, you mean?"

"That," I nodded, leaning my head back against him, "and knowing that we're all okay. That it's all over."

"Mmm," he agreed, "It's all over."

At least the worst of it was, I hoped. The world had shifted. A lot. But we were alive, we were together, and from what I could tell, we were obscenely happy.

"We should find the others for breakfast," I pulled away from him, begrudgingly. "I promise we can go for round two after this mysterious surprise of yours."

He groaned. "Why delay happiness though?"

With a laugh, I grabbed his hand, pulling him towards the stairwell.

He froze for a moment, hand tightening briefly around mine.

When I turned around, his eyes were narrowed, something unreadable flashing briefly across his features.

"Everything okay?"

He nodded, eyes locked on mine. "Just a weird sense of déjà vu."

"Bad déjà vu or good déjà vu?"

"I don't know yet." His fingers threaded through mine. "Good, I think."

"Good," I agreed, pulling him forward as the others came into view, all of them wearing matching smirks the moment I clocked the scent of fresh bacon in the air. "Personally, I think we're due for some good all around."

"Okay," Dec said. I heard the smile in her voice, even though I couldn't see it. "Grab my hand."

Her fingers were warm against mine as she pulled me out of the front seat, guiding me out so I didn't hit my head.

I gestured to the thick bandanna covering my eyes. "Can I take this off yet?"

"Not yet." Ro said, punctuating the command with the slam of a car door.

We'd taken three vans—enough to house my team, Ro, Arnell, Izzy, and Ralph. Gas and functioning vehicles were difficult to come by these days, but Mer and Charlie swore they'd be okay without these for a while.

I had no idea what 'a while' meant and no one was giving me any clues regardless.

Teleporting here—wherever 'here' was—would have been the ideal scenario, but my powers still weren't manifesting. They weren't gone, not entirely. Every once in a while, the gentle hum still flooded my veins, and when I focused, I could almost just sense them rising to the surface. But they felt different. Not bad, but strange, like they were changing or evolving.

Darius yelped behind me, a mess of chaotic grunts and shifty movements—one that sounded an awful lot like him running into the rear of the van. "This damn cat. Remind me why she needed to come again?"

Shadow purred and I grinned, knowing damn well she was nudging her head into Darius's leg.

I could picture the vampire's expression even if I couldn't

see it, an attempt at unaffected composure, but equal parts annoyance and amusement peeking through. Shadow was growing on him, but he would never admit it.

A series of four more doors slammed, the voices of the others filtering over us.

"We're all here?" Atlas called.

"Yep!" Izzy this time.

"Okay, ready?" Eli stood behind me, his breath warm on the back of my neck as he gently untied the bandanna. His touch sent chills down my spine, and my body leaned back into him of its own accord. He pulled the cloth down, his hands lingering on my shoulders, like he craved the closeness as much as I did.

"What—" it took a moment for my brain to process where we were.

Only a moment.

A familiar clearing, larger and more manicured than before. A few trees had been removed, but they were replaced by new saplings.

My throat was tight and I fought to take in the scene quickly, before my tears made it impossible.

The last time I was here, it was to watch our cabin burn to the ground.

Now, in its place, was a large, beautiful house. It took inspiration from the rustic original, but even from here, I knew it had to have at least four or five times the amount of space inside.

"I know it's not home. Not like the old one anyway. But maybe we can make it into one, eventually. All of us." Ro cleared his throat, and I turned to find him next to me, hesitation in his brows. "It's okay if you hate it. If this place holds too many bad memories. We can take it down or leave it for someone else to live in. We don't have to stay here. It was just an idea we had while you were," he shrugged, scratching the back of his head, "you know."

"Stay?" It was a miracle I got even one word out, though it sounded more like a garbled mess than English.

"A place to regroup, rebuild, while the world...settles." Ro grabbed my hand, pulling me to the back of the giant house. There was a second one, slightly smaller, but still considerably bigger than the cabin we'd grown up in. Jarrod's fire had cleared more space, and it was evident they'd all put in a ton of work on the landscaping to make everything fit together seamlessly, while still retaining the cozy charm of the original.

There was even a back pavilion already set up for training, our usual obstacle courses and tools shiny and ready for use.

Ro nodded to the second building. "This one's for me and Arnell—and Izzy or anyone else who wants to visit. Plenty of room for us all."

"I've already picked out my room and decorated it," Izzy said, her voice laced with excitement. "There's a theater too. Darius and Dec stocked it with all of our favorites. Movie marathons every weekend if we want!"

Tears carved thick, hurried stripes down my cheeks as I walked towards where we'd scattered Cy's ashes. It felt like years ago.

The tree was gone now, no doubt burnt to a crisp. But there was a small plaque there with his name etched into the surface, the writing remarkably similar to Ro's chicken scratch, along with the words "beloved father, brother, and friend."

"Did we fuck up?" Darius's nose scrunched in concern, and for a moment, he looked like he was debating whether or not he wanted to punch something. Or someone. "Are those good tears or bad?"

I smiled, my vision now just a mess of liquid until all I could parse were splotches of blotchy colors and concerned faces. "Good. I—" I swallowed, struggling to find words to shape the warmth flooding my chest, "thank you."

"What do you think?" Ro asked, brows bent, hesitant.

Ralph dropped his red ball at my feet and went hopping off towards the trees, ready and eager for a round of fetch, like he'd been waiting a lifetime to play in this forest, here and now.

I picked it up, slippery with his slobber, and beamed, my heart impossibly full. "I think we're finally home."

37

EPILOGUE

THREE YEARS LATER

MAX

"Auntie Max, Auntie Max!"

I grunted as a familiar raven-haired toddler jumped into my arms, her tiny arms trying desperately to close themselves around me. The force of her pushed me down into my usual booth.

"Easy Bishop, we don't attack our friends and family," Charlie called from behind the bar, her chastisement ringing with the undertone of laughter before she added a muttered, "this is why I told Uncle Darius not to give you that chocolate bar so late."

I pulled her up, positioning her so that she was seated on my lap. Dark ringlets framed a familiar face—carved in equal parts from both of her parents.

But it was her eyes that stole my breath, no matter how many times I'd seen them.

They were dark and warm, like Charlie's, but every now and again, they'd flare with threads of iridescent silver that seemed to almost glow.

Charlie walked over to us, grabbing the remaining square of chocolate from her daughter's reluctant fingers. "Do you want your usual, Max? Darius is in the back, going over supplies with Mer, but he should be done soon."

I nodded, my mouth already salivating with the promise of Charlie's cooking.

A year ago, we'd finished renovations on the town a few miles away from our home. The Guild's destruction had left very little to salvage, but with our numbers, we'd shaped the space into something comfortable and practical for our uses.

Charlie, and most of the others who'd been living at The Lodge, moved in immediately. Things had been...chaotic since The Ritual. To say the least. It was safest for us to stick together, and we'd carved a beautiful haven here. We had access to fresh water, food, semi-reliable electricity—more than most. Not to mention, we were a pretty damn skilled group when you accounted for our individual strengths.

Most importantly we had love. Community.

A peace I'd never experienced before cushioned our little town, filling it with safety and protection, and a calm that made it easy to breathe for the first time in our lives.

The world was different now—and it would always be dangerous—but we'd found a source of warmth here. Family.

Bishop squirmed in my lap, her eyes crinkling as a mischievous smile tugged at her lips. She blinked, and the small square of chocolate instantly transferred from her mother's hands into her own.

Charlie sighed, her eyes sparkling as they met mine—half amusement, half fear. She glanced around the small diner, the air humming with a taunting energy that I felt rumble and echo in my chest. "How am I supposed to discipline my kid, when I have to contend with her powers, and—" she waved her hand aimlessly, the lights flickering as if in laughter, "the stubborn whims of this place?"

"Not for me. For you, Auntie Max." Bishop shoved the piece of chocolate into my mouth before I could protest.

I winked at her as I let the velvety goodness melt on my tongue. Chocolate was becoming increasingly difficult to find—as were most manufactured foods—especially for us, all the way out here. But, like most of us, Darius loved spoiling the toddler. And she, in turn, loved sharing whatever treasures she was given with the rest of us. So I savored the bite for the gift that it was.

None of us understood the limits of Bishop's powers. They were inconsistent and unpredictable. Like most things these days.

Our best understanding was that The Ritual had worked... but it had come with some unexpected consequences. Namely, shards of shadow magic had scattered throughout the world, infusing people—and things—with a latent energy that occasionally made itself known.

Honestly, it made sense. We'd dissolved the barrier between realms, but all that power had to go *somewhere* once it sifted through us. Magic aside, energy that powerful didn't simply disperse into nothing.

Occasionally, we encountered people who had new abilities —abilities they hadn't had before The Undoing. Most were trivial, difficult to master, and relatively useless on the grand scale of things. I'd met one girl, for example, whose hair had turned blue. And no matter how often she tried to dye it back to its original blond, nothing seemed to stick for more than a day or two.

We were pretty sure Bishop's...unusually powerful talents resulted from Charlie's proximity to The Ritual. While most people affected by the shadow shards were affected in small, almost unnoticeable ways, Bishop was born with a stare that could only be described as supernatural. There was no hiding or denying it—power simply seemed drawn to her.

It was one of the primary reasons Charlie decided to move closer to us. My powers had come back, slowly and over time.

That made us uniquely equipped to protect her. And, hopefully one day, teach her to feel and control the magic that pulsed in her veins now.

The diner was the more puzzling case. It was newly erected and hadn't existed before the ritual, let alone been anywhere near the nexus point.

Still, there was no doubt the place hummed with a familiar, powerful energy. It was a normal restaurant most days—as normal as anything could be in this new, strange world—but every once in a while, the magic would make itself known. A hum in the air, the soft flicker of lights. Like it was sentient.

One time, Eli and Darius had been bickering about which movie we'd screen that night in the town center, and the building just—tossed them both out. They'd gone flying through the air and landed on their asses outside, all remaining threads of debate dissolving on their tongues to make way for shock.

The magic wasn't neutral. It had a mind of its own.

We just weren't sure what it was after, or what purpose it served.

For now, it didn't seem to want to hurt anyone, so we lived alongside the strangeness, almost like a ghost built into the walls of this place—as much a part of this community as the rest of us were.

"Latest run bring any new intel?" Charlie asked, her expression guarded but hopeful.

We'd been searching for Lucifer and Sam for three years. With the barrier between the realms down, Serae helped us search pockets of the hell realm that they'd been known to frequent. Nothing. They seemed to have vanished entirely after The Ritual. No bodies. No sign or sighting whatsoever. Like they were never even here to begin with.

I shook my head. "No, but we've been hearing some rumors about a group in Oregon, and another in Seattle. Call themselves Lucifer's disciples or something. Claude's keeping an ear to the ground and swears he'll let us know if anything comes of it." I sighed. "Doubt it's anything, but at least it's—"

"Something," Charlie finished, her eyes softening. "No stone unturned, Max. If they're out there, we'll find them eventually. And Levi's got eyes, too."

Levi had eventually returned at least. And while he never stuck around for too long, his visits were frequent and cherished.

Eli jumped at every chance to repair some of the hurt and history between them. It would take time, and I knew that Levi was struggling with their mother's death, with his place in this strange, new world. He kept us all at arm's length, never getting too close or attached. But he kept coming back, which I took as a good sign. I knew firsthand that those scars would never fully disappear, of course. But the wounds would mend—he just needed time.

"I don't know what exactly it is he gets up to out there." She rolled her eyes. We all wanted Levi to settle down here already, where it was reasonably safe. But he wasn't the sort who could be forced into anything. He'd stop his aimless, solo wandering when he was ready to. Not a moment before. "He'll keep us in the loop."

"Yeah," I said, offering her a watery smile.

A soft bark echoed.

I smiled at the perpetrator. Ralph waddled through the clutter of chairs and tables. He knocked three wooden stools to the ground, but paid them no attention.

Bishop's deep belly laugh vibrated through me as she leapt from my lap and buried her hands and face into the hell-hound's dark fur.

Ralph didn't generally like when people other than me touched him, but he'd made an exception for Bishop. Sometimes I was half-convinced he thought of her as his own pup.

She climbed on his back, fists clutching his fur, like the powerful creature was nothing more fearsome than a small pony.

Charlie's eyes widened as she swept her daughter into her arms. "Sorry Ralph. We're working on manners."

Ralph yipped, licking the girl's dangling leg.

Darius walked in, hair tousled in that messy way that had my stomach tightening at the sight, eyes gleaming with a knowing smirk when they met mine. "Ready, Little Protector?" He lifted up a small reusable bag. "Figured we'd dine out. Dec and the guys are finishing up a project with Seamus and Saif tonight, so they'll be home later. Seemed like a good night for a movie binge. I'm in charge of dinner. Izzy and Ro are taking care of popcorn."

"I want to go to the movie binge." Bishop shot Darius with her best puppy-dog eyes.

Charlie laughed. "You're going to bed." She ran her hand playfully through the toddler's hair. "But maybe tomorrow."

Before Bishop could argue—or Darius could fold—Charlie carried her daughter into the back. Ralph followed them out, no doubt hoping for some stray scraps of whatever snack Bishop got her hands on next.

Laughing, I pressed my lips to Darius's. "Movie night sounds great."

He deepened the kiss, groaning softly into my mouth before pulling back. "Can't believe I elected to share you tonight." He pursed his lips, pouting, and I resisted the urge to tug on his bottom lip with my teeth. "I get cuddling rights during the movie marathon for being so magnanimous. I'm thinking something with vampires this time."

"You? Shocking." I pressed my smile into his chest as his heart beat a steady rhythm against my cheek, feeling so at peace, so content—so ridiculously happy.

~

THANK you so much for joining me on this epic journey.

WHILE THIS SERIES concludes Max and her team's story (they've earned a well-deserved break, don't you think??), it is only the beginning. Check out Veil of Death and Shadow, Book One in the Order of Reapers series to learn about life post-Undoing. You'll find some familiar faces ;)

VEIL OF DEATH AND SHADOW

THE APOCALYPSE DIDN'T BREAK HER. THEY MIGHT.

Mareena is no stranger to death. It's been her constant companion. A curse that steals everyone she loves. So, she doesn't do love. She doesn't do attachment. She doesn't even do hugs—not if she can help it.

What Mareena does is survive. She runs a diner for the community that adopted her, watches over a grumpy old man she refuses to call family, and shares an apartment with the one person on earth stubborn enough to love her back (and the undead crow they can't seem to shake). But when a sardonic guardian from the afterlife shows up, claiming that she's his new charge, Mareena has to stop surviving and start fighting.

Kieran is tethered to her by fate, devastatingly beautiful, and completely forbidden. He's also the same man who saved her the day the world tore open. The same man she broke every rule for, one reckless night at a demon club. The only man who has ever made her feel like the curse she carries might not be a death sentence after all.

But Kieran isn't the only one tethered to Mareena. The man with amber eyes she's been running from since childhood is no longer content to wait in the dark. And whatever power has been sleeping inside Mareena since the day the world split is waking up hungry.

With Seattle cracking open at the seams, her best friend missing, a bounty circling through the demon underworld, and a reaper with a grudge following them both, she's running out of time to pretend she doesn't need anyone.

A gritty post-apocalyptic urban fantasy set in a fractured Seattle, where vampires and werewolves brawl in the streets, demonic cults vie for power, and humans do anything they can to stay alive.

ACKNOWLEDGMENTS

This book wouldn't be possible without the support of my family and friends. You know who you are, and I couldn't be luckier to have you in my life. Thank you for always encouraging and pushing me to chase after my writing worlds.

Special thank you to my editor, Kath, and my cover designer, Michelle. This book is so much better because you've both contributed a piece to it. Thank you.

And to my very own 'Ralph,' thanks for keeping me company while I wrote this series for hours and months and years on end. You are the best friend I could ask for and it's been the honor of a lifetime to hang out with you every day.

Finally, thank YOU. This series has been a part of my life for years. Through it, I have explored themes I've come to care so deeply about: unpacking grief, working through trauma, dealing with attachment style issues, the importance of community care and mutual aid, the value of finding yourself, the essential (often harrowing) process of unlearning. It means the world that you worked through these topics alongside me. While I sincerely hope you loved the romance, the spice, the characters, and the plot—I also hope that this series has inspired you to reflect on these themes and how they unfold in your own life. And most of all, thank you for your time. I know how very precious it is and I don't take the honor lightly. Thank you, thank you, thank you.